Friction Zone

A Slow-Burn Motorcycle Romance of Desire, Danger, and Second Chances

Melissa Lucas

Melissa Lucas

Cover Design: LeadHer Publishing

Developmental Editor: Cara Lockwood

Contents

Dedication

To you — yeah, YOU.

The one questioning their worth.

The one who wonders—Can I even do this?

Who stays up too late writing, plotting, editing, & fighting ghosts no one else can see.

You didn't imagine it. You're not crazy.

But guess what? We're still doing this!

And to everyone out there with a storm behind their eyes & no place to put it...

You're not alone.

You're not too much.

And you are not done.

Acknowledgements

To my husband—I could write 'til my fingers bleed about your hype, and it still wouldn't be enough. Thank You for saving me all those years ago. You saw something in me I hadn't even found yet. You told me who I could be, then believed in me while I became her. I will forever love you more, infinity times more!

To my kids—My world exists because you do.

Courtney—OMG, there's not enough I can say about you! I had a dream... I saw your face... the rest is magic.

Laurie—Your energy and beautiful rawness, you're my weekly spark.

Misty— You gave me the ARC experience I didn't know I needed, the friendship is bonus, XO!

Libby—You carry something rare. Keep inspiring, exactly as you are!

Jamie—Thank you for your honesty & heart, your opinion & laughter, & your teaching!

Miranda—I will never be able to Thank You enough.

Drew Bates—Chapter 20 wouldn't be what it is without your words and I'm grateful you said yes.

WesGhost—Thank you for letting me sprinkle a bit of your music throughout my story.

Shinesty—Your Ball Hammock Pouch Underwear brought more than just support, they brought personality, punchlines, and serious swagger.

Epigraph

Love is like friction. A place between control and surrender, where everything begins to move. It starts slow, building heat with every shift. Without it, there's no traction. No spark. No ride.

— Author

He touched my soul before he ever touched my skin.

— Eira

I never meant to fall in love. But I'll burn every ghost from our past if it means she feels safe in my arms.

— Andrew

Trigger Warnings & Tropes

Trigger Warnings

Betrayal and manipulation • Death • Emotional abuse • Explicit sexual content • Narcissistic control / gaslighting • Panic attacks and dissociation • Piercing play • PTSD and flashbacks • Sexual tension, edging, and safe word usage • Violence and injury

Tropes

Alpha male • Forbidden-ish / off-limits tension • Found family • Grumpy/sunshine-ish dynamic • Protective love interest • Safe word romance • Second chance at love • Slow burn • Strong female lead • Trauma bonding / healing through love

CHAPTER ONE

Eira

E ira drops to the ground at her mom's gravesite. One arm cradles her head, while the other fails to keep her balance. Tears slide down her cheeks, mingling with the sunbaked August earth beneath her. With each inhale, she breathes in the earthy scent of dirt, and each exhale carries the stark realization, she's alone again.

Still.

Tears flow so profusely that her body convulses with her hiccups. The gentle breeze echoes the rhythm of her sobs.

"Momma," she whispers, "Logan sent me a text. Said it was over, and if I didn't get my shit by Wednesday, he'd throw everything to the curb for the trashman."

Met with silence, she sobs again for the loss of her mother, taken too early from her.

Eira scoots to sit up, her back braced against the cold headstone. As Eira lifts her head, she sees the somber landscape of marble headstones, flowers, concrete pathways, and ash trees. Her fingers trail over the freshly cut grass, trying to seek solace in a place where the living connects with the departed. Tears continue to stream down her cheeks, like a never-ending waterfall. The weight of her loss suffocates her.

"Momma," she says, her voice barely recognizable above the rustle of the wind through the trees. "I miss you."

There's no comforting embrace; her mother is gone. Her dad is gone. Now, Logan is gone.

"I don't have anyone," she manages to choke out before the magnitude of loneliness pulls her into its depths. "Why can't I be somebody's person? Can I go back in time and change my design? I hate feeling like this, but I can't seem to stop." She sniffles. "I refuse to settle, but I'm getting tired of trying to find someone. I know I'm not perfect, but, Momma, are my flaws that bad?"

Eira sighs and closes her eyes as she remembers what her mom said right before she passed. *My dear, you must not let your flaws define you. They are simple facets of you. Embrace them; they make you, you. Love worth having takes time to find. And when the weight of the world feels too heavy to bear, remember to be gentle with yourself.* Eira's memory of her mom's soothing voice continues to whisper guidance. *You're worthy of love just as you are.*

And yet, Logan had left her. His accusations of her enjoying the flirting, the praise, and the attention of other men were like daggers being plunged deep into her wounded heart.

Logan is an expert at giving whiplash.

In the beginning of their relationship, he'd yell at her. Anger coursing through his body, arms slightly bent in attack mode, and fists clenched so tight they were vibrating at his sides, accusing her of being Miss High and Mighty, too good to talk to his friends. He warned her she had better learn to be friendly and not make his friends feel unwelcome ever again. Using the cruelest tone she had ever heard from his lips, he told her, "Learn to comply and we won't have any issues. Got it?"

So, she learned to ignore her cautious feelings towards his friends and began to laugh with them. Making a point to stay at the fire pit with them well past midnight. As the months went on, she started serving them beers from the coolers and whiskey shots from Logan's basement bar.

His friends started showing appreciation for her.

She occasionally made them food. They gave her praise when the shepherd's pie she'd made for them tasted just like they remembered from their childhood.

That's when Logan started to get more aggressive.

He would yell at her and then cradle her head, telling her how beautiful she was.

He would throw dinner plates and gas station cups full of soda and ice across the room, then pick her up bride-style, carry her to his bed, all the while covering her cheeks with kisses.

After each outburst, he would worship her for days, giving her the attention she craved.

Another tantrum from Logan was when she was folding his laundry. He yanked his jeans from her hands, yelling at her, "Quit auditioning for my fucking wife; you're not worth it." She could still hear the echo of his cruel laughter, feel the sting of his betrayal like a festering wound refusing to heal.

Logan apologized for that outburst by taking her away on a weekend vacation. Scenic rides on his motorcycle along the coastal highways to a charming beachfront villa. Their nights were filled with exploration of each other's bodies, and their days were filled with snorkeling, riding jet skis, and parasailing around the cove. The last night at the villa, Logan told her he loved her and couldn't see a future without her. He needed her, but most of all, he wanted her in his life. She was hopeful things would get better, but in all his words, he never promised to stop the hatefulness.

Against her better judgement, she shouldered on, refusing to give up on Logan like her father had given up on her.

Thoughts of Logan would run through her head daily. Hoping he got to work without incident, wondering if he remembered to feed Tiny, his Olive Python snake, and hoping he would have a safe ride back home.

The last outburst seemed different. One minute she was sitting on his couch, while they both scrolled through social media, and the next, a look of disgust radiated from Logan's face. He threw his phone in her lap and bellowed, "I told you I don't share."

"What're you talking about?" Eira whispered.

Looking down at the thread of texts with screenshots of her riding her bike with their friends, she blinked. "I'm riding with our friends, that's why you're screaming at me?"

His final words were spoken with haunting aggression. "I'm screaming at you because I just realized I was sharing you like a tool with my friends. I'm done. You. Leave. Now."

An orange and black butterfly landing on her knee breaks her chain of thought. The butterfly flies away. Shaking her head, she tries to clear away the self-deprecating thoughts. Her fingers chase her tears, frustration giving way as snot begins to pool at the end of her nose.

"Momma, how could he do all the right things and say all the right things, only to hurt me so badly? God, I'm a fool for not protecting myself."

Overcome with emotions, she digs her nails into her palms as she clenches her fists. She'd thought Logan was different, hoped he'd be her anchor. Instead, he'd proven himself to be just like all the others, a fleeting shadow getting pleasure from her despair.

With a trembling breath, Eira stands, her eyes scanning the horizon for a sign of hope. She's met with emptiness, an endless expanse stretching out before her like a cruel mockery of her pain.

She wipes away her tears one last time, her cool fingers brushing them from her cheeks. He's made her feel so small, so insignificant in his world, a mere speck of dust in the cosmic dance of life.

As she gazes at the horizon, that same butterfly who landed on her knee now lands on the white gas tank of her motorcycle. As a gentle smile graces her tear-streaked visage, a flicker of determination ignites within her as she says, "Thank you, Momma."

She sighs.

"Did you know people laugh at me because I'm so short? They think I'm a twelve-year-old boy riding a motorcycle. Jokes on them, huh?" Eira glances at the ground beneath her momma's headstone. "I'm gonna be okay. I just have to find myself so I can bounce back."

The butterfly swoops and lands on her momma's headstone. With a spark of determination, Eira shakes her head.

"I can only count on myself," she whispers, her voice barely audible above the roar of her own heartbeat. "I'll focus on me, find my own happiness."

With her mantra firmly intact, Eira turns away from her mom's grave. Her footsteps are firm as she walks towards her motorcycle. She may be lost in chaos, but she refuses to be swallowed by any darkness.

Her engine comes to life like a symphony of freedom in the stillness of the graveyard.

"Focus on me and find my happiness," she confirms with a nod, driving home.

CHAPTER TWO

Andrew

Andrew's world crumbles around him like the ruins of an ancient civilization. He rides alone on the sun-soaked streets of Mexico, the air heavy with the scent of tequila and regret. A bitter reminder of the nightmarish descent into chaos that has torn his heart to pieces.

His girlfriend of seven months, Claire, begged him to take her to Mexico. She'd convinced Andrew to trade his GSX-R600 for a Norton V4SV. The price was supposed to be reasonable, but that went to shit in a handbasket soon after seeing the Norton. What he'd ended up getting was a run-in with Mexican law, a concussion, robbed of thirty-five thousand dollars, and being dumped by his cheater of a girlfriend. By all accounts, none of that is what he'd considered reasonable.

Claire's been married for two years, conning her way through people trying to get them to take her to Mexico.

Claire's husband is a Policia Federal, so the concussion and theft dealt to Andrew by his hands are completely overlooked by the authorities in Mexico.

Claire brought Andrew here knowing the Norton motorcycle was a piece of shit and it wouldn't make it to the border. The heartless cunt knew he would have been stranded on the streets of Mexico and beaten until death came for him.

Where's her fucking conscience?

After Andrew was smacked on the side of his head, his survival instinct took over. Even with blood dripping from his eyebrow, his brain scrambled, forcing him to jump on his bike and ride to the border.

He could have died in Mexico, by Claire and her husband's hands or by the thugs lurking nearby. Their job had been simple–dispose of Andrew.

Now Andrew understood Claire's obsession with where the thirty-five grand was stashed on his motorcycle. She had one thought: take his cash and get her ass back to her husband.

Piece of shit or not, her words echo in his mind like a haunting melody: "Andrew, you're so damn desperate, nobody really wants you. You make for a good pity piece, but that's it." Each syllable splintered deeper into his soul, making it shatter. Claire's betrayal burned like acid in his veins, searing his flesh with the seething fury of a cauterized wound.

"Why do I give a shit?" he mutters to himself, his voice a bitter rasp against the backdrop of his chaotic thoughts. "I'm fucking done being played the fool."

After hours of riding beneath the relentless August sun, he finally sees the American border. Hopefully, his mind isn't playing tricks on him; he shakes his head lightly. Blinking to clear his sight out of habit, he notices his blurry vision has cleared. Sighing deeply, he realizes he's close to freedom.

Andrew is itching to open his Gixxer, leave Mexico, Claire, and all its troubled thoughts behind. He's just got to get out of Mexico first before anyone else can stake a claim on him.

He's fighting anxiety as he slowly advances behind the lines of vehicles, all leaving the hellish country in their past. Adding to his frustration, Claire and the intrusive thoughts in a constant loop, how close he was to dying with his most trusted person beside him crafting his demise.

Andrew's gravelly voice, hoarse from disuse, bounces inside his helmet. "How could I live with someone, cook for her, buy her fucking tampons, make stinky ass bath bombs with her just for her to create the moment I'd take my last breath! What kind of fucked up person is she?"

He must be concussed if he's talking to himself now. When did that become a thing?

The heat of the sun beating down on the black asphalt beneath his bike mixes with the bike's exhaust wrapping around his black boots. Gravity causes the sweat coating his body to travel south, making his clothes drenched as if he had been caught in a rainstorm. He exhales, hanging his head as his chin meets his chest. He gently shakes it, trying to clear the latest thoughts.

The white Audi in front of him advances, closing the distance between him and the border.

Andrew lifts his head. His thoughts are back to Claire as he duck-walks his bike towards the border patrol agents in the exit line.

Claire is gone. In her wake are feelings of betrayal, deceit, infidelity, and destruction. That didn't stop the fact that they'd been together for seven months. Seven months!

I was her fool.

While he thought they were making a future together, she was mocking him.

Lying twat.

The white Audi crosses into the United States. He's next!

Andrew lifts his visor.

The Border Patrol Agent raises his eyebrows. "I need you to remove your helmet," he says, as Andrew notices his name, Nelson, pinned to his uniform.

Andrew winces as the helmet's chin curtain brushes against his eyebrow, smearing most of the wet blood across his forehead and into his hair. Some of the blood has dried, making it flake and fall on his black gas tank. Andrew squints his eyes as he rests his helmet on his tank.

"Do you need medical attention?" Agent Nelson asks. "That looks like a nasty cut."

Andrew shakes his head. "Fucking bird came out of nowhere and smacked me. Thanks, though, I'm fine."

Agent Nelson chuckles and gives Andrew back his passport. "Free to go," he says. "Hey bud, watch out for birds that dent your head without putting a dent in your visor."

Andrew pockets his paperwork and gingerly puts his helmet back on. Nodding to the agent as he closes his visor, he drives to safety.

Crossing the border gives him a sense of security. Mexico can burn to the ground, and he wouldn't piss on the fire.

As he sets out on his motorcycle ride back to Florida, he breathes deeply. He didn't realize the tension he was carrying until he crossed the border from Mexico into the United States. He acknowledges he will leave behind the hard lessons of his loss in Mexico. Wanting more distance between Claire and him, he revs the 600cc's of his motorcycle. He silently begs the road noise to halt his self-loathing.

Can the fury of his own blood pressure drown out the racket of his self-destructing thoughts while he tears down the highway? Each mile away from Mexico is a mile closer to home.

He knows he's pushing his limit, drinking that rush, and tapping into the thrill from the speed. His blood's pumping adrenaline as he dances on the gray line of sanity. Zipping past semi-trucks and other motorists, his lookout is for the Florida state line.

No one can ever escape an adrenaline dump, and Andrew's finally hits him around Houston. He's halfway home, but his mind's mush and his body is physically drained; it's demanding sleep. The concussion pounding against his skull subsides into a pulsing headache, and his thoughts are a jumbled mess. Food doesn't even register as a concern.

Pausing the chaos of his shattered dreams, he pulls into a hotel parking lot. Securing his motorcycle for the night, he walks slowly into the hotel.

Why should he rush?

He catches his reflection off the hotel doors before they automatically open. Noticing the lack of line at the check-in desk, he wills the clerk to be uncaring and for her to ignore his bloody face, dusty jeans, and torn shirt.

Walking to the desk, Andrew asks, "Can I get a room?"

The clerk gasps and points to his face. She turns her fingers to herself and flows her finger across her face where his blood is.

"Should see the other guy," Andrew answers with a smirk.

"Oh my God, are you alright?" The clerk puts her fingers over her lips. "I'm sorry, that was stupid —"

Andrew interrupts, "I'm fine." He looks into the mirror behind the desk. "Can I get that room?"

He answers the hotel clerk's question and is soon rewarded with a room key. "I've put you on a floor that's kinda empty and no one's around you. I... um, have a good night," she tells him, but it sounds more like a question.

The ride in the elevator is silent except for the hum as he ascends each floor.

Andrew swipes the room key, adding the "Do Not Disturb" sign to the room's door handle.

After latching the locks, he's too exhausted to care. Removing nothing from his body, he tosses his helmet and gloves on the bed, then himself onto the mattress. He's asleep before his head hits the pillow of his cheap rented room.

Andrew's alarm blares like a horn on a carrier ship, making his ears want to bleed. Rolling on his back, he groans as he slaps his phone to silence. The sunlight cuts through the window like rays of a laser, making Andrew squint. He winces as pain pulses through his eyebrow. Standing to stretch has brought another moan of pain.

His headache's eased, but the remnant of a marching band is still ever present in the deep recess of his skull.

Already, there's a reminder of Claire. His toothbrush, deodorant, and change of clothes are in the bag with the money in Mexico. She had told him she was grabbing it to keep it safe.

"I just want a day without her in my fucking head!" he shouts.

Storming into the bathroom, Andrew puts the complimentary toothpaste on his finger and scrubs his teeth. Leaning over the sink to spit, his eyebrow pulses angrily.

"Fuck it," he growls, turning on both water taps in the shower. Letting the water heat, he walks back to the bedroom and plops down on the bed to untie his boots. Chunks of gravel still embedded in his laces and tan dirt have collected inside them. Standing, he kicks off his boots. He removes his clothes, tossing them onto the mattress.

He focuses his eyes on the outside view, watching the sky begin to cloud. He's staring out the window, yet he sees nothing.

He runs his fingers through his hair.

"She fucking didn't care if I died, but I made sure she had orange juice every damn morning! What. The. Fuck?"

In the morning sun, he checks out the damage; bruises decorated his arms, chest, thighs, and a particular golf ball size, dark purple bruise on the inside of his right upper thigh. The bruises remind him of the pain he feels not only mentally, but physically as well. He walks into the shower.

This is gonna burn like fire.

Closing the shower door, he holds his breath and steps under the spray. Exhaling slowly, he watches the water turn red, pink, tan, then clear. Washing the blood and dust off his body, he then finally lifts his head so his face is directly under the water. The burn he knows is coming sears across his face as he further pushes the pain of her betrayal to his "Fuck It" vault. He acknowledges that one day soon he'll have to clear out the vault but today is not the day.

Toweling dry, he walks to the bed.

He reaches past his dusty clothes for his boxers, smirking slightly. He'd worn his lucky ball hammock strip poker boxers. They're printed with playing cards of kings and queens in various stages of undress and sexual positions. He's alive and in the States; therefore, he's lucky. He shakes the rest of his clothes to remove as much dust as possible, and then he finishes dressing.

He checks his eyebrow in the mirror, making sure it isn't bleeding.

Done with the room, he heads out for breakfast and then towards the open road.

Acting on impulse, his deep thoughts have him stopping about an hour down the road.

With a sneer of contempt, Andrew veers off the highway onto a side road. His tires kick up clouds of dust as he avoids potholes in the back alleys of whatever city he's in. Andrew has no destination and no purpose here, other than to drown his sorrows in an adrenaline-fueled rush.

I'm not her fool. I'm not her victim.

Then he sees it. A flickering neon sign beckoning him from the shadows like a siren's call.

A tattoo shop blossoms before him like a lighthouse in a storm.

Without hesitation, Andrew parks and dismounts his motorcycle, his boots crunching against the gravel as he strolls towards the door with determination.

Entering the shop, he removes his helmet. The walls are covered with tattoo-filled pages as decoration.

Sketches of dragons, peacocks, lions, crosses, and skulls adorned the table for potential tattoos. The air is heavy with the scent of ink and sanitizer, the sound of buzzing tattoo irons mingling with the low murmur of conversation. A couple of chairs are empty; one has an older woman cleaning her tray. She turns and meets Andrew's eyes. "Oh you poor soul, what have they done to you?"

She has jet-black hair, black mascara on her eyelashes, and black eyeliner lines her ocean-blue eyes. She's a tiny thing. At six feet two inches, Andrew looks twice her height.

Andrew cocks his head to the right and smirks. "Well, they didn't kill me, so there's that."

"Normally, I would laugh at a comment like that, but I think you're serious. What can I do for you, Shoog?" she asks, her Southern drawl wrapping around the nickname.

"I want something to forget. And re-member," he stumbles.

She lifts her eyebrows. "Which is more important, the forgetting or the remembering?"

"I need to forget her and remember me."

"I can do that. Anything particular? Or are you my canvas?" She asks as her eyes peruse Andrew's dusty state.

He meets her gaze. "Give me something," he growls, his voice a low rumble.

"How about something that'll remind you to never put yourself through that again?"

Andrew nods in understanding. Reaching into his back pocket for his wallet, he hands her fourteen hundred dollars. She keeps forty dollars and hands the rest back to him. Andrew opens his mouth in protest, but she shakes her head, placing her palm over his hand, gently pushing their hands towards his chest.

As he pockets the money, he hears her say, "By the way, I'm Sage. Come on over and sit a spell."

As Andrew gets comfortable in the chair, she starts adding instruments and ink to the tray she had just cleaned and sanitized. She sketches the design that will forever mark Andrew's flesh. And then, with a steady hand and a determined gaze, she begins to work her magic, etching the image of a phoenix with its wings sunning as it rises onto the canvas of Andrew's skin.

As the tattoo iron bites into his flesh, Andrew grits his teeth; his jaw clenches with the sheer force of his will.

"Which is worse, the agony she put you through or the searing heat of my needle's kiss?"

In clipped words, he answers, "I fucking hate it, all of it."

As Sage continues to dip her head towards Andrew's skin, meticulously guiding the tattoo iron, she quietly whispers so only he will hear. "Shoog, I need you to know rebirth happens after the destruction, renewal after the understanding of what rebirth means, and resurrection after renewal. But you must welcome the healing process. You will go through this multiple times before your soul finds its twin flame. And each time, you will triumph over those who bring destruction to you. You will rise again because you are made of fire. Now, close your eyes and rest for a bit."

Andrew's eyelids get heavy and close, as he drifts to sleep under the caring hand of Sage.

When she's satisfied with the tattoo, she gently nudges Andrew awake.

"Slowly now. I rubbed salve on your bruises and cleaned up your eyebrow. It'll scar. Maybe a reminder?"

Andrew grunts his response.

Sage informs Andrew, "I let the pain subside a little before I woke you. I hope that was okay?"

He nods his head as he stands before the mirror with a sense of grim satisfaction. Sage gave Andrew a phoenix; a kaleidoscope of fiery red and orange blaze across his left shoulder onto his upper arm, then cascades to his left pectoral muscle. Its talons stop above his nipple and are open above his heart, as if it were to pluck any person who'd dare touch his heart. Just as Sage promised, it's a reminder. Andrew knows, even in despair, there's always the possibility of rebirth, renewal, and resurrection.

With a defiant smirk, Andrew flexes his muscles. The image of the phoenix dancing in the light of the tattoo shop gives him a spark of hope.

Andrew turns and freezes when he looks at Sage.

With tears in her eyes, she smiles and says, "Sorrow and struggles are the embers from which the phoenix rises. Just as flames consume the old, they give birth to the new. In the depths of your trials, remember this: from ashes of pain, resilience is born. Ride through the fire and emerge stronger than before."

Shocked beyond words, Andrew simply nods.

He heads outside into the Houston heat and finishes his journey home.

Chapter Three

Eira

Everyone knows Eira's an impulsive person, so her buying a motorcycle didn't surprise her aunt and uncle. Eira's always acting in haste and never regretting it. She feels each experience is a chance to grow.

Going out for the day's ride, Eira walks to the garage.

"Aunt Zia, Uncle Zio, I'm going out. Love ya," she hollers over her shoulder into the house from the open garage door. There's a murmur of voices, then her aunt shouts for Eira to wait.

Aunt Zia rushes towards Eira, hands gently landing on her shoulders.

"Please don't be reckless. I can't handle you being scraped off the highway!"

Eira gently pats her aunt's hands. "I'll be safer than you and Uncle Zio were when you were my age!" she says, winking at her aunt. "I'm fine." Eira kisses her aunt on her cheek. "You have to stop worrying so much. I know what I'm doing."

Aunt Zia wraps Eira's hands in hers, bringing them to her lips, giving them a quick peck. Aunt Zia hugs their joined hands to her breast. "I promised your momma I wouldn't let anything happen to you. And then your dad abandoned you. I failed your momma then. Please don't make me fail your momma again. Can't you just take your car and go out? Or wait until morning? It's almost dark. Please?"

Hearing the plea for safety from her aunt crushes Eira's heart. Enveloping her aunt in a big hug, she says, "You did not fail Momma; stop saying that. Stop believing that. I'm dealing with some stuff, but that doesn't mean I'm unstable. I would never do anything to add more pain to you or Uncle Zio. You have to believe that."

Aunt Zia kisses the crown of Eira's head. "Can't we talk about it? I know Logan hurt you. Let us help you."

Eira shakes her head a few times, stepping out of her loving aunt's embrace. "Aunt Zia, it's not just Logan, k. It's everything. I'm handling it. I've got an idea; I'm hoping it'll help me in a couple of ways."

Eira steps into the garage, holding the kitchen door ajar.

"You have to trust me, okay? I love you so much, you know that, right? You and Uncle Zio took me in when Momma died and after Dad left. I'll never forget everything you two have done for me. But being almost thirty has me thinking. Nothing bad, just contemplating my direction in life. Being a nurse is satisfying, but that can't be all I am."

Aunt Zia's foot props the door open, her hand resting on the handle. Shrugging her shoulders as she asks, "What do I say to that?" A concerned grin morphs into a playful smile. "Remember to look both ways before crossing the street and don't talk to strangers."

Eira chuckles, letting go of the door handle. "You know that's not what you say to a woman my age, right?"

As Eira walks to the shelf where her helmets are neatly stored, she hears Aunt Zia, "Well, crisp. Then. Make sure it's wrapped. Is that better?"

"Seriously! I'm going on a bike ride! Not sure where your mind went, but leave me out of that place!" Eira playfully laughs as she grabs her blue helmet and secures it on her head, ensuring her phone and helmet's Bluetooth are still connected.

"All playfulness aside, we love you; you need to keep yourself safe. See you in a bit." Aunt Zia closes the kitchen door, leaving Eira alone in the garage.

Eira approaches her bike; her fingertips trace the lines of her motorcycle. Smiling, she gently caresses the sleek curves and sky-blue accents with a sense of reverence. It's more than just a machine; it's become her anchor in a world tainted by pain and sorrow.

Wrapping her hands around the handlebars, she swings her leg over her bike. Getting situated on her seat, she turns the key, and with a push of a button, her motorcycle comes to life. The hum of the engine is like a life preserver being tossed to someone who's drowning. She needs this daily to unmuddle her thoughts.

She clicks the remote to open the garage door and allows gravity to coast her and her bike down to the end of the driveway. Ensuring the garage door is closed, she rides towards her therapy—the highway.

It's been a little over a month since Logan discarded her like yesterday's garbage. The tears stopped in the first week as she realized all the signs have been dancing in front of her face from the beginning. Her and Logan are like two opposing magnets, repelling one another. Try as she could, for them to come together as one, but they, unlike the magnets, continued to explode under force. Eira's desire to be someone's everything drove her to stay in a relationship that can only be described as cramming a square peg into a round hole—it just doesn't fit.

With the guidance of her therapist, she's discovering herself, her true self. What makes her smile? What flavor of ice cream do her tastebuds really enjoy? What kind of music makes her feel alive? How does it feel to have her own opinion?

By weeks two and three, she's deliberately peeled back her layers, baring herself for healing. Finding herself feels humdrum, like she's going through the motions, but not really living. She works, then goes straight home. She's not excelling; she's just surviving because there's nothing left of her. Deep in the demands of Logan, in dodging his abuse, in walking on eggshells waiting for the next blow, she's lost herself.

Her healing reminds her of a sandblaster. Finely chipping away all the unwantedness, until she reaches a foundation strong enough to rebuild. Finding herself means she's healing, and she's committed to her remodel.

The rush of wind against her arms and chest allows her mind to clear. It keeps the darkness from taking over, reminding her she's still alive.

As she rides, the highway stretches ahead. The canopy of trees are dense and green, with only a scattered hint of gold flirting on the edges of their leaves. The silhouette of the Atlantic coast faintly emerges, grounding her with its presence. Pristine blue waters lap against the sugary white beach shores.

She navigates through her feelings of abandonment and the slow process of untangling her distorted self-worth just as clearly as she guides her motorcycle along the hills and windy curves. The lingering hurt and betrayal by Logan feels like a wound gnawing at her heart, but it isn't just his actions haunting her. It's the echo of those who came before.

Her stomach growls as the low fuel light begins to flicker. With both the motorcycle and her needing fuel, she exits the highway, stopping alongside a pump at a gas station.

Still deep in thought, she grabs the gas handle, inserting the nozzle inside her tank, she squeezes to no avail. The gas doesn't flow inside her tank.

Frustration coats a thin blanket over her conscience. Shaking her head, she presses the grade of gas. She mumbles, "Sheesh, get outta your head long enough to select the fuel grade."

Finished pumping gas, she fights with the handle as she tries again, to hang up the pump.

Walking into the gas station with her helmet on and visor up, she pulls the door to the cooler case open. She finds the drink that cools both her body and her thoughts. Her fingers wrap around the neck of the apple juice bottle. She leaves the door open a minute longer than necessary. The sweat clinging to her skin cools, leaving goosebumps on her arms.

While she's in line to pay for her apple juice, she hears a familiar female voice.

"And she deserves everything she got. I just showed Logan what a conniving bitch she is, and he dumped her."

Eira tilts her head, allowing her to focus on the security mirror, reflecting the face belonging to the voice.

"Just so happens, I was there for him." She turns to her friend. "Naked and all night long."

A different voice responds, "I thought we liked Eira. Usually, I'm good at reading people. I wonder how I missed that?"

The familiar voice says, "Look, in this world if you want something, you gotta take it. I wanted Logan and I took him. If he were committed to her, I couldn't have gotten him that easy. He was looking for a way out and I gave him one. Now..." She shrugs her shoulders. "...we're all happy."

Eira pays for her drink and turns to leave. She stops in front of the familiar voice. "Wait til Logan starts throwing plates at you because you talked too much to his friends, then ask yourself if you're still happy."

Both girls open their mouths in shock, but Eira continues, "Ask him what he does to people who question him. Just make sure you are arm's length away from him. Have a great life!"

Eira's whole being vibrates as anger radiates within her. She pushes the door open so forcefully it smacks into the red protective pole, stopping the door just shy of hitting the building. She continues to walk to her bike. Not giving another thought or emotion to them, Eira climbs onto her bike and rides to the local Pancake Hut to fill her belly.

After eating her weight in pancakes, Eira leans back into the booth, releasing a determined sigh. Thinking about her plan, she realizes it could backfire, but it'll be fun and so cathartic.

Decision made, Eira reaches for her phone.

Her fingers fly across the screen as she creates new social media accounts. It's a leap of faith. An attempt to carve out a space for herself in a world intent on tearing her down. She formulates her plan, taking note of the most crucial goal–Have Fun!

She'll film her motorcycle rides, edit them with her feelings of the day, never dismissing how she feels at the moment, and she'll add the music that screams to her soul. When all is perfect, she'll post it.

She will share a piece of her healing journey and a bird's-eye view of how peaceful life on a motorcycle in Florida can be.

And maybe, just maybe, she'll become whole again, she'll find confidence in herself, and she'll stand strong for herself.

As the days turn into weeks, Eira spends her time helping people as a nurse, helping Uncle Zio and Aunt Zia, filming, editing, and posting her rides.

Weeks later, Eira's uncle asks her, "How's the media thing going?"

"Great, actually. I think I'm helping them as much as they're helping me," Eira responds, snuggling deeper under her cover on the couch. Aunt Zia absently slaps on top of the couch cushion. Finding the remote, she presses the pause button on their latest binge-watch of *Dr. Quinn, Medicine Woman.*

Uncle Zio sits in his recliner on the other side of the room. "I wish I knew how it helps being in the spotlight like that. Don't you get tired of people constantly knowing you're going and coming?"

"It's a minute of view time. The therapy's in the comments. I spend maybe an hour replying to comments."

"You're telling these people your secrets, it's stuck out there!" He flails his arms, pointing at the front door. Her uncle continues, "What happens in your future when they find out you have these thoughts?" His arms plop in his lap.

"Christ, it's not like I'm planning murder, or trying to take over the world. I'm connecting. I'm helping." She drops her voice as she looks at her uncle. "I'm healing."

Eira's eyes silently ask her aunt for help.

"Right," her uncle bellows, "you're connecting with psychopaths and helping gangbangers! This needs to stop; one of these nights you're not gonna come home. Then what, huh?"

Eira raises her voice in frustration. "Uncle Zio, I'm a nurse. I probably help nefarious people every night. And I get paid for it!"

Sitting up, she begins to fold the blanket. "I won't stop riding. Or posting. Or meeting new people. I won't close myself off again." Patting the blanket on the cushion, she rises. "I won't question my self-worth ever again."

"Munchkin, your newly found confidence brings joy to this old man's heart, but does it have to come with such a dangerous cost?" Uncle Zio glances from Eira to his wife and back. "Please tell me you see where my concern is coming from?"

"I think you still see me as the Eira before Logan," she says, taking a couple of steps towards her bedroom. "I'm not her anymore. I'm a new me, and that version of me will be better again tomorrow, and each day after that. I just need to know you'll accept this version of me that's healing?"

"Eira, I do accept you. I may not always like your choices, but I have always accepted you. And always will."

"I have to do this." Eira walks to her bedroom door. Twisting the handle, she stops to add, "For me." Before she closes her bedroom door she says, "Z's, I love you both."

Closing her bedroom door, Eira hears them echo, "I love you." She sighs as she walks to her bed.

I know he's concerned, but he's really out of touch with how this all works.

Plopping onto her bed, she remembers her last couple of weeks as her posts begin to garner attention.

She's building herself a community of like-minded people. Others have also been betrayed or their hearts broken; they offer kind words or suggestions to try to ease her pain. Many follow her account as they travel vicariously with her through the beauty of Florida. Others who follow are too deep in their hatred; they feel it necessary to spread their venom to someone who is trying to heal. She's accepted she'll have to ignore and block people, but she gets to laugh at some also. She hadn't banked on the cathartic feeling of freedom she's had because her social media account allows her to speak her mind daily. Processing through her hurt and pain, she's learning how to ignore the negative of what people think of her.

Even so, Eira finds herself overwhelmed by the tone of her direct messages. They are a cruel reminder of the toxicity lurking beneath the surface of people on social media. The females are the worst; their words dripping with venom as they attack her for her size, for her healing reflection of the new her, and for her uniqueness. From the beginning she's known she'd have to get thick-skinned. Although there are certain times when her guard is down and a direct message still stings. Like when a woman DM-ed her: *You're just a little girl playing with toys you can't handle.*

These hateful people can't understand how someone so small can command the respect of the open road.

But it isn't just women who seek to tear her down; the men are just as ruthless. Another comment from her post was filled with lewd propositions.

One man wrote: *That bike too much for you to handle honey? Come on over here, I'll show you how to ride something big.*

Eira receives her fair share of threat messages, too. Like: *Stay away from Douglas Avenue past dark; you won't make it out.*

At times, she feels her resolve wavering, her spirit sagging under the weight of their scorn. But deep down, she knows she can't let them win, can't let their cruelty snuff out the flicker of hope burning inside her. With a determined touch from her fingertip, her deletions banish those hateful and hurtful comments from her sight. She will always pay heed to the threats of where to stay away from after dark, but she will continue to ride her motorcycle.

The vibration from the engine nestled below her thighs reminds her she's in control. Her heart pounds with the rhythm of tires on the road. She feels a sense of freedom wash over her like a sinner being cleansed by a baptismal ceremony.

She's more than the sum of their cruel words, more than the scars they have left for her to decipher.

She enjoys filming her rides, documenting her journey, and meeting other bike riders, whether online or in person.

So many riders bring humor, like the brief exchange at a stoplight paving the way for her first new bike friendship. Now when Eira sees a passenger on a basketball bright orange motorcycle with pink bunny ears attached to a lime green helmet, she knows dancing is expected as the toll payment. The passenger hops off the back of her motorcycle and dances between other motorcycles while the music blasts across the Florida asphalt at the intersection of Smith and Wesson, waiting for the light to turn.

While other riders force a mortality check, like the scary exchange at the side of the road where Eira held a rider's shredded T-shirt to his torn-up shoulder blade, willing the bleeding to stop while trying to distract him from his bloody reality, praying the ambulance to hurry.

She's joined online motorcycle groups for companionship, for learning, and for a sense of purpose.

Her eyes heavy with sleep, she knows no matter what the world throws her way, she'll always find the strength to rise again.

CHAPTER FOUR

Andrew

Andrew hates being late for anything. Doesn't matter if it's for business or personal, being late just pisses him off.

His last client wouldn't reschedule; absolutely refused to. She delayed their meeting by an hour. It caused all his plans to shift. The aggravation sets deep, leaving him lacking in patience. The client was channeling Chatty Cathy, but after Andrew told her he could not schedule her installation for the next day, she turned into self-righteous Karen.

Leaving work an hour later than planned means he's now late.

Attempting to make up time, he reasons his plan, speeding. He's committed to riding through the streets of Jacksonville like the Grim Reaper's nipping at his boots.

Jonah, a good friend who sometimes takes on the role of father figure since Andrew's dad passed, texted him earlier today to be in the parking lot behind The Club at seven.

A couple of friends are getting together to practice street bike freestyle stunts. Basically, just hanging out and blowing off steam from the workweek.

As Andrew merges onto the highway, he notices a dusty white semi-truck ahead of him. Quickly calculating his approach, he maneuvers his motorcycle alongside the middle of the trailer. Maintaining speed and balance, he takes his left gloved middle finger and etches in the thick layer of the truck's dust, two vertical lines for eyes and a curve for a mouth. Pleased with his smiley face, he chuckles.

Claire chewed his ass for hours the last time he etched a smiley face into the side of a semi-trailer. He thought her concern was because she loved him, so he decided to compromise and stop.

Memories come back, full force but now they mean something entirely different. He knows she was just afraid something would happen to him, and he wouldn't be able to take her to Mexico.

Even a month later, thoughts of Claire still sour his stomach. The acid threatens to climb up his throat.

Forcing himself to ignore all thoughts of Claire, he speeds to the front of the semi-truck. Andrew extends his left arm down below his handlebars and wiggles his four fingers in a wave, as if he's fanning his fingers, trying to remove crumbs from his hand. The truck driver responds with a tug of his air horn. Andrew nods, then twists his motorcycle throttle, devouring the distance between him and The Club.

With every rev of the throttle, every weave of the tires, he fights to outrun the betrayal of Claire. She's like a ravenous beast gnawing at his soul, tearing him apart from the inside out. Andrew knows he's better off without that manipulating bitch of a girlfriend, but it still doesn't make what she did any easier to deal with. No matter how fast he rides, no matter how far he pushes himself, he can't escape the pain and distrust Claire has caused.

She decimated him. The length she connived to has bred a distrust he willingly holds against the opposite sex like a shield.

Facing the daunting task of reassembling his heart and mind, he slowly analyzes each piece to strategically rebuild them. But this time, he's solidified his exterior walls, creating an extra barrier to protect him from future harm. Staring down death does irrational things to the human mind. He can't see how he'll be able to trust again, but he knows when he's ready–if he's ever ready, it'll come after he heals.

His hands clench the handlebars with white-knuckle intensity, while his body is a coil of pent-up rage and anguish. Every screech of rubber against asphalt is a desperate attempt to drown out the echoes of her deceit. One day, he'll successfully be rid of her existence and the effect she has on him.

He's so deep in his thoughts and focused on the ride that somehow, he still misses his exit. Shaking his head to clear his thoughts, he hunkers his chest to lay as close to the gas tank as possible, looping around the highway's cloverleaf interchange. Coming out of the curve, he twists his throttle to speed up when a black Tahoe with a dented driver's side bumper crosses the merge line, coming into Andrew's lane. The Tahoe driver slams on its brakes as Andrew swerves to miss getting hit.

The Tahoe's horn blares while the vehicles around them slow down and some move to the side of the highway. Stopped in the middle of the highway, the Tahoe driver leans out their window, flailing their arms and shouting incomprehensible gibberish.

Andrew looks over his shoulder, itching to fly his middle finger at the driver of the Tahoe. He recognizes the driver; it's Chatty Cathy/Karen, his last appointment from work.

Can this day get any shittier?

He tosses a wave over his shoulder, then starts shifting gears so he can continue his ride to The Club.

"Damn near ate it, Dad," he mumbles into his helmet as he zigzags his motorcycle to miss a pothole. "I miss you, but fuck, I'm not ready for it to be today."

Ever since losing his father, Andrew has a driving need to make his father proud. It's hard with him not here, but Andrew still craves to hear those words again, just one more time.

Before passing, Andrew's father drilled into him to treat others the way you want to be treated. So, when Andrew reigns in his rage or his discontent, he can faintly hear his father's words, "I'm proud of you, son." But when his rage takes center stage, he can hear his dad say, "Not the way we handle things, son."

Andrew knows his desire to ride comes from wanting to follow in his father's footsteps, to carve out a legacy of his own accomplishments with his motorcycle. Andrew just doesn't want to end up like his father.

Andrew's raw confidence and arrogance on the road allows him to become one with his motorcycle. Some say his confidence will be what takes him out, and others say it is a form of art.

Making the final turn into The Club's parking lot, Andrew pulls into the nearest spot. An out-of-breath Jonah rushes to his side. "You're late!" he exclaims.

"I got held up," Andrew replies.

Jonah's puzzled face looks up to meet Andrew's helmet. "Where the hell have you been, man, you're never late. Is your fucking finger broke?"

Flipping up his visor, Andrew raises his middle finger at Jonah.

"Well, damn, guess it works just fine," Andrew smirks.

"You asshole, you could've texted me. Ya know, let somebody know you're late and not in a damn ditch somewhere bleeding out?" Jonah keeps needling Andrew.

Andrew sighs. "Where is everybody?"

Jonah twists at the waist, throwing his thumbs over his shoulder. "Back there." Jonah glares at Andrew. "Seriously, man, what gives?"

Andrew rolls his bike backwards and starts the engine. "I'm going around back. Think you can change your tampon and quit riding my ass?"

Jonah throws his arms in the air, stepping in front of Andrew's motorcycle. "Are you fucking serious, man?"

Jonah raises his hand, counting on his fingers as he shouts out all the things Andrew has done wrong. "You get back from Mexico a month ago and we still haven't talked. You're down thirty-five grand without the Norton. Got a gash on your eyebrow that should've had stitches. Claire's missing and you're fine with it. You got a fucking tattoo blazing across your chest."

Jonah points at Andrew. "You've got the worst self-destructive, reckless attitude I've ever seen from you. And you're calling me—" Jonah shoves his thumb to his own chest, "—a bitch because I'm concerned about you?"

Jonah falls silent as he drops his arms to his sides, closing the distance between Andrew and himself. Jonah reaches out between the handlebars and slaps the kill switch.

"We're fucking talking now," Jonah says as he extracts Andrew's motorcycle keys.

Andrew drops the kickstand, getting comfortable in his seat. "Sure, we'll have a go. Want me to braid your hair or paint your nails while we talk?" he replies with a snark as he removes his helmet, placing it on the gas tank. Andrew rests his hands on top of his helmet, tapping his thumb with aggravation.

Jonah shifts back a couple of steps. "You can be pissed all you want, but I'm not giving up. You're on a damn secret mission to meet your father. That ain't happening on my watch. Got it kid!"

Andrew drops his head in frustration, chin meeting his chest. Sighing deeply, he shakes his head.

Inhaling slowly, he lifts his head and begins. "Claire is married. The Norton bike was a scam to get money out of me and to get me to take her to Mexico. Her husband's a cop, reminds me of that actor, Danny Trejo. He decided bashing my head would make stealing my money easier. I saw the glint of sunshine off his aluminum baseball bat and ducked before it could lay my head open. He got a smack to my eye, though. Claire was fucking bouncing on her damn feet, clapping her hands, yelling at him to 'Do it again!' He raised the bat again, but I jumped off my bike to get away. There's a lot of shit that sticks out the side of a bike; that's where some bruises came from. I grabbed a handful of dirt and threw it in his face. While he's covering his eyes and screaming, 'I'm gonna end you,' I used the distraction to jump on my bike and get away before the local welcome committee could take their shots at me. I left Claire's lying ass in Mexico. Now I'm here. Working through that shit. And I'm not reckless, you fucker. I just realized we're all on borrowed time. It'll happen when it's meant to. Until then, I'll ride." Andrew finishes with a shrug of his shoulders.

Jonah stares at Andrew for a bit. Recovering, he says, "Shit, Andrew, you've been back a month and haven't said a fucking word of it. And don't call me a bitch again, or I'll bash your other eyebrow. And what's with the tattoo? You're fucking terrified of needles."

"I'm not terrified; I just don't like them," he says, rolling his eyes. "The tattoo is a daily reminder. When I look in the mirror, I'm reminded I trusted her, was building a life with her, and was going to ask her to marry me..." Andrew's thumbs start drumming on the top of his helmet. "...only for her to watch her husband try to kill me. For thirty-five thousand dollars."

Andrew stills his thumbs and raises his voice. "My life is worth more than that!"

He glances around the parking lot, hoping this is still a private conversation. "Claire betrayed me. She made me think she loved me when all along she was using me, playing me like a fucking fool. I could care less that she didn't have a job because we were making a home, a future together, or so I thought."

Andrew looks up at the sky. "Do you know the kind of shitty thoughts running through my mind thinking of what she did? While I'm making love to her, she's plotting ways to kill me?" Andrew looks at Jonah. "I thought I had her loyalty, but I read that fucking wrong also. Dude, I held her hair when she puked, rubbed her feet when she was on her period, and didn't cook meat inside the house because the smell makes her sick. What do I get in return? A fucking bat to the head served with a side of let's steal your fucking money!"

"Mother-fucking hell," Jonah murmurs.

Andrew sighs. "This isn't just Claire cheating on me. She wanted me dead. Left in the streets of Mexico to rot like a discarded piece of meat. I just can't." Andrew shakes his head as if trying to clear it.

Jonah takes his right hand and rubs the back of his neck. "Son of a bitch, how can I help if you won't tell me what's going on? I'm so fucking pissed at you right now! You rode hours with a concussion! You could have fucking died, or worse yet, killed somebody else. How reckless can you be?"

Andrew is stunned. "You think I don't know that? That I don't relive that bullshit daily? Claire is the reason I want nothing to do with women."

Andrew looks over Jonah's shoulder. "Why do you think when you mentioned getting laid last week, I said I'd pass? No fucking thank you; I'm not interested in sticking my dick anywhere. Pussy is deadly."

Andrew opens his hand and holds it in front of Jonah. "Gimme my keys."

Jonah digs in his pocket, returning Andrew's keys. "Never again. You hear me? I fucking mean it, kid!"

Andrew nods in agreement and rides towards the back lot of The Club.

Pulling up to a free parking spot, he glances around and sees about twelve different bikers, only six of which he considers friends.

Jonah walks through the open shop bay doors, pointing towards a tester bike and shouts Andrew's name. "That's ready when you are!"

Andrew hops on the tester bike, taking a couple of laps to get familiar with the bike. As Andrew makes his way around the building, picking up speed on the straightaway, he pulls the clutch in so that it slips. Twisting the throttle, he revs the engine, then lets the clutch out until the front wheel bounces up. He rides for about ten feet before he feels his back tire starting to get squirrely.

Before Andrew can save it, he and the motorcycle are whisked sideways, skimming on top of the pavement with a deafening scrape against concrete.

Coming to a stop, he realizes his first mistake. He assumed someone checked over the tester bike, so he didn't. He rests his head on the concrete with a deep sigh.

Andrew's lying on his side, still straddling the bike. Attempting to extract himself, he feels a slight tug on his upper right thigh. Looking down, he sees a screwdriver shaft disappearing into his leg. The area around the screwdriver is getting dark and wet as his jeans wick blood from the wound. The screwdriver handle is partially melted and wedged between the frame of the bike and the top of the engine.

Andrew growls, propping himself on his forearms, not sitting or lying down. He mumbles, "Someone was working on this and what, walked away?"

Pain explodes in his thigh. "Someone want to help here?" he yells. Andrew lies on his back, letting his head rest on the concrete. Breathing deeply, he tries to control his response to the pain.

Andrew hears the pounding of footsteps on the concrete as Jonah shouts, "Get back, get away from him." He kneels at Andrew's side; his face masked in concern.

"The bike is tethered to your upper thigh by a service screwdriver." Jonah shakes his head. "We can't pull it out. If that thing nicked your femoral artery, you could bleed out. We're going to untangle you from the bike, then we're going to the ER."

Andrew feels dizzy seeing the screwdriver lodged in his thigh as blood oozes from his wound.

Jonah hesitates, not wanting to hurt his friend but unwilling to waste time either. He squats, hands trembling as he begins to untangle the bike from Andrew's leg, careful not to bump the screwdriver unnecessarily.

Free of the bike, Andrew squeezes his eyes shut, his vision swimming with the haze of adrenaline. As Jonah helps him up, Andrew stumbles on his feet. "I asked earlier if this day could get any shittier. Well, I guess it can."

While Jonah was untangling Andrew, one of the service crew members started the truck. It's a couple of feet behind Jonah; the driver and passenger doors are open with the air conditioner's fan set to high. Jonah guides Andrew to the passenger side of The Club's service truck. Once Jonah has him buckled in, he jumps onto the driver's seat.

Jonah depresses the ignition button, slams the gear shifter into 'D,' then tears out of The Club's parking lot.

"Damn." Andrew clenches his jaw, his hand searching for the 'Holy Shit Handle' only to come up empty. With his palm splayed against his window for support, he growls at Jonah, "You're driving like there's a blue light special on glow in the dark lube."

Jonah glances at Andrew and winks. "You'll thank me later."

Eyes back on the road, Jonah accelerates to make it through the light before the color changes. He nearly plows into the rear of a trash truck but swerves just in time.

"Fairly certain this seat belt won't save my ass if you get us into a wreck. You wanna drive like you own a fucking brain?" Andrew growls.

Jonah skids to a stop at the ER entrance, jogging to the passenger side of the truck. He waggles his eyebrows at Andrew. Jonah steadies Andrew while helping him to stand. "I just saved your life, you ungrateful bastard. Quit giving me the shaft!" They start walking toward the ER doors. "You wanna show a little gratitude?" Jonah asks.

Jonah walks faster than Andrew can limp, zigzagging around a collection of gravel on the pavement, causing Andrew to stumble.

Andrew bellows in pain. "Shit, man, you're like a blind man strung out on speed. Quit screwing around and get me inside?"

As Jonah and Andrew approach the ER door, their motion triggers the automatic sensor, causing the door to open, just as Jonah shouts, "Shit, you're such a mouthy bitch with that stuck in you!"

The waiting room falls silent. Heads pop up and turn, staring at the open ER door while Andrew struggles to get away from Jonah as he limps to the desk. Jonah frowns, latching onto Andrew's arm.

The woman at the check-in desk smirks. "What can I help you gentlemen with?"

"He got a screwdriver embedded in his thigh about fifteen minutes ago. He's a mouthy fucker and someone needs to make him shut up," Jonah says. "Can you help with that?"

"Jesus Christ, Jonah," Andrew admonishes. "You've got about as much finesse as a rabid dog; chill out."

"Please have a seat in the waiting room, and someone will call you when it's your turn," the nurse says, handing a clipboard and a pen to Andrew. "Please fill out this form while you wait." She turns, shouting over her shoulder, "Olive, let them know we got another couple!"

CHAPTER FIVE

Eira

Returning from taking a patient's information to the lab, Eira steps out of the elevator, sidestepping a cluster of Halloween decorations. The cardboard cutouts of painted white ghosts grinning with crooked teeth are leaning against the wall. October brings with it the hospital's amusing attempt to introduce the holiday season.

A man's gruff voice bellows, "He got a screwdriver embedded in his thigh about fifteen minutes ago. He's a mouthy fucker and someone needs to make him shut up. Can you help with that?"

"Wow," Eira whispers to herself. Walking a couple of steps in the opposite direction of the roaring man, she runs into someone. "Umph." The rubber on her shoes squeak on the tiled floor as she comes to a quick stop. Masculine hands wrap around her biceps, keeping her from falling. "I'm sor —"

Dr. Gregory, the attending physician, interrupts her, "Get that loud one to room seven." He nods down the hall towards the ER.

"Then prep him for thigh stitches." He releases Eira. "I'll take care of room five and then I'll stop by to finish," he says, disappearing down the hall.

Before going to room seven, Eira checks in with the front desk. "Hey Olive, can you take the thigh injury to room seven, please?"

"Sure," Olive replies. "He's a white male, late twenties. Managing the pain well, but his friend is quite agitated. Dr. Gregory has ordered an X-ray, tox screen, CBC, and a penicillin plus tetanus shot."

Eira opens her mouth, but Olive continues, "And yes, they all know they're Stat." She points behind Eira. "Actually, here's X-ray now. I'll tell them to take him to room seven when they're done."

Sliding her badge between the reader, Eira hears a click as the door lock disengages. Shouldering her body weight into the door, she pushes it open. Stepping into the supply room, she lets the door slam shut, engaging the lock. Eira closes her eyes, drawing deep, relaxing breaths. Sometimes the ER can wreck a person's nerves.

Gathering her suturing supplies from the inventory room, she walks towards room seven.

Eira has just finished organizing the supplies on the tray beside the bed when the X-ray tech pushes the patient in a wheelchair towards the ER bed. He looks removed, stoic. He's followed by the man who was agitated in the waiting room.

The agitated guy and the X-ray tech transfer the patient to the bed, without a single noise from any of them.

The patient lies on the bed, quiet. She can tell he's in pain though, as he keeps pulsing his jaw, tightening it only to relax it. Digging his heel into the bed for leverage, he pushes with his left, rolling himself onto his right side but leaving his right leg straight. His left foot is taut on the corner of the bed, holding his position. Occasionally, he rocks from his heel to his toes, jiggling the bed ever so slightly.

"Are you uncomfortable?" Eira asks. "I can help you move into a more relaxed position."

"No," he says, in a clipped tone. The patient continues to focus on the wall with his hands clasped together under his head.

The agitated man whips his head towards the patient. "Andrew," he says, "don't be an ass to her. Shit, man, she's just trying to help." The guy looks at Eira with a smile. "He's fine where he is. You'll have to excuse the fucker. His social skills suck lately. But thanks for your concern."

She simply nods and smiles. Eira walks behind the computer screen, and soon the only sound in the room is her fingers clanking on the keyboard.

"My name is Eira and Dr. Gregory will be in shortly," she says. Lifting her head, she adds, "What's the patient's name?"

Silence.

Staring at the wall above the patient, Eira tries to hold her professionalism intact. Giving him the opportunity to answer has her wondering if he's always this cantankerous? His personality is as monotone as his voice.

"Seriously, man." Jonah looks at Eira, planting his thumb into his chest. "I'm Jonah," he says, then points his finger at the bed. "And that surly bastard is Andrew."

She nods her head, informing Jonah and Andrew, "Ok. Dr. Gregory ordered an X-ray, which you've already gotten. He ordered blood work, so I need to find out where they are—"

Jonah cuts her off. "The vampires were outside X-ray waiting for him. They already got their hit. Not sure what you're looking for, but he's clean."

"These are just routine tests for a patient in his condition," Eira explains. Leaning against the wall for support, she bends her knee as she props the sole of one foot on top of the other foot's toes. "Let's get some history, okay?"

Eira types on the keyboard, reading aloud, "It says here he was playing on his bike and got a screw... d-driver stuck in his thigh?" Eira stutters, shaking her head. "Well, that's interesting—"

"I can't believe that old bag fucking wrote that!" Jonah booms.

Andrew glares at Jonah. "That's what you told her. You think she's gonna add anything else since you were such a dick to her?"

Andrew's thumb nervously taps the bed. He keeps staring at the wall above the door.

"I was practicing stunts on a motorcycle," he says, overly enunciating the word *motorcycle*. "When the back tire got away from me. I skimmed the top of the concrete. The screwdriver was in the bike somehow, and it got stuck in my thigh."

Suddenly growing agitated, he tries to sit up. "This is bullshit," he growls. "I'm leaving."

Eira claps her gloved hands together, just once, commanding the attention of the room. Two sets of eyes lock onto hers. She snaps her fingers and points her gloved finger at Andrew. "Stay put and lie back down."

Eira removes her examination gloves. "You have a screwdriver sticking out of your leg. Can we all just calm down please?" She tosses them in the trash. "And you," she says, pointing to Jonah, "any more outbursts and you're gone."

Jonah nods his head, and Andrew sighs, lying back on the ER bed.

"Dr. Gregory has also ordered you a penicillin and tetanus shot. We usually put the tetanus in the deltoid," she says, cocking her head to the side, "so, the arm. But the penicillin goes in the glutes."

Andrew arches his eyebrow; a quiet stillness blankets the room as he slowly turns his head to Jonah. His breathing turns erratic. It's like he can't suck in enough air. "She wants to stick me in the ass!" he bellows, his voice dropping to a low rumble before cracking into a high squeak, as if he's hitting puberty all over again.

Following Andrew's stare, Eira turns her gaze to Jonah. Quietly, she asks, "Which do you think he'll want first?"

"I'm right fucking here!"

"Yes, but you're not exactly in control of your emotions. Asking you would be like asking which came first, the chicken or the egg, and that's not going to help."

She tries for compassion, but the flat look Andrew sends her way says she missed the mark.

"Just give me the damn shots," he grits. His jaw tense, but she sees the moment he shifts from fighting to acceptance.

Eira exhales slowly, seizing the crack in his stubbornness. "Think you can help me remove his left arm from his hoodie so I can give him the shot?"

Jonah silently nods his answer.

Looking closer at his hoodie, she notices an Instagram square logo on his left arm with white block letters spelling something, but it's badly frayed, making it unreadable.

Andrew lifts his left arm as Jonah walks to the other side of the bed.

Jonah lowers his voice. "Hey, sweetheart," he teases. "I've been itching to get your shirt off for a while."

Andrew mumbles under his breath, "Perverted fucker."

Chuckling, Jonah stuffs his fingers of both hands into the holes from the fray of Andrew's hoodie and rips it open, grunting like an ogre.

"Explains why you're single," mumbles Andrew.

Laughing, Jonah walks around the bed. Closing his hand into a fist, he bumps it against the side of Andrew's leg. "Just order another one, sissy."

Snapping on a fresh pair of exam gloves, Eira lets out a squeak. "Oh my God. You ripped it. That's harsh."

Tearing the alcohol wipe package, she swipes the wet square across Andrew's shoulder. Everything stills, and she gets the first good look at him.

Jet-black hair trimmed to the skin on the sides and back with bangs cascading gracefully over his forehead, all blended smoothly. What hair he has is scattered and flattened about his head since being inside his helmet. There's this piece sticking straight up as if he'd run his fingers through it in agitation.

Eira waves her hand over his arm where she's scrubbed his shoulder with the alcohol square, trying to dry it faster.

She notices a scar etched delicately through his eyebrow. Andrew's intense jaw clenches and releases, the only sign he's feeling pain. His chin is framed by a shadow of dark stubble. Andrew radiates strength, drawing her in with his raw magnetism.

His eyes have truly captivated her. Deep pools of blue, reminiscent of the Indian Ocean. Lurking below is so much pain, with a mountain high of over-thought emotions. She recognizes it because it visits her frequently.

As her gaze travels, she notices his long and solid fingers, the kind that can either build or break. There are scratches on the back of his hands, expected from the concrete he sailed over. She's mentally cataloging his lack of jewelry. Despite his accident, he has impeccably clean fingernails, neatly trimmed just short of his fingertips.

Andrew clears his throat, and his half-smile demands Eira's attention.

Wow, Andrew's smiling. He's attractively commanding when he scowls, but he's devastatingly dangerous when he smiles.

Andrew notices Eira's perusal of him, deepening his smile. His lips part as his tongue grazes over, leaving them glistening.

How can a simple act be stunning? Eira slowly blinks, a blush of red singeing her face. Twisting, she reaches for the tetanus shot. She needs to focus on work. Now is not the time to get distracted by a handsome face.

Coating her lips with a fake, saccharine smile. Eira says really fast, "Don't freak out, but after this shot, I'm cutting your jeans off."

Eira presses the needle into Andrew's waiting arm. Her thumb depresses the plunger at a controlled pace, pushing the tetanus shot into the muscle of his arm.

Two things happen at once. Andrew roars like a wounded bear, the sound echoing off the walls, and Jonah erupts into laughter. Doubling over, he hugs his stomach as the howls keep coming.

Fighting to remain professional, Eira hides her chuckle as a cough while disposing of the syringe. As she turns to address Andrew, she's met with his deep glare.

Andrew rabidly objects, "The fuck you will!"

She'd been concerned when he roared, afraid she'd hurt him. Turns out, the thought of getting his jeans cut off makes him react like a cornered beast.

Jonah rights himself, wiping the tears from his eyes. "Slow it down there, Edward Scissorhands. Can't me and you just take his jeans off?" Jonah asks.

"No," Andrew violently shakes his head. "Back the fuck up. My jeans are not coming off. At. All!" Andrew roars, rolling onto his back, propping himself on his elbows.

"I have to give you the penicillin shot. And how am I going to give you stitches if I don't remove your jeans?" Eira questions.

"I don't need stitches and I'll drop my jeans enough for you to stab my ass, that's it. Fuck, the last needle you plunged in my arm left a gaping hole. Now you wanna play arts and crafts with my leg and a needle? Not. Fucking. Happening."

Andrew swings his left leg off the bed.

Jonah stops him by placing his forearm on Andrew's right lower leg.

"Where do you think you're going?" Jonah asks Andrew.

"I'm fucking done," Andrew shouts, grabbing the screwdriver handle and jerking the shaft out of his thigh. "The screwdriver's out. I'm not dying." Dropping the bloody screwdriver between his legs, he flings his arm towards Eira. "My needle quota is spent for the year. I'm out."

Andrew snatches his leg from Jonah's grasp, trying to sit up.

Raising her voice, she says, "You two are unbelievable." She presses the sterile pads she's grabbed against Andrew's punctured leg.

"Ow. Damn," Andrew growls as he stills his movement.

Eira stands at the side of the bed. "You wanna walk around looking like you lost the battle to a DIY project?"

Andrew's lips curve into a smirk. He grunts.

Using humor, Eira tries to diffuse the situation. "Hey, how about we get you patched up," Eira teases. "Then you're free to go play on your bike again, okay?"

"MOTORCYCLE! I was on my fucking motorcycle," Andrew yells through a tense jaw.

"He'll take the stitches." Jonah's jokester banter is replaced with his father-like authority.

Andrew nods towards Jonah. "He can take my jeans off. And you keep your damn scissors away from my jeans." He points his finger at Eira.

Jonah walks to stand beside Andrew, reaching for his belt. Jonah pauses midway and looks at Eira. "Shit, I got nothing, but this is fucking weird."

Eira walks to the other side of the bed, resting her palm on his wrist; she squeezes gently. "Andrew, clearly this is making you uncomfortable, and I apologize. I don't want you hurting." Looking at Jonah and silently pleading for backup, she adds, "How about we both do this? Having someone on each side, working with you, will reduce your pain." She tips her head. "What do you say?"

"Fine," Andrew clips.

"If you behave, I'll find you a sucker," Eira suggests.

"Ooo, me too?" Jonah chimes in.

"Sure!" Eira chuckles. "Help me get him situated back on the bed, then we'll start." She glances at Jonah as he grabs Andrew by the armpits and pulls him up on the bed.

Eira stifles a snicker, taking off her exam gloves and walking towards the wall to throw the gloves into the trash.

Jonah reaches for Andrew's belt, but he slaps Jonah's hand away.

"I can do it, you fucking miscreant." Andrew starts to unbuckle his belt. Eira hears a shutter-click noise and notices Jonah has his phone pointed at Andrew.

"You did not just take a fucking photo of me?" Andrew points towards his feet. "Man, make yourself useful and take my boots off." Andrew props himself on his elbows, eyeing Jonah with unease until he puts his phone in his pocket. Andrew finishes unbuttoning his jeans when Eira walks to his side. Situating her new pair of gloves on her hands, Jonah tosses Andrew's boots into one of the chairs, walking to stand at Andrew's midsection on his other side.

Jonah looks at Andrew, then Eira, then back to Andrew. Jonah asks, "We ready?"

Both speak at the same time: "No," says Andrew; "Yes," says Eira.

Jonah and Eira look at each other, then down at a frowning Andrew.

Jonah's gaze bounces between the two of them. "Here's what we're gonna do. Andrew, push off the bed with your feet, we'll pull your jeans down past your ass, you lay back on the bed, and we will pull 'em off. Got it?"

Eira nods. "Yes."

Andrew rests his head on the mattress and groans. "Fuuuck."

Taking a deep breath, he props his feet flat onto the bed and lifts his rear off the bed. Eira and Jonah pull Andrew's jeans down his legs below his butt cheeks, fast. Not trying to add to his pain, but fast enough it's definitely testing his limits.

Andrew exhales, relaxing his butt back on the bed. He lifts his arm, allowing the crook of his elbow to drape over his eyes. Jonah and Eira together wiggle his jeans past his thighs.

"Shit," Andrew protests.

Eira and Jonah have been concerned with removing his jeans swiftly. Not really paying attention to Andrew, just the motion of removing his jeans with as little pain as possible. His jeans are down to the bend of his knees when he sucks in a breath. "Wait," he pleads.

Stopping, both Eira and Jonah look at Andrew, giving him a chance to breathe.

"Almost done," Jonah speaks softly.

Andrew exhales. "Just give me a minute."

Eira lifts her eyebrows in question.

Making sure Andrew's eyes are still covered by his arm, she looks at Jonah. Smiling, she tips her head towards Andrew's chest. Jonah follows her nod.

He tilts his head back and roars with laughter.

Andrew jostles, uncovers his eyes, and props himself on his elbows again. He glances around the room, looking confused. "What's so damn funny?"

Jonah laughs harder.

"Interesting choice of underwear," Eira offers, feeling her face blush seventeen different shades of red.

"An elephant... trunk... on your..." Jonah gasps between peals of laughter. "Fly?"

"They're my boxers, you ass. Can we hurry this along? All this pain is wearing me thin. Jonah, give me the damn cover," Andrew demands. Eira points her gloved finger to one of the chairs against the wall where a cover is folded. Jonah takes his time grabbing it and then tosses it to Andrew.

"This day just keeps getting shittier," Andrew grumbles as he catches it.

Jonah and Eira grasp Andrew's jeans by the foot holes; one tug swiftly removes them without a complaint from the patient.

Eira frowns, then cocks her head.

Getting Jonah's attention, she points to Andrew's socks.

"Oh, fuck man," Jonah wheezes. "Your socks are better than your draws. Nom Nom, ginger pussy eating tacos." Jonah nudges Andrew's foot. "You got any more surprises we need to know about?"

Eira hides her smile behind the back of her forearm, but her laughter squeaks out and mingles with Jonah's; they exchange amused glances.

Andrew throws his arm back over his eyes. "No," he sneers.

Eira gathers the tetanus shot and alcohol, giving him a moment to breathe.

"Turn to your side, bend your leg slightly. But you have to relax, ok? Keep holding the gauze here, and this will be..." She pauses, glancing around the room, making eye contact with Andrew, then Jonah. "...well, I can't lie, this may sting."

Standing behind Andrew, Eira swabs his glute and stretches the skin taut with one hand. She drives the needle into his muscle and depresses the plunger slowly, careful not to tear his muscle.

Counting in her head, she reaches two when he groans a guttural moan of pain.

"Fuck!" he barks, panting to regain control. "You said *may* sting, like maybe it wouldn't!"

"You're doing great, Andrew," she reassures him.

"Doing great? My ass is burning! You're roasting it from the inside out!"

After a few more seconds of hearing Andrew pant, she calmly states, "Done." Disposing of the needle, she asks, "You think you can roll over now, or I can help you?"

With a sigh, Andrew rolls onto his back.

Sensing his discomfort rising, Eira begins to clean Andrew's thigh in preparation for his stitches.

"I have to give you another shot," she says. "It has to be inside your wound. You know this, right?"

Andrew nods stiffly.

"Andrew, use your words. I can't proceed without your consent," Eira quietly demands.

Andrew slowly props himself up on his elbows. "You've got ten minutes," he says, taking a deep breath, "to do whatever you need to me." He exhales. "Without having to tell me what you're doing. After that, I'm leaving." He holds Jonah's stare. "Got that? I. Am. Leaving."

Andrew lies back on the bed, resting his arm over his eyes. Eira senses the seriousness of Andrew. Moving quickly, she sanitizes the area around his wound. Injecting him with anesthetic has Andrew balling up his fist and slamming it into the bed.

"Almost done," Eira promises.

Ensuring Andrew cannot feel his thigh, Eira stitches the skin together.

Alternating between stitching and checking on Andrew, she's on the second-to-last stitch when Dr. Gregory walks in.

"My apologies, Eira. The patient in room five took longer than I anticipated." Looking over her shoulder, he says matter-of-factly, "Looks like you've got it. Your expertise is great as always."

Eira nods, not breaking her stride. She's aware of the time constraint. Not having known Andrew long, but he's given her the impression he will, in fact, leave after the ten minutes are up, not caring if his wound is stitched or not.

Dr. Gregory peers at Andrew. "You'll need to keep the stitches clean and dry for the first twenty-four hours. After that, you can shower but quickly pat them to keep them dry. You can't ride your motorcycle for about a week. You'll need to set up a follow-up doctor's appointment after ten days. Any questions?"

Andrew's response is clipped. "No," he says, then shifts his glance to Eira. "Two minutes."

Tugging the final stitch tight, Eira announces, "I am done. Jonah, will you help me put his jeans on?"

"Minute twenty," Andrew states.

Eira exhales, waiting for Jonah to bring Andrew's jeans to the end of the ER bed.

Dr. Gregory scowls. "Eira, has this patient been giving you a difficult time?" His eyes track to each person in the room. "I didn't hear any more yelling. I heard some laughter, so I thought all was good. Was I incorrect?"

Eira speaks to Dr. Gregory, "It's fine. If you'll just step back, please?"

Eira glances at Jonah. "His jeans, can you get them? Before he walks out?"

Dr. Gregory looks between the faces of the three people in the room before settling on Eira. His voice is laced with rigid authority. "Eira, you did great. I'll finish here. There's another lab delivery at the front desk with Olive; will you take it up to them?"

"Of course. Thank you," she replies.

Having worked with Dr. Gregory for a bit, she's aware of the protective tendency he has towards his staff. To others who don't know him, that tendency comes off sounding like he's a prick.

Tossing her gloves into the trash, Eira walks out of the room. Before she can clear the doorway, she hears Jonah's growl as he slips into his father-like disposition again. Right outside the doorway, she hears Jonah clear his throat.

"Not sure what the hell that was all about, but we were fine," Jonah booms. "Andrew has a limit. It was approaching. I know this," Jonah aggressively points his finger at the doctor. "You made Eira feel like a heel. Your bedside manner fucking sucks!"

Eira can't stop her grin as she overhears this. She hovers by the doorway, listening.

Jonah tosses Andrew his jeans. "Get dressed, I'm not bailing you outta jail." Jonah snatches Andrew's boots from the chair.

"We're done here," Dr. Gregory says. "Next time, go to Memorial down the street. Your kind is welcome there." Dr. Gregory turns to leave. "Oh, and don't get any stupid ideas with Eira either. She has enough pain in her life; she doesn't need you two adding to it."

Eira sees Dr. Gregory heading her way, so she hustles to the front desk. She sneaks a glance behind her and sees Dr. Gregory heading in the opposite direction. "Unfuckingbelievable," she hears Jonah's voice boom.

"Take me home," floats Andrew's monotone voice down the hall. Eira hovers at the front desk, near Olive's beloved glass candy jar, fingers nudging through the nine pounds of candy. She grasps what she's been searching for.

Lifting her head, she checks the hallway mirrors as she stops to stand outside Andrew's room.

"Hey," Andrew addresses her as they leave.

Eira presents the sucker to Andrew. "I never go back on my word. Hope you like grape?"

Andrew smiles, taking the sucker. He rips the package off and plops it in his mouth. "Thanks," Andrew tells her around the sucker. Looking at Jonah, he says, "I need to sleep."

Jonah nods towards the exit. "Yep, let's go."

Eira watches them exit. Olive walks by loudly humming the theme song to *Kim Possible*. Turning to face Eira, she walks backwards, shaking her hips as she improvs a line from the chorus, *'I just can't wait until I hear Eira's cell phone ring.'*

Eira rolls her eyes and laughs. "You're ridiculous!"

Olive blows Eira a kiss, swinging her hips all the way to the front desk.

With a fading smile, Eira turns her attention back to the task at hand: the lab delivery.

For the rest of her shift, her focus is on providing the care her patients need. Every now and again, she smiles thinking of elephant boxers, cat-eating tacos socks, and a most intriguing guy.

Can I find a guy like that?

CHAPTER SIX

Andrew

A ndrew's home office chair squeaks with the constant jiggling from his restless foot. The floor lamp bathes the walls
in a warm hue. His laptop screen casts a faint glow, throwing shadows against the wall behind the desk as his fingers work through
edits. He's had the stitches removed for a couple of days now.
There's mild itching with minor aches to remind him of that day.

His fingers peck against the keys, finishing his latest post for his
social media account.

Thinking back to yesterday's motorcycle ride, he zeroes in on
his frustration with the highway having uneven lanes, making his
bike wobble. He has years of riding experience, but his concerns
are for the dangers presented to the inexperienced. His Gixxer
sustained no damage swerving between potholes, oil slicks, and
grass clippings, but it still holds the danger that he might leave for
a ride to never come back.

It's a constant possibility he long ago stopped giving headspace to.

Now he rides for one reason: his love for the ride.

He films his rides as an outlet that also funds his passion.

Andrew's desire to build a community for adventurous motorcyclists prompted the creation of his account. A place where bike enthusiasts can meet, whether online or in person, to do what they enjoy, feeling the uninhibited wind against their skin, despite wearing protective gear. It's not just a physical experience, but a visceral one, a combination of tangible and sensory inputs creating a feeling of freedom. There's a connection between rider, bike, and road.

Some people ride to see if they can outrun the ghosts of their past, even if for only a couple of hours a day; moto-therapy grants a reprieve nonetheless.

Andrew takes his viewers along with him as he rides his motorcycle between semi-trucks, weaving through traffic with calculated moves, and skillfully splitting lanes with quick reflexes.

He's known for his carefree lifestyle, perfecting the art of standing on the seat of his bike, adding more to his adrenaline-fueled experiences.

Living life to the fullest, he presses hard against societal norms.

Is Andrew reckless?

Depends on who's asking and their interpretation of reckless.

While social media has fueled his motorcycle passion, the flood of direct messages pouring into his phone is like someone has dumped gasoline on an open flame.

Ladies sending him DMs brazenly ask if they can ride the biker, not the bike. They've gone as far as asking Andrew if they can ride him, while he rides them on his bike along the salty shorelines between Amelia Island and Jacksonville.

Andrew's social media also allows him to use his passion as a distraction to move past Claire.

To fully understand how he allowed himself to be taken advantage of, he must first heal the wounds Claire created. To figure out how he's going to show up for himself, he needs to focus on himself and protect his heart.

With healing comes loneliness. Some days it's like a crippling disease, but most days, it gives him the reprieve he so craves. But recovering doesn't stop the world from spinning, and even the most disciplined man eventually tires of his own hand.

Social media is a world of easy temptation. A place where the line between reality and fantasy blurs with each passing moment. For Andrew, it's just a distraction; for others, it's their livelihood.

He scrolls through the endless stream of messages, each one offering a different sexual pleasure; most are explicit.

Andrew wonders if the answer is simply no more relationships? Thanks to Claire, trust is not easily given to anyone these days.

Oddly enough, he's landed in a space where many of the ladies are upfront in their request for booty calls, casual sex, one-night stands, and friends with benefits.

All he has to do is be present.

Come.

Leave.

The ladies are hyped up on the allure of him, of his bike, of the persona they've constructed in their minds of what being a biker means and his sexual prowess.

Simply put, it's easy; they're easy, so why couldn't he be easy?

Closing his eyes, he contemplates.

"I'll message the first one and see where it goes," he mumbles to himself. "But first, food."

He'd been so immersed at work with scheduling clients that eating continues to get pushed back, then it's time to lock up.

After dressing for the night's ride, his thumb rubs the cool metal of his motorcycle keys. Bringing them to his lips, he recites the same words he says before each ride: "Watch over me."

The soft glow of the kitchen light above the sink assures Andrew he won't be walking into a dark house upon his return. With a quick glance, he knows his house is in order before stepping into the evening air. Satisfied, he strides towards his bike. Starting his motorcycle always soothes him with the familiar hum of the engine.

Driving into the mild October night, he rides towards the sushi shop.

As Andrew waits in a booth after placing his order, he opens his phone, glancing at the first message.

If you bite my neck, I'll suck your cock.

He drops his chin to his chest, shaking his head nervously. Then, he hears a snort that did not come from him.

"Wow, to the point, that one is, huh?" A feminine voice quips while sliding Andrew's Rainbow Sushi Roll further on the table. She pulls a pair of chopsticks from her apron pocket, laying them beside his plate.

Embarrassment paints the tips of his ears pink. "It's empty in here; I didn't know I'd have to worry about a reader over my shoulder," he replies.

"Hey, don't be embarrassed. I'm just shocked there's no preamble. I guess, 'I'm here. I'm horny' really gets to the point if that's what you're into?" says the feminine voice.

"Look, can we start over? This time without you reading my phone messages?" Andrew asks, straightening himself in his booth.

"Sure, I'm Penelope," she announces. Fully coming into Andrew's view, she extends her hand for a shake.

Andrew accepts. When he lifts his gaze, he's met with a midsection adorned with a hint of creamy white skin leading up to a gray sweater snugly cradling each of her perky breasts.

Fishnet fabric peeks out from underneath her shirt, covering her arms. Her lips, outlined in matte black with the flesh of her lips a vibrant red, highlighting a trio of hoop lip rings that divides her bottom lip. Onyx-black mascara and eyeliner accentuate her eyes, with a dusting of black eyeshadow. Her hair, a mesmerizing ombre of red and black, cascades in waves around her shoulders; her bangs stop above her pierced black eyebrows.

Andrew's gaze continues downward. Leading to a black, short skirt that flares open mid-thigh. The belt, fashioned from chains, dangle the four crosses filed to a point spanning across her waist. She's wearing red and white stockings, reminiscent of candy canes. Her boots are chunky black *Doc Martens*.

As Andrew takes in the entirety of her goth appearance, he is captivated by her unique style and undeniable presence.

Clearing her throat, she tells him, "You can call me Pen."

Andrew recovers, removing his hand from hers, he tells her, "You can call me Andrew."

Pen smiles. "Shout if you need anything before I come back. Ok?" she tells Andrew as she walks out of his sight.

Andrew nods his head. Placing his phone face down on the table, he eats his sushi roll without interruption.

Wiping his mouth, Pen makes her way back to his table. Stacking his dishes in her arm, she asks, "Is there anything I can get you?"

Andrew shakes his head. "No. Thanks, though."

"Listen, I get off in about an hour. I'm heading to Utah in the morning. All my stuff is packed. Would you be interested in keeping me from being bored?"

"Pretty bold of you considering your earlier comment," Andrew says and chuckles.

"I was meaning with social media. You don't know what you're getting. Could be a dude that looks like a chick willing to suck your dick. At least with me, you know what you're getting."

Andrew raises his right eyebrow. "Well, I don't know what you're packing under that skirt."

With Pen's free hand she grabs Andrew's right hand and places it over her pelvis, patting it a few times in various places.

"Do you feel a dick hiding in there?" She asks Andrew, placing his hand back on the table. "Look, it's up to you. You were looking for some action anyway. I'm just making it easier. Simple yes or no will suffice." Pen's toe taps the floor.

"You can use the time I take to finish, to line out your next conquest. I can even help you pick her out?"

Andrew meets Pen's stare. "I don't usually do this. It feels weird... wrong. Isn't this disrespectful to you or something?"

Pen shakes her head, holding up her fingers as she counts. "One, I asked you. Two, we both are interested. Three, wait 'til we're done before you automatically assume *you* are disrespecting *me*. You could be wearing that shoe after I'm done with you." Pen winks as she walks away to dump the dishes in the kitchen sink. She twists about halfway away from Andrew. "I'm serious. Get your girls lined up. You've got about forty more minutes." She pushes the swinging doors open, disappearing to the back.

Andrew, not sure what to do, but he's determined to try 'no strings attached' with a woman like Pen, so he stays in the booth, cleaning his DMs.

Messages like, "I like mine extra nasty, you down with that?" or "I can't wait to tie you up and ride you til I come," are easy to delete.

The message making him gag at the same time Pen walked past his booth is, "I wanna put my thumb in your ass and lick pop rocks off your hairy balls."

Andrew grimaces. "What the fuck is wrong with people?"

Pen reads the message over his shoulder and laughs. Finding her laugh contagious, he releases a nervous chuckle, sounding much like a scuff.

After she recovers, she asks, "What do you post about?"

Andrew pulls up his page and flips his phone towards her. "Nothing that should make the crazies come out and wanna play."

"Oh, please." She braces herself on her forearms, getting closer to his phone. "You have the ultimate thirst trap here. Sleek, black motorcycle. Lean, sexy body, wearing a dark helmet." She scrolls slightly on his screen. "Is your visor always this dark, like you never show your face?" She asks.

"Never show my face," he confirms with a nod.

"You've tapped into the primal mix of mystery, danger, and desire." Turning her head towards his, she scrunches her face, making the piercings in her eyebrows wiggle. With a mysterious smirk, she tells him, "I think you know *exactly* what you're doing." She nods her head towards the back of the restaurant. "Come on. My apartment is upstairs. Let's see who's disrespecting who tonight."

Andrew slides out of the booth, following her up a set of rickety stairs. The wood groans beneath his weight as he climbs, gingerly stepping on each of the eighteen boards.

Pen has her apartment door open, waiting for him. Andrew steps into her kitchen looking around the area. "I thought you said you were packed up?" His distrust flares.

Pen squeezes his shoulder. "My stuff is packed. It's a furnished place. You okay? You look kinda pale. Can I get you something to drink?"

Andrew shakes his head. "Nah. Trusting lately has been like strolling blindfolded into a piranha pool. I'll get over it."

"I can take the lead if you're okay with that?" Pen shrugs her shoulders. "This is what you're chasing, right? With those girls in your DMs?" Pen lifts her voice in question. "Let me give you a taste. Tell me to stop at any time, k?"

"I'm not really *chasing* anything," he answers.

Pen drapes her arms around Andrew's neck. She kisses his neck below his ear, making Andrew shiver. The metal of her lip rings is cold while her lips are warm. He wraps his arms around her middle, leaning into her neck. He inhales deeply.

Pausing her kissing on Andrew's neck, she nudges him with her nose. "Did you just sniff me?" she asks with a smile against his skin.

"Yeah," Andrew chuckles, "you smell like sugar cookies and oranges."

He slides his fingers under her shirt, gently massaging her nipples. His fingers strumming along her jewelry has her moaning with pleasure. He pulls the top of her sweater down and gently kneads her tits, nipping at her stiff peaks. Adding his hot tongue, he swirls across her chilled breast.

Pen groans, "Mmm, that tickles my clit."

Andrew unties her top, tossing it behind him haphazardly. He wraps Pen's hair around his hand, closing it into a fist, as he pulls her head back. He teasingly traces kisses down her neck and between her breasts, sucking gently as he pulls her skin into his mouth.

"Kiss me, please," Pen begs.

Andrew shakes his head. "I can't."

He feels Pen's shoulders stiff. "It's too intimate. I'm not doing that again," Andrew replies as he sucks on her nipple. He lets go with a pop, placing his hand on her shoulder, gently pushing down as he says, "But *you* can kiss something else."

Pen chuckles, her eyes soft. "Look who's taking control. Hmm, whatever shall I do on my knees?"

She slowly lowers herself to the floor. "You want me to kiss your...?" Not waiting for his response, she grabs his jeans, unbuttoning them and pulling them down.

She's met with a hard cock straining against his red boxers; they have a seductive swirl of whipping cream and a cherry on top, boldly printed across his fly.

Pen giggles, looking up into Andrew's eyes.

"I didn't plan this, but show me how you'd lick it," Andrew smirks, nudging Pen's mouth closer to him. "I need to feel your mouth around my cock, Pen."

Dragging his boxers down to his thighs, Pen grabs his cock. Her hand milks his thick shaft, squeezing on the way down and loosening on the rise.

Andrew lets out a satisfying growl as she teases his balls with her other hand. Taking his dripping crown into her mouth, she hollows her cheeks, sucking over it. Flattening her tongue, she licks Andrew's dick from root to tip.

He groans. "Stop fucking teasing me," Andrew demands.

Pen smiles, swallowing his thickening length; her lips stretch over him. Not stopping until he touches the back of her throat, she sucks him faster, Andrew's cock pulsates against Pen's tongue.

Andrew groans. His balls tighten and his thighs vibrate as he leans back and releases. Pen's head loosely bobs on his cock. His cum dripping out of her mouth as it splats to a pool on the floor.

Andrew watches, a little shocked. He wrinkles his brow, looking at her in confusion.

Pen spits the offending sludge into her hand. "I don't swallow. That shit's fucking gross."

She stands, walking to the kitchen sink. Spitting before she washes her hands, she then cups water into her mouth. Swishing her mouth, she spits it again into the sink. Taking a paper towel, she dries her face. No rush and no apology. Turning to Andrew, she asks in a flat voice, "You need some paper towels?"

Still bewildered, he nods. "Yes."

She runs a paper towel under lukewarm water, wringing out all excess. Her movements are clipped, clinical, and completely lacking in emotion. She hands the paper towel to Andrew.

Sensing a complete frigidness radiating from Pen. He furrows his eyebrows. After cleaning himself up, he tucks himself into his boxers. His head volleys back and forth from Pen to himself. Fastening his jeans, he glances up to see Pen watching him; she's unreadable. "What about you?" Andrew asks, taking note that her lipstick isn't the least bit smeared.

"PFFT!" she scuffs. "I was proving a point, and joysticks don't satisfy me. I don't get off from being filled."

Andrew cannot fight his bewilderment, confusion clearly written on his face.

"Did you still want my help with the DM girls?

Andrew scoffs; the shifts in her personality make him dizzy. "No, I'm gonna leave. Uh, Utah, right? You have a safe trip."

He has his hand on the doorknob when he turns back to Pen. "How do I get out of here?"

"Shit, I'll have to walk you out. Follow me."

Andrew, still reeling from the puzzling end of the blow job, feels hollow. He follows Pen down the groaning stairs towards the restaurant's door.

She unlocks the door, and he walks over the threshold, guiding him outside. Standing on the sidewalk, the humidity is still thick.

Pen's personality shifts yet again. She sneers, "Tell me, Andy, who feels disrespected now?"

"Name is Andrew," he clips, "what happened?"

Pen licks her lips. "Just so you know, not all people get off all the time. Those DM girls—half of them are all show and no soul. So, I've gotta ask, how's it feel being disrespected?"

Andrew shakes his head in confusion. *How did I... is she the same... what the fuck?*

Pen nods towards Andrew's bike. "Feeling used after the blow-and-go? You'd better get used to it. Until you can be intimate, like actually *kiss* someone, how you feel right now is the only feeling you'll have. Later," she says with a wink. Closing the door in his face, he hears the click of the lock, and then she walks away.

Andrew climbs onto his bike to ride home. Navigating the streets from memory allows him to reflect on his night.

What a rollercoaster.

He waltzed with lust but ended in a tango of confusion. Andrew exhales.

Pen mentally led him down the self-loathing path he'd never dared to tread since before Claire.

Before Claire, he filled his plate from the pussy buffet. Being gluttonous, he kept going back to the buffet. His actions never weighed on his conscience. After Claire, he can no longer sample from the buffet. That lifestyle disgusts him now. He needs commitment, meaning, depth, love, and compassion, and he needs all that to be reciprocated to him.

Andrew opens his throttle; the vibration of his engine drowns out the clamor of his thoughts as he rips through the muggy Florida streets.

Pen has forced him to confront his emotions. Right now, he will not do commitment, and it appears he will not do pussy buffet either. He knows he has to work on himself, but being alone is daunting. Still, the thought of using someone else to fill the ache Pen and Claire left behind?

No, that's not him. Not anymore.

Or is it?

His indecisiveness has made him well and truly fucked.

In an attempt to clear his head, he tempts fate yet again. Riding down the streets of Jacksonville, he brings his feet to his seat, allowing him to stand tall on his motorcycle seat. Arms spread wide, balancing his body like a silhouette against the backdrop of the city skyline. Andrew wonders if his demons are always going to follow him.

Lowering his feet back onto their pegs, he sits his ass back into his seat. He's desperately searching for sanity. In a flash, he decides to go back to Texas, to Sage, for her unique brand of healing. It's a way to take back control of his body and his life and a proverbial middle finger to his own self-destructive tendencies.

Stopping off at his house, he gathers what he needs for his trip and rides towards Houston at ten thirteen at night.

He nods to himself. Knowing that in order for him to move forward, he needs to take it one day at a time, one foot in front of the other.

Navigating through his own fractured psyche is the knowledge that it is *his* journey, and he may just have to walk it alone. His vow to himself is a sense of direction and guidance, stability, and security; no longer being reactive to the happenings around him, but being unwaveringly rooted in his values and beliefs.

CHAPTER SEVEN

Eira

A lone in her room, Eira flips the month on her calendar from October to November. "Goodbye, witches," she sings. "Hello turkeys."

Hunching over her desk, she depresses the plunger of her green syringe-style ink pen. Writing her hospital shifts on each day allows Aunt Zia to fulfill her commitment to Eira's mother, keeping a watchful eye over her.

November has always been a difficult month for Eira, as it was her mother's favorite. The nostalgia of Thanksgiving brings forth the mouthwatering memories of her mom's oven-basted turkey. How they used to huddle together, looking through the window of the oven as the marshmallows double in size only to collapse seconds later as they'd melt over the sweet potatoes. And the all-knowing sulfur smell of boiled eggs.

Clicking the pen closed, she tosses it onto her desk. Stretching her back, she's surrounded by the silence of an empty house. Eira feels the weight of her loneliness pressing down upon her like a weighted anxiety blanket.

The springs in the bed squeak as she plops onto her mattress. Staring at the ceiling fan, the blades swirling tiny gusts of air over her skin; she longs for someone to hold her; to comfort her in the darkness, but she knows deep down she's better off alone.

Is it too much to ask to be genuinely loved? To be chosen for who I am, rather than what I offer.

"What's the use? Nobody really cares anyway," Eira mumbles.

Propping herself on her pillows, she leans against the headboard. Passing the time, she scrolls through her social media.

She notices a particular post has gotten significantly more views and comments than usual.

Intrigued, she taps on her post.

Smiling, she remembers. She'd felt particularly rebellious that day, feeling free, realizing she doesn't have to make herself feel small when it comes to her desires anymore. Her post reads, "**think I need to make a change to my appearance as a coping mechanism!?**"

Reading the comments, she feels the outpouring of support from her community bringing reassurance to her confused heart.

Their messages to her speak loudly, but there are three that warm her heart. These three people were the first three followers on her page. She's never met them, but she knows them.

No change is needed, says her first follower.

It's a them, not a you problem. Sometimes people are just assholes, says another.

You keep doing you, says a stay-at-home mom of six from Poland.

The uplifting comments do their job as her funky feelings fade away.

But nothing lasts forever.

Crude and vulgar messages blur together with those of edification.

How can the same message have two totally different meanings?

One drips of sexual innuendo from a guy who's always making vulgar comments to Eira and one from a girl who praises Eira for being her own champion.

Eira lets out an exasperated sigh. "Today, it's too much."

Before she closes her social media app, her eyes glance further down the screen. They land on Logan's profile icon. Curious as to why he's showing up in her DMs after three months, she clicks his message.

I love you. I miss you. Get back under me.

Eira wheezes at his message as if she were slapped. Her chest struggles to allow air inside. "He dumped me!"

She fully grasps the significance of his words; embedded inside is his unmistakable promise of pain.

She reads his words with detachment; her heart hardens again, remembering the trauma he's caused. The betrayal he's already orchestrated.

"No," she commands, her voice steady despite the storm raging within her. She replies to his message in all caps.

WE ARE OVER

She closes her eyes, breathing in the moment of calm.

Then.

Ping. Ping. P-Ping-g. Ping.

Ignoring him doesn't stop his spray of messages. Logan's responses are swift and vicious. His words are laced with venom as he hurls more poison at her with fury:

No one wants you; you're nothin' but a fuckin' cunt.

You're such a slut. Jumpin' from dick to dick tryin' to get filled the way I filled you.

You're pathetic.

You think you can be somethin' without me? I own you. You're still the same insecure little girl.

I love you, dammit! Just fucking come home! Don't make me come after you!

Eira's fingers click the three bars in the upper right corner of Logan's profile, pressing the 'Block' button.

Giving the middle finger to her phone, she mumbles, "Good riddance!"

Eira's onslaught of sadness hits deep in her chest as she realizes the person she once loved does not, and probably never did, love her in return. *How could he hate me this much?*

Logan's comments incinerate her heart as if it were the bullseye of his intended target.

She reads his messages, then reads them again.

Aggressively wiping a tear from her cheek, she tells herself aloud, "I'm done losing tears to this prick."

Eira mentally forces a hardened shell to surround her heart, forming a protective barrier. Weeks before he threw her out, Logan demanded Eira to change. Ever the people-pleaser, she'd changed just for him. Her reward for losing a little more of herself was him tossing her out like garbage.

Eira can't shake the feeling of impending doom, hanging over her like a dark cloud.

Logan has always perceived losing as a weakness. She knows he'll view her not coming back to him as him losing, and he's never allowed her to simply ignore him.

The meaning of those messages has fractured the walls of her fortress. She needs time to reinforce them. She feels unprotected, like she's teetering on the brink of emotional devastation. Refusing to let his words break her spirit, Eira forges herself as her therapist has taught her. She recognizes she's worth so much more. Accepting less is no longer an option for Eira.

Standing in front of the mirror, the glint of silver catches the light's reflection.

Smiling, she feels empowered.

Logan put his fist through one of his dining room walls, forbidding her to get her nose pierced. He'd thrown his phone at her, demanding she cancel the appointment.

No longer Logan's helpless victim, Eira is healing, becoming a warrior for herself. When others failed to protect her, she became what she wished they could be for her.

In a rebellious gesture to reclaim control over her own life, she now adorns herself with a dainty, silver-studded diamond nose ring. While it's small in gesture. It's huge symbolically. Closing her eyes, she envisions herself proudly throwing up her middle finger to Logan and anyone else trying to drag her down.

Sitting on the edge of her bed, Eira returns her attention to her social media. Scrolling through book posts, nursing humor posts, and motorcycle posts, all brought to her by her trusty social media algorithm.

Eira's learning to steer her solitude towards strength. Recognizing true independence, as well as value, stems from within oneself.

In the motorcycle community, many creators are grappling with emotional turmoil; yet one individual, FriktionZone, stirs something deep inside her each time his posts land on her FYP.

While she knows nothing about this person, she can reason from some posts that this person is a 'he'. His posts reflect the same thoughts as Eira's: happiness is solely each one's responsibility.

He embodies the typical characteristics revered in the motorcycle community: a sleek bike, a tall biker wearing protective riding gear, and a closed tinted visor on a dark helmet. His identity remains hidden, but unlike his physical features, it's left up to the viewer's imagination.

Eira has seen his posts sporadically for the past month, but this is the first time he's posted with his location visible.

He's an hour north of me, and his content makes him seem like he's a seasoned rider, someone I could learn from?

She's messaged motorcyclists in the past, as well as received offers to ride with other bikers, but for reason she can't put her finger on, she's hesitant to message him.

Closing her eyes, she sighs. With newfound confidence, her fingers tap out a message.

Do you want to meet for a ride? We're only an hour away from each other. I'm fairly new, so any help would be appreciated. She hits send.

She thinks to herself, w*ell, it's up to him now.*

Just as she begins to doubt herself, a notification appears on her phone. She's talked herself into believing her message will just get buried because of his large following. Truthfully, she wasn't expecting an answer this quickly.

Her heart skips a beat as she reads his words. *Sure. When & Where?*

Eira hesitates and then types. *Vilano Beach in about two hours?*

FriktionZone is quick to respond. *Meet at Pelican Point?*

Realizing she does not know what he looks like, she types, *how will I know it's you?*

His response is quick. *Probably be the only bike in the parking lot, but I'll be wearing a blue hoodie.*

After typing and deleting a couple of messages, Eira settles on: *Okay, see you there.* She hits send; the nervous butterflies take flight in her stomach. *Did I do the right thing? Is this being too rash, meeting a stranger?* Then she reasons, *we'll be in public. It will be fine.* Inherently, she trusts him, though she doesn't know why.

She dresses for her motorcycle ride, then lifts her backpack that she has hanging on the back of her desk chair.

She checks it for all her necessities: Lip balm, hand wipes, hoodie, moisturizing eye drops, ibuprofen, tampon, phone charger, microfiber cloth, lotion, panty liner, AA batteries, umbrella, deodorant, a pair of socks, and peppermint gum.

Tossing a bottle of apple juice in the air and catching it, she flips the light on in the pantry. Digging for her secret stash of onion chips that Uncle Zio hides in the cauliflower cracker box, she flicks off the light and stuffs them into her backpack. Sliding one arm through a strap, she slings the backpack onto her back and guides her other arm through the second strap. She tugs on the bottom to tighten it over her shoulders. Grabbing her helmet, she tucks it securely under her arm.

Her phone pings with a notification.

She'd turned the volume up on her phone when she was messaging him, and she'd forgotten to turn it down.

It pings again. Then again. Her phone pings again as she's walking across the house to the garage door.

Setting her helmet on the kitchen counter, she takes one last glance around the house. She flips on the light above the sink.

Her phone pings again.

Miffed, she places her fingerprint on her phone screen. Social media notifications line the top of her phone.

Her notifications show that someone has commented on her post about life being really hard lately and sixteen other posts.

Tapping the inbox, she sees a barrage of notifications; all from the same person. Username Space_wzrd12 has hit the heart button on forty different posts in less than a minute, officially spamming her account.

Urgh! I'm gonna get shadow banned again!

Her phone pings.

FriktionZone: We need face pics.

Eira: K, did U change your mind?

FriktionZone: Face pic

FriktionZone: Then we meet.

"Wow," she says, jutting her hip against the kitchen sink.

Eira has a tender head, and after her first motorcycle ride, her hair looked like a rat's nest. The tangles were so bad that she had to cut her hair. Aunt Zia found Eira a skullcap covered in tiny syringes, stethoscopes, hearts, and wheelchairs. Now, before every ride, Eira tucks all her hair inside.

The patience it takes for her to take a great selfie is something she's never really had. Holding her phone one-handed, she struggles to keep her face inside the camera area as her thumb skips over the shutter circle. She takes a photo just as she blinks. Sporting the just-stoned look, with her tongue barely peeking out between her lips, and not a strand of hair in sight. She chuckles and presses send.

Seconds later, she sees the status of the message change from 'Sent' to 'Seen.'

Twenty-seven minutes later, there's still no response.

"For real," she says, propping her feet onto a wooden kitchen chair.

Getting edgy, Eira decides she'll get her moto-therapy today, even if she rides alone.

As she locks her phone to stand, it pings. Unlocking it mid-stride, she stares at his picture and laughs. "Oh, that's too funny."

Balancing herself on the top step with her helmet tucked under her arm, she shuts the kitchen door to the garage. Thudding her palm against the garage wall, she hits the garage door button.

Sitting on her motorcycle, she adjusts her helmet. Engaging the clutch, she coasts backwards down the driveway.

Pressing the garage door remote attached to her motorcycle's cluster, waiting for the garage door to close, she lets her motorcycle idle while getting her mind right.

Eira's rides are purposefully south, in the opposite direction of Logan. She's used to staying out of his territory, always riding towards Melbourne.

Today, though, it's different. She fully embraces her unusual "fuck Logan" mindset. Throwing herself and caution to the wind, she rides north.

An hour later, she's pulling into the parking lot of Pelican Point.

Dropping her kickstand, she notices there's no motorcycle with a rider in a blue hoodie.

Well, the ride here was nice.

"I'll take what I can get," she says, removing her helmet. She rests it on her seat before walking to the cafe.

Pushing the door open, the heat clinging to her skin is chased away by the sharp chill of the air conditioner. The cool air bites into her sun-kissed skin as she makes her way to the restroom.

After washing her hands, she uses the damp paper towel to wrap around the door handle. Pulling, she holds the door open with her foot and tosses the paper towel into the trash can.

Leaving the cafe, she waves and tells the cashier, "Thanks."

The humid ocean air caresses her skin as she walks towards her motorcycle. The sea breeze envelops her, calming her anxious heart.

"It's always the same," she says aloud, exhaling while throwing her leg over her seat. Holding her helmet with both hands, she pulls the chin straps away from the sides of her helmet. Inside her helmet, she notices white contrasting with the black interior. Looking more intently, she sees the white cap with all the nurse vibe pictures. "I've got to get a balaclava instead of this skullcap," she mumbles as she hears a motorcycle getting closer. Pausing with the skullcap, she rests it in her lap.

The motorcycle with the rider wearing a blue hoodie pulls into the parking spot beside her. Allowing his bike to idle, he lifts the visor and squints against the sunlight.

Turning to look at Eira, his eyebrows furrow as he cocks his head to the side. "You look familiar. Do I know you?"

He removes his helmet, resting it on his gas tank.

Eira chuckles. "I'm guessing you're not talking about the picture I sent you earlier?"

His scowl bores into her. "You sound familiar, too."

Eira quips, "Where should I start?" Nodding to his thigh, she adds, "How's the hole in your thigh?"

He twists his body towards her. "Were you at The Club when that screwdriver stabbed me?"

Their gaze locks and she snorts. "Andrew, I stuck you twice with a needle. Tried to cut your pants off and laughed at your boxers." She lowers her voice to mimic his, "Then played arts and crafts with your leg and a needle." She changes her voice back to normal. "Remember me now?"

Andrew smiles with recognition. "You also laughed at my taco socks."

"Yeah, I did!" Eira laughs, nodding her head.

"So, we've been properly introduced, you ready to ride?" Eira asks, situating her helmet over her cap. Some of the anxiousness leaves her limbs; Andrew is not a complete stranger.

"I'll take the lead. I've gotta meet some friends in Jax later," Andrew says as he tightens his helmet strap under his chin.

Eira rides behind Andrew. He's careful as he navigates the pedestrian crossings of the road, keeping a more than safe distance from the car in front of him. He makes her ride to the right in her lane, which she has read this allows him to guard her from her left. He uses hand signals well before the turn or when he's going to slow down. He points to sites for her to look at. Eira senses Andrew's protectiveness. Early as it may seem, she feels she can let her guard down around him.

Despite her painful past with men, she feels he's different. There's this calming, safe, comfortable feeling she gets from his presence.

This is the first time in a long time she's allowed herself to truly relax. To enjoy a ride without the need for constant vigilance of others.

Andrew is cautious about where he rides. Steering clear of congested corners, he's showing Eira he, too, will protect her. He rides with at least a tire of distance between them. Sometimes, he lags behind her bike, forcing the car behind her to add distance while maintaining a full car length distance from the driver in front of him. One particular driver got heavy on the gas, so Andrew stopped at the intersection, waving Eira on. She was half a bike away before the driver started honking their horn and revving up their engine. Andrew casually drove off after making sure there was a sizable gap between Eira and them. Logan would never have put himself last to make sure she was protected.

I'll hang out with him just this once; it probably won't turn into anything, she thinks as she rolls her head to the side, feeling the stress melt away. *I'll happily take what I can get.*

Eira enjoys the company as well as the ride.

After riding for a couple of hours, she follows Andrew as he pulls off to the side of the road. Lifting his visor, she hears him say, "From here, you can ride that way." He points towards a highway.

"But I've gotta go this way," he adds, tossing his thumb over his shoulder.

"Thanks for showing me the area," she says as she adjusts her foot near the gear.

"Anytime, just message me."

As Eira rides home, the sun dances off the sparkling water like diamonds. Pristine sand on one side and black asphalt on the other stretches endlessly in both directions.

Singing along in her helmet, she wails the chorus while trying to make her gut stop wanting things she knows she cannot have.

CHAPTER EIGHT

Andrew

"Dammit," Andrew grumbles to himself as he leaves wet footprints on his bedroom carpet.

When he's hyper-focused, simple tasks like putting away his clothes or starting the dishwasher are forgotten.

Freshly showered, Andrew's naked body is dripping water, forming a trail with each step. He grabs the stack of towels from the top of his dryer and carries them to his bathroom. Opening the cabinet door, he stuffs the towels onto the shelves.

Between the air conditioner temperature set to brass monkey cold and the ceiling fans whirling on high in every room, the trek across his house to gather his towels has him mostly air-dried.

After the cottony soft towel absorbs the few surviving water drops from his body, he tosses it over the wet spots on the tiled bathroom floor.

His testicles rest on top of the cool quartz vanity. Goosebumps pop all over his chest and arms as a cold shiver courses through him.

"Gnomes must have built this house," he hisses.

Dropping his toothbrush on the bathroom counter, he strolls into his bedroom in search of his boxers.

Grabbing the ones called the mascot, he steps his leg into the blue stars side and the other leg into the red striped side, pulling them up his legs.

Adjusting himself, his finger finds a frayed spot over the bald eagle's beak.

I need to update my auto-order, he thinks as his mind continues to race.

Remembering what Sage said about not letting his tattoo become dry, he slathers the healing ointment on his newly tattooed chest. Smearing the excess goop across his phoenix tattoo, he tightens the lid and places the jar back on his dresser.

Standing in front of the bathroom mirror, finally ready to brush his teeth, he stares at his tattooed chest.

The fire-engine red on the tip of the needle pointing north is the only color in his tattoo. The contrast in color immediately reminds him of its meaning, just as Sage told him it would.

Andrew pauses in brushing his teeth, finding himself lost in a memory, back in Houston on Sage's table.

"Shoog, I knew I'd see you again. I already designed it. Just tell me where you want it," Sage says as she hugs a dispirited Andrew.

Leading Andrew to her table, a sense of ease wicks up his spine, sending comfort with every step.

Watching his face in the mirror's reflection, she raises her eyebrow. "Doesn't seem as bad as last time, no?"

Andrew shakes his head. "Nah."

Sage's finger taps the right side of her chest. "On the other side of your phoenix?"

"Sure," Andrew replies, tossing his shirt into a chair.

"Maybe this can be a daily reminder to keep yourself grounded. Quit giving your strength away. Something bold, telling you to stay true to your path."

Lying across Sage's table, Andrew hears her say those calming words, "Close your eyes and rest for a bit, Shoog."

Andrew's eyelids get heavy and eventually close, allowing him to drift to sleep under the caring hand of Sage.

A little while later, Sage gently wakes Andrew. "You can wake up now, Shoog."

He is hit with a dull ache across his chest. Sitting up slowly, his fingers touch a bandage on his chest. "You covered it?"

Sage nods. "I did, for your ride back home." She points to his chest and explains, "It's an anchor and a compass rose joined as one. The arm of the anchor is the bottom circle of the compass. The shank of the anchor is the north and south needle of the compass. I've added more directional needles to make them look like an eight-point star. The red-tipped needle will always point True North. The rest is black." Silence falls across the shop.

Sage hands Andrew his shirt, as a tear drops from her lash. Gravity forces it to trail down her cheek. Andrew wipes it with his thumb, then dries it on his denim-covered thigh. Slipping his shirt back on, he reaches in his pocket for his wallet. He stills when he feels a warm hand pressing against his.

"No. It's my gift. You have not met her yet. But when you do..." Sage pauses, mid-sentence. Shaking her head slightly, she sighs, "... it's going to be wonderful."

Andrew says with a scoff, "You gonna point her out to me?"

"Shoog," she slowly says, "the *One*." She clasps her hands together as if she's praying. "You'll know. She'll put your heart together while ignoring her own. You will never be lost again, you hear me?"

Excess saliva pools in his mouth, snapping him out of his thoughts. He spits in the sink and finishes his bathroom routine.

As much as his hyper focus mind skips simple tasks, it also demands fixation. His closet is meticulously organized. His clothes hang on the closet rods by their function. The jeans he wears on his motorcycle rides are first; next are his newly purchased ones mixed with the ones he wears when he's hanging out, and finally are his trashed or will get trashed ones. These are for working on his bike or mowing his and the Anderson's lawn. T-shirts are hung by sleeve size, then by color, while his hoodies are arranged by degree of warmth. First are the hoodies keeping Andrew warm like an overcooked baked potato, followed by the ones for wicking sweat, then water-resistant, and lastly lightweight sun-protectant.

Striding into his closet, he steps into his jeans, then tucks in a black T-shirt. Dressing for a motorcycle ride in November, he bounces his shoulders inside his blue, breathable but wind-blocking hoody.

Searching around his house for his boots, his mind remembers something his dad used to say to him. "Riding is cathartic," he'd say. "It's a chance to clear your mind. Experience the exhilaration of just being one with your motorcycle. To some, it's a mode of transportation; to others, it's therapy, and for the rest, well, it changes daily, son."

Motorcycle rides used to be filled with happy memories of being with Claire. Now, they're attempts to outrun those memories. She isn't at the forefront of his mind as much, but the effects of what she did to him have left scars of extreme anger, betrayal, insecurity, fear, and pain.

Intrusive thoughts still play on loop.

Was I good enough? What could I have done better? How did I let her down? How was I so blind not to see any of it?

Andrew shakes his head to clear it like a nineteen-sixties Etch-A-Sketch.

I didn't let her down. There was nothing I could have done. That shit's on her.

Before Andrew leaves for his ride, his fingers tap rhythmically against the screen of his phone, checking the endless stream of notifications flooding his social media.

A post from Eira catches his eye. They've ridden together several times each week since their first ride at Pelican Point. Life hasn't been treating her well lately. She always puts on a strong front, but Andrew can tell she's hurting.

Her ex must have done something again.

Knowing she could benefit from a mental reminder, he comments on her post using a term from the latest exercise her therapist has taught her.

Get out of Limbic Friction!

Then, he checks his DM notifications. Bodhi left him another message. So has Eira. And a slew of other people, but those he just ignores.

Meet me at my house? Bodhi asks.

Bodhi is playful, easy to talk to, and direct, but honestly, a little high-strung. Her long lime-green hair and sharp claw-like fingernails add to her craziness. Andrew's friends don't really care for her, so he avoids mixing them.

Bodhi and Andrew have dated some; and other times, she just hangs out at his house. She doesn't ride motorcycles, but she doesn't complain when he does. She said she wants easy. He decided he can do easy.

When. Where? He asks Bodhi, and then when he doesn't get a reply right away, he reads a message from Eira sent three hours earlier.

Are you free to ride today?

Seeing that Bodhi is offline and not replying to his texts, he replies to Eira.

When. Where?

In the past, Andrew has avoided female riders, but Eira's new to motorcycles. Quiet and shy, Andrew feels she hides behind her helmet. She'll learn she can't outrun her demons soon enough, and until then, he can ride with her so she's not alone.

Before Andrew puts his phone away, he sees another post from Eira.

She praises the welcoming nature of the biker community, contrasting it with the lack of acceptance she feels from her own friends and family.

Andrew makes a mental note to talk to Eira. Not all communities are as welcoming as his. Andrew's group is more about the family forged from the open road with a sense of belonging. Some can be destructive; he'll have to warn Eira.

I'll meet you at the gas station off Racetrack Rd in 15 minutes, Eira DMs him.

Andrew, gearing up for his ride, flips on the light above the kitchen sink before grabbing his motorcycle key. Bringing it to his lips, he murmurs, "Watch over me," a familiar phrase he inherited from his father.

Andrew's bike has been basking in the November sun as he planned on riding earlier today. Closing the garage door, he wraps his hands around the handlebars while swinging his leg over his seat. The day's heat is harnessed in his motorcycle's seat, immediately radiating warmth to his ass cheeks.

With a twist of his motorcycle key, the silent neighborhood is filled with the unmistakable rumble of his engine. His neighbors across the street are an older retired couple, still ornery, but he watches out for them, and they for him. They know when his kitchen light is on, he's out, leaving them to keep a watchful eye over their little part of the neighborhood.

During the eight-minute ride to the highway, he takes the opportunity to clear his mind, purging unnecessary thoughts to focus solely on the ride.

Florida's sun shines on Andrew, the heat radiating off the pavement, warming his skin.

The gusts of wind passing through vehicles give him a rush, mirroring the thrill of riding in the vortex of doom behind semi-trucks. The exhilaration of the ride pulses through his veins, filling him with freedom and adventure.

Despite the delay at the traffic lights, Andrew feels alive. Uninhibited. The weight on his shoulders pressed by Claire lessens with each new day.

Grinning behind his helmet, he leans into the curves of the road, soaking in the very essence of the ride. He cuts through the wind like arrows shot from its bow.

With "Fever" from WesGhost blasting through his helmet, Andrew can't help but feel invigorated by the beat of the music. His body grabs hold of the rhythm as he jiggles his hips a little in his seat, his head bobbing to the music as he rides.

Andrew exits the road, pulling into the gas station parking lot beside Eira. She's leaning against her motorcycle with her phone in her hands.

Lifting his visor, Andrew asks, "Hey, you ready?"

Eira moves her phone towards Andrew. "Do you know this girl?" Eira continues talking to him as he takes her phone. "I posted something from our ride last weekend. Then she comments on it, accusing me of being a 'wobbly-eyed homewrecker'? I removed the post, but now she's blowing up my messages. Weird, right?"

Andrew hands Eira's phone back. "Yeah, I know her. Bodhi's harmless."

Eira raises her eyebrows at Andrew.

"What? She slid into my DMs a while back and now..." Andrew takes a deep breath, then shrugs. "...we're kinda..." Andrew exhales. "...ya know, seeing where it goes."

Eira purses her lips together and nods her head slowly. "So, what, I just ignore her comments about me being a cock-jumper?"

Andrew shakes his head. "Fuck no. I'll talk to her. What makes me worried is how all this is affecting you. I don't want you to get hurt." His concerned gaze locks onto her. "This kind of drama shouldn't land on you."

Eira clucks her tongue. "I'll ignore her just like I do all the pervs sliding into my DMs." Eira nods towards the gas pumps. "I need gas, then we can ride." Eira guides her motorcycle to the gas pumps.

Stepping off his motorcycle, Andrew tells Eira, "I don't need fuel, but I'm gonna get a drink. You want anything?"

Eira shakes her head as she pumps her gas. "No thanks," she calls over her shoulder.

After paying for his drink, Andrew walks to Eira. She's on her bike, visor down, head tilted towards the sky.

"I know you said 'no', but I got you this anyway," Andrew says softly.

Eira lifts her visor and turns her back to him. She shrugs her shoulders a couple of times, causing her backpack to jolt. Smiling at Andrew as she's looking over her shoulder, she says, "Thanks, will you put it in my backpack, please?"

Andrew unzips her backpack, dropping the apple juice inside, and chuckles. "No shit, you have an umbrella in here?"

As he finishes zipping it closed, Eira jokes, "Do you have a problem with me being prepared?"

Walking towards his motorcycle, Andrew smirks. "Nah, just thought I'd see a needle and thread before an umbrella."

"I've got a whole sewing kit in here, but what you won't find is a screwdriver. I've seen what it can do!" she calls out as Andrew walks his bike beside hers.

With a smile, he answers, "Touché." Nodding towards the road, he asks, "You ready?"

"Yep," Eira says before shutting her visor and following Andrew onto the highway.

As they ride, Andrew can't help but notice the tension between them.

Before their second ride, they had synchronized their comms through their helmets. Typically chatty, today she's unusually quiet.

Is her shitty ex giving her a tough time again.

Andrew queues the comms. "Why was Cinderella so bad at soccer?"

Eira responds, "No clue."

"Because she kept running away from the ball."

Andrew snickers. "Shit, that was horrible."

"It wasn't thaaat bad," Eira says.

"Hmmm. Why can't you hear a pterodactyl going to the bathroom?" Andrew asks.

"Oh God, no clue."

"Because the 'P' is silent."

Andrew exhales loudly. "That wasn't any better. Okay, last one. What's the difference between a poorly dressed man on a trike and a well-dressed man on a motorcycle?" Andrew asks.

"I don't know."

"Attire." Andrew laughs. "Now that one's funny, admit it!"

"Okay, that was funny," Eira replies, "but I don't think you should quit your day job!"

The rest of the ride passes without Eira's voice or laughter in his ear.

Even with music blaring in Andrew's helmet, her silence is deafening.

Andrew will talk to Bodhi, let her know Eira and he are just friends who ride their motorcycles together, that's it. He finds himself getting irritated, thinking about the upcoming chat with Bodhi.

I will not have another female dictating to me, placing demands on me, or treating me disrespectfully.

A phone call silences his music.

"Hello."

Law asks, "You wanna grab some sushi at that new place, then ride to the fountain?"

Andrew answers, "I could eat. We're on Route 13 now."

"Who's with you?" Law questions.

"I'm with Eira. We're twenty minutes out. See you there," replies Andrew.

Law disconnects the call, allowing Andrew to queue up the comms to Eira. "Law wants to grab some sushi, then ride to the fountain. You in?"

"I'm gonna pass. I've got an early shift at the hospital tomorrow. I'm gonna head home. Thanks for the ride, though." Eira waves as she breaks away from him, riding home.

As Andrew rides to meet up with his friends, he can't help but feel pissed about what Bodhi did to Eira. He knows it's not unusual for creators to have trolls on social media, but he will not let Bodhi become Eira's troll.

"I'm not starting this shit again," he grumbles.

CHAPTER NINE

Eira

Lounging on her bed, Eira edits her post yet again. It's titled **"Hating someone you've never met, REAL fan club behavior."**

Should I even post this?

Bodhi, the girl she asked Andrew about weeks ago, is becoming a constant negative voice. Not only in her posts but also in her DMs. Before therapy, she would have internalized the words from Bodhi. But on the healing side of Logan's abuse, she's found her worth and refuses to give up her value.

Eira decides it's time for Bodhi to feel the effects of her own words.

Eira scans over the post: text on screen, music, and caption, all selected to drive the message to her community that this type of behavior is not acceptable and will not be tolerated.

She taps the post button.

When she first showed Andrew Bodhi's messages, she joked about them, trying to defuse the bite. Still early in their friendship, she hadn't expected much, so when he defended her, it warmed her, but something still feels off. The drama Andrew is bringing into Eira's life has her questioning if it's healthy for her to stay?

The recurring realization hits like an anvil against a steel beam. "It's just me. It's up to me to protect myself and to stand up for myself."

Anger surges, bubbling to the surface and making her emotions raw. *I don't like how out-of-control this is making me feel.*

She rolls around the question that she continues to ask her therapist, "Will someone ever be capable of putting me first?"

The way Andrew dealt with Eira regarding Bodhi still stings. Even though she acknowledges it shouldn't have. It has stirred up her doubts and insecurities.

Andrew is just a friend; why is this aggravating me?

Eira can't help but wonder if she's made the wrong decision in allowing herself to become friends with Andrew.

Feeling her phone vibrate, Eira checks her notifications. Instantly seeing the comment on her '**fan club**' post.

It's Bodhi and this time she writes, "Hope you blow out a front tire."

Completely shocked, Eira fumes.

Part of healing is knowing when to confront and when to protect. Eira decides another post is necessary, and then she's putting social media away for the rest of the week.

Using Bodhi's comment as her picture, she posts the screenshot.

Drawing an orange circle around the user's name from the post, Eira adds the text: **POV: when DM Girl wishes for my demise**

She adjusts the song "Crazy Bitch" by Buckcherry so the chorus plays the name of the song on loop while the video is of Eira riding her motorcycle. She's so done with this troll! Eira leaves off captions and hashtags, then clicks the post button.

Eira ends this on her terms by blocking Bodhi.

This post is intended to show her community what kind of evil souls are out there.

She tosses her phone onto her pillow. "What a witch!" she grumbles.

Shrugging off Bodhi's negative vibes, she gets ready for her birthday date.

Walking into the kitchen, she grabs the plastic bag from inside the fridge, then zips it in her backpack.

Leaving a note so they won't worry, she pens a message to her aunt and uncle. *"I'm out. Be back later. Love ya!"*

Eira makes sure all pre-ride motorcycle safety checks are good, paying special attention to her tires, especially after Bodhi's comment.

Her serotonin begins to spike as she whizzes down the highway like a hot knife slicing through butter.

Her mind stills to basal thoughts as she rides her motorcycle. The forty-five-minute drive to the cemetery flies by in a blink, as time always passes quickly on her motorcycle.

Clicking the switch, she activates her turn signal, pulling off the highway and into the entrance of her mom's final resting place.

Grief begins to wick, starting a fusion of warmth deep in her stomach. Feeling as though a hand is clenching her heart, sorrow suffocates her joy.

"Telos," she says the one word that stops the onslaught of those waves of grief and rights her world. Forcefully expelling again. "Telos. Telos!"

Eira's therapist advised her to have one word programmed in her mind to stop everything. As her brain protects itself during this time, her mouth says the word. Her ears hear it, and her body understands and executes the command—Stop. Ending all previous thoughts. The fortress locks for her protection. Each person has a different word; hers is Telos.

Slowing alongside the cemetery pathways, Eira comes to a stop, dropping her kickstand. She dismounts from her motorcycle, leaving her helmet and gloves on the seat of her bike.

Mouthing Telos is like her system reboots. No time is needed as the programming is already in place and already executes. She ends and begins with her new purpose... in milliseconds.

Walking to her mother's gravesite, she's respectful to other graves as her feet feel the crisp smashing of the grass beneath her shoes.

Dropping her backpack beside her feet, she stoops to grab the blanket. Gently shaking, she spreads the fleece-lined blanket across the grass.

December in Florida is definitely different than Tennessee.

Eira kneels on the blanket. "They lied, Momma. This pain never eases."

Eira smiles at the picture of her mom on her headstone. "Happy Birthday, Mama Llama." A sense of melancholy settles over her like a heavy fog as she lays out her mom's traditional birthday lunch. When she was alive, they'd always celebrated with chicken nuggets, chocolate milk, and Zebra Cakes.

Since losing her mother twelve years ago to a drunk driver, Eira hasn't skipped her mom's birthday; it's just celebrated in a different location now. This day used to be filled with laughter, but now it's tinged with the bittersweet ache of loss.

Ripping the clamshell box in half, Eira divides the nuggets between the two halves. She lays her mom's on the grass below her headstone.

"Sorry, but I didn't want a repeat of the bee disaster from last year, so I didn't bring you any dipping sauce." Eira chuckles. "I still have a scar where that bee stung me."

Twisting the lid of the milk open, the air bursts with the sweet aroma of chocolate.

Her breath hitches, tears threatening to blur her vision. "So, how have you been?" she asks, placing the chocolate milk beside the nugget box.

Opening the bag of onion-flavored chips, Eira looks around and nods. "Love what you've done with the place. Kind of homey, but not too boho." She places the chips on the blanket and grabs the apple juice to open it. Taking a drink of the cool liquid, her throat constricts. It feels like she has swallowed a brick. Coughing to ease her struggles, she wipes the offending tears from her eyes.

She opens the Zebra Cake package. "You know I can't sing, so just pretend you hear Marilyn Monroe belting out your birthday song," Eira says with a gentle smile. She lays the cakes with the nuggets.

The silence bothers Eira, putting her on edge.

"Momma," Eira begins, a knot forming in her throat, the weight of her words threatening to crush her. "I don't think you'd be proud of me. I've slipped into my 'villain era.'"

Eira murmurs, her voice barely above a whisper as she speaks to the silent headstone, "All I want is for them and their hatefulness to leave me alone."

The blades of grass tickle Eira's palms as she gently flutters her fingers over them.

"I find freedom when I ride, Momma. Even from them."

Eira rests her hands in her lap. "Sometimes I just want to escape the pain and loneliness."

Her past betrayals weigh heavily. Tears pool at the corners of her eyes as she wonders aloud, "When did I become the girl no one wants to treat right?" Her voice is laced with bitterness. "But also, the girl no one wants to get over. The one no one cares about until it's too late. Jady, the lab tech from work, said I am humble enough to know I'm replaceable, confident enough to know I was his downgrade. I hate this feeling!"

Eira continues to drop her fears at her mom's grave. "I'm afraid by the time I meet the right person, I'll be too broken to ever truly love again."

Eira adds while she swats a fly away from her bottle of apple juice, "I know you've always told me to reach out to my network. And I have. But my network is shrinking, Momma. I lost Dad after I lost you. I lost cousins, aunts, and uncles when Dad left. I lost friends when I went through nursing school. I lost more friends when I started dating Logan and then lost the rest when I left Logan. I'm down to Aunt Zia and Uncle Zio."

She crosses her outstretched legs. "Oh. I've gathered biker friends... maybe? Shit, it may be too early to tell. Momma, I feel so freaking isolated. It cuts deep. I know you didn't choose this, but dammit, why'd you have to leave when I was sixteen?" Eira's shoulders quake under the onslaught of fresh tears.

Remembering the rules, she swipes her fingers across her eyes. "Sorry, Momma. I know. I know, I'm crying." Eira's mom had always cherished birthdays, and tears were never allowed at birthday parties. Eira would continue to honor it. Wiping her tears with the corner of the blanket, Eira chews on her chips and sips her juice.

"You always told me to find the happy in the sad. I will, just not today. But I promise, I will soon. You left me, so I get more time on this misery train, okay? Don't judge me!" She smirks. "I'll win. Promise. I just need a little more time."

Eira continues the one-sided chat. "I know you like blue, but everyone thinks I'm a guy. So, I'm changing my motorcycle colors to teal and purple. I love riding; I feel like it saved me. The community I've started on social media is growing. It's mine to talk to daily; it feels good to have a release. They lift me up. It's like having a bunch of wise little yous dropping me tidbits just as I need them."

She turns her gaze to a nearby ash tree where a bluebird is loudly singing. "Oh, Logan's new girlfriend... mess... disaster... whatever you wanna call her, messaged me the other day. She told me I was heartless."

Eira shakes her head. "Such a fool! She didn't even know Logan was pissed off because of me. I blocked him and stopped responding to him. I won't take him back, so he thought belligerence was the answer. Nothing but a cheater. He must have been giving her an attitude, so she decided to tell me how cruel I was to him. Stupid, huh?"

Eira looks around, noticing the sun is low in the sky. Beautiful colors of orange, red, and pink cascade across the sky. "I love you,

Momma." Pointing to her face, she makes a wide circle around it. "See, no tears," she says, as her voice cracks. "I'll see you around."

Eira stands, gathering her blanket; she stuffs it into her backpack. She puts all the food in the plastic bag she brought it in.

Tossing the bag into the trash can beside her motorcycle, Eira weaves her arms through her backpack, securing it on her back. She tightens the strap on her helmet, smoothing out her gloves on her fingers, and slides onto her motorcycle.

Longing for the freedom of the open road, Eira craves the wind pressing against her body. The cadence of her motorcycle stills the clamor of her thoughts.

Despite her uncertainties, Eira can't deny the pull Andrew and his friends have on her. To belong somewhere without having to prove her worth first, without handing over every piece of herself, and without sacrificing any of her morals — that's all she's ever wanted. It's a feeling she's never experienced before, and the only one she's willing to accept for her future.

In return, she gets to share in the laughter, the camaraderie of the group rides, the unspoken bond seeming to grow stronger with each passing mile between Eira and them.

On her ride home, she decided she will continue to pursue those friendships.

She lifted a silent prayer, hoping to have perfected the ability to draw on her strength and resilience. She has reassurance, just as she knows the moon sets in the west; her prayers will be answered right on time.

CHAPTER TEN

Andrew

Andrew's parked outside Bodhi's apartment, lounging back on his motorcycle. His booted feet dangle over the handlebars as he scrolls through his social media, waiting for her to show up. Adding comments to his already posted content as well as reaching out to other biker communities, reinforcing their connection.

Bodhi walks to her front door, side-stepping around Andrew's bike. Her jacket zipper scrapes along the side of his gas tank.

"Dammit, would you be okay if someone did that to your car?" Andrew demands.

Bodhi lifts the hand holding her keys, shaking her hand as if she's waving. "That's a toy, my car is a need," she says with an attitude. "They can't be compared."

Andrew stands behind Bodhi, holding his helmet while Bodhi unlocks her apartment door. He asks, "What's with your attitude?"

Andrew closes the door with his heel and kicks off his boots. He follows Bodhi to the kitchen nook.

Scooting her mail and grocery bags across the table into a pile, she makes room for their things. She drops her purse while he places his gloves, helmet, hoodie, phone, and wallet on the kitchen table; she lays her jacket and keys across her purse. Bodhi aggressively grabs Andrew's phone, tapping the screen. Her fake nails echo with each tap. She pops her hip to the side, arching her eyebrow while holding his phone in her palm. The lock screen prompts for a passcode. Andrew takes his phone, putting it in his hoodie pocket.

Bodhi whines, "Unlock your phone, Andrew! You know what my code is, why can't I know yours?"

He glares past her tarantula-like eyelashes, beyond her smudged blue eyeliner, honing deep into the center of her purple mascara-covered eyes. "Not happening."

She walks to the rug beside the front door, kicking off her shoes. Bodhi turns, flipping her lime-green hair to one side of her shoulder. She places her hands on her hips. Twitching her nose like a rabbit, her dangling skull chain septum ring dances above her top lip. She points her claw-like fingernails at him. "I don't like you hanging around her."

Andrew raises his eyebrows in complete shock. Walking halfway towards her, he crosses his arms over his chest. "We agreed, easy. No demands. Now you're gonna tell me who I can ride with?"

"She's trying to split us. You don't see what she messages me. She makes rude comments to me all the time," she pouts.

Andrew raises his voice. "Are you fucking for real? You're the poster child for rude!"

Andrew walks to the couch, plopping down in the middle. "*All the time?*" he looks at Bodhi questioningly. "How many times have you two talked?"

Bodhi straddles Andrew's legs, wiggling her chest. She smashes her generously sized breasts into him. "We've never talked. We've messaged. Just a few times. But she's mean those times. Look, I don't want to fight about it, okay? Just stick to riding with your friends, *guy* friends, and we'll be okay."

On the kitchen table, Bodhi's phone rings.

Andrew nods toward the table. "You go answer that, and I'll order pizza."

"I already ordered it before I left work. It'll be here at seven," Bodhi replies, leaning in towards Andrew's mouth, puckering her lips for a kiss.

Andrew stills her advance, holding her back as he jerks his head to the side. Slightly turning his head, he glares at Bodhi. "No."

Bodhi playfully smacks Andrew's chest, huffing as she climbs off him. They both walk to the kitchen table to gather their phones.

Bodhi answers her phone. Talking quietly, she shuffles to the farthest corner of the kitchen. She digs into the top cabinet, making the glasses clink together. She closes the cabinet door, still empty-handed, and disconnects her call. Striding towards Andrew, she places her phone face down on the edge of the table as he puts his phone inside his hoodie pocket.

Bodhi laces her fingers through Andrew's, pulling him towards her bedroom.

His legs never move while his arm fully extends, but he doesn't follow.

"Can we just forget the first part of the night? I really think you'll enjoy the second part," Bodhi whines.

Andrew stops just before his toes meet Bodhi's. "Don't play fucking games with me. Got it?"

Bodhi nods. "I would never." Wrapping her arms around his neck, she whispers in Andrew's ear, "What kind are you wearing tonight?"

Andrew smirks. "I don't know. I think they're green."

Bodhi weaves her fingers through his, again, pulling him towards her bedroom.

Andrew sighs, dropping his chin to his chest. He shakes his head. Against a nagging feeling, he follows her.

Standing at the foot of the bed, Bodhi hugs Andrew. She tugs on his earlobe with her teeth, alternating between kissing and licking his neck. She runs her hands under Andrew's shirt, pinching his nipples.

Andrew reaches an arm behind his back, grabbing a handful of his shirt. He pulls it off and tosses it on the floor by the mirrored dresser. He gently grabs her hands, stilling their advancement. He places them on his belt buckle. Andrew threads his fingers through her jeans belt loops, pulling her closer to him.

After Bodhi unbuckles his belt, she pops the buttons of his jeans through the holes. Leaning in, she captures his nipple between her teeth. Pulling slightly.

Andrew stills her head, stopping her from pulling further. "I'm not into pain. Remember, you bite and I'm walking."

She draws away from Andrew with a coy smile. Demanding, "Let me see them."

Bodhi sits on the bed, watching Andrew. She rushes to remove her clothes. Tossing them into the basket in the corner, patiently waiting for Andrew.

Andrew tugs his jeans down his legs. The room's silence is broken with a thud of metal clanking as he drops his jeans to the floor.

He looks down and fans his arms out to his sides. "Trouser snake it is." Bodhi smiles at the snake design on his boxers.

"That's a boa constrictor, right?" Her fingers trace the green outline of the snake, making Andrew harden.

Andrew nods. Bodhi drags her finger between the snake's eyes, zig-zagging her finger over the snake's nose.

"How fitting," she whispers. Hooking her fingers between his waist and the black elastic band of his boxers, she pushes them to his knees.

She wraps one hand around Andrew's cock. Squeezing tightly as she works her fists up towards his crown. Releasing a little pressure, she drives him deeper into her palm with a hard pump. With her other hand, she glides her fingers between his balls, her middle finger pushes onto his seam as she rubs back and forth.

Andrew moans, rocking his hips to meet Bodhi's hands.

"Fuck, you keep doing that and you're about to get an eye full," Andrew growls. Pulling his dick out of Bodhi's hand, he nods to the pillows on the bed.

Bodhi crawls on all fours as Andrew walks to the side of the bed. He crawls to the middle of the mattress.

Patting the mattress, Bodhi tells Andrew, "Lay on your back, legs spread open."

Andrew squints his eyes, as if to question Bodhi, but does what she asks.

Facing Andrew, she is straddling his stomach. "Is this okay?"

Andrew scoffs, "Aren't you a little too far up?"

Bodhi places both of Andrew's hands on her thighs. His thumbs resting along her perfectly manicured Brazilian pussy. Rocking her hips forward forces his thumbs deeper into her folds.

Andrew feels each rock of her hips; he sees each bounce of her breasts as she drags her fingernails over his chest.

"If you'd scoot down, you'd rock onto my dick."

"No," she whispers.

Andrew playfully flicks one of her nipples.

Bodhi snaps her hips forward, moaning, as she starts to pant.

He presses his thumb on her button, delivering just the right amount of pressure to her clitoris. She slams her hips forward and back, then stills. Tossing her head back, her hair grazes the crown of his cock. "Oh, fuck yes," she moans.

"I want you so badly," Bodhi squeaks. Andrew lifts Bodhi, bringing her entrance to his dick. Bodhi locks her thighs onto his sides, shaking her head. She gasps, "Don't move me!"

Andrew stills.

Bodhi rocks back onto her ass a little. Reaching for his finger, she runs it through her drenched core. Bringing it to her mouth, she sucks her cream from his fingers. Bodhi drags his wet fingertip down her chin and across the pounding pulse in her neck. She grazes her taut nipple. Resting Andrew's hand on top of her thigh.

Bodhi slowly swivels her hips in a circle, as if she's working a hula hoop. She wiggles her hips down Andrew's stomach backwards, never breaking eye contact. Dragging her wet pussy across his erect cock, she situates herself between Andrew's thighs.

She puffs her warm breath against the base of his dick. Gathering her hair, she twists it to the back of her head, getting it out of her way.

Her teeth nibble on the underside of his shaft. She drags her tongue across his crown, flicking her tongue into his slit. She slides her mouth down his angry cock, gagging when it bumps the back of her throat.

Andrew wraps Bodhi's hair around his fist, tugging at the base of her neck slightly so that he tilts her head to reach the angle that's sure to bring his release. Her lips draw to his crown.

They both still when they hear the doorbell ring.

It rings two more times.

"Fuck, Bodhi," Andrew mutters, "let 'em leave it on the porch."

Bodhi untangles from Andrew. Grabbing her wrap, she walks towards the front door. "No way. Last time, someone took it," she calls over her shoulder.

Minutes later, Bodhi shrugs off her wrap as she climbs back onto Andrew's stomach. She pops a piece of Italian sausage into her mouth.

"There's more sausage down there." Andrew smirks, nodding towards his dick.

Bodhi looks into Andrew's eyes, glances at his lips, then back to his eyes. She asks, "Why won't you kiss me?"

Andrew shakes his head. "I just don't."

He drags the pad of his fingers across her nipple. Bringing both finger and thumb to his tongue, he licks them, then teases her nipples.

Bodhi snaps her waist forward, then releases a breathy moan. She places one of Andrew's thumbs on her clit. "Rub," she orders.

Focused on Bodhi's clit and nipples, he doesn't register the dip he feels in the bed between his ankles.

His mind struggles as it is split between the odd dip and pleasuring Bodhi. With his back still on the mattress, he leans to look around her. He sees a figure in the mirror, and that figure is kissing Bodhi's spine. Andrew sees snow-white hair, cut in a masculine, short style, but the naked body definitely is not a guy.

Bodhi grabs Andrew's thumbs, shoving them between her wet pussy lips. "Keep rubbing, Andrew. That's just Skye."

Skye props her chin on Bodhi's shoulder. She has six tiny barbells running through her eyebrows. White-boned swirls inside her gauged ears, and almond-shaped eyes outlined in deep black eyeliner. Her lips are blood-red with a piercing of a hoop along the bottom seam.

Skye's eyes never break from Andrew's gaze as she whispers into Bodhi's ear, "You sure?"

Bodhi nods, bringing Skye's hands to cover her tits; she squeezes. Bodhi places Andrew's hands over Skye's.

Skye's cold hands send a shiver down his spine, reminding him of death; he snatches his hands away.

Andrew shakes his head. Pulsing his lifted hands, he asks, "What the hell is this?" Andrew drops his hands to the mattress.

Bodhi lies on Andrew, her tits squish into his chest; her legs encase his sides. Bodhi whispers in his ear, "Just give it a try."

Slowly, Bodhi rolls onto her back on his chest. She sprawls her legs over Andrew's, bracing the balls of her feet into the mattress.

Skye rubs Andrew's calves as Bodhi scoots down his chest, lining her junction with his.

Skye presses Andrew's hard dick into the mattress. Releasing it, it snaps like a rubber band, slapping against Bodhi's wet pussy. Bodhi moans.

Andrew's breathing is strained. He mumbles, "What the hell did I just get roped into?"

Bodhi laces her fingers over Andrew's, resting them on her stomach. She presses into them.

Skye nestles the crown of Andrew's dick into the hood of Bodhi's clit. She licks Andrew's shaft, stopping when she reaches Bodhi's hood; she nibbles on both her clit and his crown.

"Oh, fucking hell," mumbles Andrew.

Bodhi hisses.

Skye blows her warm breath down Andrew's shaft, making Bodhi squirm.

"I can feel your breath on my pussy," moans Bodhi. She gasps, "Ah, your fucking fingers are sooo cold!"

"You're getting them soaking wet," Skye tells Bodhi.

Skye flicks her tongue over the length of Andrew's dick.

Bodhi's legs shake.

Skye croons, "That's it, Bodhi. Clench that pussy down hard like yesterday."

Andrew digests Skye's words as she sucks his dick deep into the back of her throat, swallowing around his pulsing cock.

Clarity breaks through his moan. "Yesterday?"

"Andrew, she's sucking you and when she comes up, her nose pushes against my clit. Oh God, I'm going to cum," Bodhi whines.

"Wait just a fucking minute, what is this yesterday shit?" Andrew asks, shaking his hands free from Bodhi's.

Skye keeps bobbing her head up and down on Andrew's dick as he struggles; his cock becomes overstimulated quickly.

Biology overtakes him; he has reached the point of no return.

As his spine tingles and his balls tighten, he feels a cold, wet finger circling his puckered hole. Before he can form words, the tip of Skye's finger breaches him.

Chaos erupts at once!

Andrew bucks his hips off the bed, slamming his dick deeper into Skye's throat.

Skye gags. Her green slushy she'd slurped on the ride over ejects from her stomach, splashing against his dick, balls, ass, and drenching Bodhi's pussy, Skye, and the bed.

Skye pulls her mouth off his dick and her finger out of his ass. She flicks Andrew's taint with her finger.

Andrew bucks again. Somehow slamming his dick into Bodhi's pussy.

Bodhi wails, "Oh, fucking rail me!" Another wave of liquid splatters across Andrew, Bodhi, Skye, and the bed.

Skye coos between Andrew and Bodhi's thighs. "You finally squirted!"

Bodhi squeals. Folding herself in half, she lunges into Skye's waiting arms. Smashing her lips against Skye's mouth, she kisses her.

Andrew is furious! He climbs off the bed. "How fucking long have you had a side piece?" He points from Bodhi to Skye.

Breaking their kiss, Skye shrills at Andrew. "Listen here, you dick-wielding piece of shit. We've been together for years. Then she sees you and now she's all like, 'OOO, he's so talented, imagine what he can do?' I'll tell you what he can do." Jabbing her finger in his direction. "Not a fucking thing more than I can do, that's your answer, Bodhi!"

Andrew rears his head back, shaking it. A gigantic smile spreads across his face. "Ha, jokes on you, you fucking witch. Apparently, I can make her squirt, and you can't." Andrew gathers his clothes off the bedroom floor and walks out of the bedroom door.

"You can't go! We're not done," cries Bodhi.

"The fuck I can't. I'm not staying for any more of this. And we..." Andrew points back and forth between Bodhi and himself. "...are over!"

Skye mocks, "Oh no, however will we get comic relief if you and your dipshit toy-riding gang leave us?"

Andrew looks at Bodhi, then glares at Skye. He feels a surge of anger as he realizes he has been played, yet again.

He leaves the hallway in search of a towel.

Finding nothing in the bathroom, Andrew stomps to the kitchen. Grabbing the hand towel hanging on the fridge door, he walks back to the bathroom. Throwing his clothes onto the vanity, he flings the shower curtain against the wall. He wrenches the water knobs all the way open. Not giving it time to warm, he steps under the freezing water.

Andrew runs his hands over his body, unsure who he's rinsing off: himself, Skye, or Bodhi? Not giving a damn, they both have to go. He wrenches the condom off his deflated accomplice; it rebounds into the tub with a slap.

He turns the water off as Bodhi rushes into the bathroom.

"I can explain. I'm really interested in you, but I can't lose Skye. You understand, right?"

In his haze of fury, he didn't close the shower curtain; water has puddled on her bathroom floor.

Andrew steps out of the shower and into the doorway as he dries off using the towel from the kitchen. He throws it towards the puddles on the floor by the shower, then he finishes getting dressed in the hallway.

Andrew scoffs. "I damn well don't understand. I told you don't play fucking games with me. And what's she talking about, comic relief?"

Not waiting for Bodhi to answer, he stalks down the hallway towards the kitchen.

Andrew fastens his boots, then stands in front of the kitchen table, slipping his hoodie over his head and tucks his wallet into his jeans pocket when Skye comes out of the bedroom, still naked, walking towards him.

With each word, Skye raises her voice until she's screaming at Andrew, "You're a piece of shit. Do you hear her crying in there? That's because of you!"

"Wrong. Whoever arranged this fuck fest..." Andrew points his finger between Skye and the bathroom. "...it's their fault. But I know it damn well wasn't me!"

He secures his helmet, stashes the phone in his pocket, and opens the front door.

"You walk out that door and you will NEVER come back. Do you hear me?" Bodhi yells from the bathroom doorway.

Andrew slams the front door so hard that it rattles her windows.

Stomping into her yard, he rears his boot back and lands kick after angry kick to the eight tiny reindeer lining her front lawn. Bells on a collar jingle as a reindeer's head flies through the air and lands on the neighbor's driveway. Andrew tosses Santa, making him face-plant into the fake snow before the sleigh overturns. "Merry Christmas," he yells, swiftly smacking the last reindeer on its glowing red nose.

Hopping on his motorcycle, he speeds off towards the gas station.

He's vibrating with anger.

He still can't figure out what the hell that was. *Who arranges something like that without making sure everyone involved is down with it, then tosses the blame on the only person who didn't know a fucking thing about it.*

Pulling into the nearest gas station, Andrew fills his tank. He crumples the receipt as he shoves it into his pocket. Realizing he can't ride this pissed, he walks his motorcycle away from the pumps. Dropping his kickstand, he removes his gloves and helmet.

He reaches inside his hoodie pocket for his phone.

"Fuck," he grunts when his fingers touch two phones. He taps on the screen to find his and pockets it. *We should have gotten different cases.* He taps Bodhi's phone screen, typing in her code. Her phone shines with multiple notifications. The last message reflected on her screen hits deep. It's to Skye. *I'm devoted to you. He's just a plaything, he means nothing.* Andrew grunts. *Will it ever stop? I must be the universe's fucking entertainment!*

Andrew types a message to Skye using Bodhi's phone.

> **Andrew:** Tell Bodhi I grabbed her phone by accident. I'll put it in her mailbox tomorrow.

Skye: Don't need it. It, like you, has already been replaced. Fuck off!

"Well, okay then," Andrew says as he walks to the gas station's trash can. Submerging her phone in the windshield washer bucket, then he tosses it in the trash.

He dries his hands on his jeans as he walks to his motorcycle. He plops himself onto his bike seat. With his phone, he makes a post on his social media. Grabbing a video from his gallery, he adds text, **Being respected is an illusion**. He clicks post.

Pocketing his phone, he looks out into the traffic as the night sky begins to replace the day.

He can't shake the feeling of unworthiness trying to engulf him.

Andrew stares at the sky. He sighs, wishing for a clear sign to grant him clarity. As he turns, he sees a sign, a legitimate sign. It's a large red arrow brightly illuminated above a tattoo shop.

Raising his chin to the sky. "I'm not going to Houston. And no one but Sage will ever tattoo my skin, so try again."

The red arrow keeps flashing in coordination with Andrew's annoying eye twitch. Curiosity gets the best of him.

What the hell am I doing? He asks himself as he tightens his helmet.

This is stupid. This is ridiculous. But he rides across the street. He pulls into the vacant parking lot of the tattoo shop. Cautiously, he walks inside.

His nose is met with the scent of disinfectant. Multiple strands of twinkling lights line the ceiling, flickering as instrumental music bounces off the shop's walls. *How can anyone see in here?*

A loud crash accompanied by a voice yelling, "Shit. Shit. Dammit to hell. Shit. Son of a witch! Nooo!" Then complete silence.

Holy hell, what's happening?

Andrew calls out, "Hey, you okay? Can I come back there to help you?"

A high-pitched feminine voice calls out, "Help would be nice, actually. But you're not getting anything out of this, so think really hard before you do, yeah."

He mumbles to himself, "You sound like someone I know." Andrew shouts, "I'm coming back there."

Walking into what looks like a storage room, Andrew sees an explosion of chaos. Broken ink bottles are everywhere. Different colored ink oozes from their shelves, onto other shelves, onto the floor, and on her.

She is smashed against a rack trying to hold a box on the top shelf with her hands, and her knee is balancing a box of glass containers. Gauze decorates the top shelf, zigzagging to the bottom totes and has rolled across the floor. It's like someone threw rolls of toilet paper in the air, just to unravel as they land.

Andrew tries to hide his smile, failing miserably.

His chuckle makes the girl turn her head. Seeing the dire look in her eyes, Andrew rushes towards her. His feet are slick on the floor's ink mess; he pushes the box on her knee back into the racks.

"I need that top box down, if you would. I'm a bit on the short side and my stubborn ass thought, 'I can reach it, how bad can it be,' well I'm never asking that again!"

Andrew holds the box close to his chest; he arches his eyebrows and smiles.

The girl cocks her head. "You can put that on the floor over there, unless you wanna keep holdin' on to it like it's your lifeline?"

Andrew backs away, stooping to the tiled floor. "Sorry," he says. Then he throws his head back, roaring with laughter.

She questions, "Oh, so you find this funny, huh?"

"Girl, you've got ink all over your face," Andrew informs her.

She snorts, "Well, I'm the one with the wet face, you're not telling me anything new!"

Andrew says through his laughter, "You have a blue face!"

She scowls. "Better than blue balls, yeah?"

"Ahh damn, you remind me so much of Sage," Andrew reflects.

"Oh, I would love to be a Sage. Sheesh, the level of wisdom for that, mmm-humm." She shakes her head, whipping her wet hair against her cheek. "Let me wash this off. I'll meet you out front."

Andrew is sitting in a chair when she walks back into the lobby.

"Now we can formally greet each other. Hi, I'm Rosemary. And you are?"

"Andrew," he answers.

Shaking his outstretched hand, she asks, "Do you believe in Divine Intervention or a Touchstone of Spirit?" Dropping his hand, she takes a step back.

Shrugging his shoulders slowly. "I believe I was supposed to come in here tonight," he replies softly, "as weird as that sounds."

Rosemary exhales deeply. "Here's the thing: I'm never going to see you again. So, I'm gonna cut the bullshit. I was nudged to bring this," Rosemary says as she's holding up a plastic package. On the package, in bold black letters are the words *Specialized Kit*.

Andrew arches his brow. "That tattoo kit for you?"

"So, um, a couple of things. I'm not a tattoo artist. And I don't have a penis. So no, not for me." Rosemary fans the package then tosses it to Andrew. "It's a Jacob's Ladder piercing kit," she smirks.

Andrew looks at the package, then at Rosemary, and then at the trash can. "I was led here to get a holey dick?" Andrew questions with disbelief.

Rosemary smiles and waggles her raised eyebrows. "Well?"

"Definitely ranks high for one of the dumbest things I've ever done!" Shaking his head in shock, he jokes, "Let's get my dick out and put holes in it. Said no one ever!" Andrew shakes his head and sighs deeply.

"You ready?" Rosemary asks.

Am I seriously considering this?

Andrew nods. "Let's get to it."

CHAPTER ELEVEN

Eira

E ira lounges alone in her room, her feet crossed at her ankles. Lying on her bed, she tries but fails to find the sun poking through the layers of dark gray clouds. She's already prayed for the unusual January rain-packed nimbus clouds to vanish; Mother Nature seems to ignore her.

She's picked up three extra shifts this week at the hospital, making today her only day off for the next six days. She craves a ride along her favorite highway decorated with inspiring Ash trees.

Her mind still fights through the chaos. It feels like her entire world wants her to crumble. Her ability to dissolve intrusive thoughts is now her best and most used superpower.

The loss of her mother, the abandonment of her father, the scars of past relationships, the abuse from Logan—all of it seems to crest like a tidal wave. Grief and trauma do not conform to Father Time.

Her aunt and uncle have filled the void left by her parents. They've instilled in her a sense of joy deeply embedded in her grasp. They're her rock and she's grateful for their unwavering support.

Despite her efforts to find peace and healing, Eira can't shake the feeling of being overlooked and underestimated.

The pain of her past betrayal mixes with the judgmental looks and condescending comments from those who call themselves her family and friends.

Not a single scar on my heart came from an enemy.

Those words are a disturbing reflection of her wounds, all given to her by those who claim to love her.

During her fight through her chaos, Eira finds comfort in her social media community, a judgment-free space she's created with the sole purpose of finding herself, then freely expressing herself in the name of healing.

Her community has enabled her to identify and then to enjoy the simple pleasures of her life. It's taught her to embrace the different facets of her personality with a sense of humor and self-awareness. Eira continues to discover herself, then drives to confidently be that person, without input from anyone.

Looking into the past, she sees how she's changed. With each person's praise or disapproval, they've been molding her character into someone she no longer recognizes.

All that time spent with Logan; he cultivated her personality without Eira realizing the cost. Not knowing when, she became blind to herself, pushing herself to conform to Logan's perfect view of who he thought she should be. Logan's threats amplified Eira's fear, creating a vulnerability. She didn't realize she'd freely given him dominion over her. When she walked away, she vowed Logan lost all power over her.

Eira tucks the fuzzy, thick throw blanket around her body.

A deep rumble of thunder vibrates her bedroom floor and rattles her bedroom windows. Her pulse spikes. The sound reminds her of that night.

Just as she and her therapist have practiced, she takes deep cleansing breaths, releasing a slow exhale. She closes her eyes.

Her heart starts to slam against her chest as she recalls that night and the fear because of it.

Memories vividly replay in her mind of Logan's aggressive behavior.

She was jostled awake when thumping rattled her bedroom window; deep vibrations radiated across her mattress and down the legs of her bed. She scrambled to sit up when she heard the voice she'd hoped would've forgotten her by now. Logan's been silent for weeks, making her believe he had accepted her leaving.

She was wrong.

Eira remembers Logan pounding on her front door well after midnight. Screaming into the steel planks, "I told you not to make me come after you! And here we are. Answer this fucking door before I kick it in!"

Continuing her breathing, she focuses on the pull chain hanging from her ceiling fan. Willing her heart to calm, her memory of that night continues.

She'd moved her bedroom window curtain to the side, her mind blanked when she saw her tormentor had returned.

Aunt Zia and Uncle Zio were hours away celebrating their anniversary; she was alone. Logan had threatened her in the past, and he's always been aggressive towards her, but never to this level.

"The more you make me wait, the worse it'll be for you!" Logan continued to slam his shoulder into the door.

Hoping she could talk sense into him, she opened her front door. "Quiet!" she hissed, "or someone'll call the cops." Hugging her midsection, she subconsciously put a barrier between them.

Logan took a step back, running his hands through his hair. "I love you, come home with me," he whispered as he dropped his hands to his sides.

Eira stepped out of the house, pulling the door closed behind her. Standing purposefully in line with the security camera, muscle memory forced her brain to cycle through her training from work when dealing with people demonstrating psychotic behavior. Training has taught her to speak low, slow, and to the point.

"Logan, we are done," she told him firmly but quietly.

Seeing that tick he had in his eye made her brain go blind with fear just as he lunged at her.

The ceiling fan blowing air across her face brings her back to the present, reminding her that she is in control and this is just a memory. She is forcing the processing of this incident; she wants the trauma removed like poison from a snake bite.

The blades cool the tears on her cheeks, reminding her once again of Logan, when his spittle flew across her face as he screamed, "I didn't tell you that you could leave!"

She can still feel the ghost of his hand wrapped around her throat, squeezing.

Trying to fight Logan was useless. He's six inches taller than her and has an extra hundred pounds of solid muscle, but her brain demanded that she do something. Black dots danced before her eyes while she gasped for air.

As Logan lifted Eira off the ground by her neck, her nails drew blood from his forearms. Being robbed of oxygen snapped her from pause to fight.

Eira scissor-kicked, swinging both legs, landing kick after kick to Logan's shins, knees, groin, then ramming both her knees into his stomach.

Logan dropped her, placing his hands on his knees. Both Logan and Eira gulped air. The black dots slowly disappeared from Eira's vision.

On her hands and feet, Eira crab-walked backwards, slamming her back into the shut door. Eira remembers feeling terrified because she had nowhere to go. She had boxed herself in. Standing, she had molded herself against her front door.

She rolls onto her side on the bed, snuggling deeper into her blankets. Cheeks dry, tears evaporated, and heartbeat calm, she's ready to finish the final purge of this vile memory.

Eira will never forget how Logan's smile held so much evil that night. "You done with your bullshit now?"

He'd grabbed her by her hand that was frantically searching for the doorknob.

He pulled her into his chest as he pinned her arm around her back, then grabbed her hair with his other hand, pulling.

Logan reared his head back. "Ready sweetheart?" He winked. "This is gonna hu—" Eira squeezed her eyes shut, anticipating the pain from Logan's headbutt, only to be released and hear Logan grunt.

Flying through the air, Eira landed with a thump.

Logan's scream filled the night air, "Get this fucker off me!"

She heard a dog's growl followed by Logan's shrieks of pain.

Eira shook her head, quickly forcing her mind to catch up with the last couple of seconds.

A dog barked, its growl got louder, then a thud when her back met the ground.

A piercing scream penetrated Eira's haze, "Don't just lay there, call this fucker off me!" The dog continued to drag Logan towards the street, Logan's bloody arm was leaving a trail along the sidewalk.

"Zeus, HALT!" commanded a deep voice.

The dog disengaged and sat down. Licking his jowl, he looked between Eira and Logan.

"Zeus, come," commanded the deep voice.

The dog trotted to Eira, plopped down in front of her, as if he were shielding her.

The deep voice questioned Logan, "Are we done here?"

"Your fucking dog chewed my arm; no, we're not fucking done here!" Logan yelled. Panting from the ground, he sprawled out on his back like a starfish.

Eira stood and dusted herself off.

Zeus' hind leg scratched behind his ear, rattling his metal collar.

The deep voice informed Logan, "You've got two choices. Call a friend and get the hell out of here. Or the cops are taking you and that security camera to the station. Which is it?"

The man with the deep voice snapped his fingers and pointed to the truck parked in the street with the doors still open. Zeus trotted to the truck, then jumped inside. The man with the deep voice shut his truck doors, waiting, watching.

Eira remembers how pissed Serta was that night.

"Dammit man, what part of *Don't* didn't you understand? We agreed to let her go, and this is what you do?" Serta shouted at Logan.

Serta, Logan's best friend since middle school, pulled Logan off the ground.

Serta reassured Eira, "He's done. He won't be coming back. If we leave now, will you not press charges?"

Zeus jumped out of the truck's window, barking as he ran to Eira. Plopping down at her feet, Zeus rested his chin on the top of her hip, nudging her with his nose.

Logan flinched at the sight of the dog. He cradled his bloody arm close to his body, scooting away from the dog.

Eira looks down at the dog resting its head on her. It was as if she gained confidence from Zeus as she delivered her response. "Logan must promise to never bother me ever again. I'll send you a copy of the video. But if he contacts me again. Ever. I'm taking it straight to the cops."

Serta smacked Logan in the middle of his back and nodded to Eira.

The sneer on Logan's face is one Eira had never seen before. "I'm done," he snarled.

Logan revved his bike; his engine roared throughout the sleeping neighborhood. He dropped the clutch and sped away; the rest of the motorcycles followed Logan. Zeus and his owner followed the bikes out of the neighborhood.

Serta's final words to Eira were, "I can assure you he'll never contact you again. I'm so sorry."

Eira's tears trail across the bridge of her nose, dropping to the wet spot on the blankets, breaking her from her memory, again.

Wrapping her arms around her body pillow, she smashes it against her mouth as she screams into it. Letting out a frustrated yelp. She pounds her fist on the pillow. Exhausted from the process, Eira props her head on the pillow.

His darkness no longer binds me.

Eira's goal is to keep her head held high, to be the person who will always save herself: physically, mentally, emotionally, spiritually, and financially.

In healing, there is the understanding that life will have obstacles. The challenge is to overcome, win big, and find peace. Healing each day, she continues to get stronger. Her fierce determination demands that she become who she knows she's meant to be. Her confidence in herself grows. Boundaries are established to protect herself as she recognizes her value. The voice of doubt destroying her self-worth is silenced by her working the healing process and by the magic of her motorcycle. It has saved her, healed her, and strengthened her.

Riding her motorcycle drowns out the noises of the world, especially when it tries to claim her.

Eira feels hope. Despite the pain and the uncertainty, she's committed to rebuilding herself. Whether disappointment from work or personal, she depends on the five-step healing process and her motorcycle to dissolve the disappointments from each day.

Fluffing her pillows against her headboard, she props her back against it, sighing. She's reminded how frequently she sees disappointment.

Her career as an emergency room nurse means sadness is nearby. *Sadness always hits harder when you allow yourself to care.*

There's an older gentleman, Oscar, who holds a piece of Eira's heart. He's alone in the world, sleeping on the streets in Jacksonville. He usually visits the ER at least once a month. Oscar has told her that his once-a-month visits are to check up on her. He says he needs to keep track of her, so when he comes for a visit, he just makes up an ailment so he can see her.

But Eira knows when someone needs medical assistance.

He stays long enough to get hydrated, and Eira always makes him eat something. She ensures his wounds, if he has any, are properly taken care of. Occasionally, she's given him antibiotics when he's had a high fever and terrible congestion.

Oscar has taught her that in order to fully see the world, one must look at both sides; otherwise, they are only seeing half-truths.

He's endearing. He has promised her that she will have *her* better life.

While Eira enjoys the philosophical side of Oscar, she adores his humor.

They've laughed a thousand times, sometimes they're gasping for air while tears roll down their cheeks, but last night her tears were not from his humor.

Oscar's sad truth, his choice to live off the streets, is showing signs of him slowly losing the battle of life. She's tried over the years to get him into shelters, a job, and even offered to take him home with her. He always refused, saying he loves his life as it is.

His pale skin contrasts against the white sheets of the hospital bed. His normal ragged look is now gray and hollow. He appeared worn down and defeated. Oscar still tried to make her laugh, but when he closed his eyes, Eira quickly relieved her eyes of her tears. He held her hand, gently rubbing his thumb across the back of it. Looking at the machines Oscar allowed her to hook him to, Eira watched as his vitals slowly descended.

"Won't be long now," mumbled Oscar.

Eira asked in a quivering voice, "Aren't I supposed to be the one consoling you?"

With cloudy eyes, Oscar patted the back of her hand. "No one consoles this old man. I've had the best life. It wasn't what everybody else wanted, but it was what I wanted."

Oscar cleared his throat. "You still riding?"

Thankful for the distraction, she answered with enthusiasm, "Absolutely! I've had a blast these past months. I'm aware people are talking trash about my life's choices. They keep saying because I'm a nurse, I should know better. Motorcycles are dangerous. My favorite is my cousin telling me motorcycles aren't for girls." Eira shrugged. "My family is not okay with the bike thing, but it's for me, not them."

"You need to live your life for you," Oscar rasped. "Promise me that."

"I will. I know people don't like the new me and I honestly don't care," Eira states. "I'm done letting other people choose how I'm supposed to live."

Oscar slowly turns his head towards her. "They see your decisions through their life experiences. It has nothing to do with you."

Oscar closed his eyes. "Don't let the small minds of people make you feel like you aren't worthy. Because honey, you are."

Eira stood, wiping her tears. She walked to the hall to grab another blanket from the blanket warmer. Returning, she tucked it across Oscar's chest. "I took your advice. I bought that three-sixty camera. It's great. I record all my rides. I've caught some pretty funny shots when I'm out riding with others too."

"He still messing with you?" Oscar asked as he notched his eyebrow.

"Not him, pffft, more like her. I'm not sure what her issue is; she has Logan and I'm not around. She still tries, but I just blocked her. I don't have to see her. But, like I told you before, I've been suppressing traumatic memories since I was a child. Like, don't play with me or I'll forget you too." Eira swings her hand like she's slamming a door. "Into the vault you go!"

A smile ghosts across his face.

"Remember honey, it's not your responsibility to carry other people's trauma." Oscar sweeps the bed as if clearing off crumbs.

"I know," Eira said, nodding. "Just life's been hard lately. With Mom's birthday last month and then the holidays. It always hits a little harder this time of year, and sometimes I feel like I failed at things because I wasn't in control." Eira sighed. "But I'm seeing the light at the end of the tunnel." Eira meets Oscar's gaze. "You told me to keep my head up, so that's what I keep reminding myself to do."

Oscar smiled, "How's the community?"

"I'm still mentally figuring it out, but it helps. When life hits hard, I just ride. My bike is my ultimate therapy."

"I'm gonna close my eyes for a bit. I still want my grape sucker though," Oscar said with a wink.

Purposeful trauma dumping may clear the mind, but it also makes her exhausted. She tilts her head towards her ceiling again, finding the chain to focus on. Thinking about Oscar has grief slamming into her chest. Hiccupping, she remembers Oscar's last words. Eira will always remember Oscar, especially when she digs through the candy dish at work or sees a grape sucker.

Some days I'm drowning, some days I'm swimming.

Wiping the tears from her cheeks, Eira knows the impulsive delivery today is because of Oscar's passing.

Scooting to the foot of her bed and looking out the window, she notices the rain hasn't stopped. Dreary gray clouds still scatter across the horizon as the rain pelts the ground. The wind sways the trees back and forth, making them look like they're dancing.

Eira agrees her upgrade was not only an impulsive decision but also a middle finger to all those who doubt her. A message of reinforcement. This motorcycle is for her, not them.

She jumps off her bed when she hears the delivery truck stopping at the end of her driveway. Excitement and anticipation take the place of grief and trauma.

Letting the screen door close on its own, she dodges water puddles as she jogs to meet the driver.

The excitement beams from her smile as she watches the driver unloading her brand-new stock red and green motorcycle. Signing the paperwork, she feels his eyes boring into her.

Handing the driver back the clipboard, he questions, "You're not riding this today, right?"

Eira looks towards the sky and shrugs. "I guess not."

"Good!" he says. "Be safe out there, you never know when it'll be your last ride," the driver tells her as he's walking back to his driver's seat.

As the delivery truck leaves, Eira pushes the motorcycle inside her garage. She thought about texting Andrew a picture of it. She knows he'll want to see it, but this isn't the best time. He's still edgy from the incident with Bodhi, and he has this 'sense' of knowing when she's battling her demons. She wants to show him in person. From a place of strength.

Bummed about not being able to ride today, she decides to do an unveiling for her community.

Unlocking her phone, she posts to her social media. A video of her new motorcycle with the text reading, ***Probably needed a hug but got this instead.***

It's her New Year's Resolution Motorcycle; her caption is meant to be her reminder now and in the future. It reads, *Oscar, Just as I Promised.*

She closes the garage door, remembering her next steps will be as she promised Oscar. She will live her life for no one but herself.

CHAPTER TWELVE

Andrew

A ndrew jolts at the sound of his front door whisking across the tiled entryway.

"Honey, I'm home!" Jonah jokingly yells, closing the door.

Andrew twists towards the living room, causing his elbow to bump his glass that's resting on the counter's ledge, sending his drinking glass to shatter against the tiled floor. Twisting in shock from Jonah and the breaking glass, he somehow manages to slam his dick into the handle of the kitchen drawer. Searing pain shoots along his shaft.

"Son of a bitch," Andrew hollers, slamming the cabinet drawer after he's untangled himself from it. He angrily huffs as he stomps from his kitchen to his bedroom, careful to miss the shards of glass.

Passing Jonah, Andrew asks, "What the hell do you want?" Not waiting for a response, Andrew continues to walk to his bedroom, slamming his door.

Of all the times for that fucker to just let himself in.

As he jerks his dresser drawer open, the mirror shakes from the force as he hastily grabs a pair of boxers, tossing them onto his bathroom vanity. Pulling the waistband of his boxers away from his skin, he's cautious of his injured member. He strips out of his black basketball shorts and boxers, kicking them to the side with his toe. Exhaling, he inspects his penis for blood.

He was startled when he heard the door open, quickly twisting at his waist, the inside of his elbow felt the cool of the glass right before it dropped to the floor. His brain shouted at him to catch the glass as he slammed his sensitive dick into the drawer. Attempting to guard his pierced crotch while still in motion to save the glass caused the drawer handle to catch on one of his barbells, jarring his junk.

Opening a drawer in the bathroom, he searches for a sanitary napkin. Finding one, he tosses it on the vanity alongside his clean boxers.

"If I'd known I'd be wearing pads like a chick, I wouldn't have gotten this damn piercing," Andrew mumbles as he tears the paper strip off, exposing the adhesive. Sticky side down to the groin of his clean boxers, he presses the pad, ensuring it's secure. He drops his pad-lined boxers back on the vanity.

Grabbing a red plastic cup from the dwindling stack on the vanity, he fills it with the room-temperature saline water he made earlier.

Pressing start on his phone's timer set for two minutes, he then submerges his penis into the cup of saline water.

When the sensation is overwhelming, he pulls his penis out, only to dunk himself in again.

Andrew sighs as he drops his head back, staring at his bathroom ceiling. "I'm dunking my junk like a cookie in milk. This is messed up."

When his phone timer buzzes, he pours the saline from the cup into the sink. Wrapping a handful of paper towels around his hand, he blots his penis dry.

Squishing the damp paper towels inside the red plastic cup, he chucks both into the trash can. His thumb and fingers spin each of the five titanium barbells, making sure they move freely inside their holes. He twists each end of the studs ensuring they're secure.

He steps his feet into his pad-lined boxers, pulling them on and carefully adjusting the pad to cushion his ladder piercing on his penis.

Bending to grab his shorts and boxers off the bathroom floor, he chucks them into his bedroom hamper.

Andrew's door suddenly opens, bouncing the door handle off the wall.

Startled, Andrew jumps and yells, "What the hell?"

"Dammit, man, I've been talking to you and I'm getting nothing," Jonah states.

"Boundaries, you fucker. Learn them!" he exclaims. Andrew eases his shorts over the top of his boxers, not bothering to shield himself from Jonah. He situates himself. A bit stiff-legged and slow, Andrew walks out of his bedroom while Jonah follows.

Jonah crinkles his eyebrows and asks, "Why you walkin' like that?"

Following Andrew, Jonah says, "I cleaned up the glass."

Andrew mumbles, "Thanks," as he digs around in his freezer. The peas squish under the weight of Andrew's hand; he situates them flat. Grabbing the frozen bag of corn, he slowly walks to the living room, Jonah still in tow.

Andrew eases himself onto the couch. Gingerly, he lays the frozen bag of corn over his pierced penis and clicks the television remote on.

Looking at Jonah as if nothing is amiss. "You gonna order pizza or make something?"

Rattled, Jonah tells Andrew, "Pizza, yeah. I sure as hell ain't eating corn from your place again! What the hell did you do to yourself now?"

Jonah plops on the cushion furthest from Andrew.

"You remember Bodhi?"

"Oh, damn, she broke your dick?" Jonah points and laughs, "Literally!"

Andrew glares at Jonah. "No."

"Isn't that the chick you're hanging out with?" Jonah snaps his fingers, pointing his index finger at Andrew. "She's the one who started some shit with Eira?"

Andrew nods. "A couple of weeks ago, I met her at her place. Things got weird. I mean, really fucking weird. So, I left."

Jonah asks, shaking his head. "You are landing the psychos lately! You want your usual on the pizza?"

Andrew adjusts the bag on his crotch. "Yes, but get extra cheese this time."

"What's with the bag?" Jonah nods towards the frozen bag of corn. Waiting for a reply, Jonah places the pizza order on his phone.

"After I left Bodhi's, I was in my head. Just thinking, asking myself if I really wanted another relationship? What Claire did and how easily she did it, that shit's still in here churning." Andrew taps his temple. "Bodhi tells her girlfriend to join us and that I'd be ok with her giving me a blowjob." Andrew throws his hands up. "Fuck man, I had no clue she had a girlfriend!" Andrew winces, dropping his hands to the side of his thighs.

"Wait, I thought things were getting serious between you two?"

"Well, we agreed no strings. That we'd just see where it goes."

"She didn't say anything about a girlfriend—or being exclusive?"

"Nope! I'm walking around thinking if I'm talking to you, taking you out to eat, chilling at your house watching movies, that I'm the only person. But nooo, each time, they've got a side piece." Andrew points his finger at himself. "I'm the fucking side piece!"

Jonah arches his eyebrows, and his mouth opens and closes like a guppy. "Dude, you passed on a threesome? I mean, I get why you did it, but you fucking walked out of a threesome?"

Andrew mutes the television. "It pisses me off how easy it is for women to treat me like a shiny toy, then toss me out. I don't demand shit from them, so I guess they think I'm down for anything. See, like I said, just in my head."

Andrew flips the frozen bag of corn over. "Whatever happened to one guy, one chick, dating for marriage? Not dating to get laid. There are some seriously freaky and disturbed people out there—a lot of them are sending me messages daily."

"I thought you were trying random DM dating?" Jonah questions.

"I did, name's Shonna." Andrew rests his head on the back of the couch. "First date," Andrew holds up his index finger and then drops it on the couch. "We're out eating; Shonna orders a salad. I ordered fried chicken, mashed potatoes, and fried green beans.

The server brings Shonna her salad, but she pushes it to the side. I'm thinking that's odd, but okay. The server hands me my food. I can see steam coming off my chicken; it's that damn hot."

Andrew raises his head from the back of the couch, shaking it. "Shonna takes half of my food off my plate. Not fucking joking! Grabs my chicken with her fingers. The same nasty ass fingers I just saw her stick in her ear! She peels half of the hot-as-fuck-fried chicken off the bone, dropping it on top of her salad. She puts the rest of the chicken, which is still on the bone, back on my plate. Then, she uses her spoon to scoop, like, I don't know, half of the mashed potatoes onto her salad plate. Looks me dead in the eye and tells me, 'Green beans are the devil's toothpicks; you can just have those' and starts eating my food! I'm beyond shocked, so I only eat the green beans. The bill comes, and I think the server notices something's up because she laid the bill on Shonna's side of the table. Shonna hands the bill back to the server, telling her, 'I didn't order any of this; that's his.' The server rears back like somebody just slapped her. I hand the server my card. I mean, what else am I gonna do? I finish paying, then the server asks if I want a receipt. Fucking Shonna says, 'Yes, I need it for the tax write-off.' The server hands me the receipt, and Shonna snatches it from my hands, stuffing it into her purse. Now is when I decided I'm dropping her ass off and I'm done. Hell no to a second date. I'm about to snap, so I'm silent the whole time I'm driving her home. Shonna has the nerve to ask me if I want to get ice cream. That date was an epic disaster, so I tell her I can't because I'm lactose intolerant."

Jonah's shoulders are shaking; he's trying to hold back his laughter. "What'd she look like?"

Exasperated, Andrew questions, "Does that even fucking matter?"

Jonah smirks. "Hey, if she's into kinky shit." He shrugs his shoulders. "Maybe she's totally fine with you milk farting while she's down there lubing your tube."

"What the fuck is wrong with you? Just listen. I finally get her home. Her house is in the middle of a neighborhood, porch light on but not a tree or privacy fence in sight. So..." Andrew shrugs, "...I walk her to the porch, like a gentleman should. I'm waiting for her to open the door to put an end to my misery when she drops to her knees and has my jeans around my ankles before I can even blink. Her mouth gobbles up my dick so fast, it's doing a disappearing act. Man, you know how I hate magic tricks. She grabs my ass, diving in, gagging herself. Then her grandmother opens the door—"

Andrew's doorbell chimes. Jonah is howling with laughter.

Andrew raises his eyebrows, nodding his head towards his lap and then the door. "You mind getting that?"

Jonah opens the door, still chuckling. He pays, telling the driver, "Thanks."

Jonah tosses the pizza onto the coffee table, asking Andrew, "You got any beer?"

"In the fridge," Andrew answers. Holding the now thawed bag of corn in the air, Andrew asks Jonah, "Will you put this in the freezer?"

"Fuck no, I'm not touching that!" Jonah yells.

"Grow up, man, put it in the freezer and grab some plates with the beer."

Jonah grumbles something under his breath, pinching the corner of the bag between his finger and thumb like it's a contaminated rag. He tosses it in the freezer, then returns.

Handing Andrew a beer and a plate, he shakes his head. "That shit is funny, but what does it have to do with the bag of corn?"

"I told you; I was pissed. Disappointed; it brought up those feelings I had when Claire did her shit. Discouraged; I want to be more than a shiny new toy. Defeated; I'm somehow a magnet for the same type of woman. At that moment, getting my dick pierced sounded like a great idea! Which it's not, don't ever do it! Not that there's a lot of pain. Just mostly awkward." Andrew opens the beer, then takes a large drink; he takes a bite of his pizza.

Jonah raises his eyebrows. "Bullshit, there is no way getting your dick pierced didn't hurt."

"It didn't, just an intense stinging when the piercing needle went in, like getting stung by a bee. As soon as the barbells were all in, the stinging stopped. But the ride home, now *there* was the pain! My dick smashed against my gas tank, fuck that hurt. I went back into the shop asking for more gauze to shove down my pants. Should've seen it, I looked like a damn teenager stuffing his pants with a pillow."

Jonah scratches his head. "I'm guessing that was the awkward part?" he asks, his mouth full of pizza.

"Nope. Here's awkward. Your dick's gotta be hard for them to mark the spot where the studs are going, then soft for the piercing."

"You had to jerk off in front of a stranger?" Jonah's laughter fills the room.

"No, dick-for-brains, I had privacy. But once it was hard, she's gotta rub a cloth to sterilize it, then she measures and puts black dots where the studs will go. After it gets soft, she pierces it. But that isn't the awkward part; it's having her show me how to put a pad in my boxers. You gotta use those during the first week."

Jonah points to Andrew's penis, scrunching his eyebrows. "You said a couple of weeks ago, but aren't you wearing one now?"

Andrew sarcastically answers, "Yeah, because someone yelled when they came in. Made me jump, and I ran my junk across the drawer handle in the kitchen. I didn't want it to bust open and bleed. So, I dipped it in saline water, got a pad, and added frozen veggies."

"That's a messed-up stir-fry recipe." He continues to laugh. "Man, I still can't draw the connection. You had a weird chick pull freaky shit and you turn your dick into a damn colander? Shit, Andrew, at this rate, you're gonna run out of body parts to mess with!"

"It's not just the freaky chick doing weird shit, Jonah. It's constantly the same type of person. I'm all in, and they're one foot out the door before we even get started. Don't you see? We're on borrowed time! I want to choose people who choose me and just let everyone else just be."

"Who doesn't, Andrew?" Jonah yells. "But we're not all out here tattooing and piercing our bodies each time a relationship doesn't work. That's just ridiculous!"

Andrew shakes his head. "Nah, I'm learning. Everybody's different. This is mine. I can't do anything for another five months. When I start getting hard, it fucking hurts. It's forcing me to confront my demons; ignoring them clearly wasn't working. I'm so tired of them haunting me, making me feel like 'empty' is the only thing I can have. Claire, Penelope, Shonna, Bodhi. None of them cared a thing about me; it was 'what can I get from him'? Between being robbed and almost dying to having some chick's gramma watch me getting a blowjob, I think I passed ridiculous months ago!"

Andrew struggles to stand. "Have you really looked at my DMs? Hell, even look at yours! The shit these ladies say, they're all the fucking same. They don't care about us; they just want to get fucked by a biker who wears a helmet. As soon as the newness wears off, they're off to find another new shiny toy."

Walking towards the fridge, Andrew grabs two more beers. Handing one to Jonah, Andrew eases onto the couch. "Do you really believe we can't have something real, something genuine—a connection that goes beyond this superficial shit?"

"Andrew, the person you're supposed to be stupidly happy with, she's out there. You're just not looking in the right direction. Me, I'm not ready yet. Give me all the chicks who want to fuck a biker wearing a helmet," Jonah grins. "I'm all in!"

Andrew rolls his eyes while shaking his head. "Have at it."

"Law's been wondering where you've been. I can't wait to tell him you got some new jewelry like a sissy!" Jonah says as he chuckles.

Andrew flips off Jonah. "I can't ride for a couple more weeks, then I'm back. I don't want to be riding and pull myself open. And I'm not wearing a pad on my bike again!"

Jonah grabs the remote and unmutes. "I've been wanting to see this. You need anything before I get interested in it?"

Andrew shakes his head. "Nah, I'm good, thanks though."

Both Andrew and Jonah get situated on the couch and watch reruns of *The Office*.

CHAPTER THIRTEEN

Eira

"**S**on of a bitch!" Swinging her arm behind her head, she launches it in complete frustration.

"Auhhh, Andrew!" Eira yells. Noticing the wrench flying straight toward him, her yell pierces the air, "Watch out!" She covers her eyes with her hands, holding her breath, hoping it misses him.

Andrew ducks, the wrench barely missing his head as it continues its maiden voyage through the air of her garage. A sharp metallic clang echoes as it bounces off the wall, then comes to rest on the concrete floor.

Oh my God, that was close.

She's thankful it missed him but still frustrated, as most of the screws on her motorcycle are seized up. Arching her eyebrows at Andrew, she feels the heat flush to her cheeks. Cringing her shoulders, she tells him, "Sorry."

"Maybe that's why you can't get the fairings off; you're throwing the tools instead of using them."

Eira scowls as she squats beside her motorcycle. "I asked you for your help, not your commentary," she whispers.

Andrew chuckles as he holds his hands up in front of him, as if he's surrendering.

Realizing she needs the wrench, she stomps across the garage to retrieve it.

"Nothing worse than an angry throw only to realize that's the tool you need." Andrew asks, "What's got you all riled up?"

He removes the rest of his motorcycle gear, placing it on the shelf alongside Eira's.

"I just wanna get this done, that's all." Eira crouches beside her bike again. She places the wrench on the bolt and pushes away from her, but nothing happens. Frustrated, she drops her ass to the concrete floor and sighs. Quietly, she grumbles, "Righty-tighty, lefty-loosie. Yep, I'm doing it right."

Andrew squats behind Eira. "Doubting yourself already?"

With her chin tucked in, in complete defeat, she mumbles, "Can we not, right now?"

Andrew toes his shoe forward, nudging her thigh. "Do you want me to do it, or help you?"

Eira lifts her head, then rests it on her shoulder. Her eyes narrow with her lips pinching together. She glares at Andrew.

Andrew crosses his arms over his chest. "Look, I'm not getting in the middle of you being pissed off only for you to bite my head off later because..." Andrew bobs his head side to side as he imitates Eira's voice, "...you didn't let me do it." Andrew tucks his thumbs into his front jean's pockets. "You tell me now, what do you want?

And don't think you're changing your mind later, so think real hard how you want me."

Asking for help has never been easy for her, and she had told Andrew weeks ago that she wanted to learn how to fix this flaw. Andrew told her then he would gladly help her, so now he waits for her to ask.

"Andrew, can you show me how to do it? Let me try it. And if I can't do it, do it for me?" Eira asks. "But each step, let me try?"

Andrew shakes his head. "No." His hand fans the air between them. "The way you are right now, you're gonna go from pissed to hellcat and I didn't sign up for that shit today. You're not tanking my day with your lack of patience," Andrew replies, sitting down beside Eira.

Eira puts both her hands on his thigh and pushes. She tries to push him away, only to scoot herself across the floor instead.

With a grunt, she mutters, "Fine!"

Andrew places the wrench over the bolt and pushes it loose. He pauses, turning his head towards Eira, pressing his lips together as if he's holding back his comments.

"Don't look at me like that! I've been working on that bolt for thirty minutes. It came off so easy because I loosened it for you," Eira says.

Andrew tightens the bolt so it is finger-tight. He places the wrench over the next bolt, giving it a solid push; the bolt breaks loose. He turns to look at Eira with his eyebrows scrunched. Eira holds her hands up, palms towards Andrew; she shakes her head. Andrew loosens the rest of the bolts. Moving to the other side of the motorcycle, he sits on the concrete, making his rounds, loosening each bolt, leaving them finger-loose.

With Andrew on the other side loosening the bolts, Eira stands, brushing her hands sideways across her butt, dusting it off.

She walks to the front of the new fairing kit box. She's replacing the stock green and red parts with a purple and teal fairing kit. Smiling, she lowers herself onto her knees; she sets out to remove all the protective packaging on her bike parts. She places the packaging on the concrete and lays the part on the packaging, allowing a buffer between the concrete and the new part. After she's finished, she stands with her hands on her hips.

Eira tries not to get emotional. Today is Valentine's Day. Another holiday. Another blaring message that she's in this life by herself. The constant reminder weighs heavily on her heart. She has no one to lean on, no one to laugh with, no one to hug, and no one to tell her lovingly to pull it together on the days she knows she's being irrational.

Eira's tired of being told she's a strong woman. She doesn't feel it's a compliment anymore.

She draws her shoulders up, then rubs her cheek across her shoulder, sniffling, then she does the same to the other cheek. She hears Andrew clear his throat. "You okay over there?"

"Yeah, just something in my eye. Did you need something?" She takes a deep breath. Turning, she notices Andrew resting his forearms on top of his knees with the wrench dangling from his fingers, watching her.

Andrew tosses the wrench with a flip, catching it, he points it at her motorcycle. "All the bolts are loose. We'll place the new parts on the floor around the motorcycle where that part will go. I'll start with the seat, then we'll move towards the front. Do you think you can remove the bolts on that side? We'll swap the parts, then you can put the bolts back in the holes so I can tighten them?"

After all the new parts are in their respective places on the floor, Eira stands at the rear of her motorcycle, with the bike separating Andrew and her. He raises his eyebrows as if he's asking her, *are you ok?*

"Uh, stop. It's just me feeling sorry for myself. I wanted to do it, prove to myself I could do it, but I can't," Eira rambles. "I started this at eight this morning. I've been going at it for two hours before I called you. I feel like crap because I messed up your day off by asking you for help. I know I seem ungrateful, but I'm very thankful you dropped everything to help me. I just wish it weren't this way. I wish I had someone I could count on. Not that I can't count on you."

Eira sighs. "Damn, I'm just here chewing on my foot and you're not saying a single thing. I'm gonna shut up now!"

Andrew smirks. "You can depend on me. We're both going through the same shit. Since we both get it, we can be that person. Without needing explanation, just be there. You good?"

"Yeah, I'm just a chronic overthinker. But I'm so damn tired of analyzing the last ten years. So, I try to focus on the now, but I end up overthinking that too. It's just the way I'm wired; I guess." Eira shrugs.

"So where does this go?" she asks, pointing to the shop towel.

"I see, change the subject." Andrew shakes his head. "Why did you take so long to call me?"

"You haven't been riding for about six weeks. I thought that stuff with Bodhi was still bothering you. Plus, it's always ever been just me." Eira shrugs. "I have to figure this out on my own."

Today was the first time they'd been in the same space since early January. Texts and late-night calls have kept them connected. He's been physically distant, but that's it.

Withdrawing the bolt, she swaps the green part for the new purple replacement part.

"It wasn't losing Bodhi that had me upset. It was what she did to you that had me pissed. You're good. I want to be someone you know you can count on." Eira hands the green part to Andrew. He chucks it at the empty fairing box the kit came in.

"Hey, be careful with that!" She tightens the bolts with her fingers.

Andrew looks at the box across the garage, then looks back at Eira. "You have plans for it?"

"The dealership said if I brought it back..." Eira over-enunciates, "...in good condition..." She smiles. "He'd give me an in-store credit... so maybe... not throw it like it's junk, please." Eira chastises Andrew.

"Change in plan, we'll both swap parts. I'll install and tighten the bolts while you repackage the parts into the box," Andrew suggests.

Eira nods in agreement, grabbing the Styrofoam packaging the purple and teal part was on top of from the floor, then walks to the box. She picks up and inspects the part Andrew tossed into the box. Wrapping the Styrofoam around the green part, she stoops down to put it on the floor outside the box.

Eira stands, turning quickly. She notices Andrew hastily directing his head down at the motorcycle, clearing his throat.

"I've never had a chance to thank you for including me in the bike rides these past months. So, thank you," Eira states.

Andrew nods his head. "Invitation is always open."

Eira and Andrew discover their similarities are deeper than they had thought. Working together to change out the fairings on her new bike, Andrew's agitation isn't present when he's talking to Eira. He slides another bolt into the tray and glances at her. "You ever notice how it's always the people you trust the most that twist the knife?"

Eira nods, continuing to pack the green parts into the box. Lifting her head, she watches Andrew's jaw tense. She gives him the much-needed time to process his next thought.

"Claire..." He exhales through his nose. "...it wasn't just that she was married. She was cheering her husband, like she was happy he was going to end my life."

Eira squeezes Andrew's wrist.

"Bodhi. I thought we were getting solid. Then she pulled her crap and proved me wrong." He shakes his head.

"What about Shonna? Jonah was laughing too hard for me to understand anything about her."

"Jonah, huh?"

"I hope you're not mad. I hadn't seen you for a bit, so I asked him about you, if you were ok." She holds her hand up to stop Andrew. "You always try to protect me, but it feels like you're hiding stuff, so I thought I'd get the truth outta him. Boy, was I wrong. He laughed so much that tears were rolling down his cheeks."

"Sounds like him. Asshole," he says under his breath. "I told Shonna I was pursuing other endeavors. The endeavor is me, but she didn't need to know that. I just need to work on me."

Eira's hand stills on the wrench. "Work on you," she repeats softly.

"Yeah. I'm done with letting people burn me down." He turns another bolt and tosses it into the magnetic tray. "What about you?"

She studies the part in her hands before answering. "Trust isn't my strong suit. People walk out. Break promises. Tell me I'm too much. Logan," her throat tightens, "he didn't just take my trust. He took my safe, making me question if I was losing my mind. His currency is fear. And I paid him enough that he should be a millionaire."

Andrew glances up to meet her gaze. "You shoot right over details like it's nothing, but I know it's not."

Eira offers a faint smile. "Therapy tricks help. Breathing. Writing things down. Reminding myself that I'm not in that place anymore. Doesn't mean it doesn't try to sneak back in."

Andrew rests his forearms on the tank. He taps the top of her middle finger with his knuckle. "When it does, you can call me. No explanation, just vent, or whatever."

The corner of her mouth lifts. "Only if you let me be that same person for you."

"Deal."

They both go back to their tasks, but the air feels different now—warmer, steadier. Like something unspoken had clicked into place.

"It's never easy to talk about the abuse from Logan. Thank you for not being judgmental."

"I'll never judge you," his voice drops to a whisper, "I just want to protect you." His finger playfully flicks hers. "I'll gladly be a bullet short if he ever comes near you again."

Flashing him a smile, they both get back to work.

With the last piece of the purple and teal fairing kit installed, Andrew throws their trash away and puts the tools back. Eira assembles the green and red stock fairing pieces into the box to return to the dealership.

Crouching over the box has her back muscles tight. Resting her hands on her hips, she leans backwards. Swaying slowly at her hips, she shifts her weight from one leg to the other. Stretching her neck, she slowly turns into a stretch.

Eira pauses.

She notices Andrew watching her again. Her ass, he's watching her move her ass. Smirking, she runs her hands side to side on her butt, looking over her shoulder, she asks Andrew, "Did I get it?"

Raising his eyes, Andrew's face tints a light shade of pink as a smirk ghosts his lips. "No, you're gonna have to smack that ass a lot more."

Andrew's intense stare meets Eira's frown.

Lost in another memory, she shakes her head, muttering to Andrew. "Can't smack my ass." Eira rapidly blinks the tears away. "Logan took it too far. He said I was supposed to like it." Eira shrugs. "So, I let him." She squints at the garage ceiling, closing her eyes as she sniffles. "He left huge welts. On my butt, my legs, my back. God, did it ever sting." Eira focuses above Andrew's head; she briskly wipes her tears. Rubbing their wetness on the legs of her jeans. With choppy breath, she continues. "When I told him he was supposed to give me aftercare, he told me if I was so damn worried about it to rub some lotion on it myself."

Eira gasps, struggling to breathe. "So, I locked myself in the bathroom, crying. He yelled at me to stop being such a bitch about it and started pounding on the door." Eira's eyes fill with tears as she looks at Andrew while speaking detached, "Needless to say, he exerted his dominance again and I paid him with his treasured currency that night."

Andrew seeks Eira's tear-filled eyes, demanding hers to find him.

He begins to walk towards her when she stops him. "Don't give me your pity, Andrew," Eira says as she closes the gap. "Give me anything else but your pity. We've had a rough go of it, both surviving in our own hell. But I'm sure neither one of us wants each other's pity."

Andrew reaches out, grasping the strings on her hoodie, and gently pulls down to tighten the hood, then pulling the strings towards him just a little. "I'm sorry," Andrew says as he loops the strings together, then lets them go. He wraps her in a hug, rocking her from side to side. "I will walk through hell's fire, dragging that piece of shit with me, just to make sure you get justice."

Eira is smashed against Andrew's chest. In a muffled voice, she suggests, "Let's get this dust and grease washed off us, okay?"

Eira holds the kitchen door wide open, allowing Andrew to enter first. She follows and closes the door behind them.

Toeing off her shoes, she kicks them to the side of the fridge. Eira glances at Andrew's feet, lifting her eyebrow, she tells him, "You gotta take your shoes off. Uncle Zio's like a freaking wizard. He'll know shoes went across his floor. I swear, I can vacuum and mop before they get back, but he still knows."

Andrew snickers. "No problem." He drops his shoes next to Eira's. Unzipping his jacket, he hangs it on the back of a kitchen chair.

Eira nods towards Andrew's feet, laughing as she asks, "What's this, no cat eating taco socks?"

He smirks. "Nope. Just normal socks."

Andrew and Eira head to the sink to wash and dry their hands first. "Can you grab me the jar of sliced apples from the fridge? The Greek yogurt also? Grab you something if you want it," Eira says as she spins the spice carousel on the countertop, pulling out the cinnamon and Bourbon Madagascar vanilla powder. She grabs a bowl and two spoons from the dish drain inside the left side of the sink.

Andrew hands the jar of apples and yogurt to Eira, then he grabs a vanilla pudding cup for himself. Andrew carefully watches Eira's every move as she assembles her apple pie bowl, dusting it with vanilla and cinnamon. "Will you put these back, please?" she asks as she hands him the apples and yogurt.

Eira brings her bowl and the extra spoon to the table, tossing the spoon so that it slides across the table towards Andrew.

As she's removing her jacket, hanging it on the back of a chair, Andrew holds up the spoon asking, "What's this?"

"Umm, caveman. It's a spoon. Civilized people use it when we eat," she jokes as she arches both eyebrows.

"I know what a damn spoon is, brat. I meant, why'd you give it to me?" Andrew replies, gently sliding it back to her.

"How are you gonna eat that pudding without a spoon?" Eira questions.

She watches Andrew rotate the cup to find the bend at the edge of the cup. As she continues to eat her cinnamon apples and yogurt bowl, she sees him peel back the wrapper on the top of the pudding cup, ripping it off. He brings the wrapper to his mouth, flattening out his tongue, he licks the pudding off the top wrapper. Once the wrapper is licked clean, he lays the wrapper on the table.

Eira stares, intrigued. She leans forward, resting her elbows on the table. Her fingers tent over her lips, watching Andrew attempt to eat the pudding cup without a spoon.

Their eyes lock with one another; he rests the pudding cup below his lower lip. He barely opens his mouth, just enough for his tongue to slip out, swiping across the top of the pudding. He brings the cream-colored pudding past his lips, swallowing.

Still staring at Eira, he dips his tongue into the cup again, going deeper. Eira sees his tongue widening as it captures another dollop of pudding. Curling his tongue, he slowly brings it to his mouth, swallowing. Andrew licks the pudding off his top lip. He lifts the cup a little, making a slurping sound as he sucks the pudding into his mouth, swallowing again.

Eira holds back a moan. She blows out a sigh, "No spoon, huh?"

Squirming in her seat, she imagines Andrew's tongue between her thighs, licking and sucking her the exact way he is that pudding cup.

The sounds coming from his mouth make it difficult for her to think. She's certain Andrew knows exactly what he's doing to her.

Andrew's eyes twinkle as he pinches the bottom of the pudding cup, forcing the pudding to bubble over the top. It drops onto his fingers. He licks his fingers slowly, never taking his eyes off her. He devours the pudding bulging over the top of the cup as he continues to pinch the cup together. Andrew finishes the pudding and slides the collapsed cup towards the wrapper.

"That's how you eat pudding without a spoon," Andrew taunts. "Aren't you gonna eat?" he asks, nodding his head at her untouched food.

Eira brings a bite to her mouth; she places the spoon back in the bowl. Raising her eyes, she stares heatedly at Andrew.

Eira hopes she's not reading Andrew wrong. *Is he on board with what I think he's suggesting?*

Sensing the shift in atmosphere, Andrew leans back in his chair, clenching his hands into fists. His words are laced with desire. "Stop looking at me like that."

Eira feels a surge of heat rise, wicking up her neck as Andrew's gaze holds hers.

She's certain she's never experienced these feelings before. The fluttery stomach, the swirling lust, the hardening nipples, the ache in the apex of her thighs, all because of his tongue, because he *ate* something.

She huskily states, "Your tongue is obscene—" She clears her throat. "—with that pudding." She places both hands palm-side down on the table, trying to gain some form of balance, but Andrew continues to keep her spiraling.

"Do you wanna feel my obscene tongue?" he asks. His voice deep with intention. Andrew backs away from the table; the legs of his chair screech across the floor. He stands and rounds the table.

Eira hesitates for a moment, causing Andrew to stop walking.

She checks in with herself: *Is this what I want?* Eira's heart pounds deep within her chest; she nods her head slowly as she stands, moving her chair to the side.

"Words, Eira, not nods," Andrew demands, still not moving.

"Yes, please," she says, just above a whisper.

"Please what?" Andrew smirks, lifting his eyebrow.

"L-lick me," she stutters in a whisper, moving to stand in front of Andrew, toes touching, her fingers using the table to balance herself.

Andrew bends slightly. He wraps his arms around her waist, swooping lower, he massages the cheeks of her ass with his hands, picking her up.

Eira wraps her legs around his waist, burying her face in the crook of his neck. She checks in with herself one last time. *Is this ok?*

Deciding he's worth the risk; she drags her teeth and lips across his neck. "First door down the hall on the left."

He moans as he carries her to her bedroom, kicking the door closed with his foot.

Andrew buries his nose in her hair, sighing as he takes a deep breath. "You smell like apple pie."

He eases her down his body, grunting when her pussy grazes his cock.

He lays her gently in the middle of her bed, her legs dangling off the mattress. Andrew's fingers rest on top of Eira's waistband; he looks longingly at her. "You're steering this; tell me again or I'm gone."

Eira places her hands on top of Andrew's, pushing her leggings and panties down past her ass. Not able to push them all the way down, Eira looks at Andrew.

"I need words. I need to be certain, Eira. Yes or no?" Andrew waits, his thumb rubbing her warm flesh.

"Yes," Eira whispers.

Eira lifts her legs while Andrew removes her leggings. He leaves a trail of warmth as his fingers teasingly drag her leggings down to her feet. Pulling them free from her legs, he tosses them over his shoulder.

Kissing her on the inside of her ankle, he props her heel on the bed, doing the same for the other.

Andrew instructs. "Open for me."

Eira digs her heels into the mattress, scooting herself up the bed a little.

Shaking his head, Andrew wraps his hands around her calves to pull her back down.

"Why?"

Andrew quickly responds, "I can't lay on the bed."

Lying on her back, Andrew guides her toes to the edge of the mattress, allowing her legs to fall open.

Andrew gently trails his fingers down her legs, igniting fire with just the touch of his fingertips. "Fuck, you're so wet, you shine like a thousand diamonds."

Andrew rests on his forearms on either side of her thighs. He leans forward, drawing in the enticing scent of her pussy. "Fucking apple pie."

Andrew's tongue flicks across her clit; Eira bows her back, moaning. He increases his pressure, brushing the stiff tip of his tongue across her clit as she fists the comforter.

"Oh, God," she groans.

Andrew flattens his tongue on her channel, licking her pussy like a melting ice cream cone. His tongue flicks up, then swipes to the side and up. His tongue teases her lips as her fingers grasp his hair.

"Don't stop," she pants, tightening her grip on his hair.

Leaning on his forearms, he interlocks his thumbs, forming a tent above her clit, his fingers draped across her pelvis. Andrew softly nibbles on her clit; the nibbles turn to kisses, then sucking.

Eira tightens her channel, shattering as she yells, "I'm coming."

But Andrew doesn't stop; his tongue laps at her pussy, licking her clean of her honey.

Eira wiggles on the bed. "Uhh, fuck," Eira gasps, slamming her hands palm-side down on the bed.

Her legs tighten around Andrew's head. He chuckles against her engorged clit; the vibration causes her pussy to weep.

Andrew pushes her legs down. "I'll stop if I can't breathe." He licks her pussy, teasing her clit as his tongue pushes against her button and sways side to side.

"I'm gonna come again," Eira shouts. Her fingers latch onto Andrew's hair as she grinds against his face.

His tongue dives into her core, fucking her with his tongue. Rearing back to blow across her wet lips, Eira clutches her core tight, welcoming another detonation.

Andrew nibbles on her clitoris.

"AAUHH," she exclaims, coming yet again.

Closing her knees, she tries to push his head away, but she can't get him to move. So, she taps the back of Andrew's head while shouting, "I can't. It's too much!"

Eira feels Andrew's smile against her wet and oversensitive pussy. He turns to kiss her right thigh, finishing by flattening his tongue against her thigh; he licks. Then he sucks her into his mouth, releasing her thigh with a pop.

He hovers over her aching petals, licking his lips.

Andrew stands, lifting his right leg to adjust his pulsing cock; he groans deep. "Fuck."

Wanting to ease the look of pain anchored across his face, she scoots toward Andrew. Reaching for his belt, she pulls tightly, unbuttoning his fly.

Andrew rests his hands on Eira's shoulders, rubbing his thumbs across her collarbones.

She sees yellow tape with black numbers on it. Curiosity fuels her to reach around Andrew's waist, pushing his jeans down. Running her hands down the sides of his hips, she pushes them down further. She can see pictures of tape measures, hammers, and drills. Scrunching up her brows, she pushes his jeans down to the bottom of his boxers.

Eira giggles, pointing at his boxers. "How fitting is this?" she questions.

Andrew shakes his head. "I can't," he groans. Slowly removing her hands, he gently squeezes as he pushes them to her chest.

"Andrew?"

Andrew steps back, his gaze never leaving hers. "I'm so fucking sorry. I... I just... I can't. If I stay, I won't stop." Pulling up his jeans, he quickly fastens them.

Eira can't help but feel embarrassed; she's naked from the waist down. He's fully dressed, wearing her pleasure as cologne with a look of regret etched on his face. She feels the heat on her face as the anger beats down the embarrassment. She scoots up on her bed, dragging the covers over her nakedness.

"Please don't look at me like that. I'm running from my own shit, not you." Andrew steps closer, brushing his knuckles against her knees. "I told Jonah and Law I'd meet them later." Andrew throws his thumb over his shoulder. "I gotta go."

Eira and Andrew exchange a meaningful look. His says, *please believe me,* and hers says, *how deep does your hurt go?*

Wanting to voice her pain, but she can't bring herself to hurt him further. She wills herself to be considerate; she can visibly see he's fighting another demon. "Then you should go."

"Eira, I–"

She interrupts him. "You should go," she points to her door.

Being dismissed, he leaves her bedroom door open. "I'll call you when I get home. That's a promise." She hears the front door close, then his motorcycle drives away.

She sits in silence, feeling vulnerable and exposed; and utterly fucking confused.

He'd wanted it as much as she did. He artfully pulled each orgasm from her without regret. She'd heard his moans mix with growls of pleasure. Felt the heat from his hands as they held her, his arms threading through her legs, holding her in place. She felt his lust.

But then she laughed at his boxers, ending it all. That can't be what turned him to ice; even as he was leaving, he was trying to comfort her.

He has to know I would never purposely hurt him.

One of the biggest aspects of healing is understanding that there is always another explanation.

Sifting through every moment they'd shared. The heat between them had been real, and it wasn't one-sided. This wasn't about her. Wasn't about him not wanting her. It was about armor. The kind erected to guard a wound.

She sighs. Something tells her there's more heat to come.

CHAPTER FOURTEEN

Andrew

"Oh, look who's hangin' with the peasants. What's up princess?" Law squints his eyes against the sun beaming inside the open bay door of The Club's shop.

"Fuck off, Van Gogh," Andrew replies, plopping onto a shop stool.

"Grouchy as ever, good to know. You ever gonna get over the paint mishap?" Law pokes.

Andrew scowls. "It wasn't a mishap, you idiot. You put white paint in my milk."

Law smiles while he bounces his shoulders. "I put mud in Liz's chocolate milk. She drank it just fine. You were just being a pansy."

Andrew yells, "Her parents took her to the emergency room!"

Law's face lights up with a smile. "Well, I am the only kindergartener at that school who's ever got suspended!" he states smugly, walking away.

Andrew flips his middle finger at Law.

"Grow up," Jonah mumbles. He's bent over a front tire, fixing a valve stem on a client's motorcycle. Pausing to wipe the sweat off his forehead, he asks, "Hey bud, thought you were helping Eira?"

Andrew replies, "I was. Her fairing is changed. Now, I need to ride."

"Law's gotta change his tires, then we're leaving." Jonah nods towards the shipping boxes on the shop floor.

Jonah sighs, then yells across the four bays of the shop, "Law, stop fucking with the receiving clerk and get your shit together!"

Law jogs over to Jonah and Andrew. "Cool your jets, ole man. I was asking her about her handheld." Law waggles his eyebrows.

Shaking his head, Andrew states in a raised tone, "You were looking at her tits; you're not fooling anyone."

Law loudly whispers in a shocked tone, "Did you know she has her nipples pierced? She was showing 'em to me."

"I was not; you perv!" shouts the female receiving clerk.

Jonah chuckles. "You're a fucking idiot. How many times you gotta be told your voice carries in here? She can hear everything you say."

Law cups his hand behind his ear and leans in the direction of the receiving clerk. "I don't hear what she's saying," he whispers to Jonah.

"That's because she's not speaking, asshat!"

"I don't have 'em pierced, Law, they're just always hard. So, they stick out—" she's cut off.

"Okay," Jonah shouts, interrupting her explanation. He points to the receiving clerk. "You—get to work! And you—" He swings his finger toward Law. "Change your tires so we can leave!"

Jonah grabs his drink, taking a huge gulp. He shakes his head. "Trying to get these toddlers to work is like herding fucking cats!"

Law yells while walking his bike to bay one, "I heard that!" as the receiving clerk in bay four drops a box, then yells, "I heard that!"

"We get it, everyone can hear everything in here, just get your shit done!" Andrew yells over his shoulder to Law.

Jonah glances at Andrew before getting back to the valve stem. "What'd you do now?" Jonah asks Andrew.

"I'm not an idiot. I'm not saying a damn word in here," Andrew curtly replies.

"Come on." Jonah waves to Andrew. "I gotta stand up, anyway. Let's go to my office."

Jonah and Andrew walk to the shop door. Andrew ducks under Jonah's arm, holding the shop door open. Jonah yells, "You two stick to task. No goofing off."

Jonah points in Law's direction. "When you're *DONE* changing your tires, come into my office."

Andrew is already sitting in the vintage vinyl chair in Jonah's office, jiggling his leg nervously.

Jonah enters, throwing the paper towels he's drying his hands on into his trash can. Sitting down behind his desk, he grabs a chip from inside the open bag on his desk.

"What did you do now?" Jonah asks while throwing the chip at Andrew.

The chip lands on Andrew's chest. He tosses it back to Jonah. "I fucked up. But I don't want it to be a fuckup. But I'm pretty certain I fucked up, bad."

"There's way too many fucks in that sentence for me to keep up. You wanna explain, or am I supposed to guess?" asks Jonah.

Andrew runs his hands through his hair, inhaling deeply. He tells Jonah, "I don't know if I should *actually* talk to you about this." He winces.

"Andrew, I've been listening to you and giving you advice since before your dad passed. Why can't you talk to me now?"

Jonah's jaw tenses. Slowly, Jonah drops his face into his hands as he growls. Grabbing the bag of chips from the desk, he throws the whole thing at Andrew; the bag, the chips, the binder clip attached to the bag, everything is launched at Andrew. "What did you do to Eira?" Jonah demands.

Andrew holds his hands up as if he's surrendering. "I didn't plan on it. I told you from the beginning, she's just a friend. With my past with women, that's all she can ever be. I mean, I've got two more months before I'm clear to do anything with this thing," he points to his crotch.

"Dude, you can't pull her in, only to push her away. That girl has been through more than enough."

"You don't have to tell me, I know!" Andrew yells.

"You're going to destroy her," Jonah sighs.

"I don't want that!"

Cleaning up the chips Jonah threw at him, he absentmindedly states, "It's just, when I think of my future, I can't help but feel she's in it."

Andrew stands, walking towards the window. He rests his hands on the ledge.

"But that's nuts, right? How can I be anything she needs? My heart and my head are constantly battling, and I don't want to hurt her."

Andrew turns to face Jonah. "Do you think she can accept that? Believe that I think she's it for me, even though I fear what that means?"

Jonah replies, "Living in fear isn't living; it's a mindset. So, stay out of your damn head and start living."

"Fuck, I just left her. On her bed, I rejected her." Andrew hangs his head in shame.

"What do you mean you rejected her? A minute ago, you said she's it for you. I'm lost here, what did you do to Eira?" Jonah asks.

Leaning against the windowsill, he watches the busy traffic, then spins.

"I'm not going into details with you. But I..." Andrew swirls his hand around his pelvis. "...ya know, her. Then she tried to..." He swirls his hand around his pelvis again. "...ya know, me. But I told her I was meeting you guys... and just bolted."

"You expect me to understand any of what you just said? What does 'ya know' mean? You did what? Fill in the blank for me," demands Jonah.

"Oral."

Jonah sighs. "You went down on her and she tried, fill in the blank."

"Oral. For both blanks. Fuck! I did oral to her, and she tried to oral me, but I stopped her. This is harder than it should be!" he grumbles.

Jonah snickered. "That's what she said."

Andrew points his finger at Jonah with a murderous glare, "Watch it!"

Jonah raises his hands in surrender. "Got it. So, if you feel this way about her, how could you do that to her?"

"I panicked. I feel different when I'm with her. But I felt different with each of them from my past. None of them showed me their craziness at the beginning. Later, each of them showed me they could not be trusted in a whole new way. What if she's going to do that to me too? I like her, a lot. As a friend, I can't lose her, but I know I have her. As mine, I'm not ready to trust. I can't date, and I won't have a backpack. Does that make me a bad person?"

Jonah shakes his head. "No, you're not a bad person. But you can't jerk her around like that."

"I'm not trying to. It's like I'm finally moving on from my past, which I want, but I don't know where it leads. I know who I *want* to end up with, but I don't know if that's who I'm *supposed* to end up with. I know I don't want to face a future without her in it. But I know I can't be who she needs." Andrew falls into his vacant chair.

Jonah scoots his chair across the floor a bit. He opens his last drawer in his desk, propping his boots on the lip of the drawer.

"Andrew, you need to figure out if your fear of getting your heart broken again outweighs your desire to love her."

Andrew rests his head on the back of his chair. "I never said anything about love."

"I can hear in your voice what the thought of losing Eira does to you, and you're gonna tell me it isn't love? I hear your fear, but I also hear how you feel about her, even if you're denying it."

"I can't," Andrew raises his head, shaking it. "I just can't, and especially not now. Not with Eira. I can't give her what she deserves." Andrew rubs his palms on his jeans across his thighs. "I'll just have to convince her that being friends is what's best for us."

"I know you say she deserves better, and you're convinced you're broken, but I can't see her with anyone else. Can you? How are you gonna feel the day she brings a guy with her on group rides?"

Andrew scowls.

Jonah points his finger at Andrew. "That's my point! Right there! I guess you're just gonna have to become the *better* that you say she deserves."

Jonah massages the back of his neck. "Side note. I ran into Bodhi the other day. Well, her and I guess, her girlfriend? Bodhi wanted me to tell you she misses you. She said she tried a couple of times to DM you, but you didn't respond." Jonah scoots his chair under his desk.

Andrew shakes his head before stating. "She said she didn't get what my problem was. That most men would be down for a threesome. She also told me she forgives me, so I can come back. I blocked her ass. I don't want her crazy back in my life. I ride with the guys, and that includes Eira. I'm not changing for anyone."

Andrew remembers what his father had told him. *We're all just boomerangs. Treat people great so that great comes back to you.*

Andrew had treated Claire with thoughtful consideration; he put her wants and desires above his own needs. He despised her frown, pressed for her smile, and lived for her laugh.

In the end, Claire had tried to kill him.

Penelope was a test, pure and simple. Not sure of the test, he remained skittish with her. He still gave her respect.

In the end, Penelope sought to make him feel disgusted.

Shonna was on a whole new level of crazy. Even yet, he was a gentleman to her.

Then Bodhi. He'd given Bodhi a watered-down version of what he gave Claire. He was interested in the thought of a future with her.

In the end, she betrayed him.

I put them first because I wanted them to put me first, but it never happens.

Andrew sighs, realizing not all people live by the boomerang effect.

Andrew tightly squeezes his eyes shut.

Dad, how does this work when the boomerang comes back with shit that you didn't throw?

Jonah, having known Andrew for years, knows the zoned-out look Andrew is presently wearing.

"Hey, don't go there," Jonah says. "You know damn well your dad is and always will be proud of you. Get the fuck outta your head."

Andrew slowly nods. "I know. It's all just—"

The door to Jonah's office bursts open. "You two done sniveling like little bitches?" Law drops into the last vacant chair.

"Jesus Pete! Why's everyone plopping on my furniture?" Jonah groans, pushing his chair back.

"Please. You plopped your ass on my couch a couple of weeks ago," Andrew delivers.

Laughing, Jonah says, "I told you I'm sorry for knocking your corn off your junk."

Law whips his head to the side, staring at Andrew. "You got some kink with corn on your dick?"

Andrew scrunches his eyebrows. Reaching a new level of frustration with Law. "What? No. It was keeping the swelling down, muffmonkey."

"Why's your dick swollen?" Law questions with genuine concern.

Andrew groans, rubbing his hand over his face.

"You kept that quiet for all but about three weeks," Jonah laughs.

"I smashed it into a kitchen drawer," Andrew vents.

Law squints his eyes and cocks his head to the right. "Why was your dick outta your pants in the kitchen while Jonah's on your couch?"

"Fuck no." Jonah jumps from his chair. "I see where he's taking this."

Staring at Andrew, Jonah recites, "Andrew got his dick pierced, but he doesn't want people to know."

Jonah stares at Law as if death will be knocking on his door if he so much as breathes this to anyone. "So, Shut. Your. Mouth, got it?"

Law's eyes open wide. "Did you get the double helix bar or straight barbells? How many did you get? What's next, needle man, a Prince Albert?"

"I'm not talking to you about the bars in my dick. I'm going for a ride now!" Andrew grumbles.

With Law and Jonah in tow, Andrew walks out to The Club's shop. All the employees are long gone, so the shop is eerie quiet. Their boots and sneakers squeak on the waxed shop floor with each step. Jonah locks up while Andrew and Law get situated on their motorcycles.

Reaching for his helmet, Andrew directs, "Jonah, take the lead and Law, get your ass in the middle."

Law whines, "Why I gotta be in the middle?"

"Last time you rode back door, you got us into a fight. I'm not into that tonight, so get your ass in the middle!" Andrew exclaims.

"Fucking fine! But you got too much shit in your head, so stay offa my channel!" Law yells as he tightens his helmet strap.

"No. We ride together, we sync," responds Andrew. "I'm good, Law, safety above all else."

Jonah takes the lead, while Law and Andrew follow him onto the road.

As they continue their ride, Andrew keeps coming back to his conflicting emotions. He knows he can't commit to Eira. Can't allow himself to get too close. He knows he isn't what she needs.

Andrew can't shake the maddening layers of guilt for the way he left her earlier today. He knew it made her feel rejected; he saw it on her face as she pointed at the door.

Andrew knows Eira is interested in him, and truthfully, he's interested in her, which only makes it worse.

He knows he can't return her feelings, but the thought of losing her friendship boils his insides like molten lava singeing his veins.

Will she see I'm trying to protect her?

He can't shake the feeling that he's hurting her more. He's agonizing over the decision to let her go because he simply can't. He's torn between his desire to keep her close and his fear of causing her pain.

Eira is a constant presence in Andrew's thoughts. Her loyalty, her friendship, her drive to heal from her past gives him motivation.

Licking his lips, the ghost of her taste still lingers. *Fucking apple pie*. It will forever remind him of Eira's succulent cunt. Remembering her taste, the feeling of her grinding her pussy into his face while he nibbled on her clit, has him wanting what he can't have. He can still hear her moans as her cum coats his lips, dripping down his chin. He's fascinated by the warmth of her flesh, having used his hands to hold her still as he lapped at her core.

He knows her strength, as well as her ability to wiggle her sweet ass across the bed as he pleases her with his tongue.

He shifts his hips on his motorcycle, searching to ease the growing ache in his cock.

Andrew sighs, knowing the intimacy they shared can't happen again.

Smiling at himself, he thinks of his next post, inspired by Eira. **What do women and Jello have in common? They both wiggle when you eat them.**

"I'm hungry," Law's voice rattles through Andrew's helmet, "Are you guys?"

"Sure," replies Jonah, turning on his blinker to exit the highway into the parking lot. Cautiously inching his way to the empty shaded parking spaces by the diner.

"I could eat," replies Andrew, following them.

As Jonah and Law dismount their motorcycles, leaving their gear on their bikes, Andrew stalls, willing his erection to disappear. "You guys go ahead, I've gotta check something."

Walking a few paces away, Law calls to Andrew, "Hurry up, man, this place has the best apple pie."

Andrew stuffs his gloves into his helmet and locks it onto his handlebars. Removing the key, he shakes his bike, making sure the fork lock is engaged.

He can see Law and Jonah being seated in the diner. The table they sit at has a clear sight of their bikes.

Inhaling deeply, Andrew sighs as he comes to terms with knowing he has to trust in his journey ahead and learn from his past mistakes. As he heals, he has to trust that he can be a better person. Whether he can ever truly let go of his fear and embrace the possibility of love remains to be seen.

Grinning like a Cheshire cat, Andrew walks into the diner muttering to himself, "Fucking Apple Pie."

CHAPTER FIFTEEN

Eira

Eira's GPS indicates her destination is on the right. She gasps. "Who sponsors a marathon inside a cemetery?"

Turning off the highway into the cemetery, people dart in front of her car, throwing their hands in the air as if they're thanking her for not running them over. Eira slowly follows the signs to the volunteer check-in tent. Pulling up beside a Jeep with the sides removed, Eira slams her car into park.

There are people everywhere.

Tents, porta-potties, golf carts toting people between tents, evacuation vehicles, news vans, ambulances, people. Everywhere!

"He's playing a joke on me!" Eira reaches for her phone, dialing Dr. Gregory.

"If you're not bleeding, I can't talk right now!" Dr. Gregory shouts at her.

She ignores his snark. "Is the 5k today in a freaking cemetery?" she asks, tapping her phone to speakerphone. She places the phone on her dash while she collects her stuff she brought for today.

"Yes, the Historical Society has it there every year." His voice is muffled, then he speaks louder. "Eira, is something wrong? Are you ok?"

"Me? Sure. Just fine, Doc. Not at all worried that we're celebrating one of the biggest drunk days of the year around the dead!" she shouts. A couple of passers-by turn their heads toward her. She smiles, shrugging. She stares in awe at the blue portable toilets lined under the flowering trees. *There have to be hundreds of them, literally a line of shit.* She snorts.

"It's not like you're using the headstones as seats, Eira. And the runners are in the streets."

"They can't be this dense? There are hungover people running when they should be sleeping off last night's beer and whiskey crawls. There's concrete, curbs, cracks in the asphalt, and so much gravel!"

His voice is muffled again. "Eira, I've got to go. Look, we made a deal; honor it."

The air in her car is silent. Eira looks at her phone. "He actually hung up on me? Incredible!" she shouts, smacking her palm against the steering wheel.

Taking a deep breath, Eira grabs her phone and gear and walks towards the volunteer check-in tent.

She's helped with marathons, so she knows how it goes. She's never been this on-edge, though.

Headstones! It's the freakin' headstones! Those are better suited for Halloween, not a Saint Paddy's Day 5k.

Stepping up to the check-in table, she gets her badge quickly then is shown the tent she'll be working in. It seems Dr. Gregory has already pre-verified her. It's like he knew she would back out if there was even the slightest glitch. *Hmph, like he knows me.*

Getting settled into the medical tent. She takes in all the chaos.

People are yelling orders, laughing, chatting on phones, and tossing water bottles to volunteers. Some are clinging to their marathon partner, attempting to hold themselves upright, while others are bolting past them.

One of the medical coordinators stops in front of her. He doesn't introduce himself, but Eira can see the lanyard on his badge matches the same as hers. He's got pompous asshole energy rolling off him. He's explaining the flow of the marathon to her as if she were a child, never having volunteered before. *I get it. I'm short, but I'm in scrubs!*

She can't keep up with the names he's tossing out: runners, patients, clients, volunteers, victims. She assumes he's using them interchangeably as he keeps tossing his hands in the general direction of the marathon's starting line. He's also licking his lips between every other word, reminding her of a dog eating peanut butter. He runs his hand through his hair while his other hand taps his thigh with the clipboard. Closing his eyes, he exhales a long sigh.

Eira notices he finally runs out of words. *Thank You!* She turns her head as the stench of stale whiskey wafts up her nose. *This guy is supposed to be the medical advisor for the marathon?*

She fans her hand in front of her nose. "Too much whiskey in your crawl last night?" Eira asks as she nods towards his green bracelet wrapped around his wrist.

"Oh shit!" he blurts. "Can you cut this off?" He thrusts his arm towards her, pulling his sleeve up his forearm.

Eira rolls her eyes, shaking her head. *Unbelievable!*

"The fuck. *You* gonna bust my balls?" he states arrogantly.

Reaching into her scrub pocket for scissors, Eira cuts the bracelet free from his wrist. Handing it to him, she adds, "Nope, I just think if you're going to volunteer in a medical tent, I shouldn't be able to smell Jack Daniel's on you when you open your mouth."

"It's from last night," he deadpans. Glaring at her.

"Don't care," Eira states. "Last night or today. I should not be able to smell it. That's completely unprofessional." She narrows her eyes at him. "You should know better!"

Ignoring his personality, the need to help people is still deeply rooted. Eira takes inventory of the items on her table. "You're probably dehydrated. Take two of these electrolyte tablets and drop one in your water bottle; drink it fast. Do the same with the second, only drink it slower." She hands him the tablets and the water bottles. "And try to stay out of the sun." She raises her eyebrows, nodding towards the sign-up tent, as if to shoo him away.

"Don't speak to me in that condescending tone. I'm a medical director at Mercy. I know what to do for dehydration," he says and flares his nostrils, walking out of the medical tent.

"Great to know, I'll stay away from there!" Eira mutters.

Jackass.

She was able to gather her assignment from *Jack*, that's what she's calling the whiskey-smelling medical director. She'll have another person to help her, *thank you*. They're to assess the runners as they come into the medical tent and direct them to particular rooms. Then doctors will rotate throughout the rooms as they treat them. And by rooms she means white sheets hanging from the roof of the tents, separated into six rooms, each with a music stand to hold the patient's charts, and three chairs in each of them. Currently, the curtains are open, but as they fill up, they'll get closed. There's one slightly larger room with the curtain drawn, as it holds the supplies.

Noticing there are no signs on the curtains, she grabs seven pieces of paper. She writes: supplies, injuries, mental health, dehydration, heat exhaustion, heart, and cramps. As she secures the sign to each curtain, she hears someone rustling around the main table in her tent.

A voice booms, "Who the hell thought a bunch of hungover runners in a cemetery was a good idea?"

Eira smiles, thankful her partner for today is her friend from work. "Olive, I figured you'd love this type of scenery."

"I would during All Hallows' Eve. But St. Paddy's Day, this is just creepy as shit," Olive retorts, pulling back each curtain, placing the lined trashcans in the corners. "They always forget the cans," she says, shaking her head.

Olive and Eira are standing at the front table in the medical tent, organizing their gear and making notes of where to refill their supplies.

Olive looks up and gasps, then throws her head back and laughs deeply. Eira looks at Olive, then tracks her line of sight. Laughing, she walks to the box a couple of feet behind her. Eira grabs her arms full of electrolyte tablets, scattering them onto the table.

Olive points to the tablets. "We're going to have sooo many pukers today!" she exclaims with a sadistic smile, waggling her eyebrows.

As Eira dumps another armload of tablets on the table, the person they were laughing at meets Olive under the medical tent.

He's shirtless, with his chest painted green. Some of the paint has faded; what's left is matted in his chest hair, but his entire chest is emerald-green. His eyes are glossy, his hair standing up as if he's been shocked, and he's got his hands propped on his waist, gently swaying. "Can you point me to the loo?" he belches, then gags.

"Oh buddy, you're not making it in time. Follow me," Olive leads him to the curtain marked mental health. She ushers him inside. "Blow over the can, I'll be right back."

Eira's shaking the water bottle, forcing the tablet to dissolve faster. "You put him in mental health?" she questions Olive.

Olive reaches for the bottle. "Closest one, I'm not smelling vomit the rest of the day because he couldn't make it to the dehydration room's trash can!"

"Two," Eira announces, handing the water bottle with the dissolved electrolyte tablet to a smiling Olive.

"Bullshit, that guy's a four or five!" Olive snickers. "As pissed as he is, he'll probably blow six times."

Eira's eyes narrow. "It's too quiet back there." Both turning, they see him sleeping on the floor, his body is the big spoon as the trashcan is the little spoon.

"We both lost on that one," Olive says, walking the water bottle to lay it beside him. Olive closes the curtain. "We'll just let him sleep it off, k."

The sign-up tent is getting busier as the start time draws near. Sighing, Eira sits down in a folding chair. She crosses her legs, lost in thought.

"You want to talk about it? And by it, I mean Andy?" Olive asks, pulling out her own folding chair.

Eira stares into the horizon. "Not really. I just thought there was something there, or maybe the start of something."

Smiling towards Olive, she turns her gaze to the sign-up tent. "We've been riding for the past couple of months. With the group, and sometimes, just us. I've made it abundantly clear I'm interested in him. Each time, he tells me different versions of how he's not doing relationships anymore, that one of us is going to end up hurt. He doesn't want it to be me, but it ain't gonna be him. I'm so tired of people not showing up for me the way I need them to, ya know?"

Olive nods. "Yep."

Eira looks at the grass beneath her feet. "And then he goes and confuses me. He says he can't commit, that he's been hurt too many times. So, he friend zones me, but..." Eira lifts her hand to the table like she's picking at lint. "...his show of affection confuses the hell out of me. He watches out for me when we ride, and he tries to pay for my gas. This back and forth keeps happening; I swear I've got whiplash. We were riding just the two of us last night. He rode by and brushed his fingers against my thigh." Eira shakes her head. "But he says it's nothing."

She sighs. "He always has to know where I'm at. He's got a tracker on me on his phone—"

"Girl, that's not ok," Olive interrupts.

"Oh God. No. Not like that." Eira squeezes Olive's hand. "He called me one night, and I didn't answer. It was the night that stabbing victim got belligerent in the ER, you remember?" Eira points her finger at Olive.

"Oh man, that was a scary night."

"I was driving home, and he thought I should have *already* been home. When I didn't answer, he freaked out. Like full-on, 'If you don't answer me in the next five minutes, I'm driving to your house' kind of freak out."

"Oh, damn. Did you call him in time?"

"Nope, he was already half-way to my house. He came over anyway, though. Said he needed to make sure I was safe. That's the night I asked him if he'd be ok if we both put trackers on each other's phones."

"Are you sure you're ok with that? I mean, Logan... shit."

"I suggested it, Olive, not the other way around. It also helps when I ride. Just another layer of safety." Eira taps her fingers on her chest. "Andrew is not Logan. He cares out of concern, not out of dominance." Eira chuckles. "That's why I'm so confused. Andrew makes sure I ride on the group's inside, never the outside. He's always watching me, not in a creepy way, more like... he has to protect me." Closing her eyes, she sighs. "He's got this way of looking into my soul." Eira takes a drink of her water. "Why can't guys just be straightforward?"

Olive taps Eira's shoulder; she turns to Olive. "What I'm hearing is he's into you, but he's afraid."

"So, how long do I stick around and play this game? I don't know if I should keep waiting or if I'm just wasting my time. My biggest fear is waiting for months only to not be chosen by him."

"Girl, you remember last year? Storage room. You and me. Crying because of Logan. Remember, you were faced with a choice of which direction you wanted your life to take. You decided to live for yourself. Please tell me you remember?"

Eira nods. "Yes," she sniffles. "I remember the last thing you told me was sometimes what feels like an ending is actually just the beginning."

"Let's say you stop riding with Andrew. Completely stop hanging out with him. What're you going to do then?"

"Oh, I don't want him because I'm bored. Please." Eira waves her hand in the air as if she's swatting a bug away. "I've got nursing, my crocheting, and my motorcycle. With the right playlist, I can ride for hours." Eira nods her head, punctuating each word. "By. My. Self."

"All of this and you're still praying for a chance with him?" Olive asks, pointing at someone, laughing again.

A sweat-drenched runner is limping towards the sign-in table.

"Oh, yeah. We'll be seeing her in a bit!" Eira whispers, laughing with Olive.

"To answer your question, I am. I know he's hurting, trying to heal from his past. I know he doesn't mean what my overthinking brain tells me because it feels like he's rejecting me. He's trying to protect me; he doesn't know he's hurting me though. I know I should find someone else, but Lord, I am so addicted to him. Olive, I really, really want him. And I want him to want me."

"I know he's already turned the water on in your Lady Garden, but have you thought about just kissing him?" Olive asks. "Like get the unknown out of the way?"

"I have, but right now, I know that rejection would sting. I also know he wouldn't mean it the way I'd take it, so I'll just smile for right now."

"Remember, sometimes the people in the most pain hide behind the biggest smile."

Eira shrugs, looking back to the horizon. With a gentle smile, Eira says, "Don't I know it."

"Hey, do you want to play hide-and-seek from your heavy shit? I'm gonna go check all this out, you coming with?" asks Olive.

"I'll stay here, thanks though."

Olive has barely made it past the tent when she turns back to Eira. Blowing her a kiss, she yells. "Stay out of trouble!"

"You're ridiculous! Shoo. Go on!"

Eira unlocks her phone; she's learned to ignore all the social media notifications. She's set aside time for responding to comments each day, otherwise social media will overtake her time.

She snort-laughs watching Andrew's recent post. He's sitting on his motorcycle at an angle; his back is to the camera while the text on screen fades out. **What do women and Jello have in common? They both wiggle when you eat them**.

"He freaking tagged me in it," she murmurs. *Some of the stuff he does is insane.*

Seeing Andrew makes her think about the night he gave her the best orgasm of her life, only to reject her. A snicker creeps in as she acknowledges the irony. She'd cried out, 'Oh God' both times. Once when she came and the other when he left.

His departure left Eira feeling so alone, and that's how she knows she's invested further than he is.

She wrestles with knowing he's in pain and granting him grace, while feeling hers, but wishing they both could be free of pain.

While she understands he's suffering, she doesn't like how his absence is making her feel. She's vowed to never be in a place of doubt again, yet Andrew's hesitation and indecision over the past month has her questioning her desires for their future.

She craves something more, something real with Andrew, but she's not sure he can see her through the fog of his past. His inability to leaves her feeling frustrated, making her wonder if she is enough.

Stop this shit; we agreed never to doubt again.

She can't understand why he's so afraid to take a chance on their relationship, why he's so fixated on his past. She's nothing like the other women from his past.

Eira knows she's got to make a choice. Either continue to wait for Andrew to come around, risking further heartache, or she protects herself and walks away.

She knows there's someone who will give her the love and commitment she deserves.

The thought of not seeing Andrew makes her feel like her intestines are knotting. She's decided to hold on to the hope that one day Andrew will realize she isn't like his past. Until then, she'll remain locked into her pursuit of healing from her past so she can forge her own path.

Placing her phone in her scrub pocket, Eira hears the crunching of shoes on gravel.

Olive jogs to the tent. "Eira, I need your help! Someone just went down by the merch tent."

"Oh shit, that's bad!" Eira jumps from her chair, switching to nurse mode as fast as her heartbeat pounds against her ribs.

"Blood is everywhere!" Olive shouts, grabbing the first aid kit and supplies.

Feeling the adrenaline kick, Eira thinks: *And so it begins.*

CHAPTER SIXTEEN

Andrew

The skate park is alive with the buzz of competition. Dozens of nine-year-olds, each eager to show off their skills, fill the concrete playground.

The perimeter is taped off, ensuring the aspiring athletes have space to execute their practiced routines. Family and friends shout encouragement while others clap with excitement.

Andrew stands beside Roni, Finn's mother, who's biting her nails with nervousness.

Finn bobs his head to keep his routine coordinated with Wes-Ghost's song, "Teeth", like he and Andrew practiced. Swiftly gaining speed, he pops his board onto the ramps, and rides over the rails with skill before dismounting with a hop.

Andrew cups his hands around his mouth and shouts to Finn, "Doin' great, keep your focus!"

Roni claps. Wiping the tear off her cheek, she hugs her fists to her chest.

The look of determination is etched across Finn's face. He skates to the concrete bowl in the middle of the park, rolling into the drop-in. Leaning his body towards the front of his board, he forces himself to pick up speed. Finn pops out of the bowl with enough movement, allowing him to perfectly land his last trick, a kickflip. Five judges, strategically positioned around Finn, follow him as he progresses through each set. The judges shake Finn's hand, then walk towards the next skater to begin again.

Finn's eyes twinkle with excitement. His smile radiates confidence, while his white knuckles hint at his nervousness as he grips his skateboard tightly. With a reassuring nod, Andrew watches as Finn joins the other finished competitors.

Andrew drapes his arm around Roni's shoulder, but she twists and pulls Andrew into a full hug while speaking into his chest, "I can't thank you enough for being here for him."

Stepping away from Andrew, she whispers, "I know it's heartless, but I'm so thankful he fell in front of your house that day. He's been withdrawing since his dad left," she says and starts to cry a little harder, wiping her cheeks but only managing to smear her mascara. "Then you come along, and he now has a guy to help him."

Looking at her mascara-covered fingers, Roni chuckles, "I might have grabbed the wrong tube of mascara today."

Andrew smirks, looking down at her. "I'm not sure they make any that could withstand the waterworks you're throwing at it today."

She chuckles.

She hiccups. "Finn gets so blasting upset when I cry, so I try to wait until after he's in bed." She sniffles. "Sometimes, I don't make it, and he gets so angry at his dad." She sighs. "Moving into the house on the cul-de-sac months ago was the best thing for us; we just didn't realize it then."

Using the tissue Roni has given him, he dabs it under her eye. "All good. It's all gone now," he says. He hands her back the tissue. "I can't offer much, but if you need anything, find me, ok? Anything. For either him or you," Andrew says, patting her on her shoulder.

"I promised Finn some St. Paddy's ice cream if he didn't make a single mistake today," she says and winks at Andrew. "I have no freaking clue what any of this is, so I'm saying he did perfect and we're getting some green ice cream!" She wipes her cheeks again. "Are the smears gone?"

Andrew smiles, nodding.

"You've got someone waiting for you," she says and nods towards the park bench where Andrew placed his motorcycle gear earlier.

"Come on, I'd like you to meet her," Andrew tells Roni as they walk to the bench.

"Eira, this is Roni. She and her son live in the blue house right before the cul-de-sac. Roni, this is Eira."

Roni extends her hand towards Eira. Shaking it, Roni tells Eira, "So glad to finally meet you! Finn raves about you." Roni air quotes and mimics Finn's voice, "The chick who rides like Andrew." She smiles and waves her finger at Andrew and then her son. "Not sure which of these two fangirl you the most, but you've got a loyal following."

Eira smiles, glancing at Andrew.

"I'm grabbing Finn and we're going to head out. Thanks again, Andrew. It was nice meeting you, Eira. You two be safe," Roni says before walking away.

Andrew sits on the bench. He tugs Eira's fingers, pulling her to sit beside him. "You survived the inebriated marathon yesterday?"

"Oh my God, I'm pretty sure I got contact drunk from all the puking runners! Next year, Dr. Gregory can have it." Nodding to Roni's retreating figure, Eira shyly asks, "So, you do a lot for them?"

"I've got a soft spot for the kid." Andrew shakes his head. His eyes follow Finn and Roni until they're out of sight.

He sighs. "His dad abandoned them for a job in Nigeria. Piece of shit never asked if Roni or Finn wanted to go, just told them he was leaving and then left them a week before they moved into the house. Finn was so full of rage. He reminded me of myself. When I lost my dad, I felt the same way. I mean, my dad died and his just fucking walked out on him, but grief is grief. I didn't know the Andersons were going to rent that house out again until the day there was a moving truck backed into the garage. Granny Anderson was walking up my sidewalk humming like she does. I was checking my mail when she asked me to watch out for them, that they'd had a hard year and could really use some help. A week later, the little dude had a meltdown in the street in front of my house. I felt like I was looking in a mirror at myself years ago. I wanted to be there for him. Now, each week, we help each other with our bikes, and we talk. Nothing big, but we're working through issues that he's struggling with, like why he needs to take the trash out daily. Kind of doing what Jonah did for me. I just can't help wondering what would have happened to me if I didn't

have Jonah in my life during that time. Boomerang Effect, right?"
Andrew states, watching a bird pecking at the ground near the
trash can.

Eira nods slowly. "I know that feeling. Different details, same
ache in your chest that never fully goes away." She offers a small,
knowing smile. "Sounds like you've been a Jonah for him."

Eira taps Andrew's shoulder, pointing at a little boy by one
of the ramps. A soft giggle escapes her. Andrew glances at Eira,
following her finger.

Andrew drops his forearms to his thighs, inching forward and
leaning to his right a bit. Squinting his eyes, he looks around the
mammoth oak tree to see what Eira is pointing at.

"He just walked over there, holding the puppy under one arm
and the skateboard under the other. Then sat down." Her voice is
filled with worry. "Where's his parents?"

"That little shit. His name is Connor, and his dad is gonna be
pissed at him."

Eira giggles while asking a question, "Who dressed him?"

Andrew sits back on the bench, smirking as he takes in all of
Connor's favorite idols being displayed with his clothes. Connor
and Andrew had this chat just last weekend, so he knows how
Connor's feeling. Andrew knows what he's going to say will break
Eira's heart as well as make her laugh.

He clears his throat. "Connor dresses himself. Always. Mike says
he has to pick his battles and fighting over what his son wears is not
worth it."

Eira rests her hand on Andrew's arm. "That puppy must adore
him! It hasn't even tried to get off his lap." Eira tips her head
towards Connor. "Not being mean, but Connor knows he doesn't

match, right? He's got so many colors going on." She rests her hands in her lap, and she fiddles with her silver band around her thumb.

"He doesn't care," Andrew scoffs. "His purple shorts are because his mom loved Black Panther, his yellow shirt is because she used to call him her little Wolverine, and his red cape is because all heroes have capes. That pink tutu he's wearing today means he's missing his mom."

Andrew glances at Connor. "She used to be a dancer. Connor thinks a ballerina is the only type of dancer, so that's why the tutu. I can't see from here, but I bet he's got his rocket socks on. He keeps telling Mike he's gonna build a rocket so he can shoot up in the sky to visit his mom."

Andrew rests his palm on Eira's shoulders. "Connor's mom died a year ago. His dad, Mike, his brother, James, and him are in a certain kind of hell."

Eira's eyes are glossy as she sniffs.

She points at Connor. "Andrew, he's trying to put the puppy on the skateboard. Should we do something?"

"Dammit, he's going to push that thing down the ramp." Andrew exhales, jogging towards Connor.

Andrew speaks with authority and shakes his head at Connor, "Why don't you stop and come sit with us until your dad gets back, okay?" Andrew holds his hand out, waiting. "Hand me the skateboard."

Connor stands, patting the dog's head. Vigorously shaking his head, he shouts, "NO. NO! K-nine wants a ride, Drew."

"Hand me the skateboard or I'm taking K-nine from you," Andrew demands.

Connor hugs the puppy tightly and stomps his foot as Andrew points towards the bench.

Andrew juggles the skateboard as he grabs his phone, trailing behind Connor.

Connor tells Andrew, "You not sappose ta test and walk. That's what ma dad tells James awe da time."

"I'm texting your dad and brother, letting them know I've got you with me," Andrew relays to Connor. "You know you're not supposed to walk away from them. I bet they're freaking out right now trying to find you." Andrew sits down on the bench, finishing his texts as he hears Connor tell Eira, "I'm gonna be a poles office one day. What are you?"

Eira smirks. "You mean a police officer?"

Connor nods his head yes.

Eira chuckles. "I'm a nurse. Why do you want to be a police officer?"

"I gotta save udder peepoles mommies, since no one could save mine," Connor shouts as he twirls around. "Like ma cape?" He finishes with his tiny arms squeezing tightly, trying to flex his muscles.

Eira glances her misty eyes up at Andrew. Her shock is visible in her eyes; she gently wiggles her head side to side as she whispers, "What do I say to that, Andrew?"

"Eira thinks your cape is cool, don't you?" Andrew nods towards Connor.

As Eira is reeling from her shock, Connor states, "You can pet K-nine." Connor points his finger at his puppy. "Just don't let 'em stick hims butt lickin' tongue on ya. That's what ma dad tells me awe da time."

"Not a problem," Eira says as she pets K-nine behind his ears.

Looking up, she hears arguing coming from two males who are getting louder as they walk towards her. The young masculine voice says, "Shit, Dad, I said I'm sorry already. What more do you want?"

"Watch yourself, son. I asked you to keep an eye on your brother while I changed your coach's wife's tire. Next thing I know, I'm getting a text from Andrew telling me he's got Connor. Followed by you texting me a picture of a girl. What the fuck, James?"

The commotion is halted when Connor claps his hands together.

"Dad, we don't say fuck we say fart, 'member?" Connor has his hands, palms facing, towards the sky above his shoulders, wiggling his head like a bobble-head doll.

James whispers loudly to his dad, "I sent it to you by mistake! I said I was sorry!"

Taking a deep breath, Mike kneels in front of Connor. "Fart, yep, got it. Hey, you can't keep going on adventures by yourself, bud. That's not okay. When I tell you to do something, I need you to do it, please."

Connor grunts, "But Dad, I don't wanna see hims gurl. She gots pee'nut butter on her face and strawberry jelly on her lips." Connor shivers. "No fanks Dad!"

Mike sighs, "Son, it's called makeup; we've talked about this before."

"Dad, she gots spider legs on her eyes." Connor points to his eyelashes. "That's just sac redijous!" Connor says, shaking his head. "That's what ma Toots says awe da time." Connor arches his eyebrows as he smiles at Eira.

Mike hangs his head in defeat. "The word is sacrilegious, Connor and her wearing fake eyelashes is not sacrilegious." Turning to James, Mike states, "Remind me to have a chat with your grandmother, k?"

James sighs, nodding his head as he answers, "Yes, sir."

Mike stands, ruffling Connor's hair. "Andrew, thanks again. Didn't mean to put you out any, but damn glad you were here. Let's go guys, to the truck."

Mike, James, Connor, and K-nine take a couple of steps away when Connor runs back to Eira.

The other two keep walking as they are deep in a chat when K-nine barks and sits down. Connor places his tiny hands on Eira's knees and flashes a megawatt smile at her, "Will you be mys nurse if anyfing happens ta me?"

Eira smiles at Connor as she pulls him in for a hug. "Of course, but why are you asking?"

Connor lifts his head, looking deep into her eyes. "You're prwetty ta look at."

Andrew belts out a deep laugh and shouts towards Connor's dad, "Mike, come get your kid!"

Connor rises on his tiptoes while waggling his eyebrows. He shouts, "And ya make ma insides all wiggly. Bye now!" Waving his little hands as he walks towards his dad.

"Connor, let's go. Now!" Mike hollers.

Connor darts towards his dad, yelling, "Oh God, I'm coming." He stops running, turns around to face Andrew and Eira. Connor points his finger at Andrew. "That's what ma auntie tells ma dad awe the time when she sleeps over!" Connor skips to Mike.

"Dammit, Connor, put your hand over your mouth and come on! Sorry guys," Mike says as he picks up Connor, resuming their walk towards their truck.

Eira squeals with laughter while Andrew watches her, himself also laughing.

Andrew sits back on the bench, taking Eira's hand in his. He asks, "Is this okay?"

Eira's somber expression meets Andrew's blank gaze. "What are we doing here?"

She looks around the park, looking back at their joined hands.

"You ask me to join you here, which I'm fine with. But before that, you've sent cryptic texts. We've gone on group rides, but nothing just you and me. The last time we were together, you bolted like I had the plague. And now, you're asking me if holding my hand is ok?" Eira exhales shakily, removing her hands from Andrew's.

Andrew slumps his shoulders. "I just freaked, but I felt like shit with the way I left you."

He grabs Eira's hand closest to him, placing it on his thigh. He rubs his thumb along the back of her hand.

"You're sending mixed messages and frankly, I am getting whiplash. I have, from day one, made my feelings explicitly clear. You know about Logan and all my past, and I know yours. I've sought to better myself, to push myself forward, to rise above all that baggage. But you. It's like you're using your past as a crutch to stay so despondent. Do you want to move on?"

"I do," replies Andrew.

"With or without me?" Eira quietly asks.

Andrew shifts on the bench, bringing himself closer to her. "You should know, there isn't a world for me without you in it. I can't lose you," Andrew sighs. "I want you. For a friend and more. But my history scares the hell out of me because I know if we are together, I'll eventually lose you. But if we're only friends, I won't lose you, don't you see—" Andrew cups Eira's chin, aligning her gaze with his own.

Eira scowls, her face reflecting her confusion, cutting Andrew off. She admonishes, "You don't know that!" She wrenches her chin away from Andrew.

Scooting away from him, stopping just as she reaches the end of the bench.

"Your fear of commitment is consuming you. Are you really telling me you're fine with letting your fear dictate your future? To truly be happy, you know you've got demons to confront, but you're choosing not to?" Eira attempts to rise, but Andrew applies slight pressure to her thigh, causing her to remain seated.

"Let me finish," Andrew begs.

But Eira isn't having it. Shaking her head, her voice is broken, but slightly louder, "Me and Jonah are both your friends, right? Do you rub his thigh? No. What about Riggs? Do you tighten his chin strap? No, you don't. Your hand-kissing, flirty texting, tongue-wielding, alpha shit crossed the friendship line weeks ago. Then when you realize what you've done..." She tosses her hands in the air. "...your insecurities rear their ugly heads, and you pull away again."

Eira swats at Andrew's hand, trying to nudge his hand off her thigh. "But I think we're past that, so once again, I'm expecting something from you that *you're* unwilling to give me. This is your choice! And you're choosing all those women who hurt you over me!"

"No, I'm not. I'm trying to protect you. Dammit, just let me finish!"

"Your way of trying to protect me is *actually* causing me pain!" Eira grits.

"I FUCKING AGREE..." Andrew shouts. Raking his hands through his hair, he continues, his voice dropping to a whisper. "...with you!" Scooting closer, Andrew places his fingers over Eira's lips. "Please, I'm begging you. Please. Do not say another fucking word until I finish."

Eira latches a hold of Andrew's wrist, taking a deep breath, she gently eases her fingers to his palm, slowly pushing his hand away from her lips.

"I'll be quiet," she simply states.

Andrew exhales like air being released from a punctured tire. "I feel the connection. It's more than friendship. But something tells me I won't recover when you break my heart—"

Eira opens her mouth.

Andrew holds up his hand in the air between their chests, then points his finger at Eira. He shakes his head. "You said you'd be quiet. I let you have your say, now let me have mine."

Eira's eyes mist over as he drops his arms to his side. Clearing her throat, she looks away. She hastily wipes a rogue tear, hoping Andrew doesn't see it. She quickly drops her hand to her lap, then nods yes ever so slowly.

Wiping a tear from her cheek with his thumb, Andrew lowers his voice, sounding like he's trying to talk in a room full of sleeping babies. It reverberates to the very essence of her marrow as he growls, "You fucking gut me when you cry. I'm so sorry to be the cause of them." He rests his hand on her shoulder, gently rubbing his thumb across her collarbone.

Eira shrugs his hand off, aggressively wiping her eyes. She glares at Andrew. "Then don't finish that statement," she whispers.

"All I can give you is friendship."

Eira gasps and then coughs. Tears streaming down her face, making large wet drops on her jean-covered legs.

Shaking her head, she mutters, "I don't accept—"

"Don't answer that," Andrew requests.

"You know that's the ring for the hospital, I have to," she states, reaching for her phone in her back pocket.

"Hello," Eira listens and nods. "Yep, I'll be there in less than thirty. Sure will." She sniffles and wipes her cheeks with the back of her hand. "No, I'm fine. Just allergies. No biggie." She sighs again. "Dr. Gregory, I said I'm fine." She pauses, listening. "Yes, see you then."

Eira ends the call. She leans to her left, lifting the right side of her rear off the bench, and pushing her phone into her back pocket. "I'm needed at the hospital."

She stands. "I... I'm not sure..." She fidgets with her hands. "...what am I supposed to say? I'm so mad at you right now," Eira looks towards the sky, exhaling deeply. Straightening herself, she looks at Andrew. "I just can't."

Andrew reaches for her hand, lifting the back of it to his lips. "Text me when you get to the hospital. I need to know you're safe."

Eira snatches her hand from Andrew's. "Unfuckingbelievable!"

She jerks her helmet off the bench, stomping away from Andrew, towards her motorcycle.

Andrew's words chase after her, tapping against her consciousness, "You better clear your head before you ride, Eira."

Eira lifts her left arm into the air, flipping off Andrew over her shoulder. Never glancing back, she continues her pursuit to her motorcycle.

"There's my girl," Andrew softly chuckles. His smirk fades the second she's out of sight. His gut twists. Walking away from her isn't an option.

I've got to find a way to get this right.

He waits until he hears Eira's motorcycle weave through the parking lot of the skate park. When he can no longer hear her, is when it's safe for him to think of her. More importantly, a life with her.

To fall asleep with his arms wrapped around her and wake up to her draped across his chest. What he would give to burrow his nose into her neck or bury his cock deep inside of her. To have her smile at him when he walks through the door of their house, or to hear her giggle as he tickles her with his tongue, licking over her hipbone.

He knows he wants her.

He's vowed to himself he'd no longer let his past define him.

As the sun begins its descent into the horizon, Andrew leans back, both arms outstretched across the back of the bench, legs sprawled out. He taps his thumbs against the cool metal supports.

Deep in thought, he rests his head against the back of the bench.

Can Eira silence my ghosts?

Andrew huffs.

Will she even want to?

He knows she's right about his fears and insecurities, but she's wrong about choosing those past women over her. He would set the world ablaze for Eira; the thought of losing her is like a knife to his sternum.

As he loosely dozes off, Andrew's nose picks up a distinct smell. Reminding him of how Sage's tattoo shop back in Texas smelled. He remembers her whispering to him with distraught emotion in her voice, *"From ashes of pain, resilience is born."*

Andrew is jolted awake by the shrill of his ringtone he has assigned to Eira's text notification.

Eira: HOSPITAL

Andrew: Text me when you get home. I need to know you're safe.

He shakes his head, already knowing what her reply will be.

Eira: Unfuckingbelievable

Andrew: Haven't we already had this conversation?

Figured you'd flip me off.

Andrew: There's my girl.

Knowing Eira is safe at work, he gathers his gear and rides home.

He must be feeling nostalgic tonight because the only thought on loop through his mind is Sage's words of wisdom.

"The One will put your heart together while ignoring her own broken heart."

CHAPTER SEVENTEEN

Eira

E ira has noticed the subtle shifts in Andrew's behavior over the past weeks. It's a possessive behavior, but it gives her comfort, never fear. As if he's proving to her, she's his to protect. Eira never feels like Andrew is trying to own her. She feels safe, encouraged, seen, and free.

Andrew is not Logan. He has given her no reason to fear him. Logan's brutal grip was about submission through fear, whereas Andrew's gentle caress is about keeping her safe. Logan's touch made her recoil. Andrew's caress is a marvel; he lets her breathe. If Andrew is near, his hand is never far from hers. If they're out riding, she's on the back of his bike, her thighs tightly hugging him. If they're grabbing a bite to eat, she's sitting next to him. He knows where she is at all times. For protection, though, never trying to subdue her.

Eira enjoys the tenderness. The simple touch of his fingers has her body fluttering, slowly vibrating, like waves rolling through her. The way he strokes his thumb against her collarbone feels like it ignites sheets of tingles, cascading like ice water drops across her skin. His thumb tapping on her thigh to the beat of a song makes her a gooey mess. When he presses gently between her eyebrows, where her forehead creases in a scowl, it's his way of quietly reminding her she's overthinking again.

When their time draws to a close, he pulls her into a hug. He affectionately cups her ass, using his thumb to rub across her cheek like a guitarist strumming their strings. He nestles his lips against the nape of Eira's neck; either licking, sucking, or kissing, and sometimes all three, but never kissing her lips.

Eira also sees the near-constant struggle warring inside him. She knows they're on borrowed time, like she's waiting for the final shoe to fall. But she's already decided; when the last shoe drops, she's tossing that sucker. He can't drop it again if she chucks it into the ocean!

As they make their way to the skatepark, Andrew's hand is over hers, tenderly rubbing them both against his stomach. Preparing for the turn into the parking lot, he locks his fingers around hers, tapping her hand against his chest where his heart is.

Bracing for the turn, Eira tightens her thighs around him. She continues to rub his stomach, giving him as much affection as he'll allow.

Andrew's hand disengages the clutch while his other squeezes the brake as he downshifts expertly. They come to a stop under a large tree, providing shade from the warm April sun.

Andrew extends his arm, assisting Eira's dismount from his motorcycle. She removes her backpack, which holds Connor's skateboard, resting it safely against the back tire. After hanging their helmets on the handlebars, Andrew wraps his arm around her waist, bringing her ass to rest against his thigh as he leans against his bike's seat. He drops kisses along the back of her neck.

"I'm going to take the board to Mike, while you decide where we go to eat," Andrew rubs his hand against the length of her thigh, tapping the side of her leg as to signal his request for her to take a couple of steps forward.

Stooping slightly, she grabs the skateboard from her backpack. Andrew guides his hand across her ass, skimming his touch over her hip. His hand is splayed across her pelvis, having his middle finger dangerously close to an inappropriate display at a kid's park. He pulls her back into his chest. Eira gasps as Andrew lowers his head, gently nipping at her neck below her earlobe. Releasing her, he smiles smugly.

Andrew arranges the skateboard in front of him, concealing his erection. Then he disappears into the park entrance, taking the skateboard to meet Mike at the bench where Eira and he sat last week.

Motorcycles are aplenty in warm-weathered states. After a while, they all sound the same, blending into Florida's background noise, a symphony if you will.

Eira removes snack wrappers, bottles, and wadded-up paper towels from her backpack.

Walking to the trash can, she hears a motorcycle getting louder, not an uncommon sound for a sunny day in Florida. When she turns to walk back to Andrew's motorcycle, the sun reflects off a parked car's windshield.

Raising her hand to shield her eyes, she pauses when she steps under the shade. Looking up, she sees Logan straddling his idling motorcycle right beside Andrew's.

Cold sweat trickles down her spine as her breathing becomes labored, more of a gasping for air after a mile run. Her hands begin to shake. Looking around, Eira realizes it's just her.

And that monster.

"This state just isn't big enough," Logan sneers.

"We had an agreement; you're not supposed to be around me," Eira tries for confidence; instead, her voice is saturated with fear.

"Does your new guy," Logan nudges his chin towards Andrew's motorcycle, "know to keep you away from his friends?" He laughs as if that's the punchline to a hilarious joke.

Eira steps forward, still having about ten feet of distance and Andrew's bike between the monster and herself.

Anger lights across her skin like a freshly lit match. "I never did anything with anyone but you!" She balls her fists by her sides. "It's a shame everyone knows you can't say the same," Eira shouts.

Logan stands, pointing his finger at Eira. "I should have squeezed tighter when I had your worthless throat in my hands. You're such a waste—"

"Get away from her," Andrew shouts, interrupting Logan. Andrew runs to Eira.

Logan flashes Andrew a defiant smile. His motorcycle engine roars to life as he slams it into first gear. Tires screaming, Logan leaves black marks over the concrete parking lot as he luckily makes it out into traffic without smashing into any parked cars.

Andrew rushes to Eira, looping his arms over hers.

Eira is shocked from seeing Logan; still fearing what he's capable of, mixing with the iron grip of Andrew's protective hold, dumps adrenaline into her system. It catapults her quickly into one of the worst panic attacks she's ever had.

Eira's breathing is deep, and it's coming in rapidly. She's clawing at Andrew's arms, gasping for air.

He spins her. Freeing her arms, she claws at her neck and collar. "I can't breathe," Eira screeches as tears rush down her face. Her body vibrates as all her senses are slammed into overload.

"Fuck! Look at my face, Eira," Andrew pleads. "Find my eyes. Can you hear me? What color are my eyes?"

Eira feels the warmth of his palms resting on her shoulders. She recognizes, in a small recess of her mind, that she must tether to something.

Unlike Logan's grip that used to squeeze the breath from her lungs, Andrew's hands rest gentle and steady on her shoulders. He continues to offer her space to breathe, room for her to process the chaotic emotions. His calm voice and gentle reassurance reminds her that she's safe now.

His commanding voice breaks into her internal safe space. "Eira, what color are my eyes?"

"Blue," she whispers.

"Now find my lips."

She offers him a small smile as her gaze locks onto his concerned lips.

"Do you feel my breath?" Andrew exaggerates his exhale like a child blowing on a bubble wand.

"Yes."

"Now slowly inhale through your nose and watch my mouth, you feel me blowing on your cheeks?"

"Yes."

"Now, you. Blow on my face."

Eira slowly pushes her breath towards him.

"That's it, again. In your nose, out your mouth. Slowly. You're doing good."

As Eira inhales through her nose, she hears a motorcycle in the distance. Her eyes widen in fear, then frantically bounce over Andrew's shoulders, searching for the rider, making sure it isn't Logan again. Her breath stutters and snags in her throat.

"Hey, look at me. Don't go there. Eira, stay present with me."

Her therapist has taught her to focus on her safety, then focus on her constant surroundings. In an effort to reground herself, she says, "Blue." Her eyes mist over. "You have blue eyes."

"That's really good. Do you know who I am?"

Eira glances at Andrew. Looking at his lips, his nose, and back to his eyes.

"Stay with me. Who am I?" Andrew's voice is deep with emotion.

"Andrew. You're Andrew."

"That's right. You're safe. I've got you." The motorcycle accelerates, causing Eira to stiffen.

"Look at me. Who am I?"

"Andrew."

"I need to hear your voice. What word do you say?"

"Telos."

"Again."

"Telos." Eira exhales.

"I'm so cold," she whispers as her body shivers, causing her words to garble.

"Hey, we're going to move to the grass, okay? Can I carry you?"

"So cold," Eira says, shaking her head, her body shaking with it.

"Repeat after me. 'Andrew is picking me up.'"

"You're picking me up," Eira states.

"No Eira. I need to know you feel safe. I need you to say, 'Andrew is picking me up.' Just like you taught me, you said you had to follow the process," he lightly scolds.

"Andrew is picking me up." Eira places her palms on Andrew's neck. Drawing in comfort, she says the phrase again.

Andrew swoops Eira into his arms like a bride being carried across the threshold on her wedding day.

"Andrew, where are you taking me?" Eira battles her emotions as worry begins to set in.

"I need you to look at me. I need you to trust me. Say it," Andrew demands.

She's come back into her reality enough to confidently know she can trust Andrew; he won't hurt her or let harm come to her.

Eira breathes deep through her nose and exhales as if she's purging everything from her soul. She looks up at Andrew, changing her tone to mimic his, "I need you to look at me. I need you to trust me. Say it," Eira copies him while smiling. "Telos," she says in her own voice, sharp and clear.

"There's my girl," Andrew says. "Where am I taking you?"

"To the grass, Andrew." Eira looks towards the grass when she sees a flood of people walking out of the skatepark. She squirms in his arms.

"You're fine. No one's watching. See they're all too consumed in their own shit," he advises.

Andrew, with Eira still in his arms, carefully sinks to his knees in the grass. The row of dense green shrubbery at their back gives them a sense of privacy. Eira scoots to sit on the grass as Andrew rolls from his knees to his hip, planting his butt onto the grass next to her.

"Eira, take off your shoes and socks," Andrew advises as he removes his own. Tossing them at the end of his feet on the grass.

"Run your feet over the grass. Back and forth, that's it."

Eira focuses on sliding her feet across the grass, back and forth.

Andrew softly rests his hand on her thigh; the heat from his palm brings her comfort. He asks, "Are you good over there?"

Eira's voice wavers. "There's a lot of people here, Andrew."

Andrew straightens his legs. "Come here," he says, tugging on her shoulder.

She doesn't move. Her eyes are trained on the hordes of people leaving the park when another motorcycle drives by.

"Fuck, I'm not losing you again!" Andrew scoops her up and sets her in the center of his thighs.

She releases an astonished gasp. "There're kids here, we can't sit like this!" she hisses.

"I don't care. You're all I see. Who am I?"

"Andrew," she says, lifting her hand to thread through his hair. She chokes as her tears flow down her cheeks. "I'm so sorry."

"Don't." Andrew shakes his head before kissing her nose. "Keep saying my name. You told me it'll help ground you. If you ever feel it coming, say my name or Telos, then I'll know you've been triggered."

As he rubs her thighs, a kid runs into the parking lot, a woman chasing after him.

"Hey, Mom, look at that," he stops and spins, pointing at Eira and Andrew.

Andrew's eyes squint as Eira turns, looking over her shoulder at the boy.

The boy starts laughing. "What a show!" he howls, slapping his leg for emphasis.

Eira stiffens as a grounding thought sparks in her mind, is Finn and this boy the same age?

Her breathing hitches. Eira drops her head so that it rests on her shoulder as she breathes deeply.

"I've told you what that is, son." She rushes to her son, dragging him by his collar to Eira. "Not everyone's healing looks the same, remember that!"

"Damage is done, just leave," Andrew barks. Shooing his hand, he tries to swat them away.

"Give me your drink." The woman snaps her fingers at her son. "Take the lid off," she rushes.

The woman grabs one of Andrew's socks, wads it into a loose ball, and dunks it into her son's drink. She hands it back to her son.

He raises his eyebrows and dumps the liquid out onto the grass. He's shaking his head while he mutters, "Nope. Nope. Nope," he sighs, "just hell no." He tilts his head towards his mother and smiles artfully.

"This will shock her system." She fists the sock above the grass, releasing as much liquid as possible. "You keep this on the back of her neck. Believe me, it'll help." She situates Andrew's wet sock on the back of Eira's neck.

Squeezing Eira's shoulder, she asks, "At any time, did you see dots?"

"No, ma'am," Eira states.

"Good. That's great to hear. No trip to the ER for you," the woman replies. Absentmindedly flicking her fingers, slinging water on her son. "Are you good?" she asks.

Both Eira and Andrew nod.

She turns towards her son. "Let's go, we need to get you fed." She ruffles her son's hair. "Thanks for helping me back there. Proud of you." She smiles.

"Hey, Mom, you look thirsty? Want a drink?" He's smiling as he lifts his drink, offering it to his mom.

She barks a laugh, just a single one. "Nice try. Let's save it for your dad," she says, shaking her shoulders.

Eira faces Andrew, both laughing as Andrew watches the retreating pair shrink into the horizon.

Eira touches his sock on her neck. "I have a spare pair of socks in my backpack you can wear home. I don't think you want a wet sock in your boot." She rubs her shoulder.

She brings her hand to her lips, kissing her three middle fingers, then lightly touching those fingers to Andrew's chin.

"Eira, did I do something today to make that attack worse?"

Eira slowly shakes her head. "You didn't mean to. It's not like I ever told you. It was just an overload of a bunch of stuff."

"Dammit, I need to know these things," he says.

Closing her eyes, she tells Andrew, "You should know, my arms have to move freely, or it sets me off." Eira opens her eyes, lifting her head towards the sky. "Logan used to sit on me. He would straddle my chest, sometimes crushing my breasts, pinning my arms to my sides so I couldn't move." Eira whispers, "Then he'd cover my mouth with his hands. He told me I talked too much."

Eira watches Andrew's chest as she hooks her index fingers onto the front of his shirt, resting her hands on his chest. "I've learned how to work through the trauma and anxiety from him, and normally I keep myself from getting overwhelmed; this one just hit all at once. I'm not normally like this. Sorry." Eira smiles while she meets Andrew's gaze. "But hey, we learned something today," she jokes, "A wet sock wards off a panic attack." Eira traces the outside of Andrew's ear before crushing him in a hug.

"You're something else." Andrew draws a haggard breath. "I want to watch the life drain from his fucking eyes." He closes his eyes. "Don't ever be afraid to talk to me; if it rolls through your mind, I want to hear it." He lightly taps his thumbs against her leg.

Eira gets more uncomfortable as she takes in her surroundings. "Can we go back to your place? I'm all 'peopled' out."

Scooping up their things, she stumbles. Struggling with the arm strap of her backpack, she huffs loudly. He spins her to face him as they stop by his motorcycle. Smirking as he stares deep into her eyes, he situates her backpack. He slides his hands under her knees and lifts her effortlessly onto the bike.

Eira welcomes the level of peace only a motorcycle ride can deliver as they secure their helmets before he takes to the highway. As it is for most, riding a motorcycle is a form of therapy. Even more so since Andrew insists she rides with him on the back of his motorcycle. Riding back to Andrew's place, Eira settles herself into deep thought. She knows ignoring that stunt from Logan will keep her healing stagnant. She craves calm, so her mind begins the familiar steps in the panic attack recovery process. Aligning her thoughts, she begins the questions involving her senses. From experience, she knows it'll bring her comfort and keep her fully in the present so she can process her emotions.

Eira thinks to herself, first is sight. *What do I see? Andrew's black hoodie with his social media square QR code.*

Satisfied, she proceeds to the sound. *What do I hear? The low, rhythmic hum of Andrew's motorcycle vibrating, the crosswalk signal's mechanical voice alternating between commands of walk and don't walk, and the sharp squeals of tires.*

Eira wonders about the next one, being behind Andrew, with a helmet on. The word 'taste' flits through her mind. Turning her head away from the traffic, she parts her lips. *What do I taste? The salty tang of the sea.* Eira closes her mouth. *Interesting.*

Licking her lips, she closes her eyes to block everything out. She focuses on the next sense: smell. *What do I smell?* Eira takes a deep breath. *Hmm, Andrew's signature clove cologne. Gasoline and exhaust.* Eira smiles. She leans closer to Andrew. *He smells like home.*

She can feel herself becoming fully present, leaving behind everything Logan. With each breath, she knows her grace for Logan had ended. The line has been drawn. One more interaction and she'll file her case. She believes everyone can change for the better, Logan included. He just needs the right incentive; Eira is not, and never was, the right incentive for Logan.

Part of her healing has taught her it's not up to her to fix everyone. She's accountable for only herself. The past Eira would take on everyone's failure as her own. That's what allowed her to lose herself as she magnified her people-pleasing nature. Healing has taught her she can have empathy for them, just not take on their plight.

Feeling light as air, and her calm is firmly in place, she processes her last step.

Touch. *What do I feel?* Wrapping her arms under Andrew's, she rubs his chest, rubbing lower, she centers herself on the hardness of his stomach muscles and the heat radiating from him.

She feels him vibrate as he releases a chuckle.

Chaos erupts as a pink sedan cuts them off mid-merge.

Andrew's shouts ring through their helmet comms, but she can't make it out. He brakes abruptly, causing Eira to shift forward. Her breasts smash against Andrew's back, her thighs clutch tight around him, as the heels of her hands slam against the gas tank. Andrew quickly cycles through the clutch, brake, and gears, each causing their bodies to shift on the bike. Wrenching the throttle, he accelerates as he swerves into a different lane. Eira's right hand slides off the gas tank. It splays out, covering Andrew's groin. In mid-motion, she continues to pull him to her, with her hand over his crotch.

Seconds later, Andrew pulls over to the side of the road. His feet straddle his bike. He twists slightly, asking over his shoulder, "Are you okay?"

"Yes," she responds through their joined helmet comms.

Eira feels her face flush; she knows she's blushing. Her hand is pressed over Andrew's penis. She awkwardly begins to retract her hand. She scrunches her eyebrows in question, placing her hand over his groin. With her fingers pressed firmly against Andrew's pelvis, she runs her fingers along his dick, feeling bumps.

Andrew's chest vibrates with his moan.

Eira slides her fingers side to side, counting. "One... two... three—oh. Oh?" she exclaims in disbelief. Starting the count over, she presses slightly harder as the shaft below her fingers begins to harden.

He drops his chin to his chest, shakes it, then lifts it. He places his hand over Eira's, halting her fingers.

He tells her with need laced in his words, "Woman, we're two minutes from my house. Think you can behave yourself until then?"

Eira innocently scoffs, "Please." Her fingertips tap Andrew's dick. "I can't guarantee anything."

Andrew's hand clasps over Eira's, holding it onto his thigh as she snickers.

Andrew merges into traffic, her right hand rubbing his thigh while her left hand caresses his stomach.

Staring at Andrew's back, a thought runs on loop in her nurse's mind. *He has a five-rung Jacob's Ladder piercing.* As a nurse, she knows body modifications have standards. Three rungs are the standard, pierced along the underside shaft of the penis; a longer shaft allows for more rungs. She bows her head forward, resting it against Andrew's back.

As they pull into Andrew's garage, she lets out a groan. She remembers it takes four to six months to heal from this type of piercing. Eira wonders if this is the reason he's been so erratic; his emotions towards her have been on a full pendulum swing. Hot, then cold.

When did he get it?

Andrew drops the kickstand, killing his bike's engine. Whipping his helmet off, he hangs it from his handlebars. He's off his bike in a flash. Reaching for Eira, he carries her into his house.

Eira has her helmet removed just as Andrew's foot slams the door closed.

Lowering her feet to the floor, he helps her stand.

Andrew grabs Eira's waist. With a low and dangerous voice, he tells her. "Slow it down."

Chapter Eighteen

Andrew

Standing in his kitchen, Eira pushes the palms of her hands against Andrew's chest, breaking free from his embrace.

"Slow it down! You're kidding me, right? You're pulling back!" Eira exclaims, dropping her hands against her thighs.

"No," Andrew holds up both hands in front of him as if he's surrendering. "I just think we need to slow down."

Walking into his living room, he drapes his hoodie over the back of his recliner. "We need to talk." He glances at Eira, his eyes wordlessly pleading for her to understand.

Eira, following Andrew, rests her gear on his kitchen table.

She spins to face him. "Let me guess." She puts her hands on her hips while widening her stance. "I've been hurt before; I can't do it again. I'm available for friendship, but that's where it stops?" Keeping a wide berth from Andrew as she sits down, the leather couch cushion hisses softly under her weighted plop.

Toeing off her shoes, she pushes them under the coffee table. "Unfuckingbelievable," she mumbles.

Sighing, Andrew sits in the middle of his couch, not crowding, but not allowing her space either. He rests his arm on the back of the couch, shifting towards her, making sure his knee is touching her thigh.

"Yes, but no. I've only spoken to one other person about this." Andrew rests his head on the back of his couch. "Actually, I didn't speak to him about it. He barged in here," he finishes in a whisper, "then I had to put ice on it." Andrew clears his throat, lifting his head, he locks his gaze with hers. "Otherwise, he wouldn't know either."

Confusion knits her brow. "Icing? Since when do you bake?"

"Icing. Bake. What?" Stifling his laugh while he shakes his head, Andrew states, "No. Ice. Like frozen cubes of water." He rests his palm on Eira's shoulder, rubbing his thumb across her collarbone. "I had a frozen bag of corn on my junk and Jonah wouldn't stop with the questions."

Eira sarcastically taunts, "Jeez, Andrew, doesn't Jonah know that's where everyone stores their frozen corn?"

"Are you doing okay over there?" Andrew arches one eyebrow. "This can wait."

"Andrew, don't treat me with kid gloves." Eira nervously picks at the skin around her nails. "You can't act differently now that you know I have panic attacks. Saying your name doesn't mean I'm just going to blast off into an attack; it means I'm centering myself to stop it. Now out with it!"

"I have a Jacob's Ladder piercing." Andrew's fingers cuff her chin, forcing her to meet his gaze.

"No?" She gasps while swatting Andrew's hand away. "But. You're terrified of needles!" She brings her palms to her cheeks, feigning astonishment. "I thought that was just your zipper I felt earlier!" Eira exclaims, drenched in sarcasm.

"Don't be an ass. I'm not terrified; I just don't like them."

She slightly wrinkles her brow. "But why such a secret?" she asks in a hushed tone.

Andrew drops his hands to his lap, losing himself in his thoughts. He has told no one how damaged he feels. He doesn't want to give a voice to all those thoughts. To tell Eira means he brings all his past shit into the present. Eira needs to know what's formed him into the man he is, but he still wants to be cautious in what he reveals to her. Knowing he can't have it both ways, he must decide.

Will his explanation simply give her ammunition?

He keeps telling himself his feelings for Eira are different from the feeling for the previous women, but isn't that just repeating his past again? He thought each of them was different, but their blades hit the mark and drew his blood.

This will be the first time he will voice how deep his past has cut him.

Will Eira see him as weak? Is his past slated to play on repeat?

It can't; he's out of room; he holds the physical reminder daily. Slightly shaking his head, he jolts himself into the present.

Deciding his future will not resemble his past.

He exhales with a huff. He cannot bring himself to look into her eyes.

Taking a deep breath, he releases it slowly as he explains to Eira, "I didn't wake up one morning and randomly think 'My dick needs jewelry.'" Andrew rests his hand on top of Eira's leg, fixated on her fidgeting fingers. "Five rungs for the five women. Each one blamed me. Said I wasn't worth the hassle. They tore me apart with their criticism and selfishness. They made me feel invisible, incompetent, and defective." Andrew laces his fingers through her hair that's resting on her shoulder. "You get told you're a worthless piece of shit by five people and about the third time, you start believing it. The fourth time, you think it to be true. By the fifth time..." Andrew shrugs. "...I said, 'Fuck it, ima start living for myself' and that's what I did."

Andrew gently fiddles with Eira's jade-studded earring. "Their manipulation, lies, deceit, and rejection has made me cautious. These..." Andrew points his fingers at his groin. "...barbells are not for my failed relationships. But for my limits. I'm out of room. In my head. On my dick. In my heart."

Andrew shakes his head. "I got no more room for mistakes. I'm not settling, and no one will treat me like that ever again."

Andrew tucks his fingers under her bra strap, resting his knuckles and palm on her shoulder. "I thought the tattoos would be a good enough reminder," Andrew says and smiles. "Turns out getting holes in your junk keeps you more aware of your actions than ink."

Finally looking up, Andrew meets Eira's watery gaze.

He wipes her cheek. "Hey, don't waste your tears on me."

"You're comparing me to them!" she exclaims. "You think I'll treat you like they did?" Eira pushes Andrew's knee, trying to, but unsuccessful, in moving him away. "What have I done that makes you think so little of me?" Tears steadily drip off her chin, circles swelling on her shirt to the size of quarters.

"It isn't you." Andrew points his thumb towards his chest. "It's me I don't trust. I'm the one who went after those five women and look where that got me."

Andrew drops both feet to the floor as he grabs Eira's waist, pulling her to straddle his lap. "I'm the one who wants you. But can I trust myself not to hurt you and turn you into them?"

Eira leans back at her waist. Creating space between them, she pushes her outstretched arm to Andrew's chest.

Andrew gently pops the side of his hand against the bend of her arm, forcing her arm to buckle as he effortlessly pulls her close. He rests his hands on her hips. "Stop pushing me away."

"Oh, that's rich coming from you!" Eira exclaims as she turns her head away from Andrew. "You've been pushing me away for months."

Andrew firmly holds onto Eira, gently rocking her heated seam across his dick. "I want you so badly it hurts," he says as he presses his hardness into Eira's warm, damp center, "but I won't watch your heart get hardened because of me."

Eira wraps her arms around Andrew's neck. She whispers into his ear, "Then stop pushing me away." She aggressively grinds against Andrew's erection.

He groans. "This has to be the last time," he stresses.

"Stop choosing your past over me!" Eira kisses his neck. She whispers to him, "This is what your rejection says to me: Every time you don't choose me, you're choosing them." Eira sits on Andrew's lap. "Look at me. Andrew…"

He lifts his gaze, staring deep into her eyes. The chemistry between them is evident in his longing. "Even after all these years, you're still giving them power over you," she says. "They're still manipulating you, still preying on you because you won't move past their grasp on you. Each time you don't choose your future, you're choosing to strengthen the tether binding you to them."

Eira leans back, and she lays her palm over his beating heart. "We're not all the same, you know."

Running her hands through his hair. She gets his attention by tugging on the bottom of his hair, lifting his head. "Andrew, please see me for me. Will you trust me?"

He tightens his hold on her hips. "I'm gonna fuck up. You're gonna get pissed at me. Sometimes I'm a fucking ass because I just wanna be left alone."

"Let's worry about that when it happens." Eira smiles. "Can I ask you something?"

"Anything," Andrew says, tapping his thumbs on the insides of her knees.

"Can I see your piercings?" She blushes, heat wicking from her neck to her cheeks. Showing her vulnerability by asking that question embarrassed her.

Bracing for an explosion, she realizes her past muscle memory will need to be reconditioned, as Andrew is not, and never will be, Logan. She darts her eyes to look at his thumbs.

Andrew hooks both index fingers into the collar of her shirt, pulling her to his chest. "Don't ever be afraid to ask me anything," he whispers into her ear.

Scooting off his lap, Eira stands. Holding her hand out to Andrew. "Choose us?" she questions.

"Always," he replies.

Standing, he reaches for her palm, nipping his teeth across the heel of her hand, then caresses the pulse on her wrist with his tongue.

Spinning around Andrew, Eira sits on the edge of his couch. Watching Andrew, she pulls him between her legs. As she reaches for his belt buckle, Andrew stills her fingers, "When you see my boxers, just know I didn't plan this."

Eira feels Andrew's excited length as her knuckles glide across his dick, slowly lowering his zipper.

Pulling the opening of his jeans apart, she chuckles. "Rockets, huh? Think they predicted your future?"

Eira slowly pushes his jeans over his hips, shimmying them down his legs.

Andrew clasps his hands on her shoulders as he hangs his head to watch. He snorts when he hears her laughter deepen, acknowledging the source of her humor.

Her eyes are in line with his boxers, which have a large blue rocket going up the center over his dick. The tip of the rocket is a red, triangular cone. His boxers are quite patriotic: an array of rockets scattered with white stars decorating the blue boxers.

"I think your rocket is fueled for launch." Eira coyly smiles as she traces her fingers over the length of the rocket with a slow, zig-zagging caress.

Andrew watches Eira closely. "Sprite, you better be laughing at my boxers and not my rocket."

Eira cocks her head. "Sprite, huh? Are you comparing me to the wet, tingly feeling you get in your mouth when you drink the soda?"

Andrew tracing the underside of her chin. "No," he says and grins, "there's a spark in you. Mischievous. It pulls me in. Teasing me, demanding I come back for more."

Eira tilts her head sideways, placing her lips over Andrew's hardness that so visibly begs to be released from its cloth prison. His dick jumps with excitement as his boxers wick the wetness from her mouth.

She exhales through her mouth slowly, blowing heat over his penis. He feels the warmth of her breath heating his dick and tickling his surrounding skin. Leaning back, Eira tugs the legs of his boxers down. The weight of his titanium rungs pulls gently on the underside of his cock, making it bob slightly as it rests erect before her mouth.

Sighing deeply, Eira inhales the subtle yet distinctive scent of Andrew, clove and musk, laced with desire. His spice floats to her nose, making her breath hitch with excitement.

Eira gently fondles Andrew's velvety smooth dick. Her fingers glide over the balls of his rungs from his piercings. She rubs her thumb over the mushroom tip, feeling the heat radiating from his dick.

His excitement rushes to his crown, swelling it further.

As she clenches her hand around his cock, she feels his veins. Watching them form deep purple ridges. The coolness of his piercings mix with the heat of his desire in her hand.

His size is overwhelming for sucking, yet substantial enough to guarantee her nether satisfaction.

Eira wraps around Andrew, resting her splayed hands on his ass cheeks. She pulls him into her waiting mouth.

Andrew hisses. "Oh fuck!" The unexpected intensity from her wet, warm mouth has his hips bucking, slamming his cock deep into Eira's throat.

Eira quickly pulls off. She shakes her head. "No jamming." Her eyes trace down his dick.

Taking him in her hand, she guides it to her waiting lips. Hovering over his tip, she tenderly nips it. She slips her tongue into his slit, then slides her mouth down his cock, sucking hard.

Cradling her head, Andrew rests his hands in Eira's hair.

Feeling slight jolts from Andrew's hips, she knows he's fighting the urge to rock into her mouth. He releases a sigh while he massages his fingertips into her scalp.

A feeling of empowerment spreads across Eira, igniting her soul. She is making this man, who's always in control, lose it.

The coolness from his piercings, the heat from his dick, the clicking of his barbells dragging against her teeth, the feeling of his crown tapping on the back of her throat, the tickling of his hair presses into her chin, mixing with his animalistic growls makes her pussy weep as she feels his balls tighten.

Swaying her hips on the couch, she seeks relief while continuing to suck him, sliding her tongue across his rungs, sending jolts of electricity to Andrew's aching balls.

Her mouth waters, making her lips a soppy mess.

Never before has she experienced this kind of rush. Power, as she is the one giving him this pleasure. Power, as she is the one getting pleasure from giving him this pleasure.

Andrew's slight jolts are turning into harrowed thrusts as he rocks into her mouth.

His breathing is choppy and hitches; he hisses as her teeth tug on his barbells.

Eira rests one hand on his ass cheek, pushing him towards her, and the other hand is cradling his shaft and most sensitive parts. She swivels her thumb to rest behind his balls, her fingers spread across his pelvis, pushing him back. Creating a push-pull motion that she is in control of.

Seeking more reactions from Andrew, Eira pulls off.

Andrew begs, "Why?" Pushing himself back to her lips, he pleads, "Wrap your lips around me."

Eira blows across the shaft of his dick, making it jump as Andrew adds pressure to his fingertips massaging her head.

Eira sucks Andrew's dick back into her hot mouth, groaning against the base of his hard cock. She rakes her teeth up his shaft and across the top of his head, creating gentle friction. She notices a soft, barely audible hum coming from Andrew as he glides himself over her tongue, pressing against the roof of her mouth.

Teasing him, she gently squeezes her teeth around his penis.

Andrew gasps, tapping his fingertips on her ear. "No biting, Sprite."

Eira smiles before giving way with a deep suck. She hollows her cheeks, creating a gentle, rhythmic squelching noise as her wet lips bob on Andrew's fattening cock. As she sucks his dick, he becomes slick with her spit, allowing him to glide effortlessly over her tongue.

Andrew laces his fingers together, as if he's praying, then wraps them around the back of his neck. Losing the fight for composure, he shouts as he loses his resolve.

Not having had a release in months, he showers Eira's mouth with cum. With each thrust, he gives her his iridescent pearl elixir.

Eira slows her bobbing, allowing his cum to run out of her mouth and splatter on his floor. His taste is unique: a rich sweetness balanced with a subtle hint of bitterness. He's decadent with a hard edge.

Andrew tugs his shirt off. Cupping it in his hand, he wipes her mouth. "Spit out the rest."

"Now I know what drinking from a firehose is like."

Andrew kisses her forehead. "Let me get you something to drink," he says as he's righting his jeans and walking towards the kitchen.

"I'm going to the bathroom, okay?" Eira walks into Andrew's bathroom as a shrill sound spreads through the air.

"Shit, Andrew. What's that for?" she yells, letting him know she heard her phone's alarm.

He grabs her phone, wincing from the pitch. "It says you're gonna be late to Aunt Zia's party!" Andrew yells back.

"Damn, I have to get going. I can't miss that, or Uncle Zio will have my head!" Eira rushes towards her gear. "Can I show you something tomorrow?" Eira asks Andrew as she is dressing in her motorcycle gear to leave. "Nothing big, just my favorite spot on the beach!" Eira rushes to grab her shoes stowed under the living room table. "Before you go all Neanderthal on me. No, no one has ever gone there with me."

Andrew stares at Eira's hair, hiding her face. Even as she ties her shoes, she seeks to comfort his apprehension. His hesitation displays his vulnerability yet again. Without skipping a heartbeat, Eira is reassuring him.

He hears the faint whisper of Sage, *"Shoog, The One, will put your heart together while ignoring her own broken heart..."*

Despite Andrew's initial resolve to stay single and focus on himself, he finds himself drawn to Eira. Her crafted playfulness as well as her moments of vulnerability have only deepened his feelings for her. She's challenging his notions that love doesn't exist, at least not for him. Her intense passion has stirred a sense of security deep within him.

Acknowledging his excitement and anticipation for what their future holds, he nods his head. "When and where?"

Eira slows her frenzy. She wraps her arms around Andrew's neck, hugging him tightly. She whispers, "I had an explosive time, did you?"

Andrew lets out a boisterous laugh. He spins her around and gently nudges her towards the door. "Get going, so Uncle Zio will leave your beautiful head where it belongs. Text me when you get there. I need to know you're safe."

CHAPTER NINETEEN

Eira

A distraught Eira hastily taps out a text to Andrew while the tears swelling in her eyes distort her phone's keyboard.

Eira: Just lost a patient.

Andrew: Did you do everything you could?

Eira: Yeah, just wasn't enough.

Eira: It hurts.

Eira: I need a distraction.

Andrew: I can just surprise you…Or you wanna throw axes?

Eira: IDK. Got anything to make me forget.

As she rereads Andrew's question, the three dots pulse on her screen, only to disappear, then reappear, then his next message fills the screen.

> **Andrew:** Maybe. What am I walking into tonite?

Holding this in hurts, like she's a pressure cooker, ready to blow. Her fingers fly across her phone's screen, message after message spilling out, jagged and messy. She hates how exposed this makes her feel, but she also knows Andrew is the only place she can safely fall apart without fear.

> **Eira:** Raincheck on the beach, k.

> **Eira:** I just can't

> **Andrew:** Slow down!!!!

> **Andrew:** You're getting me tonite either way, I'm not leaving you alone with this.

> **Eira:** I'm a disaster, like full on raging dumpster fire!

Why doesn't he understand?

> **Eira:** I don't think our relationship is ready for that yet.

> **Eira:** I'll see you next week.

> **Andrew:** I can't Netflix and chill alone

She's spiraling; I don't like this.

> **Andrew:** Either you come here or I'm coming to get you.

She's lost a couple of patients over the years; each one leaves its mark. *Hopefully, he knows what he's getting into with this.*

> **Andrew:** You don't have a choice, got it.

> **Eira:** See you at 6.

The alarm she set on her phone screams at six o'clock. Silencing it, she stuffs it back into her scrubs pocket. Still reeling from earlier, she pushes a little too hard, slamming her car door in Andrew's driveway. It rocks back and forth from the force.

She's eager to escape May's heatwave, hell-bent on scorching the Sunshine State, she jogs inside his garage. She clicks the close button on the garage door remote with her thumb. In an effort to control herself, she waits until the door meets the concrete floor, taking a few extra moments to right her thoughts, then she steps into Andrew's kitchen.

Steam rises from the stovetop, accompanied by a hiss, like a pissed-off kitten spitting its warning to pass with caution. The deep tapping sound of a wooden utensil striking against a metal pan has Eira arching her eyebrows in a scowl.

The feelings of anger and sorrow are still climbing that mountain, trying to reach its peak from her emotional hospital shift. She inhales a couple of times to ground herself.

The bottom of a pan scraping against the gas burner grate has her cocking her head to the side. Knowing her mood is difficult after losing a patient, she's concerned Andrew may have underestimated his ability to understand what this does to her. *Can he give me what I need?* Closing her eyes, she forces her thoughts away from the hospital and into the present with Andrew. The aroma of freshly baked bread tickles her nose, as does the fragrant smell of green peppers cooking in butter and onions with a hint of garlic.

Her stomach growls loudly.

Andrew chuckles. "You hiding a beast in there?"

He kisses her forehead as he pulls two plates from his cabinet. "Philly cheesesteak. You good with that?" he asks while tucking the plates into his arm like a football. As he passes Eira, his fingers cradle her chin. Holding it with his thumb and fingers, he tilts her face left, then right. "Humph," he says, sweeping her hair off her shoulder. Making his way back to the stove, he stirs what she now knows is shredded beef in the pan.

She places her hands on her hips. "What does 'humph' mean?"

Andrew pulls the bread out of the oven. "Still warm," he winks at Eira. With a serrated bread knife, he carefully cuts the buns in half lengthwise.

He uses his fingers to gently stretch apart the bun. "You didn't take care of yourself today. You need to put yourself first, and when you don't, it pisses me off."

He spoons peppers and onions on the bun, adds a slice of provolone cheese, lightly dusting it with black pepper and grated

Parmesan cheese. He spoons the meat next, covering it with melted white queso cheese dip. Andrew grabs the other bun, continuing his process.

"I couldn't think about food after telling his family he's not coming home," Eira's voice wobbles. "I can still hear his wife's screams. Begging him to come back!" Grabbing the hand towel dangling from his back pocket, she wipes her eyes. Tossing the towel across his shoulder, she peers around his side. She glances at the stovetop. "Did you remember the gravy?" she whispers. Her fists tightly clench the fabric of his shirt on his sides, holding her steady.

"Right here." Andrew leans to the side as he opens the microwave. He pulls out a saucepan of sausage gravy. "I know you can't eat this sandwich without gravy. But you're spooning it," Andrew pretends to gag, "it's disgusting how you drench your sandwich in that shit!"

Walking towards the table, Eira asks, "Why's there a bottle of tequila, apple juice, water, and a lavender-green tea at my spot?" She points to the beverages.

"Pick your poison. I wasn't sure what your go-to is for these types of bad days. So..." Andrew shrugs while walking their plates to the table. "...thought I'd cover all bases."

Smiling so he knows she's not ungrateful. "Alcohol is out. I'm still vibrating deep inside. I can't shake this feeling and adding tequila to this..." Eira waves her hand in front of her. "...shit-show will not end well. Are you still on board for catching the brunt of this?"

Andrew sits in his chair. "Take the good with the bad, isn't that part of this relationship thing we agreed to?" He drops the hand towel on the table between them.

"Yes, but—"

"Eira, enough. Sit. Take care of yourself." Andrew points to her plate. "I'm not listening to another word coming out of your mouth unless you've eaten your food. Got me?"

Scraping her chair on the floor, she plops down. "Sheesh, you're right. You can be a *fucking ass*," Eira huffs, pushing all her sass into that statement.

The smell of the meat sizzled to perfection, and the char marks marring the edges, has her mouth watering. Outside of her mom or aunt, no one has ever made her anything to eat before, let alone cared enough to demand that she finish her food. Realization hits like a bolt of lightning; it's only been her taking care of herself for years. The thought of allowing Andrew to care for her is a hard notion, but one she wants to welcome. That feeling of comfort reminds her of a cold winter's night snuggled up to a roaring fire. He somehow makes everything else disappear.

She feels safe. She sees only him and herself.

And food!

The fork carries a not so dainty bite to her mouth; she closes her eyes, moaning, as she gently sways her hips side to side in her chair. "Mmm, dee-lish," she says, opening her eyes. Cutting another bite off her sandwich, she hears Andrew's ragged inhale.

"I know you're hungry, but you moan like that again and we're done." Andrew takes a long pull of his beer. His hand moves swiftly beneath the table, adjusting himself. His eyes never leaving Eira's, he takes another pull of his beer.

Mischief lights up her smile. "I thought you weren't talking to me until my plate was clean?"

"Sprite, I need you to eat. Don't fight me on this, no more noises." Pointing at her plate, he adds, "Now finish your supper." Andrew takes another bite of his sandwich, watching Eira the way a predator watches its prey.

Three more bites and her stomach spasms. Maybe the cheese and gravy are too rich for her palate today? Maybe it's the seasoning on the meat? Or the vegetables?

Not sure what's causing it, she breathes slowly in through her nose and out her mouth. Eira coughs, trying to clear her throat. She reaches for her lavender-green tea, sipping as she forces herself to perform grounding techniques. She focuses on the lavender smell and the bite of the green tea. The wet, cooling sensation spreads across her tongue. Stretching forward, she places her glass precisely over the previous water ring.

Taking another cleansing breath, she can feel it ebbing in. With as much as her therapist has taught her, the hardest fact is that sometimes, *you just have to feel it so you can process it*. Sitting back in her chair, she feels tears forming. Her spine breaks out in tiny beads of sweat while her chest flushes red; she feels like she's standing on the sun. Her fingertips tingle, as if tiny needles are piercing them. Knowing her range of emotions is on the surge, she doesn't want him to witness their peak. Not out of embarrassment, but out of reverence. She feels she's lost today; she'd let a family down, as well as herself, and she has to process how that feels to her. Most people don't understand. *Compartmentalize*, they say. Which she will, but only after she processes this loss in her own way. Placing her hands down on either side of her plate, she clears her throat. "Andrew, I can't. I need to go home."

She begins to stand, but Andrew pulls her into his lap, her back against his chest.

Andrew nestles his mouth against her ear. "It's okay, just let it go. Experience the emotions. Let me be here for you, with you. Please." He kisses her neck. "It doesn't mean you're weak, just means you're still alive," he says, cradling her. He gently rocks with her. "You can't do this to yourself. You can't fix, save, and heal everyone. Beating yourself up is only hurting you," Andrew hugs her tighter, "and it pisses me off to see you hurting."

"You don't understand," she hisses. "My fingers felt his life leave. I heard those monitors screech when his heart stopped, and you want me to what...." She raises her voice. "...think about myself?"

"Yes! I need you to care for yourself the way you care for others. I need you to choose *YOU!*"

Eira jumps out of Andrew's arms, peering down at him. "It doesn't work that way. I'm..." Eira slams her fist into her chest. "...not wired that way." She squats, resting her chin on her knees. "I held his hand so he wouldn't die alone," Eira whispers, "only to find out the woman who hit him said, *my bad* to the paramedics on scene. She fucking took a life, Andrew, and all she said was *my bad!*" Eira hiccups. "She was texting a picture of her toenails and didn't see him brake."

Andrew settles behind Eira, pulling her fully onto the floor. He kisses her neck. "I'm so damn sorry," Andrew whispers to her. "You have to know if I could take this pain from you, I would."

"How is any of this fair?" Eira stretches her legs, resting them on top of Andrew's. "She actually asked Olive to call security because some woman was screaming, making her uncomfortable."

Andrew sweeps Eira's hair to her other shoulder.

"That woman screaming was the wife of the man she had just killed. Oh, God, I'm gonna be sick."

Andrew nibbles his teeth along the length of her neck. "Stay with me, Sprite." He stands, bringing Eira with him. Her breathing is dancing towards hyperventilation. He grabs the lavender-green tea and dumps it onto the hand towel, wrings out the excess over her plate, then wraps the wet, cold towel around the back of her neck.

Eira gasps and shivers as the cold tea on the towel shocks her.

"Andrew," she whispers, "I'm so sorry." Wiping the tears, she softly laughs. "At least it isn't your sock this time."

She takes a deep breath, eyeing the countertop. "Popcorn and sour patch kids for the movie, huh? Are the bags already opened?" she asks.

"Oh. Shit. Okay. We're switching up the crazy. I gotcha." Andrew bounces his head. "Are we just done with that now?" pointing to the wet towel around her neck. "Cause I feel like I'm gonna need a minute to catch up, but you're just skipping to the chill part of the night."

"This is why I told you I'd just go home. I warned you I was a disaster." Eira heatedly throws the wet towel at the table. With a soggy splat, it lands next to Andrew's plate.

"I wish you had used something else; that tea was good." She smiles nervously and looks at Andrew.

"So, we're just going to pretend the last twenty minutes didn't happen? Like, what's next so I can be prepared?"

Eira replies, "Sorry to burden you. This is a mistake. See you around," she tries to walk past Andrew.

"No." Andrew tucks her so that her back is against his chest. "I know you're processing right now, and I'm trying to be understanding. We've been over this before. We're. Not. A. Mistake."

He releases Eira, spinning her around to face him. "Have you worked through losing your patient today?"

"Sort of, until I lose another one. Then the," Eira lifts her index fingers and hooks making air quotes, "crazy starts all over again."

"Watch your sass, Sprite."

"For fuck's sake, Andrew. I just need you to make me forget." She twitches her nose. "Or feel something else?" Eira closes the gap between them, wrapping her arms around his neck. "Please, make me feel something else."

His hands land on her waist. Twirling her around, he plants his hands on her hips, tugging her closer to his chest. He runs his teeth along the outside of her earlobe. "You sure?" Andrew questions.

Eira nods as she presses herself back against him, gliding the cheeks of her ass over his hardening dick. He feels her body jolt as she's pressed against his thick cock.

Eira walks to the bag of microwave popcorn sitting on the counter, ripping it free from the plastic wrapper. She knows she's being a brat. "You invite me over, but I told you I'd be all over the place." Tossing the bag into the microwave, she presses the timer. "I've lost patients before, and I'm sure I'll lose more." Leaning against the edge of the counter, she adds, "I know how I get myself through it, but I'm probably just gonna piss you off again."

Andrew narrows his eyes. "Get yourself in check."

Eira smacks her hand against the countertop. "See!" she exclaims, throwing her hands in the air. "You know what," she spins on her heel, taking a step in the direction of the front door when two hands wrap around her biceps, stopping her.

"You know what?" Andrew mimics Eira's voice. "I've had enough of your sassy attitude. You wanna feel something? Then clothes off," he quickly demands. Giving Eira space, Andrew steps back, crossing his arms, waiting.

"What did you just tell me?" Eira heatedly replies.

Andrew leans against the countertop. "You or me. Choose."

"What does that even mean, you or me?" Eira settles her hands over her hips. "I'm not so keen on *Andrew the Pitbull*." Eira winks at him. "Now, *Andrew the Golden Retriever*, he can play any day." Rearing back, Eira starts, "Don't—"

Andrew interrupts her, "Oh, you're getting eager to please tonight. Just not like you think. You take your clothes off, or I'm ripping them off. That's what that means." Andrew steps in front of Eira.

With a fluid motion, Andrew reaches his hand to his back, his palm grabbing a handful of his shirt. Swiftly, he pulls the shirt over his head and tosses it to his side. Nodding towards Eira, Andrew demands, "Shirt."

Eira grabs the hem of her shirt, removing it. "Urgh, I'm only doing this because I don't want you to rip it. Not because you asked me to."

"Make no mistake, Sprite. I did not ask. I'm telling you." Andrew reaches one arm around her back, releasing her bra's clasp.

He drags his nose across her neck, licking her jawbone as he steps back, snapping his fingers, then holds his hand out.

Eira raises her eyebrow, laying her hand in his.

Dropping her hand, Andrew growls, "Don't be a brat, give me your fucking bra," he says, his eyes filled with lust.

Eira's wavy chestnut hair cascades over her shoulders, caressing her creamy skin.

He stares at her still-covered breasts; her blue brassiere no longer trusses them. He stops her attempt to hide them, taking her hands in his. He outstretches their arms, shaking his head slowly.

Andrew's hands cradle her breast. "They fit perfectly." He runs his thumbs over her cloth-covered nipples, watching them pebble with each stroke. "Fuck." Andrew inches closer, placing his middle finger in her cleavage and pulls her bra away from her chest, dropping it on the floor. "Don't keep these from me again."

Andrew taps his finger on her jean-covered waist. "You or me?" he questions, unbuckling his belt. Removing his jeans, he kicks them to the side.

Eira erupts into laughter, pointing at his pelvis. "Your boxers never disappoint." Stooping to get a closer look. "That's a half-peeled banana across your penis," she says, standing up. "Ahh, I love it." She continues to laugh.

Not being deterred, Andrew points to her jeans. "Last time." He bends forward, tapping the leg he needs her to lift so he can remove her socks.

"Andrew, I think your banana's growing," she says, smirking.

"It's waiting for you to peel it," Andrew jokes.

Eira hooks her thumbs into the waist of her jeans, sliding them and her panties off. Standing naked in front of Andrew, she kicks her clothes across the floor.

Andrew's dick jumps with interest. He tosses her over his shoulder in a fireman's carry, walking with her to his living room.

Wiggling in an attempt to free herself, she realizes it's useless.

Eira knows Andrew remembers her ass is an anxiety trigger; more to the point, getting it spanked is.

He gently rubs his fingers along the meaty part of her ass. "Get still," he growls, then rubs his palm down her seam. Stopping, he slowly slides her down his body. She glides over his hardness, soaking in the warmth from his skin.

Eira speaks softly, "Thank you for remembering."

Andrew cradles her head in his hands. Tilting it to his chest, he kisses her forehead. "Sprite, I'll always remember."

Eira cocks her head; she notices a dining room chair that wasn't here last week is now placed in front of his TV.

Andrew sits in the dining room chair, gently pulling her to him. She attempts to straddle him, chest to chest, but he twirls her around. Facing away from him, she can see his reflection on his TV.

"Are you wet?" Andrew asks.

Still standing, Eira shrugs. Bending forward slightly, she extends her fingertips to the floor, burying her cold fingers into the nap of the soft rug that wasn't here last time either. She murmurs, "Looks like you've been redecorating."

Andrew uses a featherlight touch to draw an X on her ass, kissing it, he makes her giggle. He digs his fingers into her waist, pulling her down to his thighs, her legs dangling over his. Resting his chin

on her shoulder, he adds, "I didn't want your feet to get cold."
Slowly dragging his hand to her sacred core, Andrew rubs his
fingers across her silky garden. "Fuck me, you're drenched."

As he parts his legs, Eira has no choice but to open hers with
him. Andrew watches her response from over her shoulder as he
traces her soaking lips with his finger.

Eira gasps, tilting her head back.

Andrew asks, "You okay, Sprite?"

"Yes."

"Do you trust me?" he questions.

"Yes."

"Close your eyes for me."

Andrew gently tips both of them to the left, his fingers dragging
against cardboard as he guides their bodies to the center of the
chair. She jumps as a coolness settles over her clit, and again when
she hears a click, then a low hum.

The hum dredges up painful memories tied to Logan, though
she reminds herself that Andrew is nothing like Logan. Calmly,
she reassures herself Andrew wouldn't try to shave her pubic hair
with an unguarded beard trimmer. Shivering, she remembers the
pain from when Logan seemed to enjoy drawing her blood as he
bounced the trimmer off her vagina lips.

Firmly staking her claim in the present, she quietly asks, "Andrew, what are you doing?"

Andrew kisses the spot behind her ear that he knows drives her
crazy with need. "Are you okay? It's just me, no one else belongs
here. You know what it is, right?"

She opens her eyes, peering into the TV's reflection of them.
"Andrew, a vibrator."

Eira's been cautious of overusing his birth name since the skate park incident. They both know it's her signal. She comforts herself in an attempt to soothe the anxiety. He'll question her if she's not careful. But she knows it's out of concern, not out of belittlement.

As if right on cue, he asks, "Eira, I need you to tell me, right now, stop or continue?"

"Andrew, continue," Eira says with a slight shake in her voice.

"Eira, what state? Close, middle, or distant?" Andrew hugs her middle, squeezing slightly. "Tell me where you're at."

"Andrew, middle, but I don't want you to stop. Please tell me you won't give up. Please, I trust you. Andrew, please keep going."

"Fuck, I love hearing you beg. But not like this. I can't push you. I won't." He turns the vibrator off.

"No, no, no, no!" Eira cries, wrapping Andrew's arms around herself. She stares at his reflection inside the black TV.

"We have to trust each other, Andrew. I'll tell you when to stop. And I'll do it before I can't recover. But you have to listen to me. Trust me in my decision. Trust me to say *Friction Zone* and we stop. Everything stops. I know this; you know this. But let me get close to where I think I need to say it. You don't get to keep me from that. Andrew, you promised me we'd both heal, but how can I if you always stop me before I'm ever close to saying the words? That's not healing." Eira runs her hand through his hair, pulling gently to get his attention. She returns her arm to cover Andrew's.

Andrew sighs. "I will die if anything happens to you. Because of me, or while I'm supposed to protect you. Can't you see what this does to me? It fucking guts me, Eira. Mentally fucks with me." Shaking his head, he adds, "I'm sorry, I can't. Knowing I'm the one who's causing it."

Eira points her finger at his reflection in the TV. "Andrew, you will do to me every last fucking thing you planned and more. My cusp is so far away now, it's disappeared. Gone! Turn the vibrator on and let's continue. Now!"

Andrew rocks his chin on her shoulder, asking her, "What do you say to get me to stop?"

"Apparently, I say your name more than twice!" Eira growls.

Andrew sucks on her earlobe. "Stop sassing; I'm trying to protect you."

"Turn it on. I'm sitting here with my legs sprawled over yours and my coochie is air drying while you're counting how many times I say your damn name. Did you count when I came on your tongue? Because I know I screamed, 'Andrew. Andrew. Annddrreeww' until I was hoarse, and you never stopped tasting me so I'm calling bullshit."

"If you're not wet, we're stopping," Andrew threatens.

"No, we're not! You scared the hell out of me a minute ago, and you've got it as cold as Antarctica in here, so of course I'm dry. I'm also naked, turning blue, and my nipples are hard enough to cut you, which I will, if you don't start that damn vibrator. Don't make me—Ahhhh!"

Eira's ranting session is cut short as sensations assault her at once: the cold silicone vibrating over her clit, hearing the hum of the vibrator as he increases the speed, and her chest flushing as desire wicks to every cell in her body.

"Damn. The power of a vibrator," Andrew chuckles. He moves it over her clit, eliciting a pleasure-filled gasp from her. He teases her with it, causing her to twitch in his lap. He glides it across her clit. "Tell me you're good?"

Resting her head on his shoulder, she closes her eyes and murmurs, "So good." She continues to slowly rock her hips. Leaning forward adds more pressure from the vibrator, backwards elicits groans from Andrew.

Her breath hitches as he traces the outside of her hood. "You want me to stop?" asks Andrew. He tucks the head of the vibrator under her hood, tapping his finger against it.

"I will squash you," she softly purrs as her first climax drips onto the chair. Pooling between their legs, it drenches his balls, wicking up his boxers.

Andrew brushes his hands down her thighs. "Sprite, can you stand up? I need to take my boxers off."

Both rising, Andrew quickly drops his boxers, sitting back down. Wrapping his hands around her hips, he guides Eira.

She slowly sinks onto Andrew, hissing as his dick stretches her pussy. Closing her eyes, she focuses on the pleasure from the bars on his dick as each one disappears inside her.

"Not drilling into you right now is so fucking hard," Andrew rumbles.

Rolling her head back to rest it on his chest, she savors the sting from the stretch. She adds, "I feel everything. You feel amazing." Eira turns her head, encouraging Andrew to shower her neck with kisses. Eira grinds her hips, her breath becoming labored. "Oh, I can feel all of them, your piercings, oh hell!"

"Stop!" he bellows. "You're just supposed to sit on my cock right now, not fuck me yet. Damn, I can't think straight when I'm in you." Andrew taps her clit with the vibrator. "We'll get you off with this again."

"Yes, please."

Andrew rubs her clit with the vibrator. She moans as her pussy clutches around his cock. She rocks forward slightly, whimpering. Fondling Andrew's balls, she feels them tighten as she gently tugs.

"Fuck. Slow it down, I don't want to cum yet," Andrew confesses.

Her fingers touch where they're joined, feeling him gasp as she tightens around him like a vice. He's slick with her arousal, knowing he will be getting wetter, she brings her fingers to his mouth. He sucks her sweet nectar from her fingers.

"Touch your tits," he pleads.

Her hands glide up her stomach to her breasts, teasing them. As she massages her breasts, she rolls her hips over Andrew's throbbing dick nestled deep inside her wet channel. Eira grunts as she pulses around him.

Andrew rests his chin on her shoulder, grunting as his hips jut into her. "Ahh fuck," he groans.

Squeezing tighter, she keens as her cum drips onto the leather chair. Eira sighs, head falling forward, pulling Andrew's hand with the vibrator off her clit.

"That feels like a lot?" she asks.

"Yes." Resting his forehead against her back. She moves to get up. He grabs her hips. "Stay."

She wiggles a little. "I'd rather look at you handsome, than at the television. Can I turn around?" Eira teases him by grinding her tight cunt on his cock. She feels his dick jolt as he thrusts his pelvis.

"I can feel you growing beneath me." She continues with her hips, smearing them onto his lap.

He kisses her spine. "Yes." His hands are on her hips as he lifts her up his cock and glides her down, gently easing his hips to meet hers just as his dick fully seats inside her.

Eira moans, "Andrew," as she tightens around his thick cock.

"Fuck, Sprite, I need you to loosen up some."

With a wicked smile, she pulses her channel around him. "Rock into me, please, Andrew."

He stands up, bringing her with him as his dick is still buried inside her. Scooting the chair back across the floor with his foot, he gently pushes between her shoulder blades. He walks his fingers down her spine until her fingertips rest inside the rug's nap. With his foot, he taps at her ankle, silently asking her to widen her stance, making Eira stand on her tiptoes. With his knees bent and fingers digging into her waist, he slowly pulls out just to thrust back in.

"Yes. Don't stop," Eira begs. A couple more thrusts have her whimpering. "Andrew, you're too tall. I can't," she gasps.

Andrew pulls her back against his chest. Nibbling at her shoulder, hard enough for her to feel it but not hard enough to break her skin, he sucks at the base of her neck. Wrapping his arm around the underside of her breast, he lifts her. Eira moans and Andrew grunts while he drills into her as they both cum together.

Andrew's fingers trace the line on her inner left forearm. "Is that implant still bothering you?"

"Not anymore, but my legs are. They're like Jell-O." She playfully swings her legs. "I need to clean up. You're running out of me." Setting her feet on the floor, she turns towards the window, noticing the darkness outside. A small laugh escapes her. "We've been tangled up since before sunset."

Andrew cups his hand as far down her legs as he can. He scoops their come back into her deliciously satisfied pussy.

Eira asks Andrew as he swirls his thumb on her sensitive clit, adding pressure. "Mmm, what are you doing to me?"

"Making up for all the orgasms I missed giving you while I was stuck in my head."

"Oh." She leans her head against his shoulders. "Okay, but can we go a little slower?"

"You're in charge, Sprite. Always." He winks. "With you, I could go all night." Andrew smiles while carrying her to his bedroom. Gently laying her down, her legs dangle over the bed. Bending forward, he takes Eira's nipple into his mouth. Worshipping it with his tongue, he finishes with a gentle tug from his teeth.

"Is this, ok?"

"Oh fuck, yes Andrew."

He teases her on his way down her body. Nipping at the underside of her breasts, kissing, and licking his way to the center of her stomach. He flattens his tongue, circling her navel.

Eira tangles her fingers in Andrew's hair, massaging his scalp while he trails kisses down her body, stopping at her clit. She pulls his hair. "What are you doing?" she asks.

He smirks as he inserts his middle finger into her slick cunt. Never breaking eye contact, Andrew moves his finger inside her and curls his finger with a come-hither motion.

Eira whimpers. "Oh God, yes!"

Andrew sucks on her inner thigh until he's sure she's marked. He releases with a pop when she bucks her hips like a wild mustang.

"That's it, ride my hand. Take what you need."

Andrew drags his cum-coated finger across Eira's bottom lip. He quietly asks, "Lick?"

She relaxes her body as she shakes her head.

He wraps her legs around his waist, locking them behind his back. Andrew runs his finger across her slit, then traces his soaked finger along her top lip. Growling at her. "Sprite, lick."

"No," Eira states.

Andrew growls. "Lick. Your. Fucking. Lips."

Smiling, she shakes her head, taunting him. "You first."

Andrew dips two fingers inside her, scissoring his fingers to completely coat them.

He traces her lips with their mixed cum, then he sucks his fingers clean, watching her, watching him. Bending forward, he lets his thick cock rest against her weeping cunt. He braces his forearms on both sides of her head on the bed, making sure his weight isn't hurting Eira.

Andrew glides his tongue across her bottom lip, sweeping over her top, then both lips. When he lifts his head, his gaze locks with hers.

Eira quietly scolds, "I respect your condition of no kissing on the lips, but you can't tease me like this."

"What if I want your lips?"

"Don't tease me."

Andrew sucks her bottom lip between his teeth, tugging and gently sucking, hard enough to get her attention.

He stares deep into Eira's eyes. "I want all of your lips, forever."

He brings his head towards Eira's nose, giving her Eskimo kisses.

"Andrew," she moans.

He closes his eyes and sighs.

Concern knocks at her heart. "Now is not the time for you to pull away from me," she admonishes, "from us."

Staring into her eyes, he says, "Can't you see what I feel for you, how deep it runs?"

"Show me?" Eira whispers.

Andrew's breath warms the small space between them as his gaze pins hers. His lips gently peck the seam of her lips.

"More," she begs.

With exact knowing, he covers her lips, letting his tongue reveal what his words could not.

Andrew

Andrew moans as he deepens the kiss, his lips molding against hers with a slow, deliberate pressure. The faintest hint of honey lingers on her breath from her tea. The steady thrum of their joined heartbeats fills the silence, his world narrowing to just her.

Eira's hands find their way to the back of his neck, her fingers tangling in his hair, drawing him closer as their tongues dance to the same lustful beat.

This kiss, it's everything. Months of restraint, pain, and longing melting into something entirely new. He pours all the emotion he feels for her into this kiss. Adoration, respect, and protection. Need, desire, and hunger. Devotion, fascination, and obsession.

Kissing is something he hasn't brought himself to do since Claire.

But this. Her. He knows Eira feels right.

This is so much more than either of them expected. This is what happiness feels like. This is love.

Smiling out of the kiss, he slips his throbbing dick inside Eira, and she shrieks.

"Ahhh, a little warning next time, before you just jump right in." Shifting her hips, she asks, "How are you even ready again?" Eira pants while Andrew's hips start their slow dance into her silken heat.

"It's all you, Sprite." He silences her by running his tongue across her lips. With a wink, he straightens. Andrew drapes the back of her legs up his chest so that her feet are up by his head. He wraps his hands around her thighs. "I love watching your tits bounce," he says while continuing to pump his pierced hardness into her.

Leaning onto her side, she tries to get her hand behind her back. "Andrew, I can't grab it. Can you move this pillow?"

Andrew twists at his hips a little but keeps pumping into her. She moans. "Fuck, Andrew, there!" she exclaims.

"I can't quite grab it!" Andrew shouts, not understanding why she just yelled.

"Oh, God, leave it. Leave it there. Don't stop. Keep fucking me, don't slow down!"

Andrew glances down and notices the pillow slightly pushing Eira onto her side. It's making his cock hit Eira differently. He slows his thrusts.

"Nooo, don't stop!" Eira yells, slamming her fists on the mattress in frustration.

Andrew pulls out, lifting Eira by the hips. He repositions the pillow under Eira's ass, then places a kiss on her nose. "Are you ready?" he asks.

Eira whispers, "Oh, God, please!"

Andrew slowly enters her pussy. Her wet lips jostle each rung, causing electrical pulses to shoot to his engorged dick.

Eira moves her hips, forcing him to hurry while also pushing him deeper.

He thrusts in exaggerated strides, going deep as he pushes his hips to his right with a slight jolt.

Eira moans, "Do that again!"

Andrew gets into a push at his hip jerk rhythm when Eira whines, "Oh, shit. Andrew stop. Something doesn't feel right."

Andrew stops but doesn't pull out. "Did I hurt you?"

"No, it doesn't hurt. It feels weird. Like a pressure down there."

Andrew withdraws to his crown, then slowly slides in deep. Her breathing has turned into slow, shallow gasps. Slowly withdrawing only to slide his cock inside her channel. Her pussy is clutching around him, pulsing, tightening its hold as if she's spasming around him.

"Andrew, I feel it again," she blurts. "Shit, stop." She arches up on her forearms and tries to pull away from him.

"I. Have. To. Pee! I can't on you!"

"Oh, you're not," he says, understanding what she's getting ready to do. He grabs her hips. "You're going to soak us both. Let it go. Relax, Sprite, give it to me."

Eira trusts Andrew. She calms her concerns as Andrew continues fucking her. The bed groans under the relentless thrust of his hips.

Andrew tells Eira, "Eyes on me when you cum, you hear me?"

One last push-hip-jerk-jolt causes Eira to topple over the edge. Looking deep into Andrew's eyes, she screams her release, "Yes. Yes. There, yes, fuc—what is that wetness?" She shrieks in alarm. "Oh my God, Andrew, I just peed on you?" Eira erupts into tears, closing her eyes. Bringing her hands to cover her face, still crying.

Andrew commands, "Eyes on me."

Gently pulling her hands away from her face, he leans over her and stops a breath away from her lips. "You squirted. You did nothing wrong; you gave me a gift," he says with a smile. "Fuck, I can't hold it back!" he moans.

Resting his forehead on hers, he slams his release deeper inside her heated core.

Completely spent, he reassures her, "You just squirted. You didn't pee."

"Well, I've never done that before. So, now I need a shower!" she grumbles.

Pulling out, he stands and kisses her shoulder, her collarbone, her neck, and lastly, her lips.

Usually, he's a one and done kind of guy, but the undying need for Eira proves otherwise. His dick is famished for her; she's a balm to his insatiable appetite. Months of healing from his piercing and desiring what he thought could never be for him has him greedy for her taste. Her squirting for him has brought an all-new high to him.

Grinding his half-hard cock against Eira's stomach, she pulls away. "How? No! Shower!"

Andrew smiles, pulling her into the bathroom. He guides her to the toilet. Lifting the lid, he nudges her to sit. Smirking, confident, standing naked in front of Eira, he says, "Let gravity do its job."

Eira giggles while shaking her head. "Your shameless attempt at humor."

He twists the knobs, sending a rush of water roaring to life. When the temperature warms, he lifts her into his arms and carries her to the shower, setting her feet gently on the tiled floor. Andrew grabs the shampoo to wash her hair. She moans as his fingertips massage her scalp. He lathers the loofah with his body wash, gently guiding it over her body.

Eira runs her hands across her body, rinsing the suds off when she feels Andrew's tongue graze her nipples. She sighs.

"Can I wash you?" she asks Andrew.

"Nope, you said you needed a break." Andrew stands under the stream of water. "One touch from you and we're at it again. Go on, get out and dry off."

Leaning his head back into the spray of water, he hears Eira whisper, "I want to trace the veins of your dick with my tongue."

Andrew groans, "Yes." He steps out of the water, but Eira rests her palms on his chest.

"Nuh-uh, you get back to washing your hair."

Andrew raises his eyebrow, stepping back under the stream of water as instructed. She nods towards the shampoo. Andrew drops a dollop in his hands, then scrubs his hair.

Eira fists his cock, tugging up and down. Andrew hisses as water and shampoo are viciously flung around the shower. She jiggles each metal bar, eliciting a grunt from Andrew; his hips jab forward.

After the water running off Andrew's body is free from suds, Eira rests her hand on his thighs, sucking him down to the root and up to the tip. She traces his cock's veins as she gently tugs on his sack. With her other hand, she grabs his ass, holding him still as she sucks him deep into her throat. Opening her mouth, her tongue slips out to lick his balls.

"Fuck, I can't!" Andrew gruffly replies as he pulls Eira's mouth off his dick.

"Hey, I wasn't—" Her words are cut off as Andrew's lips slam into hers, feasting on her like a starving animal. He picks her up, and she wraps her legs around his waist. Andrew holds her just above the head of his cock. As he walks, his crown rubs against her pussy, making her moan.

Still damp from their shower, Andrew carries her to the dry side of the bed, crawling between her thighs.

"You're so fucking beautiful!" Andrew says, lowering himself over Eira. He lets his balls tap against her wet folds, teasing her. Andrew wiggles his hips side to side, making his soaking balls rub against her pussy lips while the bulge at the base of his shaft drives friction over Eira's clit. Andrew kisses deeply, making love to her tongue. Eira reaches for his ass, but she's too short; she can't grab it. She drags her toes up the back of Andrew's legs, opening her legs wider. He nibbles on her shoulder, then starts to suck. Pulling on her skin as he tortures her with his hip movements.

Breaking the kiss, Eira begs, "Andrew, please? I need you."

He leans his weight on his left forearm, taking his cock in his right hand, stroking his crown through her slit, and taps her clit a couple of times. He drags down her core again, but just as his dick gets to her entrance; she thrusts her hips forward, causing him to impale her.

"Ahhh. Yes. Deeper. Move," she growls.

Andrew slowly dips further into heaven, sliding inside until the tip of his cock kisses her womb, then painstakingly slow, pulls out.

"Who owns this pussy?" Andrew's deep voice vibrates in her ear as she clenches around him, tightening like she's holding back the world's largest dam.

Eira grabs Andrew's neck, bringing him closer. "You," she says before kissing him.

With a hitch in her breath, she breaks the kiss. Andrew notices tears rolling out of her beautiful chocolate eyes and stops mid-thrust. "Fuck, Sprite. What'd I do?" Eira hiccups, shaking her head.

"Come on, baby, you've gotta tell me," Andrew replies in anguish. "Eira, I'd rip out my own heart before I ever let my bullshit hurt you. You know your tears gut me. What's going on?"

"They're pleasure tears," Eira says with a sniffle. "I feel you, Andrew. Not just your cock..." Eira squeezes her pussy around Andrew's dick.

Andrew growls, "Stop smashing my dick and talk to me!"

"...but all of you," she continues. "Everywhere. I feel your heart racing; I feel your breath on my skin; I feel the heat from your body. I'm connected to you; I feel your vulnerability, your fear, your desires as if they're my own. I feel you so deep within my soul, I'm buzzing inside." Clearing her throat, as it fills with emotion. "I can't explain it, really, but what I feel is so deep, it's like you're just mine, you know. Do you feel it?"

"Yeah, I feel it," Andrew answers. "I'm going to cum," he stills, then moves his hips, dragging his bars across her entrance, meeting him thrust for thrust.

"Stop moving but stay deep. Ahh, there it is. I can feel your cock pulsing deep, filling me with your cum."

Andrew centers Eira's clit between his two fingers, gently squeezing and tugging. He slides his thumb sideways along his fingers, flicking her clit.

"Oh, yes," she yells.

She squeezes Andrew's cock. He finishes, sending ropes of warmth deep inside the only person that truly matters to him.

Draped across Andrew's chest, her eyes droop closed, and her breathing slows. She curls into him, her heart still humming from the last time.

He's never felt this way about anyone. Smiling as he thinks back on their night, trying to count. But it's early morning, and he's already lost track. He smiles as he remembers her snarky-ass comment about *quality, not quantity*, runs through his mind.

Andrew knows this moment is more than just sex; it's about their commitment to each other.

With the heat of their bodies still lingering in the air, he whispers three simple words that hold the power to change their lives forever: "I love you."

CHAPTER TWENTY

Andrew

Each year Andrew organizes a charity motorcycle ride in May, called Ride for Their Heartbeat. It supports the local children's hospital, known for exceptional pediatric cardiac care. The ride brings together hundreds of supporters for the children who are battling cardiovascular disease.

Donors are welcome to gather at Nymera's Bluff, an expansive outdoor venue, where administrators and mascots of children's foundations unite for this cause.

"Chill out, fuck stick, she'll be here," chuckles Law, using humor as his shield from his emotions.

Andrew unlocks his phone, his fingers urgently tapping out his text.

Andrew: You're cutting it close.

Eira: I can't get out of here!!!

Andrew: Simply walk out the doors you walked into this morning!

Eira: Can't. Incoming.

Andrew: Shit don't rush it then.

Eira: I don't want to miss the ride!!!

Andrew: It's fine, I need you safe.

Eira: They need me here. I'll text before I leave.

Andrew: Forget the ride. Remember my badge and I'll meet you at Nymera's Bluff.

"She just got an emergency; she won't make the ride," Andrew states, clearing his throat.

Bending so his head shields his phone from the sun's rays, Andrew pauses before responding. *I know she loves her work, but every damn time...* he shakes his head while reading her next text.

Eira: It's a Code 30. Gotta go.

Andrew: Text me when you leave the hospital. I need to know you're safe.

> **Andrew:** Meet me by the prop bike at Nymera's.

> **Andrew:** And don't forget my badge.

Experience has taught him that Code 30 means the victim has suffered severe physical injury and will need assistance from both medical and law enforcement. He knows Eira can handle herself, but he's not there to protect her. He's agitated by the silent phone, but the lack of a reply from Eira confirms that she's already prepping for the accident. Tension rides up his spine as he's forced to pocket his phone. "Law, are you still good with taking the lead?"

As the organizer, Andrew's motorcycle is one of the first to lead the charity ride, followed by anyone who has lost someone to this disease. Wanting to ride beside Eira this year, Andrew asked Law to take his place in the lead. Andrew knows Law has firsthand knowledge of the impact of this disease, how it mentally and physically affects the baby's parents. Law suffers in silence, but he's always supported Andrew in his desire for this cause.

"Yeah," he clears his throat, swallowing the erratic emotion of having made it through yet another year without his son.

"Man, you don't have to be here. You don't have to torture yourself," Andrew tells Law.

"Nah, it's fine. I mean, it still hurts like a motherfucker. I feel their pain," Law coughs, "and-da. I struggle. To not go back there," he taps his temple, "ya know. But that won't... won't ever go away. Being here helps." Law nods his head. "If I can help at least one person each year, then Mataeo's death wasn't in vain."

Law pivots on his heel, voice laced with pain, he tells Andrew, "I'm going to make my way to the front. See ya at Nymera's." Law throws his arm above his head, tossing up a wave as the crowd engulfs him.

Andrew sighs as he glances around the crowd. Finding Jonah, he walks to him. Andrew fist-bumps both Jonah and Riggs. "I'll meet you guys at Nymera's."

Anticipation builds as the minutes are counted down by a timer. Bikers and riders settle into line, getting their safety gear secured as they mount their motorcycles.

An air horn blares, signaling the timer's end.

An announcer yells into the microphone, "Light 'em up!"

Volunteers with megaphones along the starting line shout, "Light 'em up!" as the chorus of engine reverberations bounces off the asphalt.

Andrew shivers as goosebumps pop on his arms. *It says a lot about a person if they don't get chills when hundreds of motorcycle engines start.*

Being front and center, he can feel the cadence of their throttle rap-outs resonating deep in his marrow. He shivers with a sigh, knowing every rider has a different reason for being here, and in the end, it's for the babies.

These supporters are just trying to ease their pain, one mile at a time.

The memories of Law and what this disease took from him threatens to overtake Andrew, but he, like many others, harnesses pain through the power of music.

Andrew and hundreds of riders take to the road for the charity motorcycle ride. The stress of the day dissolves into the miles of ocean views along Florida's sun-kissed beaches. Riders soaking up the state's rich history are welcomed with smiles and thumbs up from members of the communities.

Because this event is meant as a celebration of babies, Andrew and motorcycle riders celebrate May 2nd, National Baby's Day, with a cause. Each mile ridden is a donation received, representing hope for babies' hearts.

Turning into the last curve of the ride, Andrew exhales deeply. He fights with the bittersweet feelings of the ride's success. Again, an impressive turnout, each year gaining more participation than the last, but the emotional turmoil of it is ever present.

Pulling into the parking area reserved for today's event at Nymera's Bluffs, Andrew smiles when he sees Eira leaning against the prop motorcycle. Her chestnut hair pulled into a high ponytail, swaying in the breeze.

Andrew chuckles, shaking his head. He couldn't find this year's hoodie earlier today, and now he knows why. The oversized and plunky Ride for Their Heartbeat hoodie that Eira is wearing is his.

Steadying his helmet on his handlebar, his eyes lower their peruse of her. His palms itch to glide over her curves like her ripped jeans do.

Eira smiles at him as his head ticks up. She waves at him like a contestant in a beauty pageant.

In a rare moment of subdued chaos, Andrew mouths, "You good?" as he tucks his gloves into his back pocket.

Uncrossing her ankles, she walks towards him, nodding.

Andrew snakes his arms around her, both hands rubbing over her ass. Wrapping his arms around her back, he squeezes a little tighter than usual, dragging his tongue along her earlobe, making her gasp.

Draping her arms over his shoulders, she states, "There's a bunch of people here."

Threading their fingers together, they walk towards the entrance. Bringing Andrew's hand to her lips, she kisses his knuckles. "Sorry I didn't make the ride; will you show it to me later?"

Andrew bears a playful smirk. "I already had plans to show you something later."

"I'm going to hold you to that!"

The walkway from the parking lot to the entrance is lined with yellow-painted bricks. The path sparkles like a disco ball as the sun bounces off the glitter scattered across the walkway.

As Andrew and Eira walk into the venue, they stop in front of the two sculptures of the Ride for Their Heartbeat logo. Standing a towering 15 feet high and 10 feet wide on each side of the entrance to the banquet area is a motorcycle with a white heartbeat pulse in the middle of a red heart, symbolizing the delicate balance of life and struggle.

"So much detail. I love you used the motorcycles as another donation drop-off," Eira says.

She runs her fingers along the edge of the gas tank. Its handle is fashioned after the symbol for hope. A rainbow. Lifting it, she points to the inside of the gas tank and squeaks, "It's painted gold in there."

"It's supposed to be a reminder that the contributions will hopefully fuel a cure for the babies," Andrew says softly and smiles at her.

As they move past these powerful statements, her eyes widen when the venue opens, revealing a feast laid out in bistro style. Stepping down the three wide stairs, they find themselves in the grand outdoor dining area. Rich green grass softens their steps as they walk to the shade from the scattered trees.

"Nymera really outdid herself," Andrew comments.

Mahogany tables overflowing with fresh vegetables, succulent meats, seafood pastas, and vibrant fruits arranged in a bullseye design with juices, teas, and fruity drinks nestled in the middle. Every detail of the meal was thoughtfully planned for the riders and their guests as a 'Thank You.'

Looking around, Eira says, "This is amazing. How many donations before you beat last year's?"

Andrew shakes his head. "I can't know numbers; it tarnishes the effort. For me, the focus needs to be about the babies." Pulling Eira into his chest, he kisses the top of her head. "I get what you're asking, though." He rests his chin on the top of her head, and he draws her closer. "It's successful when I see Law chatting with other people affected by the disease."

"Was this always for Law?" she mumbles into his chest, her fingertips rubbing circles on his back.

"He was a big part. But also, I needed something to take my mind off Claire," he says, shrugging his shoulders. "I chose this."

"You're a good person; you know that, right?"

"Pfft, last night you said I was fantastic and now I'm just good, what gives, Sprite?"

Pulling out of his arms, Eira playfully swats Andrew's bicep.

He weaves his fingers through hers, guiding her to the food. "You hungry? You probably didn't eat anything today."

Releasing her hand, he raises his arm, holding his index finger in the air.

"I'll go grab something to eat while you do your..." She uses her fingers to create air quotes. "...organizer stuff."

"Where's my badge?" Andrew raises his chin into the air, nodding and giving a thumbs up towards someone else in the distance.

"I've got it," she says and taps the hoodie pocket. "Go on, they're waiting for you."

"Let me get this over with," he says before kissing her temple.

Walking into the private conference room, Andrew's jaw clenches in distaste. This is the part of being the charity ride organizer he could do without. He has to sign tax documents in the presence of a notary public, ensure addresses and tax identifications are correct, then shake some hands and network with hospital representatives.

He tells the charity administration he wants to use this venue again next year, and they nod in agreement. And so, the preparations begin for next year's event.

Tolerating as much as he can, he holds his hands up in front of his chest, as if he's surrendering. "I'm not here for numbers. I'll see you all later."

There's a chorus of 'Thanks' and 'Chat soon' that bombards his retreating form as he leaves in search of Eira.

He spots Jonah and Riggs arguing about how a high-side is completely preventable. The crowd forming around them has split views; some are extremely vocal about their beliefs. Nodding his head in acknowledgement towards the group, he pats Jonah on the shoulder, continuing his search for Eira.

This place is packed, he thinks, just as his elbow connects with Olive's chest.

Reaching out to steady her, he asks, "Shit, Olive, you okay?"

Balancing what's left of her drink in her hand, she pinches her white shirt between her fingertips, pulling it away from her chest. "Well, I'm walking around a bunch of bikers in a wet t-shirt, you should probably ask them if *they're* okay," she states, nodding to the crowd.

Andrew, holding onto Olive's elbow, continues his search for Eira in the crowd.

"She's about five or six tables down that way," Olive says, pointing into the seating area.

"Thanks," he mumbles while he removes last year's Ride for Their Heartbeat hoodie. He hands it to Olive. "Here. We don't want to traumatize anyone today," he says and chuckles.

"Ass," Olive quips, slipping his hoodie over her head.

"Call me if you need anything. I'm going to find Eira."

Andrew walks in the direction Olive pointed. Seeing Law sitting on a bench, he feels a wave of calm as he notices Eira is with him.

That calm leaves abruptly; in its place is a jealous rage threatening to spin out of control. He growls.

Sitting with Law and Eira is Nymera's son, Tre. Andrew has had limited dealings with him, but what he has, hasn't left a great impression. Tre's an arrogant, bullish, entitled pissant that Nymera should've wiped off in a towel.

Andrew cocks his head to the side, trying to pop his neck while flexing his fists at his sides. Tre smiles flippantly at Andrew.

Tre's palm lies on the back of Eira's hand, resting on the table. Law pulls her with him as he scoots as far as he can on the bench.

Unable to shake the feeling of possessiveness gnawing at him, Andrew grits out her name, "Eira, come here." His feet stop at the beginning of the table.

Startled by the tone of Andrew's voice, she looks over her shoulder at Law, raising her eyebrow questioningly.

"About fucking time," Law mumbles as he stands up. Walking into the crowd, he shouts over his shoulder towards Andrew. "I'm going to get backup."

Eira wrinkles her eyebrows as she looks at Andrew. "What does Law mean?" she asks, still sitting on the bench. The bottom of her shoe rests on the bench between her and Tre.

Fueled by insecurity, Andrew desired to be the only one to experience today with her. But he can't be angry at her, since he left her to fend for herself, not the other way around. He knows he only has himself to blame, but there's a war raging inside him. It's déjà vu, seeing another one of his girlfriends openly flirt with no regard for him. Rationale pummels at his haze; Eira would never do that to him. *She probably doesn't even think Tre's flirting with her.*

Tre bounces his gaze between Andrew and Eira, smirking. He reaches for her knee.

Andrew sees red.

In a flash, Andrew reaches for Eira, picking her off the bench and plopping her to her feet behind him.

Facing Tre, Andrew growls, "Touch her again," his every being vibrating with anger, "and I'll break you."

Andrew's voice seems foreign even to his own ears.

"Andrew," she gasps.

He sees Eira's eyes flicker for a moment, something he recognizes as alarm, but it's gone as fast as it came. Her hand presses softly against his back, rubbing gentle circles in a calming rhythm.

Andrew's hand splays along Eira's lower back, guiding her to the exit. The throng of guests split like the Red Sea. Not getting there fast enough for Andrew's liking, he hisses, "Damn, your little legs." Andrew stoops behind Eira, his forearm pops against the back of her knees, causing her to fall back into his waiting arms. Standing, he is struggling to get his emotions in check. Side-stepping around people or dodging them altogether, he hustles to the exit.

Setting her on the back of his motorcycle, he demands, "Stay."

Eira crosses her arms over her chest. "I'm nothing like them, you know. A simple act of respect instead of this caveman bullshit will work."

Andrew jams his fingers in his pocket, digging out his phone as Law, Riggs, and Jonah stop at Andrew's back tire.

Their heads swivel when they hear Eira say, "Andrew, think about what you're doing." She warns, "My allowance for your crap is running thin."

"Law said you needed backup, what are we doing out here?" Jonah asks.

Andrew spins to glare at Eira. She's perched on the back of his bike, her arms crossed, forehead scowling while she flexes her dangling feet. "Your allowance, huh? Were you fucking enjoying that?" Andrew angrily points to the venue.

In shock, she raises her eyebrows. Turning sharply towards Andrew, she steadies herself on his bike, pointing at him, "Listen here—" She's cut off when Law grabs Andrew's shoulder, pulling him away from Eira and the guys.

"Have you lost your damn mind?" Law yells while corralling Andrew.

"Get outta my fucking face." Andrew shoves at Law.

Law has his hand on Andrew's chest. "Look at her, man," Law says, pointing to Eira. "Does she look like you need to attack her? Bro, she did nothing wrong."

Reaching into his pocket, Law unlocks his phone. "Shit man, Dillion says Tre is heading our way. The way you are right now, we need to leave," Law says as he pockets his phone.

"Who the hell is Dillion?" Andrew questions, looking around in confusion.

Law quickly explains, "He's over the panel of directors at the hospital. Don't start shit here, let's go."

Law jogs to retrieve Eira's helmet and backpack from her motorcycle, then walks them to her, corralling Andrew in front of him.

Handing her helmet to Eira, he asks Andrew, "Are you good to ride?"

Andrew nods; the realization of what just happened, what he just did, hits like an arrow piercing its target.

Law tells his friends, "We need to leave. Meet us at the gas station on the corner of Crossroads and Pine."

Turning his head to check the entrance, he stands before Eira. "A little more allowance, please," Law begs. Holding out Eira's backpack, Law helps her arms through it, cinching the straps securely.

Andrew looks at the entrance, then back to Eira. She's moving her hands in a splayed-out manner, palms up, above his seat like Vanna White asking what tile to flip. Her fingers make the come-hither motion and then point to his seat.

Andrew grabs his helmet, forcefully sliding it onto his head. Anger courses through his veins. Anger over how he treated Eira, and anger at himself for ever thinking she was like them.

She deserves someone better than me.

Straddling his seat, Andrew's bike comes to life with the turn of the key. Riding a motorcycle with a clouded mind is not just stupid; it's dangerous. Going through the motions allows Andrew to quiet his mind and focus.

Popping the kickstand, he speeds up. Running through the gears, he feels Eira's hand rubbing his stomach. He takes comfort in knowing she's trying to soothe him.

With his blinker indicating his direction, he sweeps his gaze to the road ahead before coming back to her reflection in the mirror. The only thing that matters is keeping Eira safe. He pulls out of the parking lot with Law close behind.

Eira presses the comms button on the side of his helmet, allowing it to synchronize with hers.

Andrew sighs, knowing he has messed up. He can feel the sting on his soul like a grasshopper hitting his knee at high speed. He's focused on the road, but knows he needs to apologize to Eira.

Words drip from him. "I messed up," he confesses, his words heavy with regret. "There's so much on the line here." Andrew shakes his head. He shifts gears. "I can't lose you. I'll lose everything."

"I can't be the one who pays for their mistakes," she says and dips her helmet to rest on his spine. "It's not fair to me." Her fists clench the fabric of his hoodie at his sides. "I know those scars run deep, but I'm with YOU, not you and *THEM!*"

Andrew turns the blinker on as he downshifts into the turn to the gas station.

"You need to understand, while I may understand why you did what you did, and I trust you with my life, do not ever disrespect me again. My scars run just as deep, and I will only have so much understanding before I'll choose to protect myself."

Andrew pulls up to the gas pump and turns off the motorcycle. Hanging his head. "I'm so fucking sorry. When I saw you and him talking, I just saw red."

"I was cheated on and humiliated, too. I know what that feels like; I would never do that to you," Eira says as she removes her helmet. "You do realize, I will talk to men, and it doesn't mean I'm flirting. I'm just talking to them. Occasionally, I'll even laugh with them. But they mean nothing to me like you do."

After Andrew removes his helmet, dangling it from the handlebars, he says, "You don't even realize how beautiful you are. The men you're talking to are flirting with you, even though you don't see it."

"So, not only am I paying for the crimes of the women from your past, but also the crimes of every man who talks to me? That's bullshit and you know it. Do I treat you that way?" Eira taps his shoulder. "Are you going to get off?"

Andrew carefully dismounts, cautious of his foot not to hit her.

He steps up to help her off, like he always does. But instead of taking his help, she slides off, handing her helmet to Andrew. "I'll be back."

Andrew watches Eira as she walks into the gas station.

Hearing laughter has him turning his head. He notices Law, Jonah, and Riggs leaning against their bikes under a tree, laughing and throwing cheese puff balls at each other.

"I can't take you kids anywhere." Andrew playfully scolds in their direction.

He's met with two middle fingers, and Jonah blows him a kiss.

Shaking his head, Andrew hangs up the gas nozzle, waiting for a receipt.

"You'll have to go inside for a receipt!" Riggs informs Andrew.

"And stop pissing Mom off, would ya!" Law chimes in, laughing at his own joke.

It's Andrew's turn to throw the middle finger.

As he walks inside the gas station, moving towards the closest cashier, he asks, "Can I get a receipt for pump five? It's out of paper."

Then he hears Eira speak loudly, "I've got it, just please stop."

The cashier farthest away from the door yells, "I've got paying customers here, take your shit outside!"

Andrew's eyes scour the entire store, trying to locate Eira, when the cashier thrusts his receipt towards him, rustling it in front of him. "Here!" Andrew scowls at the cashier and snatches the receipt. He notices Tre through the window in front of the store, and then he sees Eira.

Crumpling the receipt, he hustles to the exit. Aggressively pushing the door open, wider than needed, he sees Tre's hand grab hold of Eira's wrist, spinning her into his chest.

Andrew yells, "I told you not to touch her!"

Jonah, Riggs, and Law rush towards Andrew and Tre.

Andrew's fist wrenches Tre's jacket collar while Tre holds onto Eira. Andrew powers his finger towards Tre's infraorbital nerve, applying pressure while aggressively rubbing the ridge of his hand inward and upward under Tre's nose. Tre releases Eira's wrist with a grimace, dropping to his knees on the ground.

"I told you not to..." Andrew rears his boot back. "...touch her!" he yells.

Jonah shoves Andrew in the shoulder, causing the kick to miss its intent.

Riggs helps Tre off the ground as Andrew yells, "Get the fuck outta here."

Jonah's behind Andrew, hands wrapped around Andrew's biceps while Law is in front of Andrew, pushing his palms into Andrew's chest, smashing him steadily against Jonah.

Tre jerks away from the helpful Riggs, stomping to his motorcycle. As Tre passes Eira, he sneers, "This bitch isn't even worth it."

Eira scoffs as she twists the tip of her shoe, tripping Tre.

Tre lunges at Eira.

In a fluid motion, Riggs's meaty hands latch onto Tre's neck in mid-air, tossing Tre at his bike.

Riggs folds his arms over his chest, growing at least three feet taller. He slowly advances towards Tre. "You gonna make good life choices, number three?" he taunts Tre.

Jonah yells, "Riggs, stop. Tre, shut your mouth and leave!"

Jonah and Law release Andrew once they see Tre's motorcycle vanish onto the highway.

Riggs walks behind Eira. "You should probably stick to people your own size, Pint."

"Come on man, now you're gonna have her brawling with pubescent—"

Eira interrupts, "Don't finish that sentence!" pointing her finger at Law.

Andrew hugs Eira, kissing the crown of her head.

Riggs asks, "You think you can stay outta trouble? We've gotta get on."

"Where are you going?" Jonah asks Andrew.

Just then, Eira's alarm cuts through the air as Andrew groans.

Andrew throws his arms in the air and lets them drop, slapping them down to his sides. "What does that mean?" He cocks his head, staring at Eira.

"I didn't have a chance to tell you. I have a late-night shift at the hospital."

Andrew starts as he shakes his head. "This is too much, Sprite. Why?" he demands.

Eira shuffles to Andrew's bike. "Just until the night nurse can get in." Picking up her helmet, she adds, "She and her husband had a delay on the freeway. So, I'm going to cover until she gets in."

Slipping on her helmet, she lifts her visor, waving to Jonah, Law, and Riggs. "See you all later."

She pats the seat of Andrew's bike.

Andrew lies awake, feet bare crossed at his ankles. He reclines on his bed, knowing Eira's at the hospital, safe. Every day, she erodes even more of his carefully laid protection, the one his heart is encased in. She shows him daily that she's different from the other women in his past.

He didn't set out to fall in love with her. His only intent was to befriend her, show her the riding community, have a couple of laughs, and teach her the safety of numbers.

Andrew reflects on something Jonah said.

Funny how you'll always find what you're not looking for when you give up looking for it.

Scrolling through his gallery, he finds a video of Eira and himself riding their motorcycles around historical Cedar Key last week.

Using the clip of Eira emptying the trash from her backpack in front of a bottlebrush tree, he types the text. '**When you want her not just for sex.... But for the way she calms your mind and quiets your Demons...That is a different type of love!!!**'

Smiling, he clicks submit.

Scrolling through his text messages, he smirks playfully as he types.

> **Andrew:** Eira, keeper of my heart, be safe tonite.

> **Eira:** Lol, why are you acting weird?

> **Andrew:** Ffs, play along!

> **Eira:** So grouchy…FINE!!!

> **Eira:** Andrew, keeper of my soul, sleep well tonite.

Eira: Better grump ass?

Andrew: It'll do Sprite.

Eira: What were you going to show me?

Andrew: Nothing now, you left.

Eira: OMG, U R so dramatic!!!!

Andrew: You facing my mirror, riding me.

Eira: GREAT! I'm totally wet now!!!

Andrew: My bed keeps asking why you're not here…soaking it.

Eira: STOP! I still have to face ppl, you get some sleep, I'll see you later.

Andrew: Text me when you leave the hospital. I need to know you're safe.

Eira: Of course, XOXO

CHAPTER TWENTY-ONE

Eira

F lorida in the middle of June is like being in an oven that's set to sizzle. Thankful for the air conditioner, Andrew lies naked on top of his comforter, his limbs stretched out like a starfish.

Eira shifts onto her side, recovering from a different kind of heat. Her head rests in the crook of Andrew's arm. His thumb brushing swift strokes from her fingertips to her shoulder and back again. Andrew's heavy legs thrown over hers, holding her tight. His breath tickles the back of her neck, causing goosebumps to erupt along her skin.

Andrew squeezes her hip. "You okay?"

"Thank you," she whispers, wiggling her butt, causing it to graze against his still softening cock.

"Not what I meant," he says, and cradles her breast in his hand.

"Mm-hmm," Eira pats Andrew's hand.

"Bullshit, spill it." Andrew holds his head in his hand as he rests on his forearm behind Eira. His other arm drapes over her hip, holding her against him.

Closing her eyes, she softly asks, "Do you ever wonder about sex things?" Eira feels the heat blossom on her neck from her blush.

Andrew scoots back as he urges her to lie on her back. "Like what?"

Tracing his fingers along her jaw, he gently draws her chin to look at him. "I've had my tongue all over you, don't go getting shy now," he says with a chuckle.

"Not helping," she says, staring over his shoulder.

"I'm nothing like him. I want to know what's rolling through your head."

Completely embarrassed, she says the next six words as if they were one, "Howdoyoufeelaboutcockwarming?"

Andrew raises his eyebrows in question. "Soaking?"

"What? No, you heard me," Eira corrects.

"Can't have an opinion on something I haven't had." He runs the pad of his thumb over her nipple, causing her to moan. "That something you want?"

She whispers without confidence, "Please?"

"Sprite, you know better than to talk like that," he scolds her.

Clearing her throat, Eira circles his heart with her fingertips. "Yes," she says, her words spoken with confidence and unbridled lust.

Eira sits up, pushing Andrew onto his back. "Lay down." She hovers above Andrew's now hardening length. "I read it's about the emotional connection, not really about the act of coming."

Andrew folds his arms behind his head. "So I'm not tempted."

Her fingers line Andrew's cock into her waiting warmth. Sinking onto him, she moans. "Oh God. I hope we can do this."

"Tell me what I'm supposed to do again." Andrew's breathing labors. "My thoughts disappear faster than my cock when you sink down on me," he grinds.

"Lay back and be still. No movement." Grinding into him, she groans, "This is harder than I thought."

Andrew raises his eyebrow in question. "I can't move, or neither one of us is supposed to?"

"Neither!" Slowing her rocking hips to a halt, her walls clench tight around him.

"Then stop fucking moving or this is gonna end fast!" Andrew warns.

Eira's eyes are closed, wanting to enhance her ability to feel this. "What do you feel?"

"Wet. Hot. Tight, so fucking tight." Andrew draws a haggard breath. "It's similar to Karezza."

"That's Italian, right?" Eira opens her eyes. Looking at Andrew, she feels a spark of electricity dance across every nerve deep in her soul. Andrew is more than expected; in fact, she only thought he would be a friend to guide her into the community of motorcyclists. In the blink of an eye, he's become so much more to her.

Eira stills, asking Andrew, "Do you hear that?"

Andrew lifts his head, cupping his hand behind his ear. He furrows his eyebrows. "Hear what?"

Eira smirks. "Your dick begging me to move," she teases, clutching tight around his heat.

Andrew's hands encircle her hips, stopping them from swaying. "Have you ever heard of Pompoir or a Singapore Kiss?"

"No," Eira whispers.

"It's where your vagina tilts, grips, sucks, and pulses around my dick."

"So basically, what I'm hearing is, we suck at cockwarming!" Eira laughs.

Andrew nods in agreement. "Tighten up like you're holding your pee," Andrew rasps, "oh, damn, just like that."

Eira tightens. "Have you done this with your piercings because Oh. Fucking. Hell. I don't think this will last long!" she moans and releases the hold her pussy has on his cock.

Andrew rushes, "I've never done it, only read about it. You have to hold, then let go, then hold and let go again for like a count of fifty, but let's start off with...." His hips faintly thrust into her channel. "...ah, five."

Eira concentrates, tightening her vagina and releasing it. Breathing deeply, she fights her building orgasm.

"Stop!" he begs.

"What'd I do?"

Andrew growls. "Nothing." His chest expands as he fills his lungs with air, exhaling like a popped balloon, he quietly instructs. "Tighten and hold for a count of five, then let go, then do it again."

"Gimme your hands." Eira flexes her fingers, waiting for them. Grasping Andrew's hands and sucking in her stomach, she pulls Andrew's dick deep into her cunt.

"Oh, fucking damn, don't do that again," Andrew breathes out, sweat beading on his forehead.

"I didn't even get done with one!"

Closing his eyes, Andrew grates, "Don't move!"

"Andrew, everybody knows, closing your eyes only intensifies the feeling."

"Nope. Not for me. I'm thinking of Jonah's old, sweaty socks."

Eira laughs. "I think I should be offended!"

"Dammit, have you always tightened your pussy when you laugh?"

Tilting her head, she answers, "I don't know." She scrunches her nose. "I've never thought to check."

"Well, you do. When I tell you not to move, Don't. Fucking. Move!"

"Grouchy. Sheesh, can I at least breathe?"

Andrew takes a couple of calming breaths. "This next move is called milking. Do. Not. Move. Listen to me explain it."

Eira challenges him. "You've turned into a grump ass; I'm not liking this international kissing!"

Andrew ignores Eira's sass. "Tighten your pussy, then suck in your stomach, then tighten a little bit more, pulling deeper until you're clutching as tight as you can, hold for five seconds, then slowly release in the same way." Andrew flexes his jaw. "Begin."

Eira, ever eager to impress, barely tightens her vagina. She tightens a little more, drawing in her stomach with each pulse.

Her eyes widen. "What do I do if I want to cum?" she whispers to Andrew, still tightening her pussy and sucking in her stomach.

Eira notices Andrew's body slightly twitching. "Oh, fuck, just cum," he shouts.

Eira releases at once as she's overtaken with her orgasm. She sees her look of pleasure reflected on Andrew's face as he growls her name through his release, "Eira."

Still holding his hands, Eira smiles. "It's nice being a pillow princess, isn't it?"

Andrew rubs his thumbs over the back of her hand. "I've never come so hard in my life. Pretty sure I blacked out. Thank you."

Deciding to practice cockwarming again, Eira sinks deeper onto him. "Can I ask you a question?"

"Anything," he mutters.

"Backpack. It means I can trust you with my life, with my heart, with me, and..." She tightens her fingers around his as mist forms in her eyes. "...you'll protect me." Eira's voice wavers. "We're doing this thing together. With laughter, tears, and my unwavering devotion to you. I want this journey with you. Only you."

Andrew nods his head. "It's more than just a passenger, Sprite. It's trust. It's raw. It's knowing how to beat our vulnerability." He wipes the tears off her cheeks with the back of their joined hands. "I need to know whoever's back there can handle me. All of me. That they'll support me." Andrew smiles as he caresses his fingers lazily along her thighs. "That they'll always have my back."

Eira mutters, "Claire."

"You sure you wanna talk about her right now?"

Eira clips her head.

Andrew closes his eyes, releasing a sharp breath. Realizing he hasn't thought of Claire in a while, he releases a sinister snark. "She was supposed to be the only one." Andrew gazes deep into Eira's eyes.

"Is it still too soon?" Eira questions.

"No, Sprite. What's your question?"

"Will you allow me to be your last?" Eira chews on her lower lip, waiting anxiously.

Andrew's hands cup Eira's cheeks, fingertips sinking into her hair. Lifting his head to meet hers, he pulls her to him. He pecks a kiss on her forehead, on her nose, and on each corner of her mouth.

Smirking, he tells her, "You're done brooding on my dick like a bird." He lifts her off his cock. Lying flat on his back, he draws Eira to him, his tongue making love to her mouth throughout the entire descent.

Eira's need for oxygen forces her to break the kiss. "You've never given me an answer," she quietly states.

"Do you realize how much you mean to me?"

Eira sits up on Andrew's stomach, shaking her head. She chuckles. "No, I don't want to interpret how I think you feel about me. I need words."

Andrew pulls Eira into him, hugging her to his chest. She stretches her legs across the top of his. "I think about you all day long. Overthinking, actually, if I'm being honest. I don't think I'm good enough for you. I sure as fuck know I could be easily replaced."

Eira's body quakes as she shakes her head, but Andrew tightens his hold. "Shhh, I've got you."

Eira lies her head on his chest.

"I know you haven't been loved right. Hell, neither have I. The only thing I can promise you is my unconditional love. I already told you I'd mess up, but the one thing I can promise you is, you're mine. Unequivocally mine. How's those words for you?"

Eira lifts herself, chuckling softly as she feels gravity returning Andrew's gift.

She tries to move so she can sit beside him on the bed. Andrew hugs her deeper into his chest.

"I'm making a mess all over you!" Swaying her pelvis on his stomach, she whispers, "You're dripping out of me."

"Don't care."

Andrew questions, "Why the intense need for the label?"

Eira raises her fingertips, tracing his tattoo. "I've never really felt like I had a place I belonged to, where people wanted me there, like, they chose me. I mean, the closest place to them choosing me was the hospital. But they chose me because of what I could give them, like Logan." Eira clears her throat. "Don't get me wrong, I know my mom loved me and I know my aunt and uncle do too. But each time, I was given to them." She shrugs. "I want a home where people believe in me, where they choose me." Eira's voice cracks. "Because I'm worth it. Me. I'm worthy of their time." Eira's tears form a puddle on his heated skin. She smears the remainder of her tears into Andrew's tattoo, then tries to swipe them off his chest.

Andrew's fingers wrap around her hand. Tucking it into his chest, he says, "I accept you. I'll keep you safe." He tips his chin at her. "I'll even let you warm my cock whenever you want." He winks.

Eira brushes the back of her hand across Andrew's nipple. "It comes back to the worthiness of love and understanding, but why do people always think that's just desperate?"

Andrew scoffs. "We're not desperate, Sprite." Andrew rubs Eira's back. "We're just unfortunate to know how it feels to be ignored by those who told us they loved us. We accepted being taken for granted, as fucked as that sounds."

Andrew draws the comforter up around Eira. Tucking her along his side, he drapes the covers across them both.

Eira settles into all that Andrew freely offers. "We should get cleaned up."

"We'll take a shower together when we wake up." Andrew flops Eira's hair away from her neck.

"Are we having a nap date?" She snuggles deeper into his side.

"Shush so we can." Andrew flattens his tongue, licking from the base of her neck to her earlobe, causing her to shiver.

His breathing evens, and his limbs twitch as Andrew drifts into sleep. Drawing Eira closer, his hand rests between her closed thighs.

In the quiet moments before sleep takes her under, Eira exhales a deep, content breath. Although her vulnerability is laid as bare as her nakedness, she accepts Andrew's promise of her belonging to him.

As the sunshine in Andrew's bedroom disappears, leaving darkness in its path, she whispers to the ears of their destiny, three simple words, "I love you."

CHAPTER TWENTY-TWO

Andrew

Not a day goes by that Andrew and Eira aren't in touch. When her hospital shifts overlap with his work, they text or video call, depending on the time of day and what the other is doing. This past week, their schedules have barely aligned, leaving little time for each other. On Tuesday night, she video-called him, and they laid their phones beside themselves in bed, talking and laughing until sleep claimed them with each other on the screen. Thursday night, their messages stretched late into the night, teasing and playful as always.

Tonight, all the screens, texts, and calls are gone. Andrew finally has her in the same room, just for him.

His nose brushes Eira's neck. He whispers near her ear, "Not sure which lips I want more, just know I need them around my cock."

A blush so deep he can feel the heat radiating from Eira's cheeks. She bows her head, hiding behind the curtain of her hair. Reaching out, she cradles her glass with her wrists, seeking the shock from the coolness of her drink.

"That helping?" Andrew nods towards her glass with a smirk. Knowing the effect his whispering words have on her, he grabs his glass. Using his tongue, he searches for his straw, his attention fixed on Eira. Curling his tongue around his straw, he brings it to his lips. Wrapping his lips around it, he sucks his caramel-colored drink into his mouth, making a loud slurping sound around the ice cubes.

Eira shifts in her seat beside Andrew. Jiggling her leg under the table. She places a hand on Andrew's thigh, squeezing as she murmurs, "You're making things a little sticky." She runs her hands down her legs, trying to release the budding tension from her heated seam. Pressing her back to the booth and the tips of her shoes into the floor, she slightly lifts her ass as her hands tug at her jeans. Adjusting in her seat, she rests her folded arms on the table. Eira lays her thickly wrapped bandaged finger across her bicep.

Jonah taunts as he plops into the seat beside her. "Aw, did you get a wittle paper cut today?"

"Hardly," she says and chuckles. "Dr. Gregory dropped the freaking sterilized scalpel today, and me, like an idiot, tried to catch it." She shrugs. "Better on my finger than stuck in my foot," Eira says, waving her finger at Jonah.

"Sprite, stop belittling yourself," Andrew lectures, shooting daggers towards the filled booth across the room.

Andrew sits back, swinging his arm across the back of the booth, his palm resting on Eira's shoulder. "Do you know any of them?" He tips his head toward the booth.

Eira shakes her head in refusal, her attention never leaving her menu.

"Do you two know them?" Jonah asked Riggs and Law, who were already comfortable. He blatantly points to the booth.

Riggs presses a button on the side of his phone, laying it face down on the table. He leans his forearms on the table and looks over his shoulder at the booth. Meeting Andrew's glare, he informs him, "We saw them in the parking lot, but I don't know them."

Law, ever the comedian, adds, "Yep," he slowly nods. "Tragic, really." He snaps his fingers, pointing at Eira. "Those are the Oompa Loompas Willy Wonka kicked out of his chocolate factory. Said they couldn't find the bean." Law waggles his eyebrows before winking at Eira.

Looking at Andrew, he raises his head in question. "What's your problem?"

Andrew scoffs. "I'm just shocked that I thought you could be serious for once."

Jonah throws his balled-up napkin at Law while Riggs laughs. "Your head is like a Rolodex of fuckery, isn't it?"

"Oh, wait, the one on the left looks like he was recently a patient." Eira rubs her finger above her eyebrow. "HIPAA laws and all that, but I would definitely compliment the person who stitched him. They did a fantastic job." Eira smiles, returning her attention to her menu.

Riggs looks back to the booth again, then asks Andrew, "What are we doing here?"

"Order a steak, medium; asparagus; and a baked potato, without sour cream or butter," says Eira as she folds her hands over the top of her menu. "And if you all don't know what you want when our waitress gets here, I'm ordering that for all of you." She glances at Riggs, Law, Jonah, and then raises her eyebrow to Andrew as if saying, '*Don't push me on this.*' "Got me?"

"You're a sadist!" wails Law. "No one asks for a fucking dry baked potato!"

A ringtone fills the air. Eira does a little dance in the booth. "Yes, it isn't me this time," she says and smiles as she leans into Andrew's arm.

Andrew smiles back, bringing his lips to the crown of her head.

Riggs grabs his phone, standing. "If she comes and I'm not back, order me what I normally get," he says. Offering no other explanation, he hustles out of the restaurant.

"I'm ordering that asshole a wedge salad." Law drops his hand on his menu. "With extra wedge!" Pulling the wrapper off his straw, he jabs it into his tea glass. "Who pays attention to what the hell he orders?" Law sucks his straw until half his drink is gone.

Eira admonishes, "Stop," and points her finger at Law. "I'll order for him."

The server delivers the basket of rolls with tubs of honey butter, then leaves to enter their supper order. The air is heavy with the fragrant smell of freshly baked bread.

Andrew notices Eira looking at the booth of guys who had been staring earlier. Law is playing a game on his phone, winning if the near-constant ringing of bells is any indication, while Jonah stares intently at the perched television. The Jacksonville Armada is handing another winning game over to the New Orleans Jesters.

"Like what you see?" Andrew's elbow nudges Eira.

Eira exhales, perching her chin on top of her steepled fingers. "When I see you, yes." She tilts her head to look at Andrew. "Careful." Her gaze bores into him.

Andrew dismisses her steepled fingers under her chin, bringing her lips in front of him. "You know how possessive I am," he says and pecks her lips. "They need to know who you belong to."

He captures her lips. In acceptance, she tilts her head. Andrew deepens the kiss, effortlessly gliding his lips over hers as if this is the end of time. Eira's lips taste of freshly squeezed apples, sun-ripened to perfection. Nipping at her lower lip, he growls. His hand captures the back of Eira's head, pulling her further into him.

A throat clears. "So that's what two vacuums stuck together looks like." Law's smile emerges as he lifts his head. "Here comes our food."

Breaking the kiss, Eira blushes, suddenly interested in a gash embedded deep within the table.

Andrew tilts her chin upward, forcing her to look at him. "Don't hide." He raises it higher. "We don't hide from each other," he says and kisses the tip of her nose.

Riggs patiently stands behind the server as she hands out the steak orders to Andrew, Eira, Jonah, and Law. Eira points to the place where Riggs was sitting. "That chicken-fried steak goes there, please."

Riggs looks at the door, then at Andrew, his jaw tightening with each word as he slides into the booth. "Skye and Bodhi are in the parking lot, heading this way."

Andrew closes his eyes, taking a deep breath, then opens his eyes as he exhales. "Figured our paths would cross eventually," he says.

Looking at his plate, he cuts a piece of steak, bringing it to his mouth.

Eira gasps as her fork drops onto her plate.

"Oh. Fuck. Hell no!" Jonah exclaims.

"Dude, did you forget *ALL* forms of birth control?" Law heatedly asks Andrew.

Andrew glances around the table, noticing the shocked expressions from his friends, while Riggs refuses to make eye contact with him. Andrew looks at the entrance.

He chokes, reaching for his glass, hoping a drink can be the proverbial F5 key, refreshing the scene in front of his eyes.

"That isn't mine!" he shouts, pointing his fork towards a very pregnant Bodhi being escorted by Skye. She has her hand on the small of Bodhi's back all the while staring at Andrew, the same menacing stare she threw his way months ago when he bolted out of their door.

"How do you even know?" Eira scolds.

Pushing Andrew's shoulder, she whispers, "Let me up."

Formidable anger radiates from Eira, and she pushes Jonah. "Please, I need out."

"Jonah, don't!" Andrew hisses. "Eira, fucking listen to me. We agreed not to talk about past relationships, but Sprite, That. Isn't. Mine!"

"How are you so positive? Accidents happen all the time."

"I promise you! I was wrapped. Every damn time!" Andrew threads his fingers through her hair, palming the back of her neck. "Calm the fuck down!"

Yanking away from Andrew's hold, she seethes, "A condom? That's your defense? Your only defense? You come like a freaking geyser exploding, but I shouldn't worry because you used a condom? How is that comforting to me? And everyone knows you never tell a woman to calm down." She presses her finger into his chest. "It only pisses her off more!" Her jaw tenses in anger.

Pushing her plate in front of Jonah, she taps her finger on the table in front of Riggs. "Please get me out of here," she pleads to Riggs.

Riggs furrows his eyebrows. He shifts his gaze between Andrew and Eira as she drags her feet into her seat, ducking around the light as she steps on the table. Riggs holds his hand up to assist her in jumping off the table.

Pushing Riggs' hand away, Andrew threads his fingers with Eira's.

"One of you pay my bill," Andrew says. Tossing his free hand in the air, "or better yet, give it to that witch over there." He points toward Skye.

As the whole restaurant dining area noise comes to a halt, Skye yells back, "See ya soon, baby daddy."

Andrew sends his middle finger flying as he ushers a fuming Eira outside.

Andrew attempts to pick up Eira, but she pushes his arms away. "I can walk by myself!"

"Dammit, Eira, I know you can," he places her into the passenger seat, buckling her seatbelt. As he withdraws from the truck, he gently tilts her face towards him. "This changes nothing; you're still mine."

Andrew slams the passenger door.

Walking around the front, he takes a couple of deep, cleansing breaths.

Letting his mind wander. *What kind of shit is Skye pulling now?*

Andrew slams the driver's side door. He turns to Eira, noticing her nearly shaking in her seat from shivering. He starts the truck, increases the heat to eighty degrees, and cranks the fan to full blast, pointing the vents at Eira.

"I was not leaving because of you. I needed to leave because of her." Eira continues to look out the window, her chin resting in her hand.

"I didn't do that to her," he says, and turns towards her. "Look at me when I'm talking to you," Andrew growls.

Snapping her head towards him, she seethes, "Do not ever growl at me like that again." Eira visibly vibrates.

Andrew snaps his seatbelt into the buckle, drops the shifter, and drives in the direction of his house.

"You missed my turn!" Eira says.

Andrew holds his hand up. "Just focus on calming down until we get to my place."

"Stop telling me to fucking calm down, I am fucking calm!" Eira yells, stomping her foot. She slams her fist against the top of her thigh.

"You aren't calm, you don't fucking say fuck! You're one step away from going nuclear!"

Eira twists in her seat towards Andrew. "You need to be making sure your kid's okay, not me!"

"That's not my fucking kid; I told you I wore a condom!"

"Andrew, you're ridiculous if you think a condom is going to hold your cum. You probably blew right through it and kept going!" she accuses.

"That's because of you!" Andrew stops at a red light, breathing heavily. "I only do that with you," he grumbles. "I don't normally have that much; that's your fault!"

Driving the next twenty minutes in silence has done nothing for Andrew's agitation.

Turning into his driveway, Andrew lowers his visor, pressing the button to open the garage door. He jams his truck into park and shuts it off. Twisting towards Eira, he demands, "What's the real issue here?"

"You need to be with her through it all. You need to be all in; parenting isn't a part-time job." Eira responds, continuing to look out her window.

Andrew steps out of his truck, rounding the front of it to open Eira's door. "In the less than one percent chance that kid is mine, it's gonna have three moms because you're not going anywhere, got me?"

Andrew releases her seatbelt, turning her so he can step between her legs. "You're mine, Sprite," he says and rubs his hands across her thighs, "and I'm not letting you go."

"Your kid is..." Her voice squeaks. "...worth more than me." She smiles, but not as radiant as she normally does.

"You are so wrong. First off, and particularly important," he says, holding up a finger, "that kid is not mine. Second off," he holds up another finger, "you need to stop doubting your worth. I see more of you than you'll ever let yourself see." He threads her fingers in his, rubbing his thumb across the back of her hand. "I see your cute-as-hell smile and that sparkle in your eyes. I see your determination to help people, and your happiness when you heal your patients, and I've seen you self-destruct when they don't."

Andrew cups her chin. "You're not seeing how strong you are or the battles you've overcome as victories." Andrew kisses her forehead. "You're complex." He kisses the tip of her nose. "You're wonderful." He kisses one cheek. "You're courageous." Then the other cheek. "Please believe me when I say you are worth more than all the stars in the galaxy, but you're the only one I need in mine."

Pulling Eira out of his truck, he wraps his arms around her waist. Over the last few months, Andrew has gotten comfortable with Eira. In his comfort, when tense moments happen, he uses goofiness to make her smile. She's gotten used to this and responds with a smile. He whispers in her ear, "I'm sad. Can I suck on your tits so I can feel better?"

"Pfft," she says and hugs him back, "you're a mess."

Eira walks around Andrew into the house. "And no, you're not sucking on my tits. I've got a long shift tomorrow."

Andrew closes the garage door, walking in behind Eira. "What does your shift tomorrow have to do with your tits now?"

"Have you forgotten already?"

Andrew chuckles. "I told you not to move last night; you thought I was joking, not my fault you couldn't walk afterwards."

Eira pulls off her shirt as she walks towards Andrew's bathroom. "You have no idea how difficult my shift was today because of you!" she teases. "I'm taking a shower."

Making sure the house is locked up and all the lights are turned off, Andrew sheds his clothes. He swooshes them into his clothes hamper like a basketball sinks into a net.

He steps into the shower behind her. "Give me the loofah and I'll get your back."

Hugging his chest to her back, his elbows hold on to her waist while his palms splay against her lower stomach. Resting his chin on her shoulder, he peers over her as she plops soap and lathers the loofah. "You know we'll get through this, right?"

Eira nods, handing him the loofah. "I'm sorry. She gets so much joy out of hurting people; it just makes me blind."

Andrew takes the loofah and starts rubbing it on her stomach, breasts, and brushes light strokes across her pelvis.

"I've already washed that, silly; you said my back." Eira wiggles her ass, trying to get free from his embrace.

"Just making sure, you did say you were blind." Andrew turns her, wrapping her in a hug. Rubbing the loofah over her back and ass, he walks them both under the spray, rinsing the soap from their bodies. Dropping the loofah onto the bench in the shower, he steps them out of the stream. He covers her lips with his. She lifts her head, allowing him deeper access.

Andrew moans as he picks her up, resting her haven above his crown. Eira wraps her legs around Andrew, locking her ankles behind his back.

Turning the water off, he carries her to his bed. "Andrew, we're gonna get the bed wet," she shrieks.

Andrew lays her on top of the fluffy towel. "I already put a towel down, but I'd happily sleep in a puddle of you if it meant waking up with you every morning."

As they cling to each other, Eira makes Andrew glow from the inside out, a quiet warmth spreading through his chest. Every brush of skin, every slow, steady beat of her heart against his, speaks a language no passion alone could ever reach. Their legs curl together, locking them in place, anchoring them in this perfect, still night. Just holding her like this, close and completely seen, makes his chest ache with a contentment he never knew he needed.

Eira's head rests on his chest. The pads of her fingers trace his tattoo. Andrew trails his fingertips along her arm as her breath softens. Lulling her to sleep, Andrew whispers into her hair, "You have to know I love you."

A light flashes in the darkness. His phone vibrates against his nightstand. Andrew turns towards it, wondering if it's a text or a call. In the past, he would answer it. Anytime.

Kissing Eira's hair, he sighs.

He's changed by choice, not because she demanded it or even asked, but because he wants to be a better man. He wants to be the version of himself her magnetism draws out. For the first time, he isn't anxious about seeing that person.

Eira has an early shift tomorrow, and because it isn't urgent, he'll ignore it until tomorrow.

He smiles, realizing his satisfaction now comes from protecting her comfort.

CHAPTER TWENTY-THREE

Eira

Anal retrieval at four in the morning on the Fourth of July. Just a normal holiday shift in the emergency room. The prize, a carrot, not one of those skinny ones, but rather plump and thick with the frilly greens still somewhat intact.

Securing the carrot and the supplies in a red biohazard bag, Eira continues to clean and restock the room.

Crossing the threshold, Dr. Gregory holds his hand out toward Eira, flexing his finger to his thumb repeatedly, the motion silently asking her to give him the bag. "J.J. Jackson is screaming on your phone again."

"Oh. God. Has Olive heard—" but her question is cut off by a familiar screech echoing off the hallway walls, growing louder with each passing second.

Olive slides past the doorway and starts dancing the Watusi from the sixties. She's belting out the lyrics of "But It's Alright" singing along to the ringtone's music streaming from Eira's phone.

Done with her entertainment, Olive presents Eira's phone to her. "Andy's been calling for like..." She taps on Eira's phone screen. "...um thirteen times." She winks. "And he's texting some seriously juicy stuff!"

"Give me that." Eira attempts to grab her phone, but it crashes to the floor, screen against tile. Looking down, Eira squeaks, "Please tell me that's not blood."

Three heads bow to examine the spot on the floor.

Olive snickers. "Are we doing a prayer here or a seance?"

Dr. Gregory offers, "My gelatin must have dropped earlier."

Olive twists her head as she rears back. "Dude, you brought food into an exam room; that's beyond disgusting!"

"Ewwah, for real?" screeches Eira.

"No! I was just trying to make you feel better about picking up your phone." Dr. Gregory shakes the biohazard bag. "I'm going to trash this little gem while you two figure out if your phone's going to join this carrot."

Olive squats, nudging Eira's phone with her finger. "How confident are you that this," she points to the spot on the floor, "isn't blood?"

"Not!" Eira kneels. "Tonight, I've had an accidental bullet wound, vomit, a carrot in the ass, and a broken foot. It could seriously be blood!"

"When are people gonna realize guns don't accidentally shoot themselves and you can't use vegetables as butt plugs. Sheesh girl, this room's getting more action than me!"

"Too much!" Eira shakes her hands in front of her chest.

"Maintenance closed the other two rooms. It's just been this one."

Olive swipes the back of her fingernail at the red dot on the floor. "It's an effing sticker, Eira!"

Eira grabs her phone as a message previews across the screen before it goes black.

"Did that message have the word 'kid' in it?" Olive asks, raising her eyebrows.

Eira shrugs. "Maybe. We were out eating and in walks a very pregnant Bodhi." Eira shuffles to the door. "And Skye decided to announce to the whole restaurant that Andrew is now a baby daddy."

Olive gives Eira a shoulder hug. "I'm invested now; I've gotta see what Andy sent you."

Eira pockets her phone. "I've got notes to add. I'll check later."

Olive rests her hands on Eira's shoulders, stopping her. "No. Please look now," Olive glances around them. "It's quiet for a minute. This is important, and I'm here for support."

"You're just nosy," Eira says. "I'm kinda scared."

Olive reaches into Eira's scrub pocket, pulling out her phone. She tells Eira, "Type in your code."

Olive reads the text. Her eyes bounce over the top of Eira's phone and then back to the phone.

"Well, what's taking so long?" Eira picks at the skin around her thumbnail.

"I'm just looking at his massive d—"

Eira cuts her off. "He doesn't send those!" Trying to grab her phone, she adds, "And you're not helping!"

Olive smiles as she flips the screen, thrusting it in Eira's face. "It's not his kid," she says, giggling like a loon.

Eira snatches her phone, flipping through the texts from Andrew. "He says Bodhi confirmed it isn't his."

Walking away, Eira asks Olive, "If you've got this, I'm gonna grab a quick break?"

Nodding, she tells Eira, "You go on."

Lost in a tunnel where only she and he exist, she walks to the cafeteria, reading the texts from Andrew.

> **Andrew:** Imagine meeting someone who wants to learn your past because they want to know how you need to be loved?

Eira walks to the table farthest from the cafeteria door. The chair legs screech across the waxed floor as she drags it back. Curling one leg beneath her, she sinks into the seat. Draping the other leg over her bent knee, Eira gently jiggles her foot. She rests her hands on top of her leg as she types a response to Andrew's text.

> **Eira:** I'd say you found a keeper!

> **Andrew:** I've realized I've never been loved before.

> **Eira:** Before what?

> **Andrew:** Before you...

> **Eira:** What's the one thing in the world you want me to do for you?

Andrew: Honestly, stop making yourself small to please others.

Eira: I don't do that!!!

Andrew: You do, CONSTANTLY.

Eira: I guess I don't want others to feel less, so I try to make them feel more.

Andrew: Yeah, at your expense. I think you're beautiful and funny. Like a little crazy, sexy nerd that just needs to own it!

Eira: Confession?

Andrew: I mean, I'm no priest, but sure.

Eira: I'm kinda scared.

Andrew: Let's be kinda scared together...

Eira: Sure!

Eira: You ever gonna tell me where my surprise tonight is at?

Andrew: That's a need to know piece of information and RN, you don't need to know.

Eira: Can you at least tell me where I'm driving to?

Andrew: No, you'll pull up maps and get on street view. You're horribly impatient!

Eira: I'm a planner and this not knowing is setting me on edge!

Andrew: Only because I don't like you on edge. Here's a hint: plan to hug me til I smell like you…

Eira: OMG, are cuddles my surprise?

Andrew: Sprite, you're thinking too small…

Eira: Then just tell me. PLEASE!!!!

Andrew: NO. You need to learn self control

Eira: I need to know how to dress, you have to tell me!!!!

Andrew: I like you naked

Eira: FR RN!!!!! GIVE ME SOMETHING!

Andrew: *sends pin location*

Eira: A zoo?

Andrew: Told you you'd look! I'm not telling you until I am ready for you!!

Eira: Give me a time frame, I'm freaking out here!

Andrew: Soon. Now I have to stop texting you so I can finish.

Eira: Whatcha finishing?

Eira: Andrew…

Eira: ANDREW!!!

Eira: R U kidding me!

Eira: Fine!!! I'll see you soon.

CHAPTER TWENTY-FOUR

Andrew

"**O**h shit!" blurts Jonah.

"What now?" Andrew asks Jonah as he continues to arrange the placemats under the utensils on the card table, dressed up with a fancy tablecloth.

Jonah chuckles as he rounds his van. "Nothing, just wanted to see you freak out again."

Andrew watches Jonah tests the stability of the tiki torches stuck in the sand. He glances at the fire no more than a couple of feet away from the table; the three pieces of wood stacked into a tepee still burning bright. Jonah puts his hands on the side of the two large tree stumps placed in front of the fire, checking to see if they're hot. Assessing quietly as he opens the cooler between the stumps to pop another piece of chocolate into his mouth.

"Kinda looks like you're the one freaking out," Andrew jokes.

"I think the food table needs to be on the other side of the dining table, not in between the table and the fire."

"That's where I planned on putting it." Andrew furrows his brow in question.

"Dude, if I'd known that, I would've put a torch over there for some lighting!"

"Relax, man. We don't need more light. With the moonlight bouncing off the water." Andrew motions towards the fire. "That roaring sea of flames." He puts his hands on his hips. "And the fifteen tiki torches, I won't be shocked when the fire department visits us tonight."

Andrew's phone buzzes with an incoming text.

> **Eira:** Your directions from your text tell me when I'm at the ceramic shop, I'll be 10 minutes out. I just passed it. Still don't see why you couldn't just send me a pin!

> **Andrew:** Your curiosity would've spoiled your own surprise! Pull up in front of the row of trees.

"She's just about here," Andrew announces, looking up to see Jonah filling the glasses and meticulously placing them back on the round, handmade coaster.

"Don't forget to light the wick." Andrew tips his head towards the center of the table.

"Did you tear off the paper cup around the candle?" Jonah asks as he lights the wick, then presses on the side of the round loaf of bread in the middle of the table.

"Did you seriously put a candle in the middle of the sourdough bread?" Andrew asks.

Shaking his head, Jonah grumbles, "What does she even see in you? That," Jonah points, "is called a butter candle. You melt butter, add some herbs, and freeze it. Then, when you're ready, you light the wick and place it in the middle of the bread." He nods. "I think you're all set." Dusting his hands against his thighs. "Call me when you leave. Law and I are gonna watch the game with ole man Sam, so we'll be waiting to clean everything up." Closing his van door, Jonah taps his thumb on the outside of the driver's door. "You did good, Andrew. She's gonna love it. This cool weather for July worked for your benefit, also. I'm really happy for you two."

"Will you make sure Sam knows I appreciate him letting me use his beach?"

Jonah nods, shifts into reverse, and drives off just as Eira pulls into the vacant spot.

Andrew leans against a turned-up tree root, abrasive edges smoothed by years of wind and sand. He watches Eira gracefully walk to him. The top of her sundress dips gradually between her breasts while the lacy bottom hem gently taps the top of her knees with each step. Eira stops just before their toes touch; she cocks her head.

"Your silence is kinda eerie," she whispers.

Andrew leans forward, placing a kiss on her forehead, the tip of her nose, then presses his lips to hers. "Mmm, your lips taste like apple pie." His hand cradles her chin, tilting her head up and to the side so he can deepen the kiss. His lips glide across hers as if he's teaching her a slow, seductive dance, only to part as he drags his tongue along their seam. Sliding his thumb along her jaw, he wraps his hand around the back of her neck lovingly, drawing her to him. Dipping his tongue into her warm mouth, Andrew flicks it against hers, wrapping his other arm around her waist, infusing her into him. Moaning, Andrew breaks the kiss.

Pulling back, he shifts his feet. His growing erection presses the limits of his zipper while he tries to hide his excitement by adjusting his stance.

Eira's smirk tells him he failed, miserably.

"You look beautiful, Sprite."

"So, not the zoo, huh?" she says with a cheeky grin.

Andrew scoffs, offering his arm, and she loops hers through his. Together, he leads Eira to her surprise.

Andrew has been here since mid-afternoon, making sure everything is set up, but only now does he truly see the gift of his effort in their surroundings.

Their footsteps are muted as they walk on the carpet runner Andrew gently laid on top of the whitewashed sand. The entire area Jonah and he worked on pays off with just two words from her.

"It's beautiful," Eira gasps.

Andrew takes her hand and escorts her to her seat.

"This is just wow," Eira says. She takes a sip of her water while focusing on the ship-wheel-shaped coaster.

Noticing her nervousness, Andrew quietly clears his throat. "Hey, are you okay over there?"

"I'm fine, really." Eira grants him a smile shining brighter than the moonlight.

"You could stop right here, and this would be more than what anyone has ever done for me. It's absolutely beautiful."

"Well, we're just getting started." Andrew tilts his head and grins.

Eira reaches for her stemless wine glass, raising her eyebrows in question.

"Watermelon green tea," he offers.

Eira swallows and smiles. "It's delicious." She points to the table. "Why is there a candle in the middle of the bread?"

"Jonah," Andrew states with a sigh. "The candle is actually melted butter with herbs added to it. Pull pieces of bread from the loaf, dip them, then enjoy."

"Didn't know Jonah had it in him," Eira comments, taking another drink of her tea.

Andrew delivers the first course to Eira, a bowl of salad he made earlier. "Spinach and Strawberry Salad, minus the almonds. A trip to the ER is not in my plan for tonight."

Andrew, not touching his salad, rests in his chair, taking in the person before him.

"You're not eating?" Eira arches her brow.

Andrew, spearing his sliced strawberries, forks them into his mouth. "Satisfied?"

"Well, since you won't eat," she says, cocking her head, "tell me something about you that no one knows."

Taking a deep breath, he exhales. "I have dyslexia."

Eira scrunches her face as if she's sucked on a lemon wedge. "What?" she gently shakes her head. "But you don't show any signs." She asks in astonishment, "How?"

"When I was younger, I worked with a private reading specialist to make it manageable. I still have it; I just know how to work with it," Andrew answers, shrugging off his awkwardness.

Noticing his discomfort, Eira switches to a safer topic. "Is there any more watermelon tea?"

"Sure," Andrew says and stands to get the tea, taking with him their salad plates. He stows them in a plastic tote for Jonah to clean up later.

Pouring more tea into Eira's glass, he put the pitcher of tea back into the cooler.

Cautiously opening the cooler marked HOT, Andrew steps back, allowing the steam to billow over the top of the cooler. It's positioned on its side so when it's opened, the lid rests on the table. Andrew carefully places the stuffed acorn squash onto a plate and serves it and the drink to Eira.

"This smells wonderful. What's in it?"

"Seared sausage with caramelized onions and mushrooms over cauliflower rice, and an ass load of spices." Andrew winks. "All on your acceptable list."

Settling back into his seat, he watches Eira. She closes her eyes and tilts her head towards the sky.

Her skin glows with the vibrant orange and reds of the fire while her hair sways in the breeze.

A smile drifts across his lips. He's acknowledged. His body doesn't seize up as his mind keeps chanting, *She's the one*. As it already knew she was, but it was giving his head the time it needed to come into agreement.

Opening her eyes, she's met with his smile and a fork presenting a bite of squash and sausage.

"Open." Andrew rests the utensil on the edge of her bottom lip.

Eira's mouth encases the fork, and her lips drag across the tines as Andrew gently pulls it back. Eira moans. "This is delicious."

Sitting back a bit, Andrew points to her plate with his fork. "Eat," he urges, then adds, "tell me something about yourself."

"Um," she chuckles, "let me think." She taps her finger on her bottom lip, then sighs.

Eira snaps her fingers. "Okay." Taking a deep breath, she delves into the story. "My aunt and uncle were having marriage problems right around the time I moved in with them. I don't know what it was about; I just remember Uncle Zio fixing it. That's when I realized I wanted what they had."

Andrew smirks. "You wanted marriage problems?"

Eira waves her hands above her plate. Hiding her mouth with her other hand, she continues. "No, no. Not that. I want their kind of love, to share that kind of passion with someone. Like, I can see their devotion and their connection is so real. They showed me I don't have to settle."

"How'd he fix it?" He rubs his eyebrow, perching his elbows on the table.

Eira lays her fork down, her gaze focusing above Andrew's shoulder. "He created a scavenger hunt. The clues were based on times in their lives when they were there for each other."

"Seriously?"

"I'll never forget the twinkle in her eye as she moved from one hint to the next. She transformed from my starchy aunt into a sensual woman who craved the memories of love she relived with each clue. I could see her yearning for physical touch from the person she said she wanted to be with through all times. She would pull the notes to her chest and sigh. I swear, she would go back to the time each hint came from." Eira shrugs. "Life happened; I guess. They both got so caught up in their own thing, each one having their own hobbies, oftentimes the other not being present for the other." She slowly blinks. "They used to yell, like a lot, and there wasn't a door in that house that wasn't slammed off its hinges." Slowly, shaking her head, she adds, "I'll never live that again."

"Tell me more about this scavenger hunt," Andrew says, pushing his plate aside.

"Oh man. Uncle Zio told me later he spent months planning it, all completely personal to their life, their love, their game. He said it was his last shot at making Aunt Zia see him. The last hint I couldn't go with her, though. It was in the middle of a corn maze." She rests her elbow on the table, propping her chin in her hand. "Their first date was at a corn maze. And at the scavenger hunt corn maze, they were doing some stuff back there I didn't want to know about!"

Smiling, Eira continues. "Back then, that is. But now..." She clears her throat. "...now I know what they were doing is needed for a healthy relationship. The desire to feel love is ageless, and I think people forget that."

"Forget what, Sprite?" He doesn't look away, letting her feel the weight of his focus. "How just the touch of a lover's fingers can make someone ache for more? How they'd willingly work day and night to build something real together?"

He clears his throat. "You should know, just the thought of fucking you makes me harder than I've ever been before. You make me burn hotter and brighter, and it's like my sole purpose is being the reason you smile." Andrew's voice deepens. "That it's natural for me to want your love, and to show you on every surface of our house just how delicious your hot cunt tastes? Knowing I'll still desire you when we're forty, fifty, sixty, hell, even seventy. Obviously, it'll change, but I know I'm still gonna want you, always."

She wiggles in her chair. "I thought you didn't want that?" she questions.

Slowly nodding his head, he tells her, "Making you scream my name isn't the only way to show love."

"What's another way?" Eira whispers.

Andrew reaches for her hand as he stands. Walking towards the fire, he settles Eira onto a stump of wood. "I want to give you something no one has ever given you before."

Andrew bends, whispering in her ear, "Yourself."

"Huh?" She rears back, confusion flickering across her face.

Andrew squats to meet her gaze, his hands rubbing the length of her thighs. "Not just the parts you've kept safe, but also the parts you thought you lost. The pieces no one else bothered to see. I want you to have freedom, to be yourself fully, without fear or apology."

Not knowing how to respond, she turns to the flames dancing in the breeze.

Andrew reaches for the cooler between their stumps and pulls out a telescopic metal stick. He twists the shaft to lock it in place. Then, he skewers two extra-large marshmallows on the fork of the metal stick and thrusts it into the fire.

Sitting on his stump, he says, "Will you reach into that cooler and get the graham crackers and three squares of chocolate, please?"

Andrew eases the marshmallows into the fire. Turning the stick, trying to get a perfect char, one of the marshmallows takes to flame, burning just as bright as the surrounding tiki torches. "Shit!"

Gasping, Eira laughs. "You're burning it!"

Bringing the flaming marshmallows to a safe distance in front of Eira, Andrew smirks. "Blow."

Eira inhales, slowly blowing until the flame is extinguished. Smiling, she tosses her sass at Andrew, "Was it as good for you as it was for me?"

Andrew chuckles. "Behave." He nods. "Can you bring those crackers over here?" Andrew places the toasted marshmallow on top of the chocolate and cracker. "Place the other cracker over the top and squeeze a little while I pull out."

Eira suggestively snickers while she presses the crackers against each side of the brown, crunchy-gooey marshmallow. Smirking, Andrew withdraws the stick, leaving the white sticky goodness sandwiched between the crackers while the heat melts the chocolate. Andrew tosses the stick with the burned marshmallow into the fire, and the smell of toasted confection fills the air.

Noticing her brow crinkle, Andrew says, "Jonah and the guys are cleaning up after we leave tonight; they'll take care of it."

Andrew's fingers wrap around Eira's hand holding the s'more, drawing it to his mouth. He bites the cracker. Crumbs lightly sprinkle onto his lap. Chewing, he gently tugs her hand. Pulling her towards his lap, he guides her legs to straddle him. The heat from her Duchess warms his aching cock.

He takes the s'more from her hand, resting a corner of it on her bottom lip. Her gaze flicks from the s'more to his eyes before she leans in for a bite. Pulling back, she lifts a hand. "I got some on my mouth, didn't I?"

Andrew sweeps her hand away. "Uh-huh. C'mere."

He clasps her chin, drawing her to him; his tongue licks the corner of her mouth. "Got it," he says with a smile. Bringing the s'more back to her lips. "You know I love you, right?"

Eira's breath hitches as she flattens her hand over his heart. His heart is pounding, filling her palm with the impact of each beat.

"What's wrong?" he asks.

"Nothing," she says, and her voice cracks, "it's just the first time you've said it."

"Pfft, I've said it plenty." Andrew tilts his head in mock shock.

"Only when I'm drifting into sleep."

"Bite?" he questions, his fingers bringing the s'more even with her lower lip.

"Did you want...?" she asks with a nod towards the s'more.

Andrew shakes his head.

Eira grabs the s'more and throws it over his shoulder.

She leans back onto his lap, her fingertips strumming against his heart; it's still pounding like a racehorse taking the lead. "I hold a pure heart for you." She traces her middle finger over his bottom lip.

Andrew leans towards the cooler again. He pulls a small white box from the cooler and sets it in her lap. Lifting the lid, he murmurs, "Close your eyes."

Doing as requested, Eira jolts when she feels a chill, as thin metal is settled against her throat. Andrew's warm fingertip traces over the top of the cold length, releasing the pendant to rest between the tops of her breasts.

Shivering, she questions, "Andrew?"

Andrew runs his fingers between her breasts, nestling the coolness in his palm, holding it just above her skin. "You can open now."

Eira glances at Andrew and then at the pendant on his fingers. "It's beautiful," she whispers as her glossy eyes meet Andrew's blue eyes. "It's just like yours."

"I made sure the star matched the one inside my compass tattoo." Andrew quietly adds, "You helped me find myself. When I was lost and didn't know I needed to be found. You'll always be my North Star." He gently lets the star pendant fall between her breasts, clasps the back of her neck, and slowly brings her lips to his. "You're my everything. I love you."

"I'll never get tired of hearing you say that," declares Eira.

The opening riff of deep drums to WesGhost's "Switchblade" cuts through the night air. "Is that your phone?"

Andrew huffs, "It's probably Jonah." He clears the box from her lap. "Let me check it."

Walking to his motorcycle, he grabs his phone from his seat and scrolls through his notifications. Dismissing some, but not finding anything an emergency, he goes into Jonah's thread, making sure he isn't overlooking anything. Hearing a rustling behind him, he twists. Nothing could have prepared him for the sight before him.

Eira is pulling her dress over her head while slowly walking towards him.

The dancing flames from the fire cast blue and yellow hues along her pale skin as the darkness coats a shadow over her legs. Waves crash onto the beach, bringing a cool breeze with them. The breeze makes Eira's nipples harden and sweeps her hair off her shoulder.

He stops scrolling on his phone. "Holy hell, Sprite."

Folding her dress in half, she lays it on the sand and kneels before him. Looking up at Andrew, she sasses, "What? I don't want to get sand all over me." She reaches for his belt buckle.

Andrew tosses his phone on his bike seat, gathering her wayward hair into his fist. Tugging just enough to get her head to raise. "This wasn't what I planned for you."

Continuing her pursuit of his cock, Eira raises an eyebrow as she tilts her head. "Are you refusing?"

Shaking his head, "Bfffk, no!" he growls.

Andrew's pants are down past his feet when Eira hums with anticipation. "What am I gonna see tonight?"

Andrew chuckles, dropping his chin to rest on his chest. "They're all black with a green stem holding a red rose over my dick."

"Mmm, what are they called?"

"The right reasons," he says and smiles.

Eira hooks her fingers over the top of his black waistband as she gently tugs his boxers to meet his jeans. Bracing her palms against his thighs, the tip of her tongue traces each barbell rung on his dick, slightly lifting each one from their sides, eliciting a growl from Andrew. Cautious of his Jacob's Ladder piercings, she nibbles the vein at the union of his shaft and sack, then widens her tongue and licks him from base to crown.

"Eira," Andrew growls, flexing his fists, reminding his hips not to move.

He threads his fingers through her hair. His chest struggles to breathe while Eira continues her sweet torture of him.

His shoulders tense as Eira nibbles along his velvet ridge, then blows her hot breath across his leaking peak. Her wet tongue and sharp teeth alternate between licks and nips along the top of his shaft.

A forced plea escapes him, caught somewhere between his locked fingers and the slow, shuddering exhale that follows. "Enough!"

Eira smiles. Her hands skate across his thighs until she's cradling his balls with one hand and has her other wrapped around his aching cock. She pulses her grip, knowing it deepens his arousal.

"Fuck, Sprite," he says and pulls her up to him. "This was supposed to be your night."

The star on her necklace catches the moonlight's reflection, reminding him of his plans. Toeing off his jeans, he nudges them behind him with his foot. "What have you always wanted but not had the courage to ask for?"

Smirking, she looks at the bike, then back at his dick.

Raising his eyebrows, he questions, "You sure?"

A nod of her head has him removing his shirt, draping it across the gas tank. Cradling his phone onto the handlebars, he adjusts his naked ass and treasured jewels on his motorcycle seat. His fingers snap, pointing to her pelvis. "Panties."

Stepping free from them, she gives them a little shake. Fashioning them into a bracelet, she threads them around his wrist.

Andrew pats the gas tank. "You ready?"

"I didn't think this through," she stalls, "how's this gonna work?"

Andrew scoots as far back as he can in his seat. "Face me, put your legs over mine."

"Andrew, I can't even reach a pedal," she hisses.

Andrew leans towards her, wrapping his hands around her waist. "Trust me?"

Eira nods.

In one fluid motion, he lifts her up, hovers her cunt over his cock, giving her just a moment to prepare before he sinks inside her. She clutches her walls, her pussy quivering around his swelling shaft.

"Oh, fucking hell," she says as her forehead falls to his chest.

He bows his head to kiss her hair. "You say the word and we're done, you understand?"

"I don't wanna stop, I just..." She pulses her cunt around him.

"That pussy better stop sucking my dick or we're finished before you get a pump outta me!"

"Okay, what now?" she asks, resting her feet on the tops of his.

She draws her hands along the sides of his neck. "I'm losing it here. Stop touching me," he growls. Being inside her on his bike is a whole new experience, and he's struggling for control.

Eira brings her hands between them, shaking them. "What am I supposed to do with these then?"

"I don't know, but you've got me fucking primed to blow," he grits out.

"Fine!" Eira shouts and raises her arms in the air.

"For fuck's sake, Eira, your damn tits are in my face now!" He exhales across her nipples making them hard. He stoops to nip it, then sucks it before Eira pulls back.

Her fingers thread through his hair, pulling at the base to get his attention. "Andrew, you've got about five seconds before my vagina sucks the life force out of your body, so figure out how you want this and fast!"

Toeing Eira's dress towards his pants, he braces his heels in the sand on each side of his motorcycle, guiding her legs around him so her feet rest on the back pedals. He places his hand on her lower back, slightly pulling her towards him. Her back arches making his dick push deeper inside her, both moaning. Protecting her back from the edges of the gas tank, he lays his palm against the tank. "Lie back," he coaxes.

She lays her back on his protective hands, wrapping her fingers around the handlebars, drawing her feet off the pedals, and bracing her heels against the ridge of the back seat.

Andrew stands, sinking deeper into her center. Slowly thrusting his cock inside her, he feels her tighten around him. Withdrawing, he only leaves his crown inside her. "I'm not gonna last." He pounds into her sloshing pussy like a beast in rut.

"Lift me up, I want to feel all of you," she squeaks.

Raising both hands, he lifts her to sit on him as she tightens around him. Her walls quiver around his dick. "Oh, God. Yes. Yes. Oh, yes!" Her chant scatters across the top of the water, sending her pleasure-filled screams with the wind down the beach.

He slams into her. "Oh, fuck, take it all, Sprite," he roars, burying himself deep in the sanctuary of her warmth, filling her with every last drop of the storm he's held back for so damn long.

Chest heaving as he sits back in his seat, he nuzzles her neck. "I love you, Sprite."

Before she can reply, his phone's notification of WesGhost's "Switchblade" pings into the night air.

Sighing, Andrew reaches for his phone at the same time Eira hugs him, causing his hand to jump; his fingertip accidentally hits the video icon.

"You better be glad it's me calling and not Law!"

"Shit, don't move Sprite!" Andrew barks as he clicks the icon to flip the video screen.

Jonah yells, "What the hell is wrong with you? Screaming like a banshee is tearing you limb from limb? There are calls blasting over the scanner. One's about ole man Sam's beach on fire and the other is to Animal Control because the eighty-year-old woman three doors down thinks she heard a deranged beast! You two get your asses out of there, now!"

Eira's laughing against Andrew's chest, turning her head to the side, she asks, "Jonah, they ever say what the banshee said?"

"Haha. Fuck no, they didn't. But old man Sam wants to know why the beast is yelling for someone to take all the soda pop, so there's that. Leave. Now. We're almost there and I'm not interested in seeing Andrew's pushpin of a dick! Hurry up!" Jonah ends the call.

Dressing in a hurry, Andrew throws on his boxers and his shirt as Eira shakes her dress free of sand, as much as she can, then quickly puts it on. Grabbing her phone from the table, she shouts, "I see headlights, we've gotta go!"

Andrew grabs his phone off his motorcycle, running for Eira's car. "Have you seen my pants?"

"Just go without!" Eira slams her passenger door shut.

Andrew pulls his door closed, and it rocks from the force. He tears out of ole man Sam's beach just as Jonah's van comes to a halt. People flock out of all sides of the van like chickens being chased out of their pen.

The long silence of the drive is broken when Eira's laughter turns into a mumble and ends with a whine.

Seemingly hitting every red light from the beachfront to his doorstep, he slows to a stop at the next red light. "What are you going on about?"

"I don't have panties on, and you didn't wear a condom!" she rushes.

Andrew takes the last turn to get to his house. "We agreed not to wear one! But I will if that's what you want?"

Eira flops her head against her headrest. "Andrew, there's nothing catching you." She opens her legs. "You're running all over the place. Damn, your sperm is undisciplined!" Huffing, she snaps her legs closed.

Andrew smirks. "Just tuck your dress," he says and reaches over to the passenger seat, shoving his hand between her legs. Her boho dress is short, and the force of his hand sliding it between her thighs causes her head and neck to bow involuntarily. When he pulls his hand from her legs, it is wet. Toggling his attention between the road and his wet hand, he shrugs his shoulders and wipes his hand across the shoulder of her dress.

"Did you seriously just wipe that on me?" she snipes.

Andrew chuckles. "Possession is nine-tenths of the law, and right now, you possess enough to be called my personal cum dumpster." He roars with laughter.

She shrieks, "What did you just say?"

"Laugh, you know that's funny!"

"Why do you have so freaking much?" she whines. "It ran down my ass crack two stoplights back." She throws her thumb over her shoulder. "And at that stoplight, it started pooling in my seat!" she exclaims. "I think you make more than a stallion!"

Feeling guilty, he quietly says, "I'm sorry this wasn't a great night." Pulling into his driveway, Andrew glances at Eira waiting for the garage door to open.

"Nah. Best night ever. Even with me marinating in your sandy juices over here." She swirls her hand above her legs. "I wouldn't trade it."

Andrew pulls the car in beside his truck, shutting it off as the garage door rests on its threshold. Eira looks at Andrew, and a huge smile spreads across her face. In a quick vault, she launches herself at Andrew.

Straddling his very hairy, naked leg. She says, "I love you, Andrew." She giggles as she kisses him. Circling her waist, she grinds her leaking treasure on his thighs, returning his essence.

Andrew chuckles. "Let's get inside," he says and kisses her forehead, "so we can clean up." He kisses her nose. "So we can get dirty again." He kisses her lips.

CHAPTER TWENTY-FIVE

Eira

"**D**ammit," Eira hisses.

She stubs her toe on her full-length mirror. "Was this really the best place for *you*?"

Hopping on one foot, her hands grip the sides of the mirror tight, determined to dance it to safety.

Settling the mirror, Eira shrieks, "Seven years of bad luck, no effing way!" She straightens with a huff, her eyes catching the reflection of the compass rose necklace Andrew gave her last night.

She will always hold those memories of the beachfront close to her heart. Andrew definitely showed her what it means to be seen and heard. Everything he did was for her because he had listened to her throughout the last months. He learned her likes and dislikes, learned when she was too shy to ask for something, and demanded that she ask with confidence.

I want to be better for myself because of him.

Smiling, she thinks back to the way he makes her laugh, even in the tense moments.

The fluffy towel wrapped around her already dried body has shifted, while the towel on her head holding her wet hair has fallen askew during her mirror dance.

As if in slow motion, the mirror's reflection shows everything. The unmade bed, the half-full glass of water by her bedside, the momentary puffs from her air diffuser scented with frankincense, her cracked laptop lid, her chipped nail polish on her big toe, but the most stunning reflection: her smile.

Not that guarded one, whose only purpose was to mask her pain she never wanted anyone to see. No, this one's different. It reveals the truth now, without care or concern. This smile is the kind that creeps up on you one day when you aren't paying attention, then you see it and realize you are simply... Happy.

While still taking in her reflection, she pulls the towel from her head. Letting her damp strands tumble free while she pats her hair dry. She stills as she revels in the version of herself she once was.

Twelve months ago, that reflection told a different story. One of pain, loss, and uncertainty.

But now? Now, the truth is so very different.

A mirror never lies. Its job is to reflect, not just the current image, but everything you've been through to become that reflection.

Eira feels comforted; that person in the mirror is not trapped anymore, not lost, and most certainly, not stumbling about, trying to find her worth.

"I found me," Eira says quietly, as if telling a secret, hugging the wet towel to her chest.

Her reflection smiles back, tearfully so.

Eira notices the subtle differences between the person she was a year ago and the person she has become. She wipes the lone tear clinging to her eyelashes; a smile ghosts her lips as she remembers.

Twelve months have passed since Logan kicked her out. She's now elated because that forced her to face her unresolved pain. Eleven months since she bought her first motorcycle, kick-starting her healing journey and sharing it on social media. It's become her therapy, and her place of self-discovery. Ten months since her first introduction to Andrew and Jonah's odd father-son-like relationship. Nine months since being accepted into the riding community, which has given her more approval than that of her own family. Seven months since changing the fairing on her motorcycle, leading to one of the biggest breakthroughs for her. While working with Andrew in her garage, she learned a valuable lesson. Sometimes being independent means knowing when to ask for help and that you are not less for needing it.

All this has led to the change in her acceptance, her value, her protection of herself, and her knowing her worth. Going after what she wants from a place of confidence, rather than hope. Seeing all this reflected in the woman staring back at her, knowing all the pain had to happen to bring her here, home, True North.

The last six months of getting to know Andrew have been nothing short of beautiful. Watching him heal himself while helping her to heal as well. The way he cares for others, the way he shows up for those he loves, and giving anything less is not an option.

But the most breathtaking act is Eira getting to know the real her, finding the capacity to accept herself in her true form. The mirror now reflects a woman who has a love for herself.

Her past still tries to whisper doubt into her mind. Constantly making her question whether she's doomed to repeat the mistakes of yesterday. She acknowledges her imperfections, but she now knows how to manage them. Not forging a riot against herself but forging herself because of them.

Eira sighs. "Mirror, mirror on the... floor, we always got up when our hearts were sore, through every storm, with every break, our last breath it could never take."

A pounding on her door startles her. "Andrew's here," bellows her uncle.

"Yikes!" Eira jumps up, throwing her towels on her bed. She runs into her closet, yelling, "I'm not ready yet!"

"Well, you better hurry. He doesn't look like he's messing around!" her aunt yells back.

"Keep him busy until I'm ready, please!" she pleads.

"Rrr, damn it. Can't he be late just once?" she asks, getting dressed in a hurry.

CHAPTER TWENTY-SIX

Andrew

T he olfactory nerve is a demanding little thing. With only a single scent to remind you of a past memory.

He had just swiped his card at the pump when the sweet smell of apple pie drifted under his nose.

One minute, Andrew's straddling his motorcycle filling up his gas tank, and the next he's guided by the pea-sized bundle of nerves because of his newfound craving for apple pie.

Helmet and gloves off, he's now sitting at a picnic table inside a food truck's courtyard, scarfing down not one, but two of the flakiest-crusted apple pie empanadas ever made.

His taste buds explode in pleasure as the spicy warmth of cinnamon and sugar mixes with the lemon glaze drizzled across the pastry's top.

Looking at his last one, he shakes his head, amazed at how one little treat can remind him of someone so special.

Continuing to eat as if on autopilot, he's deep in thought, realizing it's not just Eira's moans that entice him. It's also when
she gives herself grace to ask him for help, when she uses her toes
to pinch his calf, or when she leaves all the kitchen cabinet doors
open. The tenacity she has towards challenges, her desire to make
him laugh daily, and her dainty little snores greeting his ears each
night. All these things people take for granted, but he finds grati-
fication in them. They are her. And she's choosing him.

Looking out at the horizon, he smiles.

Just inside his line of sight, Andrew sees a little boy whose ice
cream cone is melting under the August sun. Jerking his cone away
from the little girl, the top scoop slides off, landing with a splat
on the ground. Andrew hears the panicked screech of a mother
screaming, *no,* as she lunges, but it's too late. The little girl swipes
the scoop of ice cream off the ground. Squishing the brown lump
between her fingers, she fists it to her lips. Shoving the dirt-covered
scoop into her mouth. In her haste to eat the ice cream, she has
smeared it on her cheeks and chin. Andrew chuckles as the upset
mother escorts the crying boy and an ice cream-covered girl out of
the courtyard.

Wiping his hands on a napkin, he glances at the time. Eira's
pulling a shift at the hospital. In six more hours, she's all his. This
time they are really aiming to watch a movie and just chill. It
never fails, halfway through the movie, she'll get cold. He'll get
her the fluffy sherpa blanket from his bedroom, only to come back
to the living room to see her lounging on his couch in her shirt
and underwear. To date, they've not made it through a full movie
without having to rewind it.

Just thinking of her makes him close his eyes. His thoughts flash to her lying on his bed, nipples hardened as the cool air sweeps across them. Her panties are soaking wet from her desire for him. She pleads for relief while the smell of apple pie floats around him, making his mouth water.

How can a pastry make his dick fight his zipper as savagely as a honey badger?

He rests his elbows on the table, propping his chin on the backs of his hands over his empanada. Breathing deeply, he opens his eyes to the lemony-sweet glaze drizzling over the top. Another lust-filled memory of Eira shrieking and laughing as he rubs the mess they's made on her last night into her skin. Moaning, he eats the last bite.

The door of the empanada food truck slams shut. The owner steps out, hands on her hips, face angles towards the sun, and takes a deep breath. Isabella wipes her hands on a brightly colored cloth tucked over the front tie of her apron. Her warm, brown eyes soften, as she looks at Andrew, then back to his empty plate.

Andrew stares down at his plate with a deep scowl.

She approaches, her voice gentle. "Mijo, is something wrong with your empanadas?"

Andrew's head snaps up, a little too quickly. "No! No... it's...," he exhales, rubbing a hand over his face before glancing at the empty plate of apple pie empanada. He shifts uncomfortably, aware of her expectant gaze. "It smells like... my girlfriend..." he rushes, meeting her eyes.

Isabella blinks in confusion, then smirks. "Your girlfriend smells like deep-fried dough?"

He groans, dragging a hand through his hair. "No, not dough. Apples, sugar, cinnamon." He smiles. "Her shampoo, her lotion, her... ah–" His cheeks tint red. "Hell, just her, she smells like apple pie, and I can't seem to get my fill of it."

For a moment, Isabella simply watches him, then a slow, knowing smile spreads across her face. She chuckles, shaking her head. "Ah, Mijo." She pats his arm as a mother comforting her son. "I believe that's called love."

"It definitely is," he says quietly.

She gives him a playful wink before heading back to the truck. Stopping halfway, she calls over her shoulder, "Are you going to make that pie yours, or just let her sit around smelling delicious for someone else to claim?"

Isabella disappears into the truck, while a thought that's been bouncing around Andrew's mind takes root.

With Eira by his side, Andrew knows anything is possible. They may have faced their fair share of struggles, but they've emerged stronger and wiser.

Mind made up, he throws his trash away. Andrew duck-walks his motorcycle away from the courtyard filled with people, then starts it.

As he rides away, he remembers the joy in Eira's voice when she was talking about her aunt and uncle's scavenger hunt. He's already thought of five clues around his house, with the last being in the bedroom with a ribbon and a ring.

For Andrew, this isn't just the end of a chapter; it's the beginning of a beautiful new adventure.

CHAPTER TWENTY-SEVEN

Andrew

E ira shifts her car into park at the top of Andrew's driveway. She sighs in anticipation of the muggy night's air as she reads Andrew's text. It's a simple request, but the butterflies in her stomach flutter.

> **Andrew:** Hey, Sprite, can you grab your gloves from the garage before you come in?

> **Eira:** Yep

Closing her car door, she feels the sultry Florida evening air clinging to her skin like a wet spaghetti noodle flung on the ceiling. The distant rumble of an engine fades as she walks into the garage. Sweat trickling down her spine, causing her scrubs to stick to her skin without any give. Kicking off her shoes, she drops her socks over the top of each shoe. Her feet soak up the coolness from the concrete floor as she walks towards her riding gloves.

The garage light casts a shadow over the aluminum rack where their organized chaos of riding gear rests. There's a faint scent of motor oil because the catch pan still sits full on the floor. Sighing, she notes, *I need to get this to Jonah.*

Grabbing her gloves from the third shelf, she hears a crinkling sound, like paper being squished. "What is this?" she asks.

There's a pink piece of paper, like a post-it note, inside her glove. Slipping her fingers inside, she pinches the note between her thumb and finger, pulling it out.

She presses the adhesive to her finger as she reads, *"Just like that ride, life can throw gravel our way. But we take the hit together. Now, for what soothed your stress after that rough day last week."*

She presses her hands between her breasts, as if she's giving the note a hug. "Did he really?" she murmurs.

She grabs her gloves and walks to the kitchen door. Using her middle finger, she presses the garage door remote button to close it. Walking into the kitchen, she recalls the day Andrew's clue refers to.

She'd had a grueling day, and he researched the best tea for relieving stress. Andrew ran her a bath with lavender essential oil and Epsom salt. While she soaked in the fragrant, stress-relieving hot water, he drove to the store to get the tea.

When he came back, he helped her dry off and slipped her favorite t-shirt of his over her head. Leading her to his bedroom, she spotted her teacup sitting on Andrew's nightstand as a sweet, delicate floral aroma filled the room.

After he tucked her in, he gave her the teacup. He explained Jasmine Dragon Phoenix Pearl Tea is the best for both uplifting and relaxing, and he wasn't wrong.

She opens the cabinet holding all the tea. Inhaling, she breathes in the deeply tantalizing aroma.

The only light comes from the faint glow of the stove's clock. The scent of green tea and jasmine lingers in the air, a reminder of all the times Andrew has made her tea after a long, exhausting shift.

Her breath catches. Stuck to the sealed tea bag is another note. *"You work hard, you carry the weight of the world, and sometimes, you just need something warm to hold on to. Just like this tea, I'll always be here to soothe your soul. But you know what else brings comfort? Seven somethings hanging nearby."*

She turns, already knowing where to look. Seven aprons hang in a neat row, one for each day of the week. Andrew enjoys cooking. *Pfft, who are we kidding? He only cooks because he knows I have no patience for it.*

Smiling, she reaches for the pockets of her favorite apron. Her fingers trail over the bright pink one with a chicken standing on a tree stump holding a beer bottle. Over the beer bottle are the words 'Grandma's Secret Ingredient.' It's soft, worn from years of use. Eira squishes the pockets, pulling the note free.

"Love is in the little things. Like the meals we make, the messes we clean, the laughter we share; and speaking of things getting hot in this house... think back to a certain time when your reflection vibrated."

Heat rises in her cheeks, and her core tightens. She knows exactly where to go next.

Darting into the living room, she smooths the notes over one another on her finger. The same chair is in front of the TV. Eira slides into it, spreading her legs slightly. She remembers his fingers curling onto her thighs and wrapping around her hips, leaving marks only she could see. The TV, where he brought her pleasure, now shows her own reflection again. She remembers his head resting on her shoulder, both beautifully lost in each other's pleasure. Her eyes focus on the note on the corner of the television. "*I remember the way you looked at me that night—how you finally saw yourself through my eyes. That was the moment I knew, without a doubt, you were mine. Now it's time for you to find me. I've been waiting for you.*"

There's a soft glow radiating from under Andrew's bedroom door. Her pulse quickens. She cracks the door slightly, a sliver of golden light spilling out. She pushes it open, and her world slows.

Candle's glow, painting the room with soft shadows. The scent of clove and something faintly floral hangs in the air.

Her eyes follow the white calla lily flower petals scattered in a trail on the floor leading to the bed.

To Andrew.

To a naked Andrew lying on the bed.

Eira is entranced by the flickering light catching on his skin, highlighting every stroke of his tattoos like an inked history book. He's stretched out, one arm behind his head, the leg closest to the edge of the bed is bent at the knee. His foot is tucked under the other knee, hiding his manhood from her.

His eyes bore into hers. "Sprite," he says, his voice low, with an edge of something raw beneath it. "Took you long enough."

Her throat tightens as Andrew leisurely lowers his bent knee. "Did you like your clues?"

Eira slowly nods as her mouth opens. "Yes," she whispers.

"You have one more."

"Wh—where?" Eira stutters.

Watching intently as Andrew lowers his knee, she sees a thin white ribbon tied around the base of his fully erect cock that is tethered to a white bag resting against his groin. A note is tucked between his fingers.

Eira steps closer, stopping when her knees meet the side of the bed.

Andrew hands her the note.

She reads it out loud, *"Every road, every ride, every fall, and every rise has led me here, to you."*

Eira tries to wipe her tears away, but Andrew takes her hand and laces his fingers through hers, resting them on his thigh. "Has a nice ring to it, don't you think?" he says with a smirk.

Eira clears her throat.

"Sprite, are you doing ok?"

"Yes," she says, nodding slowly. Shyly smirking, she adds, "I just don't know which head to thank."

"I'd be happy with either," he smiles. Bringing her hands to his lips, he kisses her fingertips.

"Marry me?"

"Yes," she answers without hesitation.

"This scavenger hunt is different; you get a little something to wear at the end."

"You?" she questions.

"Yes. No. Well, you get two tokens." Andrew guides her hands to the white velvet bag. Her fingers tremble as she loosens the ribbon and taps the bag against her palm.

A sparkling diamond on a smooth band slips into her palm. Eira immediately closes her fist, her attention bouncing from her fist where the ring lies, to Andrew, to what was once tethered to the white bag, and back. Tears pool in her eyes as they finally meet Andrew's loving gaze.

He draws her fist open. Placing the ring on the third finger of her left hand, he tells her, "I choose you. You choose me. End. Of. Story."

From the author

I didn't plan on becoming a writer... **healing led me here**.

Healing doesn't always come with a halo. It can be messy, sensual, and unexpectedly empowering. Sometimes, a steamy scene is actually about reclaiming your voice, and a suspenseful chapter is the escape you didn't know you needed. It's about finding yourself between the pages.

Healing is a personal journey. While self-help books are for those actively searching for answers, a great story finds you when your walls are down. When you least expect it, a character's strength becomes your own, and you suddenly see a new way forward.

If my stories make you smile, cry, or throw the book or e-reader across the room, then I've effectively done my job.

Check out my website for future books. themelissalucas. com

Let's stay connected: [TikTok] | [Instagram]